Edward Bulwer Lytton

The Pilgrims of the Rhine to Which is Prefixed the Ideal World the coming race

Edward Bulwer Lytton

The Pilgrims of the Rhine to Which is Prefixed the Ideal World the coming race

ISBN/EAN: 9783337298883

Printed in Europe, USA, Canada, Australia, Japan

Cover: Foto ©Andreas Hilbeck / pixelio.de

More available books at **www.hansebooks.com**

THE

PILGRIMS OF THE RHINE

TO WHICH IS PREFIXED

THE IDEAL WORLD

THE COMING RACE

BY

EDWARD BULWER LYTTON

(LORD LYTTON)

WITH ILLUSTRATIONS

BOSTON

ESTES AND LAURIAT

1892

THE PILGRIMS OF THE RHINE

THE PILGRIMS OF THE RHINE

TO HENRY LYTTON BULWER.

ALLOW me, my dear Brother, to dedicate this Work to you. The greater part of it (namely, the tales which vary and relieve the voyages of Gertrude and Trevylyan) was written in the pleasant excursion we made together some years ago. Among the associations — some sad and some pleasing — connected with the general design, none are so agreeable to me as those that remind me of the friendship subsisting between us, and which, unlike that of near relations in general, has grown stronger and more intimate as our footsteps have receded farther from the fields where we played together in our childhood. I dedicate this Work to you with the more pleasure, not only when I remember that it has always been a favourite with yourself, but when I think that it is one of my writings most liked in foreign countries ; and I may possibly, therefore, have found a record destined to endure the affectionate esteem which this Dedication is intended to convey.

Yours, etc.

E. L. B.

LONDON, *April* 23, 1840.

ADVERTISEMENT TO THE FIRST EDITION.

Could I prescribe to the critic and to the public, I would wish that this work might be tried by the rules rather of poetry than prose, for according to those rules have been both its conception and its execution; and I feel that something of sympathy with the author's design is requisite to win indulgence for the superstitions he has incorporated with his tale, for the floridity of his style, and the redundance of his descriptions. Perhaps, indeed, it would be impossible, in attempting to paint the scenery and embody some of the Legends of the Rhine, not to give (it may be, too loosely) the reins to the imagination, or to escape the influence of that wild German spirit which I have sought to transfer to a colder tongue.

I have made the experiment of selecting for the main interest of my work the simplest materials, and weaving upon them the ornaments given chiefly to subjects of a more fanciful nature. I know not how far I have succeeded, but various reasons have conspired to make this the work, above all others that I have written, which has given me the most delight (though not unmixed with melancholy) in producing, and in which my mind for the time has been the most completely absorbed. But the ardour of composition is often disproportioned to the merit of the work; and the public sometimes, nor unjustly, avenges itself for that forgetfulness of its existence which makes the chief charm of an author's solitude, — and the happiest, if not the wisest, inspiration of his dreams.

PREFACE.

With the younger class of my readers this work has had the good fortune to find especial favour; perhaps because it is in itself a collection of the thoughts and sentiments that constitute the Romance of youth. It has little to do with the positive truths of our actual life, and does not pretend to deal with the larger passions and more stirring interests of our kind. It is but an episode out of the graver epic of human destinies. It requires no explanation of its purpose, and no analysis of its story; the one is evident, the other simple, — the first seeks but to illustrate visible nature through the poetry of the affections; the other is but the narrative of the most real of mortal sorrows, which the Author attempts to take out of the region of pain by various accessories from the Ideal. The connecting tale itself is but the string that binds into a garland the wild-flowers cast upon a grave.

The descriptions of the Rhine have been considered by Germans sufficiently faithful to render this tribute to their land and their legends one of the popular guide-books along the course it illustrates, — especially to such tourists as wish not only to take in with the eye the inventory of the river, but to seize the peculiar spirit which invests the wave and the bank with a beauty that can only be made visible by reflection. He little comprehends the true charm of the Rhine who gazes on the vines on the hill-tops without a thought of the imaginary world with which their recesses have been peopled by the graceful credulity of old; who surveys the steep ruins that overshadow the water, untouched by one lesson from the pensive morality of Time. Everywhere around us is the evidence of perished opinions and departed races; everywhere around us, also, the rejoicing fertility of unconquerable Nature, and the calm progress of Man himself through the infinite cycles of decay. He who would judge adequately of a landscape must regard it not only with the painter's eye, but with the poet's. The feelings which the sight of any scene in Nature conveys to the mind — more especially of any scene on which history or fiction has left its trace — must depend upon our sympathy with those associations which make up what may be called the spiritual character of the spot. If indifferent to those associations, we should see only hedgerows and ploughed land in the battle-field of Bannockburn; and the traveller would but look on a dreary waste, whether he stood amidst the piles of the Druid on Salisbury plain, or trod his bewildered way over the broad expanse on which the Chaldæan first learned to number the stars.

To the former editions of this tale was prefixed a poem on "The Ideal," which had all the worst faults of the author's earliest compositions in verse. The present poem (with the exception of a very few lines) has been entirely rewritten, and has at least the comparative merit of being less vague in the thought, and less unpolished in the diction, than that which it replaces.

EMS, 1849.

CONTENTS.

THE PILGRIMS OF THE RHINE.

CHAPTER I.

CHAPTER II.

CHAPTER III.

CHAPTER IV.

CHAPTER V.

CHAPTER VI.

CONTENTS.

CHAPTER XXVII.

CHAPTER XXVIII.

CHAPTER XXIX.

CHAPTER XXX.

CHAPTER XXXI.

CHAPTER XXXII.

CHAPTER THE LAST

LIST OF ILLUSTRATIONS.

THE IDEAL WORLD

THE IDEAL WORLD.

I.

THE IDEAL WORLD, — ITS REALM IS EVERYWHERE AROUND US; ITS INHABITANTS ARE THE IMMORTAL PERSONIFICATIONS OF ALL BEAUTIFUL THOUGHTS; TO THAT WORLD WE ATTAIN BY THE REPOSE OF THE SENSES.

AROUND "this visible diurnal sphere"
  There floats a World that girds us like the space;
On wandering clouds and gliding beams career
  Its ever-moving murmurous Populace.
There, all the lovelier thoughts conceived below
  Ascending live, and in celestial shapes.
To that bright World, O Mortal, wouldst thou go?
  Bind but thy senses, and thy soul escapes:
To care, to sin, to passion close thine eyes;
Sleep in the flesh, and see the Dreamland rise!
Hark to the gush of golden waterfalls,
Or knightly tromps at Archimagian Walls!
In the green hush of Dorian Valleys mark
  The River Maid her amber tresses knitting;
When glow-worms twinkle under coverts dark,
  And silver clouds o'er summer stars are flitting,
With jocund elves invade "the Moone's sphere,
Or hang a pearl in every cowslip's ear;" [1]
Or, list! what time the roseate urns of dawn
  Scatter fresh dews, and the first skylark weaves
Joy into song, the blithe Arcadian Faun
  Piping to wood-nymphs under Bromian leaves,

---

[1] "Midsummer Night's Dream."

While slowly gleaming through the purple glade
Come Evian's panther car, and the pale Naxian Maid.

Such, O Ideal World, thy habitants!
    All the fair children of creative creeds,
All the lost tribes of Fantasy are thine, —
From antique Saturn in Dodonian haunts,
    Or Pan's first music waked from shepherd reeds,
To the last sprite when Heaven's pale lamps decline,
Heard wailing soft along the solemn Rhine.

II.

OUR DREAMS BELONG TO THE IDEAL. — THE DIVINER LOVE FOR WHICH YOUTH SIGHS NOT ATTAINABLE IN LIFE, BUT THE PURSUIT OF THAT LOVE BEYOND THE WORLD OF THE SENSES PURIFIES THE SOUL AND AWAKES THE GENIUS. — PETRARCH. — DANTE.

Thine are the Dreams that pass the Ivory Gates,
    With prophet shadows haunting poet eyes!
Thine the belov'd illusions youth creates
    From the dim haze of its own happy skies.
In vain we pine ; we yearn on earth to win
    The being of the heart, our boyhood's dream.
The Psyche and the Eros ne'er have been,
    Save in Olympus, wedded !   As a stream
Glasses a star, so life the ideal love;
Restless the stream below, serene the orb above!
Ever the soul the senses shall deceive;
Here custom chill, there kinder fate bereave:
For mortal lips unmeet eternal vows!
And Eden's flowers for Adam's mournful brows!
We seek to make the moment's angel guest
    The household dweller at a human hearth;
We chase the bird of Paradise, whose nest
    Was never found amid the bowers of earth.[1]

---

[1] According to a belief in the East, which is associated with one of the loveliest and most familiar of Oriental superstitions, the bird of Paradise is never seen to rest upon the earth, and its nest is never to be found.

Yet loftier joys the vain pursuit may bring,
　　Than sate the senses with the boons of time;
The bird of Heaven hath still an upward wing,
　　The steps it lures are still the steps that climb;
And in the ascent although the soil be bare,
More clear the daylight and more pure the air.
Let Petrarch's heart the human mistress lose,
He mourns the Laura but to win the Muse.
Could all the charms which Georgian maids combine
Delight the soul of the dark Florentine,
Like one chaste dream of childlike Beatrice
Awaiting Hell's dark pilgrim in the skies,
Snatched from below to be the guide above,
And clothe Religion in the form of Love?[1]

III.

GENIUS, LIFTING ITS LIFE TO THE IDEAL, BECOMES ITSELF A PURE
IDEA: IT MUST COMPREHEND ALL EXISTENCE, ALL HUMAN SINS
AND SUFFERINGS; BUT IN COMPREHENDING, IT TRANSMUTES
THEM. — THE POET IN HIS TWO-FOLD BEING, — THE ACTUAL AND
THE IDEAL. — THE INFLUENCE OF GENIUS OVER THE STERNEST
REALITIES OF EARTH; OVER OUR PASSIONS; WARS AND SUPER-
STITIONS. — ITS IDENTITY IS WITH HUMAN PROGRESS. — ITS
AGENCY, EVEN WHERE UNACKNOWLEDGED, IS UNIVERSAL.

Oh, thou true Iris! sporting on thy bow,
　　Of tears and smiles! Jove's herald, Poetry,
Thou reflex image of all joy and woe,
　　Both fused in light by thy dear fantasy!
Lo! from the clay how Genius lifts its life,
　　And grows one pure Idea, one calm soul!
True, its own clearness must reflect our strife;
　　True, its completeness must comprise our whole:
But as the sun transmutes the sullen hues
　　Of marsh-grown vapours into vermeil dyes,

[1] It is supposed by many of the commentators on Dante, that in the form
of his lost Beatrice, who guides him in his Vision of Heaven, he allegorizes
Religious Faith.

And melts them later into twilight dews,
  Shedding on flowers the baptism of the skies;
So glows the Ideal in the air we breathe,
  So from the fumes of sorrow and of sin,
Doth its warm light in rosy colours wreathe
  Its playful cloudland, storing balms within.

Survey the Poet in his mortal mould,
  Man, amongst men, descended from his throne!
The moth that chased the star now frets the fold,
  Our cares, our faults, our follies are his own.
Passions as idle, and desires as vain,
Vex the wild heart, and dupe the erring brain.
From Freedom's field the recreant Horace flies
To kiss the hand by which his country dies;
From Mary's grave the mighty Peasant turns,
And hoarse with orgies rings the laugh of Burns.
While Rousseau's lips a lackey's vices own,—
Lips that could draw the thunder on a throne!
But when from Life the Actual GENIUS springs,
  When, self-transformed by its own magic rod,
It snaps the fetters and expands the wings,
  And drops the fleshly garb that veiled the god,
How the mists vanish as the form ascends!
How in its aureole every sunbeam blends!
By the Arch-Brightener of Creation seen,
  How dim the crowns on perishable brows!
The snows of Atlas melt beneath the sheen,
  Through Thebaid caves the rushing splendour flows.
Cimmerian glooms with Asian beams are bright,
And Earth reposes in a belt of light.
Now stern as Vengeance shines the awful form,
Armed with the bolt and glowing through the storm;
Sets the great deeps of human passion free,
And whelms the bulwarks that would breast the sea.
Roused by its voice the ghastly Wars arise,
Mars reddens earth, the Valkyrs pale the skies;
Dim Superstition from her hell escapes,

With all her shadowy brood of monster shapes;
Here life itself the scowl of Typhon[1] takes;
There Conscience shudders at Alecto's snakes;
From Gothic graves at midnight yawning wide,
In gory cerements gibbering spectres glide;
And where o'er blasted heaths the lightnings flame,
Black secret hags "do deeds without a name!"
Yet through its direst agencies of awe,
Light marks its presence and pervades its law,
And, like Orion when the storms are loud,
It links creation while it gilds a cloud.
By ruthless Thor, free Thought, frank Honour stand,
Fame's grand desire, and zeal for Fatherland.
The grim Religion of Barbarian Fear
With some Hereafter still connects the Here,
Lifts the gross sense to some spiritual source,
And thrones some Jove above the Titan Force,
Till, love completing what in awe began,
From the rude savage dawns the thoughtful man.

Then, oh, behold the Glorious comforter!
  Still bright'ning worlds but gladd'ning now the hearth,
Or like the lustre of our nearest star,
  Fused in the common atmosphere of earth.
It sports like hope upon the captive's chain;
Descends in dreams upon the couch of pain;
To wonder's realm allures the earnest child;
To the chaste love refines the instinct wild;
And as in waters the reflected beam,
Still where we turn, glides with us up the stream,
And while in truth the whole expanse is bright,
Yields to each eye its own fond path of light,—
So over life the rays of Genius fall,
Give each his track because illuming all.

[1] The gloomy Typhon of Egypt assumes many of the mystic attributes of
the Principle of Life which, in the Grecian Apotheosis of the Indian Bacchus,
is represented in so genial a character of exuberant joy and everlasting youth.

IV.

FORGIVENESS TO THE ERRORS OF OUR BENEFACTORS.

Hence is that secret pardon we bestow
  In the true instinct of the grateful heart,
Upon the Sons of Song.   The good they do
  In the clear world of their Uranian art
Endures forever; while the evil done
  In the poor drama of their mortal scene,
Is but a passing cloud before the sun;
  Space hath no record where the mist hath been.
Boots it to us if Shakspeare erred like man?
  Why idly question that most mystic life?
Eno' the giver in his gifts to scan;
  To bless the sheaves with which thy fields are rife,
Nor, blundering, guess through what obstructive clay
The glorious corn-seed struggled up to day.

V.

THE IDEAL IS NOT CONFINED TO POETS. — ALGERNON SIDNEY REC-
OGNIZES HIS IDEAL IN LIBERTY, AND BELIEVES IN ITS TRIUMPH
WHERE THE MERE PRACTICAL MAN COULD BEHOLD BUT ITS
RUINS; YET LIBERTY IN THIS WORLD MUST EVER BE AN IDEAL,
AND THE LAND THAT IT PROMISES CAN BE FOUND BUT IN
DEATH.

But not to you alone, O Sons of Song,
The wings that float the loftier airs along.
Whoever lifts us from the dust we are,
  Beyond the sensual to spiritual goals;
Who from the MOMENT and the SELF afar
  By deathless deeds allures reluctant souls,
Gives the warm life to what the Limner draws, —
Plato but thought what godlike Cato was.[1]
Recall the Wars of England's giant-born,
  Is Elyot's voice, is Hampden's death in vain?

---

[1] What Plato thought, and godlike Cato was. — POPE.

Have all the meteors of the vernal morn
  But wasted light upon a frozen main?
Where is that child of Carnage, Freedom, flown?
The Sybarite lolls upon the martyr's throne.
Lewd, ribald jests succeed to solemn zeal;
And things of silk to Cromwell's men of steel.
Cold are the hosts the tromps of Ireton thrilled,
And hushed the senates Vane's large presence filled.
In what strong heart doth the old manhood dwell?
Where art thou, Freedom?   Look! in Sidney's cell!
There still as stately stands the living Truth,
Smiling on age as it had smiled on youth.
Her forts dismantled, and her shrines o'erthrown,
The headsman's block her last dread altar-stone,
No sanction left to Reason's vulgar hope,
Far from the wrecks expands her prophet's scope.
Millennial morns the tombs of Kedron gild,
The hands of saints the glorious walls rebuild,—
Till each foundation garnished with its gem,
High o'er Gehenna flames Jerusalem!
O thou blood-stained Ideal of the free,
Whose breath is heard in clarions, — Liberty!
Sublimer for thy grand illusions past,
Thou spring'st to Heaven,— Religion at the last.
Alike below, or commonwealths or thrones,
Where'er men gather some crushed victim groans;
Only in death thy real form we see,
All life is bondage,— souls alone are free.
Thus through the waste the wandering Hebrews went,
Fire on the march, but cloud upon the tent.
At last on Pisgah see the prophet stand,
Before his vision spreads the PROMISED LAND;
But where revealed the Canaan to his eye? —
Upon the mountain he ascends to die.

VI.

Yet whatsoever be our bondage here,
All have two portals to the phantom sphere.
What hath not glided through those gates that ope
Beyond the Hour, to MEMORY or to HOPE!
Give Youth the Garden, — still it soars above,
Seeks some far glory, some diviner love.
Place Age amidst the Golgotha,— its eyes
Still quit the graves, to rest upon the skies;
And while the dust, unheeded, moulders there,
Track some lost angel through cerulean air.

Lo! where the Austrian binds, with formal chain,
The crownless son of earth's last Charlemagne,—
Him, at whose birth laughed all the violet vales
    (While yet unfallen stood thy sovereign star,
O Lucifer of nations).   Hark, the gales
    Swell with the shout from all the hosts, whose war
Rended the Alps, and crimsoned Memphian Nile,—
    "Way for the coming of the Conqueror's Son:
Woe to the Merchant-Carthage of the Isle!
    Woe to the Scythian ice-world of the Don!
O Thunder Lord, thy Lemnian bolts prepare,
The Eagle's eyry hath its eagle heir!"
Hark, at that shout from north to south, gray Power
    Quails on its weak, hereditary thrones;
And widowed mothers prophesy the hour
    Of future carnage to their cradled sons.
What! shall our race to blood be thus consigned,
And Até claim an heirloom in mankind?
Are these red lots unshaken in the urn?
Years pass; approach, pale Questioner, and learn

Chained to his rock, with brows that vainly frown,
The fallen Titan sinks in darkness down!
And sadly gazing through his gilded grate,
Behold the child whose birth was as a fate!
Far from the land in which his life began;
Walled from the healthful air of hardy man;
Reared by cold hearts, and watched by jealous eyes,
His guardians jailers, and his comrades spies.
Each trite convention courtly fears inspire
To stint experience and to dwarf desire;
Narrows the action to a puppet stage,
And trains the eaglet to the starling's cage.
On the dejected brow and smileless cheek,
What weary thought the languid lines bespeak;
Till drop by drop, from jaded day to day,
The sickly life-streams ooze themselves away.
Yet oft in HOPE a boundless realm was thine,
   That vaguest Infinite, — the Dream of Fame;
Son of the sword that first made kings divine,
   Heir to man's grandest royalty, — a Name!
Then didst thou burst upon the startled world,
And keep the glorious promise of thy birth;
Then were the wings that bear the bolt unfurled,
   A monarch's voice cried, "Place upon the earth!"
A new Philippi gained a second Rome,
And the Son's sword avenged the greater Cæsar's doom.

VII.

EXAMPLE OF MEMORY AS LEADING TO THE IDEAL, — AMIDST LIFE
HOWEVER HUMBLE, AND IN A MIND HOWEVER IGNORANT. — THE
VILLAGE WIDOW.

But turn the eye to life's sequestered vale
   And lowly roofs remote in hamlets green.
Oft in my boyhood where the moss-grown pale
   Fenced quiet graves, a female form was seen;
Each eve she sought the melancholy ground,

And lingering paused, and wistful looked around.
If yet some footstep rustled through the grass,
Timorous she shrunk, and watched the shadow pass;
Then, when the spot lay lone amidst the gloom,
Crept to one grave too humble for a tomb,
There silent bowed her face above the dead,
For, if in prayer, the prayer was inly said;
Still as the moonbeam, paused her quiet shade,
Still as the moonbeam, through the yews to fade.
Whose dust thus hallowed by so fond a care?
What the grave saith not, let the heart declare.
  On yonder green two orphan children played;
By yonder rill two plighted lovers strayed;
In yonder shrine two lives were blent in one,
And joy-bells chimed beneath a summer sun.
Poor was their lot, their bread in labour found;
No parent blessed them, and no kindred owned;
They smiled to hear the wise their choice condemn;
They loved — they loved — and love was wealth to them!
Hark — one short week — again the holy bell!
Still shone the sun; but dirge like boomed the knell, —
The icy hand had severed breast from breast;
Left life to toil, and summoned Death to rest.
Full fifty years since then have passed away,
Her cheek is furrowed, and her hair is gray.
Yet, when she speaks of *him* (the times are rare),
Hear in her voice how youth still trembles there.
The very name of that young life that died
Still heaves the bosom, and recalls the bride.
Lone o'er the widow's hearth those years have fled,
The daily toil still wins the daily bread;
No books deck sorrow with fantastic dyes;
Her fond romance her woman heart supplies;
And, haply in the few still moments given,
(Day's taskwork done), to memory, death, and heaven,
To that unuttered poem may belong
Thoughts of such pathos as had beggared song.

VIII.

HENCE IN HOPE, MEMORY, AND PRAYER, ALL OF US ARE POETS.

Yes, while thou hopest, music fills the air,
  While thou rememberest, life reclothes the clod;
While thou canst feel the electric chain of prayer,
  Breathe but a thought, and be a soul with God!
Let not these forms of matter bound thine eye.
  He who the vanishing point of Human things
Lifts from the landscape, lost amidst the sky,
  Has found the Ideal which the poet sings,
Has pierced the pall around the senses thrown,
And is himself a poet, though unknown.

IX.

APPLICATION OF THE POEM TO THE TALE TO WHICH IT IS PRE-
FIXED. — THE RHINE, — ITS IDEAL CHARACTER IN ITS HISTORI-
CAL AND LEGENDARY ASSOCIATIONS.

Eno'! — my song is closing, and to thee,
  Land of the North, I dedicate its lay;
As I have done the simple tale to be
  The drama of this prelude!
                                        Far away
Rolls the swift Rhine beneath the starry ray;
But to my ear its haunted waters sigh;
Its moonlight mountains glimmer on my eye;
On wave, on marge, as on a wizard's glass,
Imperial ghosts in dim procession pass;
Lords of the wild, the first great Father-men,
Their fane the hill-top, and their home the glen;
Frowning they fade; a bridge of steel appears
With frank-eyed Cæsar smiling through the spears;
The march moves onwards, and the mirror brings
The Gothic crowns of Carlovingian kings:
Vanished alike! The Hermit rears his Cross,
And barbs neigh shrill, and plumes in tumult toss,

While (knighthood's sole sweet conquest from the Moor)
Sings to Arabian lutes the Tourbadour.
  Not yet, not yet; still glide some lingering shades,
Still breathe some murmurs as the starlight fades,
Still from her rock I hear the Siren call,
And see the tender ghost in Roland's mouldering hall!

X.

APPLICATION OF THE POEM CONTINUED. — THE IDEAL LENDS ITS
AID TO THE MOST FAMILIAR AND THE MOST ACTUAL SORROW OF
LIFE. — FICTION COMPARED TO SLEEP, — IT STRENGTHENS WHILE
IT SOOTHES.

Trite were the tale I tell of love and doom,
(Whose life hath loved not, whose not mourned a tomb?)
But fiction draws a poetry from grief,
As art its healing from the withered leaf.
Play thou, sweet Fancy, round the sombre truth,
  Crown the sad Genius ere it lower the torch!
When death the altar and the victim youth,
  Flutes fill the air, and garlands deck the porch.
As down the river drifts the Pilgrim sail,
Clothe the rude hill-tops, lull the Northern gale;
With childlike lore the fatal course beguile,
And brighten death with Love's untiring smile.
Along the banks let fairy forms be seen
"By fountain clear, or spangled starlike sheen." [1]
Let sound and shape to which the sense is dull
Haunt the soul opening on the Beautiful.
And when at length, the symbol voyage done,
Surviving Grief shrinks lonely from the sun,
By tender types show Grief what memories bloom
From lost delight, what fairies guard the tomb.
Scorn not the dream, O world-worn; pause a while,
New strength shall nerve thee as the dreams beguile,
Stung by the rest, less far shall seem the goal!
As sleep to life, so fiction to the soul.

       [1] " Midsummer Night's Dream."

THE

PILGRIMS OF THE RHINE.

CHAPTER I.

IN WHICH THE READER IS INTRODUCED TO QUEEN NYMPHALIN.

In one of those green woods which belong so peculiarly to our island (for the Continent has its forests, but England its woods) there lived, a short time ago, a charming little fairy called Nymphalin. I believe she is descended from a younger branch of the house of Mab; but perhaps that may only be a genealogical fable, for your fairies are very susceptible to the pride of ancestry, and it is impossible to deny that they fall somewhat reluctantly into the liberal opinions so much in vogue at the present day.

However that may be, it is quite certain that all the courtiers in Nymphalin's domain (for she was a queen fairy) made a point of asserting her right to this illustrious descent; and accordingly she quartered the Mab arms with her own,—three acorns vert, with a grasshopper rampant. It was as merry a little court as could possibly be conceived, and on a fine midsummer night it would have been worth while attending the queen's balls; that is to say, if you could have got a ticket,— a favour not obtained without great interest.

But, unhappily, until both men and fairies adopt Mr. Owen's proposition, and live in parallelograms, they will always be the victims of *ennui*. And Nymphalin, who had been disappointed in love, and was still unmarried, had for the last five or six months been exceedingly tired even of giving balls. She yawned very frequently, and consequently yawning became a fashion.

"But why don't we have some new dances, my Pipalee?" said Nymphalin to her favourite maid of honour; "these waltzes are very old-fashioned."

"Very old-fashioned," said Pipalee.

The queen gaped, and Pipalee did the same.

It was a gala night; the court was held in a lone and beautiful hollow, with the wild brake closing round it on every side, so that no human step could easily gain the spot. Wherever the shadows fell upon the brake a glow-worm made a point of exhibiting itself, and the bright August moon sailed slowly above, pleased to look down upon so charming a scene of merriment; for they wrong the moon who assert that she has an objection to mirth,— with the mirth of fairies she has all possible sympathy. Here and there in the thicket the scarce honeysuckles — in August honeysuckles are somewhat out of season — hung their rich festoons, and at that moment they were crowded with the elderly fairies, who had given up dancing and taken to scandal. Besides the honeysuckle you might see the hawkweed and the white convolvulus, varying the soft verdure of the thicket; and mushrooms in abundance had sprung up in the circle, glittering in the silver moonlight, and acceptable beyond measure to the dancers: every one knows how agreeable a thing tents are in a *fête champêtre!* I was mistaken in saying that the brake closed the circle *entirely* round; for there was one gap, scarcely apparent to mortals, through which a fairy at least might catch a view of a brook that was close at hand, rippling in the stars, and checkered at intervals by the rich weeds floating on the surface, interspersed with the delicate arrowhead and the silver water-lily. Then the trees themselves, in their prodigal variety of hues,— the blue, the purple, the yellowing tint, the tender and silvery verdure, and the deep mass of shade frowning into black; the willow, the elm, the ash, the fir, and the lime, "and, best of all, Old England's haunted oak;" these hues were broken again into a thousand minor and subtler shades as the twinkling stars pierced the foliage, or the moon slept with a richer light upon some favoured glade.

It was a gala night; the elderly fairies, as I said before, were chatting among the honeysuckles; the young were flirting, and dancing, and making love; the middle-aged talked politics under the mushrooms; and the queen herself and half-a-dozen of her favourites were yawning their pleasure from a little mound covered with the thickest moss.

"It has been very dull, madam, ever since Prince Fayzenheim left us," said the fairy Nip.

The queen sighed.

"How handsome the prince is!" said Pipalee.

The queen blushed.

"He wore the prettiest dress in the world; and what a mustache!" cried Pipalee, fanning herself with her left wing.

"He was a coxcomb," said the lord treasurer, sourly. The lord treasurer was the honestest and most disagreeable fairy at court; he was an admirable husband, brother, son, cousin, uncle, and godfather,— it was these virtues that had made him a lord treasurer. Unfortunately they had not made him a sensible fairy. He was like Charles the Second in one respect, for he never did a wise thing; but he was not like him in another, for he very often said a foolish one.

The queen frowned.

"A young prince is not the worse for that," retorted Pipalee. "Heigho! does your Majesty think his Highness likely to return?"

"Don't tease me," said Nymphalin, pettishly.

The lord treasurer, by way of giving the conversation an agreeable turn, reminded her Majesty that there was a prodigious accumulation of business to see to, especially that difficult affair about the emmet-wasp loan. Her Majesty rose, and leaning on Pipalee's arm, walked down to the supper tent.

"Pray," said the fairy Trip to the fairy Nip, "what is all this talk about Prince Fayzenheim? Excuse my ignorance; I am only just out, your know."

"Why," answered Nip, a young courtier, not a marrying fairy, but very seductive, "the story runs thus: Last summer a foreigner visited us, calling himself Prince Fayzenheim: one of your German fairies, I fancy; no great things, but an excellent waltzer. He wore long spurs, made out of the stings of the horse-flies in the Black Forest; his cap sat on one side, and his mustachios curled like the lip of the dragon-flower. He was on his travels, and amused himself by making love to the queen. You can't fancy, dear Trip, how fond she was of hearing him tell stories about the strange creatures of Germany,—about wild huntsmen, water-sprites, and a pack of such stuff," added Nip, contemptuously, for Nip was a freethinker.

"In short?" said Trip.

"In short, she loved," cried Nip, with a theatrical air.

"And the prince?"

"Packed up his clothes, and sent on his travelling-carriage, in order that he might go at his ease on the top of a stage-pigeon; in short — as you say — in short, he deserted the queen, and ever since she has set the fashion of yawning."

"It was very naughty in him," said the gentle Trip.

"Ah, my dear creature," cried Nip, "if it had been *you* to whom he had paid his addresses!"

Trip simpered, and the old fairies from their seats in the honeysuckles observed she was "sadly conducted;" but the Trips had never been *too* respectable.

Meanwhile the queen, leaning on Pipalee, said, after a short pause, "Do you know I have formed a plan!"

"How delightful!" cried Pipalee. "Another gala!"

"Pooh, surely even you must be tired with such levities: the spirit of the age is no longer frivolous; and I dare say as the march of gravity proceeds, we shall get rid of galas altogether." The queen said this with an air of inconceivable wisdom, for the "Society for the Diffusion of General Stupefaction" had been recently established among the fairies, and its tracts had driven all the light reading out of the market. "The Penny Proser" had contributed greatly to the increase of knowledge and yawning, so visibly progressive among the courtiers.

"No," continued Nymphalin; "I have thought of something better than galas. Let us travel!"

Pipalee clasped her hands in ecstasy.

" Where shall we travel? "

"Let us go up the Rhine," said the queen, turning away her head. "We shall be amazingly welcomed; there are fairies without number all the way by its banks, and various distant connections of ours whose nature and properties will afford interest and instruction to a philosophical mind."

"Number Nip, for instance," cried the gay Pipalee.

"The Red Man!" said the graver Nymphalin.

"Oh, my queen, what an excellent scheme!" and Pipalee was so lively during the rest of the night that the old fairies in the honeysuckle insinuated that the lady of honour had drunk a buttercup too much of the Maydew.

CHAPTER II.

THE LOVERS.

I wish only for such readers as give themselves heart and soul up to me,— if they begin to cavil I have done with them; their fancy should put itself entirely under my management; and, after all, ought they not to be too glad to get out of this hackneyed and melancholy world, to be run away with by an author who promises them something new?

From the heights of Bruges, a Mortal and his betrothed gazed upon the scene below. They saw the sun set slowly amongst purple masses of cloud, and the lover turned to his mistress and sighed deeply; for her cheek was delicate in its blended roses, beyond the beauty that belongs to the hues of health; and when he saw the sun sinking from the world, the thought came upon him that *she* was his sun, and the glory that she shed over his life might soon pass away into the bosom of the "ever-during Dark." But against the clouds rose one of the many spires that characterize the town of Bruges; and on that spire, tapering into heaven, rested the eyes of Gertrude Vane. The different objects that caught the gaze of each was emblematic both of the different channel of their thoughts and the different elements of their nature: he thought of the sorrow, she of the consolation; his heart prophesied of the passing away from earth, hers of the ascension into heaven. The lower part of the landscape was wrapped in shade; but just where the bank curved round in a mimic bay, the waters caught the sun's parting smile, and rippled against the herbage that clothed the shore, with a scarcely noticeable wave. There are two of the numerous mills which are so picturesque a feature of that country, standing at a distance from each other on the rising banks, their sails perfectly still in the cool silence of the evening, and adding to the rustic tranquillity which breathed around. For to me there is something in the still sails of one of those inventions of man's industry peculiarly eloquent of repose: the rest seems typical of the repose of our own passions, short and uncertain, contrary to their natural ordination; and doubly impressive from the feeling which admonishes us how precarious is the stillness, how utterly dependent on every wind rising at any moment and from any quarter of the heavens! They saw before them no living forms, save of one or two peasants yet lingering by the water-side.

Trevylyan drew closer to his Gertrude; for his love was inexpressibly tender, and his vigilant anxiety for her made his stern frame feel the first coolness of the evening even before she felt it herself.

"Dearest, let me draw your mantle closer round you."

Gertrude smiled her thanks.

"I feel better than I have done for weeks," said she; "and when once we get into the Rhine, you will see me grow so strong as to shock all your interest for me."

"Ah, would to Heaven my interest for you may be put to such an ordeal!" said Trevylyan; and they turned slowly to the inn, where Gertrude's father already awaited them.

Trevylyan was of a wild, a resolute, and an active nature. Thrown on the world at the age of sixteen, he had passed his youth in alternate pleasure, travel, and solitary study. At the age in which manhood is least susceptible to caprice, and most perhaps to passion, he fell in love with the loveliest person that ever dawned upon a poet's vision. I say this without exaggeration, for Gertrude Vane's was indeed the beauty, but the perishable beauty, of a dream. It happened most singularly to Trevylyan (but he was a singular man), that being naturally one whose affections it was very difficult to excite, he should have fallen in love at first sight with a person whose disease, already declared, would have deterred any other heart from risking its treasures on a bark so utterly unfitted for the voyage of life. Consumption, but consumption in its most beautiful shape, had set its seal upon Gertrude Vane, when Trevylyan first saw her, and at once loved. He knew the danger of the disease; he did not, except at intervals, deceive himself; he wrestled against the new passion: but, stern as his nature was, he could not conquer it. He loved, he confessed his love, and Gertrude returned it.

In a love like this, there is something ineffably beautiful, — it is essentially the poetry of passion. Desire grows hallowed by fear, and, scarce permitted to indulge its vent in the common channel of the senses, breaks forth into those vague yearnings, those lofty aspirations, which pine for the Bright, the Far, the Unattained. It is "the desire of the moth for the star;" it is the love of the soul!

Gertrude was advised by the faculty to try a southern climate; but Gertrude was the daughter of a German mother, and her young fancy had been nursed in all the wild legends and the alluring visions that belong to the children of the Rhine. Her imagination, more romantic than classic, yearned for the vine-clad hills and haunted forests which are so fertile in their spells to those who have once drunk, even sparingly, of the Literature of the North. Her desire strongly expressed, her declared conviction that if any change of scene could yet arrest the progress of her malady it would be the shores of the river she had so longed to visit, prevailed with her physicians and her father, and they consented to that pilgrimage along the Rhine on which Gertrude, her father, and her lover were now bound.

It was by the green curve of the banks which the lovers saw from the heights of Bruges that our fairy travellers met. They were reclining on the water-side, playing at dominos with eye-bright and the black specks of the trefoil; namely, Pipalee, Nip, Trip, and the lord treasurer (for that was all the party selected by the queen for her travelling *cortége*), and waiting for her Majesty, who, being a curious little elf, had gone round the town to reconnoitre.

"Bless me!" said the lord treasurer; "what a mad freak is this! Crossing that immense pond of water! And was there ever such bad grass as this? One may see that the fairies thrive ill here."

"You are always discontented, my lord," said Pipalee; "but then you are somewhat too old to travel,—at least, unless you go in your nutshell and four."

The lord treasurer did not like this remark, so he muttered a peevish pshaw, and took a pinch of honeysuckle dust to console himself for being forced to put up with so much frivolity.

At this moment, ere the moon was yet at her middest height, Nymphalin joined her subjects.

"I have just returned," said she, with a melancholy expression on her countenance, "from a scene that has almost renewed in me that sympathy with human beings which of late years our race has well-nigh relinquished.

"I hurried through the town without noticing much food for adventure. I paused for a moment on a fat citizen's pillow, and bade him dream of love. He woke in a fright, and ran down to see that his cheeses were safe. I swept with a light wing over a politician's eyes, and straightway he dreamed of theatres and music. I caught an undertaker in his first nap, and I have left him whirled into a waltz. For what would be sleep if it did not contrast life? Then I came to a solitary chamber, in which a girl, in her tenderest youth, knelt by the bedside in prayer, and I saw that the death-spirit had passed over her, and the blight was on the leaves of the rose. The room was still and hushed, the angel of Purity kept watch there. Her heart was full of love, and yet

of holy thoughts, and I bade her dream of the long life denied
to her,—of a happy home, of the kisses of her young lover,
of eternal faith, and unwaning tenderness. Let her at least
enjoy in dreams what Fate has refused to Truth! And, passing from the room, I found her lover stretched in his cloak
beside the door; for he reads with a feverish and desperate
prophecy the doom that waits her; and so loves he the very
air she breathes, the very ground she treads, that when she
has left his sight he creeps, silently and unknown to her, to
the nearest spot hallowed by her presence, anxious that while
yet she is on earth not an hour, not a moment, should be
wasted upon other thoughts than those that belong to her;
and feeling a security, a fearful joy, in lessening the distance
that *now* only momentarily divides them. And that love
seemed to me not as the love of the common world, and I
stayed my wings and looked upon it as a thing that centuries
might pass and bring no parallel to, in its beauty and its melancholy truth. But I kept away the sleep from the lover's
eyes, for well I knew that sleep was a tyrant, that shortened
the brief time of waking tenderness for the living, yet spared
him; and one sad, anxious thought of her was sweeter, in
spite of its sorrow, than the brightest of fairy dreams. So I
left him awake, and watching there through the long night,
and felt that the children of earth have still something that
unites them to the spirits of a finer race, so long as they retain amongst them the presence of real love!"

And oh! is there not a truth also in our fictions of the Unseen World? Are there not yet bright lingerers by the forest
and the stream? Do the moon and the soft stars look out
on no delicate and winged forms bathing in their light? Are
the fairies and the invisible hosts but the children of our
dreams, and not their inspiration? Is that all a delusion
which speaks from the golden page? And is the world only
given to harsh and anxious travellers that walk to and fro in
pursuit of no gentle shadows? Are the chimeras of the passions the sole spirits of the universe? No! while my remembrance treasures in its deepest cell the image of one no more,
—one who was "not of the earth, earthy;" one in whom

love was the essence of thoughts divine; one whose shape and mould, whose heart and genius, would, had Poesy never before dreamed it, have called forth the first notion of spirits resembling mortals, but not of them,— no, Gertrude! while I remember you, the faith, the trust in brighter shapes and fairer natures than the world knows of, comes clinging to my heart; and still will I think that Fairies might have watched over your sleep and Spirits have ministered to your dreams.

CHAPTER III.

FEELINGS.

GERTRUDE and her companions proceeded by slow and, to her, delightful stages to Rotterdam. Trevylyan sat by her side, and her hand was ever in his; and when her delicate frame became sensible of fatigue, her head drooped on his shoulder as its natural resting-place. Her father was a man who had lived long enough to have encountered many reverses of fortune, and they had left him, as I am apt to believe long adversity usually *does* leave its prey, somewhat chilled and somewhat hardened to affection; passive and quiet of hope, resigned to the worst as to the common order of events, and expecting little from the best, as an unlooked-for incident in the regularity of human afflictions. He was insensible of his daughter's danger, for he was not one whom the fear of love endows with prophetic vision; and he lived tranquilly in the present, without asking what new misfortune awaited him in the future. Yet he loved his child, his only child, with whatever of affection was left him by the many shocks his heart had received; and in her approaching connection with one rich and noble as Trevylyan, he felt even something bordering upon pleasure. Lapped in the apathetic indifference of his nature, he leaned back in the carriage, enjoying the bright weather that attended their journey, and sensible — for he

was one of fine and cultivated taste — of whatever beauties of nature or remains of art varied their course. A companion of this sort was the most agreeable that two persons never needing a third could desire; he left them undisturbed to the intoxication of their mutual presence; he marked not the interchange of glances; he listened not to the whisper, the low delicious whisper, with which the heart speaks its sympathy to heart. He broke not that charmed silence which falls over us when the thoughts are full, and words leave nothing to explain; that repose of feeling; that certainty that we are understood without the effort of words, which makes the real luxury of intercourse and the true enchantment of travel. What a memory hours like these bequeath, after we have settled down into the calm occupation of common life! How beautiful, through the vista of years, seems that brief moonlight track upon the waters of our youth!

And Trevylyan's nature, which, as I have said before, was naturally hard and stern, which was hot, irritable, ambitious, and prematurely tinctured with the policy and lessons of the world, seemed utterly changed by the peculiarities of his love. Every hour, every moment was full of incident to him; every look of Gertrude's was entered in the tablets of his heart; so that his love knew no languor, it required no change: he was absorbed in it, — *it was himself!* And he was soft, and watchful as the step of a mother by the couch of her sick child; the lion within him was tamed by indomitable love; the sadness, the presentiment, that was mixed with all his passion for Gertrude, filled him too with that poetry of feeling which is the result of thoughts weighing upon us, and not to be expressed by ordinary language. In this part of their journey, as I find by the date, were the following lines written; they are to be judged as the lines of one in whom emotion and truth were the only inspiration: —

I.

> As leaves left darkling in the flush of day,
>   When glints the glad sun checkering o'er the tree,
> I see the green earth brightening in the ray,
>   Which only casts a shadow upon me!

II.

What are the beams, the flowers, the glory, all
  Life's glow and gloss, the music and the bloom,
When every sun but speeds the Eternal Pall,
  And Time is Death that dallies with the Tomb?

III.

And yet — oh yet, so young, so pure! — the while
  Fresh laugh the rose-hues round youth's morning sky,
That voice, those eyes, the deep love of that smile,
  Are they not soul — *all* soul — and *can* they die?

IV.

Are there the words "No More" for thoughts like ours?
  Must the bark sink upon so soft a wave?
Hath the short summer of thy life no flowers
  But those which bloom above thine early grave?

V.

O God! and what is life, that I should live?
  (Hath not the world enow of common clay?)
And she — the Rose — whose life a soul could give
  To the void desert, sigh its sweets away?

VI.

And I that love thee thus, to whom the air,
  Blest by thy breath, makes heaven where'er it be,
Watch thy cheek wane, and smile away despair,
  Lest it should dim one hour yet left to Thee.

VII

Still let me conquer self; oh, still conceal
  By the smooth brow the snake that coils below;
Break, break my heart! it comforts yet to feel
  That *she* dreams on, unwakened by my woe!

VIII.

Hushed, where the Star's soft angel loves to keep
  Watch o'er their tide, the morning waters roll;
So glides my spirit, — darkness in the deep,
  But o'er the wave the presence of thy soul!

Gertrude had not as yet the presentiments that filled the soul of Trevylyan. She thought too little of herself to know her danger, and those hours to her were hours of unmingled sweetness. Sometimes, indeed, the exhaustion of her disease tinged her spirits with a vague sadness, an abstraction came over her, and a languor she vainly struggled against. These fits of dejection and gloom touched Trevylyan to the quick; his eye never ceased to watch them, nor his heart to soothe. Often when he marked them, he sought to attract her attention from what he fancied, though erringly, a sympathy with his own forebodings, and to lead her young and romantic imagination through the temporary beguilements of fiction; for Gertrude was yet in the first bloom of youth, and all the dews of beautiful childhood sparkled freshly from the virgin blossoms of her mind. And Trevylyan, who had passed some of his early years among the students of Leipsic, and was deeply versed in the various world of legendary lore, ransacked his memory for such tales as seemed to him most likely to win her interest; and often with false smiles entered into the playful tale, or oftener, with more faithful interest, into the graver legend of trials that warned yet beguiled them from their own. Of such tales I have selected but a few; I know not that they are the least unworthy of repetition,— they are those which many recollections induce me to repeat the most willingly. Gertrude loved these stories, for she had not yet lost, by the coldness of the world, one leaf from that soft and wild romance which belonged to her beautiful mind; and, more than all, she loved the sound of a voice which every day became more and more musical to her ear. "Shall I tell you," said Trevylyan, one morning, as he observed her gloomier mood stealing over the face of Gertrude,— "shall I tell you, ere yet we pass into the dull land of Holland, a story of Malines, whose spires we shall shortly see?" Gertrude's face brightened at once, and as she leaned back in the carriage as it whirled rapidly along, and fixed her deep blue eyes on Trevylyan, he began the following tale.

CHAPTER IV.

THE MAID OF MALINES.

It was noonday in the town of Malines, or Mechlin, as the English usually term it; the Sabbath bell had summoned the inhabitants to divine worship; and the crowd that had loitered round the Church of St. Rembauld had gradually emptied itself within the spacious aisles of the sacred edifice.

A young man was standing in the street, with his eyes bent on the ground, and apparently listening for some sound; for without raising his looks from the rude pavement, he turned to every corner of it with an intent and anxious expression of countenance. He held in one hand a staff, in the other a long slender cord, the end of which trailed on the ground; every now and then he called, with a plaintive voice, "Fido, Fido, come back! Why hast thou deserted me?" Fido returned not; the dog, wearied of confinement, had slipped from the string, and was at play with his kind in a distant quarter of the town, leaving the blind man to seek his way as he might to his solitary inn.

By and by a light step passed through the street, and the young stranger's face brightened.

"Pardon me," said he, turning to the spot where his quick ear had caught the sound, "and direct me, if you are not much pressed for a few moments' time, to the hotel 'Mortier d'Or.'"

It was a young woman, whose dress betokened that she belonged to the middling class of life, whom he thus addressed. "It is some distance hence, sir," said she; "but if you continue your way straight on for about a hundred yards, and then take the second turn to your right hand — "

"Alas!" interrupted the stranger, with a melancholy smile, "your direction will avail me little; my dog has deserted me, and I am blind!"

There was something in these words, and in the stranger's voice, which went irresistibly to the heart of the young woman. "Pray forgive me," she said, almost with tears in her eyes, "I did not perceive your —" misfortune, she was about to say, but she checked herself with an instinctive delicacy. "Lean upon me, I will conduct you to the door; nay, sir," observing that he hesitated, "I have time enough to spare, I assure you."

The stranger placed his hand on the young woman's arm; and though Lucille was naturally so bashful that even her mother would laughingly reproach her for the excess of a maiden virtue, she felt not the least pang of shame, as she found herself thus suddenly walking through the streets of Malines along with a young stranger, whose dress and air betokened him of rank superior to her own.

"Your voice is very gentle," said he, after a pause; "and that," he added, with a slight sigh, "is the only criterion by which I know the young and the beautiful!" Lucille now blushed, and with a slight mixture of pain in the blush, for she knew well that to beauty she had no pretension. "Are you a native of this town?" continued he.

"Yes, sir; my father holds a small office in the customs, and my mother and I eke out his salary by making lace. We are called poor, but we do not feel it, sir."

"You are fortunate! there is no wealth like the heart's wealth,— content," answered the blind man, mournfully.

"And, monsieur," said Lucille, feeling angry with herself that she had awakened a natural envy in the stranger's mind, and anxious to change the subject — "and, monsieur, has he been long at Malines?"

"But yesterday. I am passing through the Low Countries on a tour; perhaps you smile at the tour of a blind man, but it is wearisome even to the blind to rest always in the same place. I thought during church-time, when the streets were empty, that I might, by the help of my dog, enjoy safely at least the air, if not the sight of the town; but there are some persons, methinks, who cannot have even a dog for a friend!"

The blind man spoke bitterly,— the desertion of his dog

had touched him to the core. Lucille wiped her eyes. "And does Monsieur travel then alone?" said she; and looking at his face more attentively than she had yet ventured to do, she saw that he was scarcely above two-and-twenty. "His father, and his *mother*," she added, with an emphasis on the last word, "are they not with him?"

"I am an orphan!" answered the stranger; "and I have neither brother nor sister."

The desolate condition of the blind man quite melted Lucille; never had she been so strongly affected. She felt a strange flutter at the heart, a secret and earnest sympathy, that attracted her at once towards him. She wished that Heaven had suffered her to be his sister!

The contrast between the youth and the form of the stranger, and the affliction which took hope from the one and activity from the other, increased the compassion he excited. His features were remarkably regular, and had a certain nobleness in their outline; and his frame was gracefully and firmly knit, though he moved cautiously and with no cheerful step.

They had now passed into a narrow street leading towards the hotel, when they heard behind them the clatter of hoofs; and Lucille, looking hastily back, saw that a troop of the Belgian horse was passing through the town.

She drew her charge close by the wall, and trembling with fear for him, she stationed herself by his side. The troop passed at a full trot through the street; and at the sound of their clanging arms, and the ringing hoofs of their heavy chargers, Lucille might have seen, had she looked at the blind man's face, that its sad features kindled with enthusiasm, and his head was raised proudly from its wonted and melancholy bend. "Thank Heaven!" she said, as the troop had nearly passed them, "the danger is over!" Not so. One of the last two soldiers who rode abreast was unfortunately mounted on a young and unmanageable horse. The rider's oaths and digging spur only increased the fire and impatience of the charger; it plunged from side to side of the narrow street.

"Look to yourselves!" cried the horseman, as he was borne on to the place where Lucille and the stranger stood against the wall. "Are ye mad? Why do you not run?"

"For Heaven's sake, for mercy's sake, he is blind!" cried Lucille, clinging to the stranger's side.

"Save yourself, my kind guide!" said the stranger. But Lucille dreamed not of such desertion. The trooper wrested the horse's head from the spot where they stood; with a snort, as it felt the spur, the enraged animal lashed out with its hind-legs; and Lucille, unable to save *both*, threw herself before the blind man, and received the shock directed against him; her slight and delicate arm fell broken by her side, the horseman was borne onward. "Thank God, *you* are saved!" was poor Lucille's exclamation; and she fell, overcome with pain and terror, into the arms which the stranger mechanically opened to receive her.

"My guide! my friend!" cried he, "you are hurt, you—"

"No, sir," interrupted Lucille, faintly, "I am better, I am well. *This* arm, if you please,— we are not far from your hotel now."

But the stranger's ear, tutored to every inflection of voice, told him at once of the pain she suffered. He drew from her by degrees the confession of the injury she had sustained; but the generous girl did not tell him it had been incurred solely in his protection. He now insisted on reversing their duties, and accompanying *her* to her home; and Lucille, almost fainting with pain, and hardly able to move, was forced to consent. But a few steps down the next turning stood the humble mansion of her father. They reached it; and Lucille scarcely crossed the threshold, before she sank down, and for some minutes was insensible to pain. It was left to the stranger to explain, and to beseech them immediately to send for a surgeon, "the most skilful, the most practised in the town," said he. "See, I am rich, and this is the least I can do to atone to your generous daughter, for not forsaking even a stranger in peril."

He held out his purse as he spoke, but the father refused the offer; and it saved the blind man some shame, that he could not see the blush of honest resentment with which so poor a species of renumeration was put aside.

The young man stayed till the surgeon arrived, till the arm was set; nor did he depart until he had obtained a promise from the mother that he should learn the next morning how the sufferer had passed the night.

The next morning, indeed, he had intended to quit a town that offers but little temptation to the traveller; but he tarried day after day, until Lucille herself accompanied her mother, to assure him of her recovery.

You know, at least I do, dearest Gertrude, that there *is* such a thing as love at the first meeting,— a secret, an unaccountable affinity between persons (strangers before) which draws them irresistibly together,— as if there were truth in Plato's beautiful fantasy, that our souls were a portion of the stars, and that spirits, thus attracted to each other, have drawn their original light from the same orb, and yearn for a renewal of their former union. Yet without recurring to such fanciful solutions of a daily mystery, it was but natural that one in the forlorn and desolate condition of Eugene St. Amand should have felt a certain tenderness for a person who had so generously suffered for his sake.

The darkness to which he was condemned did not shut from his mind's eye the haunting images of Ideal beauty; rather, on the contrary, in his perpetual and unoccupied solitude, he fed the reveries of an imagination naturally warm, and a heart eager for sympathy and commune.

He had said rightly that his only test of beauty was in the melody of voice; and never had a softer or more thrilling tone than that of the young maiden touched upon his ear. Her exclamation, so beautifully denying self, so devoted in its charity, "Thank God, *you* are saved!" uttered too in the moment of her own suffering, rang constantly upon his soul, and he yielded, without precisely defining their nature, to vague and delicious sentiments, that his youth had never awakened to till then. And Lucille — the very accident that had happened to her on his behalf only deepened the interest she had already conceived for one who, in the first flush of youth, was thus cut off from the glad objects of life, and left to a night of years desolate and alone. There is, to your beautiful and kindly sex, a natural inclination to *protect*. This makes them the angels of sickness, the comforters of age, the fosterers of childhood; and this feeling, in Lucille peculiarly developed, had already inexpressibly linked her compassionate nature to the lot of the unfortunate traveller. With ardent affections, and with thoughts beyond her station and her years, she was not without that modest vanity which made her painfully susceptible to her own deficiencies in beauty. Instinctively conscious of how deeply she herself could love, she believed it impossible that she could ever be so loved in return. The stranger, so superior in her eyes to all she had yet seen, was the first who had ever addressed her in that voice which by tones, not words, speaks that admiration most dear to a woman's heart. To *him* she was beautiful, and her lovely mind spoke out, undimmed by the imperfections of her face. Not, indeed, that Lucille was wholly without personal attraction; her light step and graceful form were elastic with the freshness of youth, and her mouth and smile had so gentle and tender an expression, that there were moments when it would not have been the blind only who would have mistaken her to be beautiful. Her early childhood had indeed given the promise of attractions, which the smallpox, that then fear-ful malady, had inexorably marred. It had not only seared the smooth skin and brilliant hues, but utterly changed even the character of the features. It so happened that Lucille's family were celebrated for beauty, and vain of that celebrity; and so bitterly had her parents deplored the effects of the cruel malady, that poor Lucille had been early taught to con-sider them far more grievous than they really were, and to exaggerate the advantages of that beauty, the loss of which was considered by her parents so heavy a misfortune. Lu-cille, too, had a cousin named Julie, who was the wonder of all Malines for her personal perfections; and as the cousins were much together, the contrast was too striking not to occa-sion frequent mortification to Lucille. But every misfortune has something of a counterpoise; and the consciousness of personal inferiority had meekened, without souring, her temper, had given gentleness to a spirit that otherwise might have been too high, and humility to a mind that was naturally strong, impassioned, and energetic.

And yet Lucille had long conquered the one disadvantage she most dreaded in the want of beauty. Lucille was never known but to be loved. Wherever came her presence, her bright and soft mind diffused a certain inexpressible charm; and where she was not, a something was absent from the scene which not even Julie's beauty could replace.

"I propose," said St. Amand to Madame le Tisseur, Lucille's mother, as he sat in her little salon,— for he had already contracted that acquaintance with the family which permitted him to be led to their house, to return the visits Madame le Tisseur had made him, and his dog, once more returned a penitent to his master, always conducted his steps to the humble abode, and stopped instinctively at the door,— "I propose," said St. Amand, after a pause, and with some embarrassment, "to stay a little while longer at Malines; the air agrees with me, and I like the quiet of the place; but you are aware, madam, that at a hotel among strangers, I feel my situation somewhat cheerless. I have been thinking"—St. Amand paused again — "I have been thinking that if I could persuade some agreeable family to receive me as a lodger, I would fix myself here for some weeks. I am easily pleased."

"Doubtless there are many in Malines who would be too happy to receive such a lodger."

"Will you receive me?" asked St. Amand, abruptly. "It was of *your* family I thought."

"Of us? Monsieur is too flattering. But we have scarcely a room good enough for you."

"What difference between one room and another can there be to me? That is the best apartment to my choice in which the human voice sounds most kindly."

The arrangement was made, and St. Amand came now to reside beneath the same roof as Lucille. And was she not happy that *he* wanted so constant an attendance; was she not happy that she was ever of use? St. Amand was passionately fond of music; he played himself with a skill that was only surpassed by the exquisite melody of his voice; and was not Lucille happy when she sat mute and listening to such sounds as in Malines were never heard before? Was she not happy in gazing on a face to whose melancholy aspect her voice instantly summoned the smile? Was she not happy when the music ceased, and St. Amand called "Lucille"? Did not her own name uttered by that voice seem to her even sweeter than the music? Was she not happy when they walked out in the still evenings of summer, and her arm thrilled beneath the light touch of one to whom she was so necessary? Was she not proud in her happiness, and was there not something like worship in the gratitude she felt to him for raising her humble spirit to the luxury of feeling herself beloved?

St. Amand's parents were French. They had resided in the neighbourhood of Amiens, where they had inherited a competent property, to which he had succeeded about two years previous to the date of my story.

He had been blind from the age of three years. "I know not," said he, as he related these particulars to Lucille one evening when they were alone,— "I know not what the earth may be like, or the heaven, or the rivers whose voice at least I can hear, for I have no recollection beyond that of a confused but delicious blending of a thousand glorious colours,— a bright and quick sense of joy, A VISIBLE MUSIC. But it is only since my childhood closed that I have mourned, as I now unceasingly mourn, for the light of day. My boyhood passed in a quiet cheerfulness; the least trifle then could please and occupy the vacancies of my mind; but it was as I took delight in being read to, as I listened to the vivid descriptions of Poetry, as I glowed at the recital of great deeds, as I was made acquainted by books with the energy, the action, the heat, the fervour, the pomp, the enthusiasm of life, that I gradually opened to the sense of all I was forever denied. I felt that I existed, not lived; and that, in the midst of the Universal Liberty, I was sentenced to a prison, from whose blank walls there was no escape. Still, however, while my parents lived, I had something of consolation; at least I was not alone. They died, and a sudden and dread solitude, a vast and empty dreariness, settled upon my dungeon. One old servant only, who had attended me from my childhood, who had known me in my short privilege of light, by whose recollections my mind could grope back its way through the dark and narrow passages of memory to faint glimpses of the sun, was all that remained to me of human sympathies. It did not suffice, however, to content me with a home where my father and my mother's kind voice were *not*. A restless impatience, an anxiety to move, possessed me, and I set out from my home, journeying whither I cared not, so that at least I could change an air that weighed upon me like a palpable burden. I took only this old attendant as my companion; he too died three months since at Bruxelles, worn out with years. Alas! I had forgotten that he was old, for I saw not his progress to decay; and now, save my faithless dog, I was utterly alone, till I came hither and found *thee.*"

Lucille stooped down to caress the dog; she blessed the desertion that had led him to a friend who never could desert.

But however much, and however gratefully, St. Amand loved Lucille, her power availed not to chase the melancholy from his brow, and to reconcile him to his forlorn condition.

"Ah, would that I could see thee! would that I could look upon a face that my heart vainly endeavours to delineate!"

"If thou couldst," sighed Lucille, "thou wouldst cease to love me."

"Impossible!" cried St. Amand, passionately. "However the world may find thee, *thou* wouldst become my standard of beauty; and I should judge not of thee by others, but of others by thee."

He loved to hear Lucille read to him, and mostly he loved the descriptions of war, of travel, of wild adventure, and yet they occasioned him the most pain. Often she paused from the page as she heard him sigh, and felt that she would even have renounced the bliss of being loved by him, if she could have restored to him that blessing, the desire for which haunted him as a spectre.

Lucille's family were Catholic, and, like most in their station, they possessed the superstitions, as well as the devotion of the faith. Sometimes they amused themselves of an evening by the various legends and imaginary miracles of their calendar; and once, as they were thus conversing with two or three of their neighbours, "The Tomb of the Three Kings of Cologne" became the main topic of their wondering recitals. However strong was the sense of Lucille, she was, as you will readily conceive, naturally influenced by the belief of those with whom she had been brought up from her cradle, and she listened to tale after tale of the miracles wrought at the consecrated tomb, as earnestly and undoubtingly as the rest.

And the Kings of the East were no ordinary saints; to the relics of the Three Magi, who followed the Star of Bethlehem, and were the first potentates of the earth who adored its Saviour, well might the pious Catholic suppose that a peculiar power and a healing sanctity would belong. Each of the circle (St. Amand, who had been more than usually silent, and even gloomy during the day, had retired to his own apartment, for there were some moments when, in the sadness of his thoughts, he sought that solitude which he so impatiently fled from at others) — each of the circle had some story to relate equally veracious and indisputable, of an infirmity cured, or a prayer accorded, or a sin atoned for at the foot of the holy tomb. One story peculiarly affected Lucille; the narrator, a venerable old man with gray locks, solemnly declared himself a witness of its truth.

A woman at Anvers had given birth to a son, the offspring of an illicit connection, who came into the world deaf and dumb. The unfortunate mother believed the calamity a punishment for her own sin. "Ah, would," said she, "that the affliction had fallen only upon me! Wretch that I am, my innocent child is punished for my offence!" This idea haunted her night and day; she pined and could not be comforted. As the child grew up, and wound himself more and more round her heart, his caresses added new pangs to her remorse; and at length (continued the narrator) hearing perpetually of the holy fame of the Tomb of Cologne, she resolved upon a pilgrimage barefoot to the shrine. "God is merciful," said she; "and He who called Magdalene his sister may take the mother's curse from the child." She then went to Cologne; she poured her tears, her penitence, and her prayers at the sacred tomb. When she returned to her native town, what was her dismay as she approached her cottage to behold it a heap of ruins! Its blackened rafters and yawning casements betokened the ravages of fire. The poor woman sank upon the ground utterly overpowered. Had her son perished? At that moment she heard the cry of a child's voice, and, lo! her child rushed to her arms, and called her "mother!"

He had been saved from the fire, which had broken out seven days before; but in the terror he had suffered, the string that tied his tongue had been loosened; he had uttered articulate sounds of distress; the curse was removed, and one word at least the kind neighbours had already taught him to welcome his mother's return. What cared she now that her substance was gone, that her roof was ashes? She bowed in grateful submission to so mild a stroke; 'her prayer had been heard, and the sin of the mother was visited no longer on the child.

I have said, dear Gertrude, that this story made a deep impression upon Lucille. A misfortune so nearly akin to that of St. Amand removed by the prayer of another filled her with devoted thoughts and a beautiful hope. "Is not the tomb still standing?" thought she. "Is not God still in heaven? — He who heard the guilty, may He not hear the guiltless? Is He not the God of love? Are not the affections the offerings that please Him best? And what though the child's mediator was his mother, can even a mother love her child more tenderly than I love Eugene? But if, Lucille, thy prayer be granted, if he recover his sight, *thy* charm is gone, he will love thee no longer. No matter! be it so, — I shall at least have made him happy!"

Such were the thoughts that filled the mind of Lucille; she

cherished them till they settled into resolution, and she secretly vowed to perform her pilgrimage of love. She told neither St. Amand nor her parents of her intention; she knew the obstacles such an announcement would create. Fortunately she had an aunt settled at Bruxelles, to whom she had been accustomed once in every year to pay a month's visit, and at that time she generally took with her the work of a twelvemonths' industry, which found a readier sale at Bruxelles than at Malines. Lucille and St. Amand were already betrothed; their wedding was shortly to take place; and the custom of the country leading parents, however poor, to nourish the honourable ambition of giving some dowry with their daughters, Lucille found it easy to hide the object of her departure, under the pretence of taking the lace to Bruxelles, which had been the year's labour of her mother and herself,— it would sell for sufficient, at least, to defray the preparations for the wedding.

"Thou art ever right, child," said Madame le Tisseur; "the richer St. Amand is, why, the less oughtest thou to go a beggar to his house."

In fact, the honest ambition of the good people was excited; their pride had been hurt by the envy of the town and the current congratulations on so advantageous a marriage; and they employed themselves in counting up the fortune they should be able to give to their only child, and flattering their pardonable vanity with the notion that there would be no such great disproportion in the connection after all. They were right, but not in their own view of the estimate; the wealth that Lucille brought was what fate could not lessen, reverse could not reach; the ungracious seasons could not blight its sweet harvest; imprudence could not dissipate, fraud could not steal, one grain from its abundant coffers! Like the purse in the Fairy Tale, its use was hourly, its treasure inexhaustible.

St. Amand alone was not to be won to her departure; he chafed at the notion of a dowry; he was not appeased even by Lucille's representation that it was only to gratify and not to impoverish her parents. "And *thou*, too, canst leave me!" he said, in that plaintive voice which had made his first charm to Lucille's heart. "It is a double blindness!"

"But for a few days; a fortnight at most, dearest Eugene."

"A fortnight! you do not reckon time as the blind do," said St. Amand, bitterly.

"But listen, listen, dear Eugene," said Lucille, weeping.

The sound of her sobs restored him to a sense of his ingratitude. Alas, he knew not how much he had to be grateful for! He held out his arms to her. "Forgive me," said he. "Those who can see Nature know not how terrible it is to be alone."

"But my mother will not leave you."

"She is not you!"

"And Julie," said Lucille, hesitatingly.

"What is Julie to me?"

"Ah, you are the only one, save my parents, who could think of me in her presence."

"And why, Lucille?"

"Why! She is more beautiful than a dream."

"Say not so. Would I could see, that I might prove to the world how much more beautiful thou art! There is no music in *her* voice."

The evening before Lucille departed she sat up late with St. Amand and her mother. They conversed on the future; they made plans; in the wide sterility of the world they laid out the garden of household love, and filled it with flowers, forgetful of the wind that scatters and the frost that kills. And when, leaning on Lucille's arm, St. Amand sought his chamber, and they parted at his door, which closed upon her, she fell down on her knees at the threshold, and poured out the fulness of her heart in a prayer for his safety and the fulfilment of her timid hope.

At daybreak she was consigned to the conveyance that performed the short journey from Malines to Bruxelles. When she entered the town, instead of seeking her aunt, she rested at an *auberge* in the suburbs, and confiding her little basket of lace to the care of its hostess, she set out alone, and on foot, upon the errand of her heart's lovely superstition. And erring though it was, her faith redeemed its weakness, her affection made it even sacred; and well may we believe that the Eye which reads all secrets scarce looked reprovingly on that fanaticism whose only infirmity was love.

So fearful was she lest, by rendering the task too easy, she might impair the effect, that she scarcely allowed herself rest or food. Sometimes, in the heat of noon, she wandered a little from the roadside, and under the spreading lime-trees surrendered her mind to its sweet and bitter thoughts; but ever the restlessness of her enterprise urged her on, and faint, weary, and with bleeding feet, she started up and continued her way. At length she reached the ancient city, where a holier age has scarce worn from the habits and aspects of men the Roman trace. She prostrated herself at the tomb of the Magi; she proffered her ardent but humble prayer to Him before whose Son those fleshless heads (yet to faith at least preserved) had, eighteen centuries ago, bowed in adoration. Twice every day, for a whole week, she sought the same spot, and poured forth the same prayer. The last day an old priest, who, hovering in the church, had observed her constantly at devotion, with that fatherly interest which the better ministers of the Catholic sect (that sect which has covered the earth with the mansions of charity) feel for the unhappy, approached her as she was retiring with moist and downcast eyes, and saluting her, assumed the privilege of his order to inquire if there was aught in which his advice or aid could serve. There was something in the venerable air of the old man which encouraged Lucille; she opened her heart to him; she told him all. The good priest was much moved by her simplicity and earnestness. He questioned her minutely as to the peculiar species of blindness with which St. Amand was afflicted; and after musing a little while, he said, "Daughter, God is great and merciful; we must trust in His power, but we must not forget that He mostly works by mortal agents. As you pass through Louvain in your way home, fail not to see there a certain physician, named Le Kain. He is celebrated through Flanders for the cures he has wrought among the blind, and his advice is sought by all classes from far and near. He lives hard by the Hôtel de Ville, but any one will inform you of his residence. Stay, my child, you shall take him a note from me; he is a benevolent and kindly man, and you shall tell him exactly the same story (and with the same voice) you have told to me."

So saying the priest made Lucille accompany him to his home, and forcing her to refresh herself less sparingly than she had yet done since she had left Malines, he gave her his blessing, and a letter to Le Kain, which he rightly judged would insure her a patient hearing from the physician. Well known among all men of science was the name of the priest, and a word of recommendation from him went further, where virtue and wisdom were honoured, than the longest letter from the haughtiest sieur in Flanders.

With a patient and hopeful spirit, the young pilgrim turned her back on the Roman Cologne; and now about to rejoin St. Amand, she felt neither the heat of the sun nor the weariness of the road. It was one day at noon that she again passed through Louvain, and she soon found herself by the noble edifice of the Hôtel de Ville. Proud rose its spires against the sky, and the sun shone bright on its rich tracery and Gothic casements; the broad open street was crowded with persons of all classes, and it was with some modest alarm that Lucille lowered her veil and mingled with the throng. It was easy, as the priest had said, to find the house of Le Kain; she bade the servant take the priest's letter to his master, and she was not long kept waiting before she was admitted to the physician's presence. He was a spare, tall man, with a bald front, and a calm and friendly countenance. He was not less touched than the priest had been by the manner in which she narrated her story, described the affliction of her betrothed, and the hope that had inspired the pilgrimage she had just made.

"Well," said he, encouragingly, "we must see our patient. You can bring him hither to me."

"Ah, sir, I had hoped — " Lucille stopped suddenly.

"What, my young friend?"

"That I might have had the triumph of bringing you to

Malines. I know, sir, what you are about to say, and I know, sir, your time must be very valuable; but I am not so poor as I seem, and Eugene, that is, M. St. Amand, is very rich, and — and I have at Bruxelles what I am sure is a large sum; it was to have provided for the wedding, but it is most heartily at your service, sir."

Le Kain smiled; he was one of those men who love to read the human heart when its leaves are fair and undefiled; and, in the benevolence of science, he would have gone a longer journey than from Louvain to Malines to give sight to the blind, even had St. Amand been a beggar.

"Well, well," said he, "but you forget that M. St. Amand is not the only one in the world who wants me. I must look at my notebook, and see if I can be spared for a day or two."

So saying, he glanced at his memoranda. Everything smiled on Lucille; he had no engagements that his partner could not fulfil, for some days; he consented to accompany Lucille to Malines.

Meanwhile, cheerless and dull had passed the time to St. Amand. He was perpetually asking Madame le Tisseur what hour it was,— it was almost his only question. There seemed to him no sun in the heavens, no freshness in the air, and he even forbore his favourite music; the instrument had lost its sweetness since Lucille was not by to listen.

It was natural that the gossips of Malines should feel some envy at the marriage Lucille was about to make with one whose competence report had exaggerated into prodigal wealth, whose birth had been elevated from the respectable to the noble, and whose handsome person was clothed, by the interest excited by his misfortune, with the beauty of Antinous. Even that misfortune, which ought to have levelled all distinctions, was not sufficient to check the general envy; perhaps to some of the damsels of Malines blindness in a husband would not have seemed an unwelcome infirmity! But there was one in whom this envy rankled with a peculiar sting: it was the beautiful, the all-conquering Julie! That the humble, the neglected Lucille should be preferred to her; that Lucille, whose existence was well-nigh forgot beside Julie's, should become thus suddenly of importance; that there should be one person in the world, and that person young, rich, handsome, to whom she was less than nothing, when weighed in the balance with Lucille, mortified to the quick a vanity that had never till then received a wound. "It is well," she would say with a bitter jest, "that Lucille's lover is blind. To be the one it is necessary to be the other!"

During Lucille's absence she had been constantly in Madame le Tisseur's house; indeed, Lucille had prayed her to be so. She had sought, with an industry that astonished herself, to supply Lucille's place; and among the strange contradictions of human nature, she had learned during her efforts to please, to love the object of those efforts, — as much at least as she was capable of loving.

She conceived a positive hatred to Lucille; she persisted in imagining that nothing but the accident of first acquaintance had deprived her of a conquest with which she persuaded herself her happiness had become connected. Had St. Amand never loved Lucille and proposed to Julie, his misfortune would have made her reject him, despite his wealth and his youth; but to be Lucille's lover, and a conquest to be won from Lucille, raised him instantly to an importance not his own. Safe, however, in his affliction, the arts and beauty of Julie fell harmless on the fidelity of St. Amand. Nay, he liked her less than ever, for it seemed an impertinence in any one to counterfeit the anxiety and watchfulness of Lucille.

"It is time, surely it is time, Madame le Tisseur, that Lucille should return? She might have sold all the lace in Malines by this time," said St. Amand, one day, peevishly.

"Patience, my dear friend, patience; perhaps she may return to-morrow."

"To-morrow! let me see, it is only six o'clock, — only six, you are sure?"

"Just five, dear Eugene. Shall I read to you? This is a new book from Paris; it has made a great noise," said Julie.

"You are very kind, but I will not trouble you."

"It is anything but trouble."

"In a word, then, I would rather not."

"Oh, that he could see!" thought Julie; "would I not punish him for this!"

"I hear carriage wheels; who can be passing this way? Surely it is the *voiturier* from Bruxelles," said St. Amand, starting up; "it is his day,— his hour, too. No, no, it is a lighter vehicle," and he sank down listlessly on his seat.

Nearer and nearer rolled the wheels; they turned the corner; they stopped at the lowly door; and, overcome, overjoyed, Lucille was clasped to the bosom of St. Amand.

"Stay," said she, blushing, as she recovered her self-possession, and turned to Le Kain; "pray pardon me, sir. Dear Eugene, I have brought with me one who, by God's blessing, may yet restore you to sight."

"We must not be sanguine, my child," said Le Kain; "anything is better than disappointment."

To close this part of my story, dear Gertrude, Le Kain examined St. Amand, and the result of the examination was a confident belief in the probability of a cure. St. Amand gladly consented to the experiment of an operation; it succeeded, the blind man saw! Oh, what were Lucille's feelings, what her emotion, what her joy, when she found the object of her pilgrimage, of her prayers, fulfilled! That joy was so intense that in the eternal alternations of human life she might have foretold from its excess how bitter the sorrows fated to ensue.

As soon as by degrees the patient's new sense became reconciled to the light, his first, his only demand was for Lucille. "No, let me not see her alone; let me see her in the midst of you all, that I may convince you that the heart never is mistaken in its instincts." With a fearful, a sinking presentiment, Lucille yielded to the request, to which the impetuous St. Amand would hear indeed no denial. The father, the mother, Julie, Lucille, Julie's younger sisters, assembled in the little parlour; the door opened, and St. Amand stood hesitating on the threshold. One look around sufficed to him; his face brightened, he uttered a cry of joy. "Lucille!

Lucille!" he exclaimed, "it is you, I know it, *you* only!" He sprang forward *and fell at the feet of Julie!*

Flushed, elated, triumphant, Julie bent upon him her sparkling eyes; *she* did not undeceive him.

"You are wrong, you mistake," said Madame le Tisseur, in confusion; "that is her cousin Julie,—this is your Lucille."

St. Amand rose, turned, saw Lucille, and at that moment she wished herself in her grave. Surprise, mortification, disappointment, almost dismay, were depicted in his gaze. He had been haunting his prison-house with dreams, and now, set free, he felt how unlike they were to the truth. Too new to observation to read the woe, the despair, the lapse and shrinking of the whole frame, that his look occasioned Lucille, he yet felt, when the first shock of his surprise was over, that it was not thus he should thank her who had restored him to sight. He hastened to redeem his error — ah! how could it be redeemed?

From that hour all Lucille's happiness was at an end; her fairy palace was shattered in the dust; the magician's wand was broken up; the Ariel was given to the winds; and the bright enchantment no longer distinguished the land she lived in from the rest of the barren world. It is true that St. Amand's words were kind; it is true that he remembered with the deepest gratitude all she had done in his behalf; it is true that he forced himself again and again to say, "She is my betrothed, my benefactress!" and he cursed himself to think that the feelings he had entertained for her were fled. Where was the passion of his words; where the ardour of his tone; where that play and light of countenance which her step, *her* voice, could formerly call forth? When they were alone he was embarrassed and constrained, and almost cold; his hand no longer sought hers, his soul no longer missed her if she was absent a moment from his side. When in their household circle he seemed visibly more at ease; but did his eyes fasten upon her who had opened them to the day; did they not wander at every interval with a too eloquent admiration to the blushing and radiant face of the exulting Julie? This was not, you will believe, suddenly perceptible in one day or one week, but every day it was perceptible more and more. Yet still — bewitched, ensnared, as St. Amand was — he never perhaps would have been guilty of an infidelity that he strove with the keenest remorse to wrestle against, had it not been for the fatal contrast, at the first moment of his gushing enthusiasm, which Julie had presented to Lucille; but for that he would have formed no previous idea of real and living beauty to aid the disappointment of his imaginings and his dreams. He would have seen Lucille young and graceful, and with eyes beaming affection, contrasted only by the wrinkled countenance and bended frame of her parents, and she would have completed her conquest over him before he had discovered that she was less beautiful than others; nay, more, — that infidelity never could have lasted above the first few days, if the vain and heartless object of it had not exerted every art, all the power and witchery of her beauty, to cement and continue it. The unfortunate Lucille — so susceptible to the slightest change in those she loved, so diffident of herself, so proud too in that diffidence — no longer necessary, no longer missed, no longer loved, could not bear to endure the galling comparison between the past and the present. She fled uncomplainingly to her chamber to indulge her tears, and thus, unhappily, absent as her father generally was during the day, and busied as her mother was either at work or in household matters, she left Julie a thousand opportunities to complete the power she had begun to wield over — no, not the heart! — the *senses* of St. Amand! Yet, still not suspecting, in the open generosity of her mind, the whole extent of her affliction, poor Lucille buoyed herself at times with the hope that when once married, when, once in that intimacy of friendship, the unspeakable love she felt for him could disclose itself with less restraint than at present, — she would perhaps regain a heart which had been so devotedly hers, that she could not think that without a fault it was irrevocably gone: on that hope she anchored all the little happiness that remained to her. And still St. Amand pressed their marriage, but in what different tones! In fact, he wished to preclude from himself the possibility of a deeper ingratitude than that which he had incurred already. He vainly thought that the broken reed of love might be bound up and strengthened by the ties of duty; and at least he was anxious that his hand, his fortune, his esteem, his gratitude, should give to Lucille the only recompense it was now in his power to bestow. Meanwhile, left alone so often with Julie, and Julie bent on achieving the last triumph over his heart, St. Amand was gradually preparing a far different reward, a far different return, for her to whom he owed so incalculable a debt.

There was a garden, behind the house, in which there was a small arbour, where often in the summer evenings Eugene and Lucille had sat together,— hours never to return! One day she heard from her own chamber, where she sat mourning, the sound of St. Amand's flute swelling gently from that beloved and consecrated bower. She wept as she heard it, and the memories that the music bore softening and endearing his image, she began to reproach herself that she had yielded so often to the impulse of her wounded feelings; that chilled by *his* coldness, she had left him so often to himself, and had not sufficiently dared to tell him of that affection which, in her modest self-depreciation, constituted her only pretension to his love. "Perhaps he is alone now," she thought; "the air too is one which he knows that I love:" and with her heart in her step, she stole from the house and sought the arbour. She had scarce turned from her chamber when the flute ceased; as she neared the arbour she heard voices,— Julie's voice in grief, St. Amand's in consolation. A dread foreboding seized her; her feet clung rooted to the earth.

"Yes, marry her, forget me," said Julie; "in a few days you will be another's, and I — I — forgive me, Eugene, forgive me that I have disturbed your happiness. I am punished sufficiently; my heart will break, but it will break in loving you." Sobs choked Julie's voice.

"Oh, speak not thus," said St. Amand. "I, *I* only am to blame,— I, false to both, to both ungrateful. Oh, from the hour that these eyes opened upon you I drank in a new life; the sun itself to me was less wonderful than your beauty.

But — but — let me forget that hour. What do I not owe to Lucille? I shall be wretched, — I shall deserve to be so; for shall I not think, Julie, that I have embittered your life with our ill-fated love? But all that I can give — my hand, my home, my plighted faith — must be hers. Nay, Julie, nay — why that look? Could I act otherwise? Can I dream otherwise? Whatever the sacrifice, *must* I not render it? Ah, what do I owe to Lucille, were it only for the thought that but for her I might never have seen thee! "

Lucille stayed to hear no more; with the same soft step as that which had borne her within hearing of these fatal words, she turned back once more to her desolate chamber.

That evening, as St. Amand was sitting alone in his apartment, he heard a gentle knock at the door. "Come in," he said, and Lucille entered. He started in some confusion, and would have taken her hand, but she gently repulsed him. She took a seat opposite to him, and looking down, thus addressed him:—

"My dear Eugene, that is, Monsieur St. Amand, I have something on my mind that I think it better to speak at once; and if I do not exactly express what I would wish to say, you must not be offended with Lucille: it is not an easy matter to put into words what one feels deeply." Colouring, and suspecting something of the truth, St. Amand would have broken in upon her here; but she with a gentle impatience motioned him to be silent, and continued:—

"You know that when you once loved me, I used to tell you that you would cease to do so could you see how undeserving I was of your attachment. I did not deceive myself, Eugene; I always felt assured that such would be the case, that your love for me necessarily rested on your affliction. But for all that I never at least had a dream or a desire but for your happiness; and God knows, that if again, by walking barefooted, not to Cologne, but to Rome — to the end of the world — I could save you from a much less misfortune than that of blindness, I would cheerfully do it; yes, even though I might foretell all the while that, on my return, you would speak to me coldly, think of me lightly, and that the penalty to me would — would be — what it has been!" Here Lucille wiped a few natural tears from her eyes. St. Amand, struck to the heart, covered his face with his hands, without the courage to interrupt her. Lucille continued: —

"That which I foresaw has come to pass; I am no longer to you what I once was, when you could clothe this poor form and this homely face with a beauty they did not possess. You would wed me still, it is true; but I am proud, Eugene, and cannot stoop to gratitude where I once had love. I am not so unjust as to blame you; the change was natural, was inevitable. I should have steeled myself more against it; but I am now resigned. We must part; you love Julie — that too is natural — and *she* loves you; ah! what also more in the probable course of events? Julie loves you, not yet, perhaps, so much as I did; but then she has not known you as I have, and she whose whole life has been triumph cannot feel the gratitude that I felt at fancying myself loved; but this will come — God grant it! Farewell, then, forever, dear Eugene; I leave you when you no longer want me; you are now independent of Lucille; wherever you go, a thousand hereafter can supply my place. Farewell!"

She rose, as she said this, to leave the room; but St. Amand seizing her hand, which she in vain endeavoured to withdraw from his clasp, poured forth incoherently, passionately, his reproaches on himself, his eloquent persuasion against her resolution.

"I confess," said he, "that I have been allured for a moment; I confess that Julie's beauty made me less sensible to your stronger, your holier, oh! far, far holier title to my love! But forgive me, dearest Lucille; already I return to you, to all I once felt for you; make me not curse the blessing of sight that I owe to you. You must not leave me; never can we two part. Try me, only try me, and if ever hereafter my heart wander from you, *then*, Lucille, leave me to my remorse!"

Even at that moment Lucille did not yield; she felt that his prayer was but the enthusiasm of the hour; she felt that there was a virtue in her pride,— that to leave him was a duty to herself. In vain he pleaded; in vain were his embraces, his prayers; in vain he reminded her of their plighted troth, of her aged parents, whose happiness had become wrapped in her union with him: "How,—even were it as you wrongly believe,—how, in honour to them, can I desert you, can I wed another?"

"Trust that, trust all, to me," answered Lucille; "your honour shall be my care, none shall blame *you;* only do not let your marriage with Julie be celebrated here before their eyes: that is all I ask, all they can expect. God bless you! do not fancy I shall be unhappy, for whatever happiness the world gives you, shall I not have contributed to bestow it? — and with that thought I am above compassion."

She glided from his arms, and left him to a solitude more bitter even than that of blindness. That very night Lucille sought her mother; to her she confided all. I pass over the reasons she urged, the arguments she overcame; she conquered rather than convinced, and leaving to Madame le Tisseur the painful task of breaking to her father her unalterable resolution, she quitted Malines the next morning, and with a heart too honest to be utterly without comfort, paid that visit to her aunt which had been so long deferred.

The pride of Lucille's parents prevented them from reproaching St. Amand. He could not bear, however, their cold and altered looks; he left their house; and though for several days he would not even see Julie, yet her beauty and her art gradually resumed their empire over him. They were married at Courtroi, and to the joy of the vain Julie departed to the gay metropolis of France. But, before their departure, before his marriage, St. Amand endeavoured to appease his conscience by obtaining for M. le Tisseur a much more lucrative and honourable office than that he now held. Rightly judging that Malines could no longer be a pleasant residence for them, and much less for Lucille, the duties of the post were to be fulfilled in another town; and knowing that M. le Tisseur's delicacy would revolt at receiving such a favour from his hands, he kept the nature of his negotiation a close secret, and suffered the honest citizen to believe that his own merits alone had entitled him to so unexpected a promotion.

Time went on. This quiet and simple history of humble affections took its date in a stormy epoch of the world,— the dawning Revolution of France. The family of Lucille had been little more than a year settled in their new residence when Dumouriez led his army into the Netherlands. But how meanwhile had that year passed for Lucille? I have said that her spirit was naturally high; that though so tender, she was not weak. Her very pilgrimage to Cologne alone, and at the timid age of seventeen, proved that there was a strength in her nature no less than a devotion in her love. The sacrifice she had made brought its own reward. She believed St. Amand was happy, and she would not give way to the selfishness of grief; she had still duties to perform; she could still comfort her parents and cheer their age; she could still be all the world to them: she felt this, and was consoled. Only once during the year had she heard of Julie; she had been seen by a mutual friend at Paris, gay, brilliant, courted, and admired; of St. Amand she heard nothing.

My tale, dear Gertrude, does not lead me through the harsh scenes of war. I do not tell you of the slaughter and the siege, and the blood that inundated those fair lands,— the great battlefield of Europe. The people of the Netherlands in general were with the cause of Dumouriez, but the town in which Le Tisseur dwelt offered some faint resistance to his arms. Le Tisseur himself, despite his age, girded on his sword; the town was carried, and the fierce and licentious troops of the conqueror poured, flushed with their easy victory, through its streets. Le Tisseur's house was filled with drunken and rude troopers; Lucille herself trembled in the fierce gripe of one of those dissolute soldiers, more bandit than soldier, whom the subtle Dumouriez had united to his army, and by whose blood he so often saved that of his nobler band. Her shrieks, her cries, were vain, when suddenly the troopers gave way. "The Captain! brave Captain!" was shouted forth; the insolent soldier, felled by a powerful arm, sank senseless at the feet of Lucille, and a glorious form, towering above its fellows,— even through its glittering garb, even in that dreadful hour, remembered at a glance by Lucille,— stood at her side; her protector, her guardian! Thus once more she beheld St. Amand!

The house was cleared in an instant, the door barred. Shouts, groans, wild snatches of exulting song, the clang of arms, the tramp of horses, the hurrying footsteps, the deep music sounded loud, and blended terribly without. Lucille heard them not,— she was on that breast which never should have deserted her.

Effectually to protect his friends, St. Amand took up his quarters at their house; and for two days he was once more under the same roof as Lucille. He never recurred voluntarily to Julie; he answered Lucille's timid inquiry after her health briefly, and with coldness, but he spoke with all the enthusiasm of a long-pent and ardent spirit of the new profession he had embraced. Glory seemed now to be his only mistress; and the vivid delusion of the first bright dreams of the Revolution filled his mind, broke from his tongue, and lighted up those dark eyes which Lucille had redeemed to day.

She saw him depart at the head of his troops; she saw his proud crest glancing in the sun; she saw his steed winding through the narrow street; she saw that his last glance reverted to her, where she stood at the door; and, as he waved his adieu, she fancied that there was on his face that look of deep and grateful tenderness which reminded her of the one bright epoch of her life.

She was right; St. Amand had long since in bitterness repented of a transient infatuation, had long since distinguished the true Florimel from the false, and felt that, in Julie, Lucille's wrongs were avenged. But in the hurry and heat of war he plunged that regret — the keenest of all — which embodies the bitter words, "TOO LATE!"

Years passed away, and in the resumed tranquillity of Lucille's life the brilliant apparition of St. Amand appeared as something dreamed of, not seen. The star of Napoleon had risen above the horizon; the romance of his early career had commenced; and the campaign of Egypt had been the herald of those brilliant and meteoric successes which flashed forth from the gloom of the Revolution of France.

You are aware, dear Gertrude, how many in the French as well as the English troops returned home from Egypt blinded with the ophthalmia of that arid soil. Some of the young men in Lucille's town, who had joined Napoleon's army, came back darkened by that fearful affliction, and Lucille's alms and Lucille's aid and Lucille's sweet voice were ever at hand for those poor sufferers, whose common misfortune touched so thrilling a chord of her heart.

Her father was now dead, and she had only her mother to cheer amidst the ills of age. As one evening they sat at work together, Madame le Tisseur said, after a pause,—

"I wish, dear Lucille, thou couldst be persuaded to marry Justin; he loves thee well, and now that thou art yet young, and hast many years before thee, thou shouldst remember that when I die thou wilt be alone."

"Ah, cease, dearest mother, I never can marry now; and as for love — once taught in the bitter school in which I have learned the knowledge of myself — I cannot be deceived again."

"My Lucille, you do not know yourself. Never was woman loved if Justin does not love you; and never did lover feel with more real warmth how worthily he loved."

And this was true; and not of Justin alone, for Lucille's modest virtues, her kindly temper, and a certain undulating and feminine grace, which accompanied all her movements, had secured her as many conquests as if she had been beautiful. She had rejected all offers of marriage with a shudder; without even the throb of a flattered vanity. One memory, sadder, was also dearer to her than all things; and something sacred in its recollections made her deem it even a crime to think of effacing the past by a new affection.

"I believe," continued Madame le Tisseur, angrily, "that thou still thinkest fondly of him from whom only in the world thou couldst have experienced ingratitude."

"Nay, Mother," said Lucille, with a blush and a slight sigh, "Eugene is married to another."

While thus conversing, they heard a gentle and timid knock at the door; the latch was lifted. "This," said the rough voice of a *commissionaire* of the town, "this, monsieur, is the house of Madame le Tisseur, and *voilà mademoiselle !*" A tall figure, with a shade over his eyes, and wrapped in a long military cloak, stood in the room. A thrill shot across Lucille's heart. He stretched out his arms. "Lucille," said that melancholy voice, which had made the music of her first youth, "where art thou, Lucille? Alas! she does not recognize St. Amand."

Thus was it indeed. By a singular fatality, the burning suns and the sharp dust of the plains of Egypt had smitten the young soldier, in the flush of his career, with a second — and this time with an irremediable — blindness! He had returned to France to find his hearth lonely. Julie was no more,— a sudden fever had cut her off in the midst of youth; and he had sought his way to Lucille's house, to see if one hope yet remained to him in the world!

And when, days afterwards, humbly and sadly he re-urged a former suit, did Lucille shut her heart to its prayer? Did her pride remember its wound; did she revert to his desertion; did she reply to the whisper of her yearning love, "*Thou hast been before forsaken*"? That voice and those darkened eyes pleaded to her with a pathos not to be resisted. "I am once more necessary to him," was all her thought; "if I reject him who will tend him?" In that thought was the motive of her conduct; in that thought gushed back upon her soul all the springs of checked but unconquered, unconquerable love! In that thought, she stood beside him at the altar, and pledged, with a yet holier devotion than she might have felt of yore, the vow of her imperishable truth.

And Lucille found, in the future, a reward, which the common world could never comprehend. With his blindness returned all the feelings she had first awakened in St. Amand's solitary heart; again he yearned for her step, again he missed even a moment's absence from his side, again her voice chased the shadow from his brow, and in her presence was a sense of shelter and of sunshine. He no longer sighed for the blessing he had lost; he reconciled himself to fate, and entered into that serenity of mood which mostly characterizes the blind.

Perhaps after we have seen the actual world, and experienced its hollow pleasures, we can resign ourselves the better to its exclusion; and as the cloister, which repels the ardour of our hope, is sweet to our remembrance, so the darkness loses its terror when experience has wearied us with the glare and travail of the day. It was something, too, as they advanced in life, to feel the chains that bound him to Lucille strengthening daily, and to cherish in his overflowing heart the sweetness of increasing gratitude; it was something that he could not see years wrinkle that open brow, or dim the tenderness of that touching smile; it was something that to him she was beyond the reach of time, and preserved to the verge of a grave (which received them both within a few days of each other) in all the bloom of her unwithering affection, in all the freshness of a heart that never could grow old!

Gertrude, who had broken in upon Trevylyan's story by a thousand anxious interruptions, and a thousand pretty apologies for interrupting, was charmed with a tale in which true love was made happy at last, although she did not forgive St. Amand his ingratitude, and although she declared, with a critical shake of the head, that "it was very unnatural that the mere beauty of Julie, or the mere want of it in Lucille, should have produced such an effect upon him, if he had ever *really* loved Lucille in his blindness."

As they passed through Malines, the town assumed an interest in Gertrude's eyes to which it scarcely of itself was entitled. She looked wistfully at the broad market-place, at a corner of which was one of those out-of-door groups of quiet and noiseless revellers, which Dutch art has raised from the Familiar to the Picturesque; and then glancing to the tower of St. Rembauld, she fancied, amidst the silence of noon, that she yet heard the plaintive cry of the blind orphan, "Fido, Fido, why hast thou deserted me?"

CHAPTER V.

ROTTERDAM. — THE CHARACTER OF THE DUTCH. — THEIR RE-
SEMBLANCE TO THE GERMANS. — A DISPUTE BETWEEN VANE
AND TREVYLYAN, AFTER THE MANNER OF THE ANCIENT
NOVELISTS, AS TO WHICH IS PREFERABLE, THE LIFE OF
ACTION OR THE LIFE OF REPOSE. — TREVYLYAN'S CON-
TRAST BETWEEN LITERARY AMBITION AND THE AMBITION
OF PUBLIC LIFE.

OUR travellers arrived at Rotterdam on a bright and sunny
day. There is a cheerfulness about the operations of Commerce, — a life, a bustle, an action which always exhilarate
the spirits at the first glance. Afterwards they fatigue us;
we get too soon behind the scenes, and find the base and
troublous passions which move the puppets and conduct the
drama.

But Gertrude, in whom ill health had not destroyed the
vividness of impression that belongs to the inexperienced,
was delighted at the cheeriness of all around her. As she
leaned lightly on Trevylyan's arm, he listened with a forgetful joy to her questions and exclamations at the stir and live-
liness of a city from which was to commence their pilgrimage
along the Rhine. And indeed the scene was rife with the
spirit of that people at once so active and so patient, so daring on the sea, so cautious on the land. Industry was visible everywhere; the vessels in the harbour, the crowded boat
putting off to land, the throng on the quay, — all looked bus-
tling and spoke of commerce. The city itself, on which the
skies shone fairly through light and fleecy clouds, wore a
cheerful aspect. The church of St. Lawrence rising above
the clean, neat houses, and on one side trees thickly grouped,
gayly contrasted at once the waters and the city.

"I like this place," said Gertrude's father, quietly; "it has
an air of comfort."

"And an absence of grandeur," said Trevylyan.

"A commercial people are one great middle-class in their habits and train of mind," replied Vane; "and grandeur belongs to the extremes,— an impoverished population and a wealthy despot."

They went to see the statue of Erasmus, and the house in which he was born. Vane had a certain admiration for Erasmus which his companions did not share; he liked the quiet irony of the sage, and his knowledge of the world; and, besides, Vane was at that time of life when philosophers become objects of interest. At first they are teachers; secondly, friends; and it is only a few who arrive at the third stage, and find them deceivers. The Dutch are a singular people. Their literature is neglected, but it has some of the German vein in its strata,— the patience, the learning, the homely delineation, and even some traces of the mixture of the humorous and the terrible which form that genius for the grotesque so especially German — you find this in their legends and ghost-stories. But in Holland activity destroys, in Germany indolence nourishes, romance.

They stayed a day or two at Rotterdam, and then proceeded up the Rhine to Gorcum. The banks were flat and tame, and nothing could be less impressive of its native majesty than this part of the course of the great river.

"I never felt before," whispered Gertrude, tenderly, "how much there was of consolation in your presence; for here I am at last on the Rhine,— the blue Rhine, and how disappointed I should be if you were not by my side!"

"But, my Gertrude, you must wait till we have passed Cologne, before *the glories* of the Rhine burst upon you."

"It reverses life, my child," said the moralizing Vane; "and the stream flows through dulness at first, reserving its poetry for our perseverance."

"I will not allow your doctrine," said Trevylyan, as the ambitious ardour of his native disposition stirred within him. "Life has always action; it is our own fault if it ever be dull: youth has its enterprise, manhood its schemes; and even if infirmity creep upon age, the mind, the mind still triumphs over the mortal clay, and in the quiet hermitage, among books, and from thoughts, keeps the great wheel within everlastingly in motion. No, the better class of spirits have always an antidote to the insipidity of a common career, they have ever energy at will — "

"And never happiness!" answered Vane, after a pause, as he gazed on the proud countenance of Trevylyan, with that kind of calm, half-pitying interest which belonged to a character deeply imbued with the philosophy of a sad experience acting upon an unimpassioned heart. "And in truth, Trevylyan, it would please me if I could but teach you the folly of preferring the exercise of that energy of which you speak to the golden luxuries of REST. What ambition can ever bring an adequate reward? Not, surely, the ambition of letters, the desire of intellectual renown!"

"True," said Trevylyan, quietly; "that dream I have long renounced; there is nothing palpable in literary fame,— it scarcely perhaps soothes the vain, it assuredly chafes the proud. In my earlier years I attempted some works which gained what the world, perhaps rightly, deemed a sufficient need of reputation; yet it was not sufficient to recompense myself for the fresh hours I had consumed, for the sacrifices of pleasure I had made. The subtle aims that had inspired me were not perceived; the thoughts that had seemed new and beautiful to me fell flat and lustreless on the soul of others. If I was approved, it was often for what I condemned myself; and I found that the trite commonplace and the false wit charmed, while the truth fatigued, and the enthusiasm revolted. For men of that genius to which I make no pretension, who have dwelt apart in the obscurity of their own thoughts, gazing upon stars that shine not for the dull sleepers of the world, it must be a keen sting to find the product of their labour confounded with a class, and to be mingled up in men's judgment with the faults or merits of a tribe. Every great genius must deem himself original and alone in his conceptions. It is not enough for him that these conceptions should be approved as good, unless they are admitted as inventive, if they mix him with the herd he has shunned, not separate him in fame as he has been separated in soul. Some Frenchman, the oracle of his circle, said of the poet of the 'Phêdre,' 'Racine and the other imitators of Corneille;' and Racine, in his wrath, nearly forswore tragedy forever. It is in vain to tell the author that the public is the judge of his works. The author believes himself above the public, or he would never have written; and," continued Trevylyan, with enthusiasm, "he *is* above them; their fiat may crush his glory, but never his self-esteem. He stands alone and haughty amidst the wrecks of the temple he imagined he had raised ' TO THE FUTURE,' and retaliates neglect with scorn. But is this, the life of scorn, a pleasurable state of existence? Is it one to be cherished? Does even the moment of fame counterbalance the years of . mortification? And what is there in literary fame itself present and palpable to its heir? His work is a pebble thrown into the deep; the stir lasts for a moment, and the wave closes up, to be susceptible no more to the same impression. The circle may widen to other lands and other ages, but around *him* it is weak and faint. The trifles of the day, the low politics, the base intrigues, occupy the tongue, and fill the thought of his contemporaries. He is less known than a mountebank, or a new dancer; his glory comes not home to him; it brings no present, no perpetual reward, like the applauses that wait the actor, or the actor-like murmur of the senate; and this, which vexes, also lowers him; his noble nature begins to nourish the base vices of jealousy, and the unwillingness to admire. Goldsmith is forgotten in the presence of a puppet; he feels it, and is mean; he expresses it, and is ludicrous. It is well to say that great minds will not stoop to jealousy; in the greatest minds, it is most frequent.[1] Few authors are ever so aware of the admiration they excite as to afford to be generous; and this melancholy truth revolts us with our own am-

---

[1] See the long list of names furnished by Disraeli, in that most exquisite work, "The Literary Character," vol. ii. p. 75. Plato, Xenophon, Chaucer, Corneille, Voltaire, Dryden, the Caracci, Domenico Venetiano, murdered by his envious friend, and the gentle Castillo fainting away at the genius of Murillo.

bition. Shall we be demigods in our closets at the price of sinking below mortality in the world? No! it was from this deep sentiment of the unrealness of literary fame, of dissatisfaction at the fruits it produced, of fear for the meanness it engendered, that I resigned betimes all love for its career; and if, by the restless desire that haunts men who think much to write ever, I should be urged hereafter to literature, I will sternly teach myself to persevere in the indifference to its fame."

"You say as I would say," answered Vane, with his tranquil smile; "and your experience corroborates my theory. Ambition, then, is not the root of happiness. Why more in action than in letters?"

"Because," said Trevylyan, "in action we commonly gain in our life all the honour we deserve: the public judge of men better and more rapidly than of books. And he who takes to himself in action a high and pure ambition, associates it with so many objects, that, unlike literature, the failure of one is balanced by the success of the other. He, the creator of deeds, not resembling the creator of books, stands not alone; he is eminently social; he has many comrades, and without their aid he could not accomplish his designs. This divides and mitigates the impatient jealousy against others. He works for a cause, and knows early that he cannot monopolize its whole glory; he shares what he is aware it is impossible to engross. Besides, action leaves him no time for brooding over disappointment. The author has consumed his youth in a work,— it fails in glory. Can he write another work? Bid him call back another youth! But in action, the labour of the mind is from day to day. A week replaces what a week has lost, and all the aspirant's fame is of the present. It is lipped by the Babel of the living world; he is ever on the stage, and the spectators are ever ready to applaud. Thus perpetually in the service of others self ceases to be his world; he has no leisure to brood over real or imaginary wrongs; the excitement whirls on the machine till it is worn out—"

"And kicked aside," said Vane, "with the broken lumber

of men's other tools, in the chamber of their son's forgetfulness. Your man of action lasts but for an hour; the man of letters lasts for ages."

"We live not for ages," answered Trevylyan; "our life is on earth, and not in the grave."

"But even grant," continued Vane — "and I for one will concede the point — that posthumous fame is not worth the living agonies that obtain it, how are you better off in your poor and vulgar career of action? Would you assist the rulers? — servility! The people? — folly! If you take the great philosophical view which the worshippers of the past rarely take, but which, unknown to them, is their sole excuse, — namely, that the changes which *may* benefit the future unsettle the present; and that it is not the wisdom of practical legislation to risk the peace of our contemporaries in the hope of obtaining happiness for their posterity, — to what suspicions, to what charges are you exposed! You are deemed the foe of all liberal opinion, and you read your curses in the eyes of a nation. But take the side of the people. What caprice, what ingratitude! You have professed so much in theory, that you can never accomplish sufficient in practice. Moderation becomes a crime; to be prudent is to be perfidious. New demagogues, without temperance, because without principle, outstrip you in the moment of your greatest services. The public is the grave of a great man's deeds; it is never sated; its maw is eternally open; it perpetually craves for more. Where, in the history of the world, do you find the gratitude of a people? You find fervour, it is true, but not gratitude, — the fervour that exaggerates a benefit at one moment, but not the gratitude that remembers it the next year. Once disappoint them, and all your actions, all your sacrifices, are swept from their remembrance forever; they break the windows of the very house they have given you, and melt down their medals into bullets. Who serves man, ruler or peasant, serves the ungrateful; and all the ambitious are but types of a Wolsey or a De Witt."

"And what," said Trevylyan, "consoles a man in the ills that flesh is heir to, in that state of obscure repose, that se-

rene inactivity to which you would confine him? Is it not
his conscience?   Is it not his self-acquittal, or his self-
approval?"

"Doubtless," replied Vane.

"Be it so," answered the high-souled Trevylyan; "the same
consolation awaits us in action as in repose. We sedulously
pursue what we deem to be true glory. We are maligned;
but our soul acquits us. Could it do more in the scandal and
the prejudice that assail us in private life? You are silent;
but note how much deeper should be the comfort, how much
loftier the self-esteem; for if calumny attack us in a wilful
obscurity, what have we done to refute the calumny? How
have we served our species? Have we 'scorned delight and
loved laborious days'? Have we made the utmost of the
'talent' confided to our care? Have we done those good deeds
to our race upon which we can retire, — an 'Estate of Benefi-
cence,'— from the malice of the world, and feel that our deeds
are our defenders? This is the consolation of virtuous actions; is it so of — even a virtuous — indolence?"

"You speak as a preacher," said Vane, — "I merely as a
calculator; you of virtue in affliction, I of a life in ease."

"Well, then, if the consciousness of perpetual endeavour
to advance our race be not alone happier than the life of ease,
let us see what this vaunted ease really is. Tell me, is it not
another name for *ennui?* This state of quiescence, this ob-
jectless, dreamless torpor, this transition *du lit à la table, de
la table au lit,*— what more dreary and monotonous existence
can you devise? Is it pleasure in this inglorious existence to
think that you are serving pleasure? Is it freedom to be the
slave to self? For I hold," continued Trevylyan, "that this
jargon of 'consulting happiness,' this cant of living for ourselves, is but a mean as well as a false philosophy. Why this
eternal reference to self? Is self alone to be consulted? Is
even our happiness, did it truly consist in repose, really the
great end of life? I doubt if we cannot ascend higher. I
doubt if we cannot say with a great moralist, 'If virtue be
not estimable in itself, we can see nothing estimable in following it for the sake of a bargain.' But, in fact, repose is

the poorest of all delusions; the very act of recurring to self brings about us all those ills of self from which, in the turmoil of the world, we can escape. We become hypochondriacs. Our very health grows an object of painful possession. We are so desirous to be well (for what is retirement without health?) that we are ever fancying ourselves ill; and, like the man in the 'Spectator,' we weigh ourselves daily, and live but by grains and scruples. Retirement is happy only for the poet, for to him it is *not* retirement. He secedes from one world but to gain another, and he finds not *ennui* in seclusion: why? Not because seclusion hath *repose*, but because it hath *occupation*. In one word, then, I say of action and of indolence, grant the same ills to both, and to action there is the readier escape or the nobler consolation."

Vane shrugged his shoulders. "Ah, my dear friend," said he, tapping his snuff-box with benevolent superiority, "you are much younger than I am!"

But these conversations, which Trevylyan and Vane often held together, dull as I fear this specimen must seem to the reader, had an inexpressible charm for Gertrude. She loved the lofty and generous vein of philosophy which Trevylyan embraced, and which, while it suited his ardent nature, contrasted a demeanour commonly hard and cold to all but herself. And young and tender as she was, his ambition infused its spirit into her fine imagination, and that passion for enterprise which belongs inseparably to romance. She loved to muse over his future lot, and in fancy to share its toils and to exult in its triumphs. And if sometimes she asked herself whether a career of action might not estrange him from her, she had but to turn her gaze upon his watchful eye,—and lo, he was by her side or at her feet!

CHAPTER VI.

GORCUM. — THE TOUR OF THE VIRTUES: A PHILOSOPHER'S TALE.

IT was a bright and cheery morning as they glided by Gorcum. The boats pulling to the shore full of fishermen and peasants in their national costume; the breeze freshly rippling the waters; the lightness of the blue sky; the loud and laughing voices from the boats,— all contributed to raise the spirit, and fill it with that indescribable gladness which is the physical sense of life.

The tower of the church, with its long windows and its round dial, rose against the clear sky; and on a bench under a green bush facing the water sat a jolly Hollander, refreshing the breezes with the fumes of his national weed.

"How little it requires to make a journey pleasant, when the companions are our friends!" said Gertrude, as they sailed along. "Nothing can be duller than these banks, nothing more delightful than this voyage."

"Yet what tries the affections of people for each other so severely as a journey together?" said Vane. "That perpetual companionship from which there is no escaping; that confinement, in all our moments of ill-humour and listlessness, with persons who want us to look amused — ah, it is a severe ordeal for friendship to pass through! A post-chaise must have jolted many an intimacy to death."

"You speak feelingly, dear father," said Gertrude, laughing; "and, I suspect, with a slight desire to be sarcastic upon us. Yet, seriously, I should think that travel must be like life, and that good persons must be always agreeable companions to each other."

"Good persons, my Gertrude!" answered Vane, with a smile. "Alas! I fear the good weary each other quite as much as the bad. What say you, Trevylyan,— would Virtue be a pleasant companion from Paris to Petersburg? Ah, I see you intend to be on Gertrude's side of the question. Well now, if I tell you a story, since stories are so much the fashion with you, in which you shall find that the Virtues themselves actually made the experiment of a tour, will you promise to attend to the moral?"

"Oh, dear father, anything for a story," cried Gertrude; "especially from you, who have not told us one all the way. Come, listen, Albert; nay, listen to your new rival."

And, pleased to see the vivacity of the invalid, Vane began as follows:—

THE TOUR OF THE VIRTUES:

A PHILOSOPHER'S TALE.

ONCE upon a time, several of the Virtues, weary of living forever with the Bishop of Norwich, resolved to make a little excursion; accordingly, though they knew everything on earth was very ill prepared to receive them, they thought they might safely venture on a tour from Westminster Bridge to Richmond. The day was fine, the wind in their favour, and as to entertainment,— why, there seemed, according to Gertrude, to be no possibility of any disagreement among the Virtues.

They took a boat at Westminster stairs; and just as they were about to push off, a poor woman, all in rags, with a child in her arms, implored their compassion. Charity put her hand into her reticule and took out a shilling. Justice, turning round to look after the luggage, saw the folly which Charity was about to commit. "Heavens!" cried Justice, seizing poor Charity by the arm, "what are you doing? Have you never read Political Economy? Don't you know that indiscriminate almsgiving is only the encouragement to Idleness, the mother of Vice? You a Virtue, indeed! I'm ashamed of you. Get along with you, good woman;— yet stay, there is a ticket for soup at the Mendicity Society; they'll see if you're a proper object of compassion." But Charity is quicker than Justice, and slipping her hand behind her, the poor woman got the shilling and the ticket for soup too. Economy and Generosity saw the double gift. "What waste!" cried Economy, frowning; "what! a ticket and a shilling? *either* would have sufficed."

"Either!" said Generosity, "fie! Charity should have given the poor creature half-a-crown, and Justice a dozen tickets!" So the next ten minutes were consumed in a quarrel between the four Virtues, which would have lasted all the way to Richmond, if Courage had not advised them to get on shore and fight it out. Upon this, the Virtues suddenly perceived they had a little forgotten themselves, and Generosity offering the first apology, they made it up, and went on very agreeably for the next mile or two.

The day now grew a little overcast, and a shower seemed at hand. Prudence, who had on a new bonnet, suggested the propriety of putting to shore for half an hour; Courage was for braving the rain; but, as most of the Virtues are ladies, Prudence carried it. Just as they were about to land, another boat cut in before them very uncivilly, and gave theirs such a shake that Charity was all but overboard. The company on board the uncivil boat, who evidently thought the Virtues extremely low persons, for they had nothing very fashionable about their exterior, burst out laughing at Charity's discomposure, especially as a large basket full of buns, which Charity carried with her for any hungry-looking children she might encounter at Richmond, fell pounce into the water. Courage was all on fire; he twisted his mustache, and would have made an onset on the enemy, if, to his great indignation, Meekness had not forestalled him, by stepping mildly into the hostile boat and offering both cheeks to the foe. This was too much even for the incivility of the boatmen; they made their excuses to the Virtues, and Courage, who is no bully, thought himself bound discontentedly to accept them. But oh! if you had seen how Courage used Meekness afterwards, you could not have believed it possible that one Virtue could be so enraged with another. This quarrel between the two threw a damp on the party; and they proceeded on their voyage, when the shower was over, with anything but cordiality. I spare you the little squabbles that took place in the general conversation,—how Economy found fault with all the villas by the way, and Temperance expressed becoming indignation at the luxuries of the City barge. They arrived at Richmond, and Temperance was appointed to order the dinner; meanwhile Hospitality, walking in the garden, fell in with a large party of Irishmen, and asked them to join the repast.

Imagine the long faces of Economy and Prudence, when they saw the addition to the company! Hospitality was all spirits; he rubbed his hands and called for champagne with the tone of a younger brother. Temperance soon grew scandalized, and Modesty herself coloured at some of the jokes; but Hospitality, who was now half seas over, called the one a milksop, and swore at the other as a prude. Away went the hours; it was time to return, and they made down to the water-side, thoroughly out of temper with one another, Economy and Generosity quarrelling all the way about the bill and the waiters. To make up the sum of their mortification, they passed a boat where all the company were in the best possible spirits, laughing and whooping like mad; and discovered these jolly companions to be two or three agreeable Vices, who had put themselves under the management of Good Temper.

"So you see, Gertrude, that even the Virtues may fall at loggerheads with each other, and pass a very sad time of it, if they happen to be of opposite dispositions, and have forgotten to take Good Temper with them."

"Ah," said Gertrude, "but you have overloaded your boat; too many Virtues might contradict one another, but not a few."

"Voilà ce que veux dire," said Vane; "but listen to the sequel of my tale, which now takes a new moral."

At the end of the voyage, and after a long, sulky silence, Prudence said, with a thoughtful air, "My dear friends, I have been thinking that as long as we keep so entirely together, never mixing with the rest of the world, we shall waste our lives in quarrelling amongst ourselves and run the risk of being still less liked and sought after than we already are. You know that we are none of us popular; every one is quite contented to see us represented in a vaudeville, or described in an essay. Charity, indeed, has her name often taken in vain at a bazaar or a subscription; and the miser as often talks of the duty he owes to *me*, when he sends the stranger from his door or his grandson to jail: but still we only resemble so many wild beasts, whom everybody likes to see but nobody cares to possess. Now, I propose that we should all separate and take up our abode with some mortal or other for a year, with the power of changing at the end of that time should we not feel ourselves comfortable,— that is, should we not find that we do all the good we intend; let us try the experiment, and on this day twelvemonths let us all meet under the largest oak in Windsor Forest, and recount what has befallen us." Prudence ceased, as she always does when she has said enough; and, delighted at the project, the Virtues agreed to adopt it on the spot. They were enchanted at the idea of setting up for themselves, and each not doubting his or her success,— for Economy in her heart thought Generosity no Virtue at all, and Meekness looked on Courage as little better than a heathen.

Generosity, being the most eager and active of all the Virtues, set off first on his journey. Justice followed, and kept up with him, though at a more even pace. Charity never heard a sigh, or saw a squalid face, but she stayed to cheer and console the sufferer,— a kindness which somewhat retarded her progress.

Courage espied a travelling carriage, with a man and his wife in it quarrelling most conjugally, and he civilly begged he might be permitted to occupy the vacant seat opposite the lady. Economy still lingered, inquiring for the cheapest inns. Poor Modesty looked round and sighed, on finding herself so near to London, where she was almost wholly unknown; but resolved to bend her course thither for two reasons: first, for the novelty of the thing; and, secondly, not liking to expose herself to any risks by a journey on the Continent. Prudence, though the first to project, was the last to execute; and therefore resolved to remain where she was for that night, and take daylight for her travels.

The year rolled on, and the Virtues, punctual to the appointment, met under the oak-tree; they all came nearly at the same time, excepting Economy, who had got into a return post-chaise, the horses to which, having been forty miles in the course of the morning, had foundered by the way, and retarded her journey till night set in. The Virtues looked sad and sorrowful, as people are wont to do after a long and fruitless journey; and, somehow or other, such was the wearing effect of their intercourse with the world, that they appeared wonderfully diminished in size.

"Ah, my dear Generosity," said Prudence, with a sigh, "as you were the first to set out on your travels, pray let us hear your adventures first."

"You must know, my dear sisters," said Generosity, "that I had not gone many miles from you before I came to a small country town, in which a marching regiment was quartered, and at an open window I beheld, leaning over a gentleman's chair, the most beautiful creature imagination ever pictured; her eyes shone out like two suns of perfect happiness, and she was almost cheerful enough to have passed for Good Temper herself. The gentleman over whose chair she leaned was her husband; they had been married six weeks; he was a lieutenant with £100 a year besides his pay. Greatly affected by their poverty, I instantly determined, without a second thought, to ensconce myself in the heart of this charming girl. During the first hour in my new residence I made many wise reflections such as — that Love never was so perfect as when accompanied by Poverty; what a vulgar error it was to call the unmarried state 'Single *Blessedness;*' how wrong it was of us Virtues never to have tried the marriage bond; and what a falsehood it was to say that husbands neglected their wives, for never was there anything in nature so devoted as the love of a husband — six weeks married!

"The next morning, before breakfast, as the charming Fanny was waiting for her husband, who had not yet finished his toilet, a poor, wretched-looking object appeared at the

window, tearing her hair and wringing her hands; her husband had that morning been dragged to prison, and her seven
children had fought for the last mouldy crust. Prompted by
me, Fanny, without inquiring further into the matter, drew
from her silken purse a five-pound note, and gave it to the
beggar, who departed more amazed than grateful. Soon after,
the lieutenant appeared. 'What the devil, another bill!'
muttered he, as he tore the yellow wafer from a large,
square, folded, bluish piece of paper. 'Oh, ah! confound the
fellow, *he* must be paid. I must trouble you, Fanny, for
£15 to pay this saddler's bill.'

"'Fifteen pounds, love?' stammered Fanny, blushing.

"'Yes, dearest, the £15 I gave you yesterday.'

"'I have only £10,' said Fanny, hesitatingly; 'for such
a poor, wretched-looking creature was here just now, that
I was obliged to give her £5.'

"'Five pounds? good Heavens!' exclaimed the astonished
husband; 'I shall have no more money this three weeks.' He
frowned, he bit his lips, nay, he even wrung his hands, and
walked up and down the room; worse still, he broke forth
with — 'Surely, madam, you did not suppose, when you married a lieutenant in a marching regiment, that he could afford
to indulge in the whim of giving £5 to every mendicant who
held out her hand to you? You did not, I say, madam,
imagine' — but the bridegroom was interrupted by the convulsive sobs of his wife: it was their first quarrel, they were
but six weeks married; he looked at her for one moment
sternly, the next he was at her feet. 'Forgive me, dearest
Fanny, — forgive me, for I cannot forgive myself. I was too
great a wretch to say what I did; and do believe, my own
Fanny, that while I may be too poor to indulge you in it, I
do from my heart admire so noble, so disinterested, a generosity.' Not a little proud did I feel to have been the cause
of this exemplary husband's admiration for his amiable wife,
and sincerely did I rejoice at having taken up my abode with
these *poor* people. But not to tire you, my dear sisters, with
the minutiæ of detail, I shall briefly say that things did not
long remain in this delightful position; for before many

months had elapsed, poor Fanny had to bear with her husband's increased and more frequent storms of passion, unfollowed by any halcyon and honeymoon suings for forgiveness: for at my instigation every shilling went; and when there were no more to go, her trinkets and even her clothes followed. The lieutenant became a complete brute, and even allowed his unbridled tongue to call me — me, sisters, *me!* — 'heartless Extravagance.' His despicable brother-officers and their gossiping wives were no better; for they did nothing but animadvert upon my Fanny's ostentation and absurdity, for by such names had they the impertinence to call *me*. Thus grieved to the soul to find myself the cause of all poor Fanny's misfortunes, I resolved at the end of the year to leave her, being thoroughly convinced that, however amiable and praiseworthy I might be in myself, I was totally unfit to be bosom friend and adviser to the wife of a lieutenant in a marching regiment, with only £100 a year besides his pay."

The Virtues groaned their sympathy with the unfortunate Fanny; and Prudence, turning to Justice, said, "I long to hear what you have been doing, for I am certain you cannot have occasioned harm to any one."

Justice shook her head and said: "Alas! I find that there are times and places when even I do better not to appear, as a short account of my adventures will prove to you. No sooner had I left you than I instantly repaired to India, and took up my abode with a Brahmin. I was much shocked by the dreadful inequalities of condition that reigned in the several castes, and I longed to relieve the poor Pariah from his ignominious destiny; accordingly I set seriously to work on reform. I insisted upon the iniquity of abandoning men from their birth to an irremediable state of contempt, from which no virtue could exalt them. The Brahmins looked upon *my* Brahmin with ineffable horror. They called *me* the most wicked of vices; they saw no distinction between Justice and Atheism. I uprooted their society — that was sufficient crime. But the worst was, that the Pariahs themselves regarded me with suspicion; they thought it unnatural in a Brahmin to care for a Pariah! And one called me 'Madness,'

another, 'Ambition,' and a third, 'The Desire to innovate.'
My poor Brahmin led a miserable life of it; when one day,
after observing, at my dictation, that he thought a Pariah's
life as much entitled to respect as a cow's, he was hurried
away by the priests and secretly broiled on the altar as a fitting reward for his sacrilege. I fled hither in great tribula-
tion, persuaded that in some countries even Justice may do
harm."

"As for me," said Charity, not waiting to be asked, "I
grieve to say that I was silly enough to take up my abode
with an old lady in Dublin, who never knew what discretion
was, and always acted from impulse; my instigation was irresistible, and the money she gave in her drives through the
suburbs of Dublin was so lavishly spent that it kept all the
rascals of the city in idleness and whiskey. I found, to my
great horror, that I was a main cause of a terrible epidemic,
and that to give alms without discretion was to spread poverty without help. I left the city when my year was out,
and as ill-luck would have it, just at the time when I was
most wanted."

"And oh," cried Hospitality, "I went to Ireland also. I
fixed my abode with a squireen; I ruined him in a year, and
only left him because he had no longer a hovel to keep
me in."

"As for myself," said Temperance, "I entered the breast
of an English legislator, and he brought in a bill against ale-
houses; the consequence was, that the labourers took to gin;
and I have been forced to confess that Temperance may be
too zealous when she dictates too vehemently to others."

"Well," said Courage, keeping more in the background
than he had ever done before, and looking rather ashamed of
himself, "that travelling carriage I got into belonged to a
German general and his wife, who were returning to their
own country. Growing very cold as we proceeded, she wrapped
me up in a polonaise; but the cold increasing, I inadvertently
crept into her bosom. Once there I could not get out, and
from thenceforward the poor general had considerably the
worst of it. She became so provoking that I wondered how

he could refrain from an explosion. To do him justice, he did at last threaten to get out of the carriage; upon which, roused by me, she collared him — and conquered. When he got to his own district, things grew worse, for if any *aide-de-camp* offended her she insisted that he might be publicly reprimanded; and should the poor general refuse she would with her own hands confer a caning upon the delinquent. The additional force she had gained in me was too much odds against the poor general, and he died of a broken heart, six months after my *liaison* with his wife. She after this became so dreaded and detested, that a conspiracy was formed to poison her; *this* daunted even me, so I left her without delay,— *et me voici!* "

"Humph," said Meekness, with an air of triumph, "I, at least, have been more successful than you. On seeing much in the papers of the cruelties practised by the Turks on the Greeks, I thought my presence would enable the poor sufferers to bear their misfortunes calmly. I went to Greece, then, at a moment when a well-planned and practicable scheme of emancipating themselves from the Turkish yoke was arousing their youth. Without confining myself to one individual, I flitted from breast to breast; I meekened the whole nation; my remonstrances against the insurrection succeeded, and I had the satisfaction of leaving a whole people ready to be killed or strangled with the most Christian resignation in the world."

The Virtues, who had been a little cheered by the opening self-complacence of Meekness, would not, to her great astonishment, allow that she had succeeded a whit more happily than her sisters, and called next upon Modesty for her confession.

"You know," said that amiable young lady, "that I went to London in search of a situation. I spent three months of the twelve in going from house to house, but I could not get a single person to receive me. The ladies declared that they never saw so old-fashioned a gawkey, and civilly recommended me to their abigails; the abigails turned me round with a stare, and then pushed me down to the kitchen and the fat scullion-maids, who assured me that, 'in the respectable families they had the honour to live in, they had never even heard of my name.' One young housemaid, just from the country, did indeed receive me with some sort of civility; but she very soon lost me in the servants' hall. I now took refuge with the other sex, as the least uncourteous. I was fortunate enough to find a young gentleman of remarkable talents, who welcomed me with open arms. He was full of learning, gentleness, and honesty. I had only one rival,—Ambition. We both contended for an absolute empire over him. Whatever Ambition suggested, I damped. Did Ambition urge him to begin a book, I persuaded him it was not worth publication. Did he get up, full of knowledge, and instigated by my rival, to make a speech (for he was in parliament), I shocked him with the sense of his assurance, I made his voice droop and his accents falter. At last, with an indignant sigh, my rival left him; he retired into the country, took orders, and renounced a career he had fondly hoped would be serviceable to others; but finding I did not suffice for his happiness, and piqued at his melancholy, I left him before the end of the year, and he has since taken to drinking!"

The eyes of the Virtues were all turned to Prudence. She was their last hope. "I am just where I set out," said that discreet Virtue; "I have done neither good nor harm. To avoid temptation I went and lived with a hermit to whom I soon found that I could be of no use beyond warning him not to overboil his peas and lentils, not to leave his door open when a storm threatened, and not to fill his pitcher too full at the neighbouring spring. I am thus the only one of you that never did harm; but only because I am the only one of you that never had an opportunity of doing it! In a word," continued Prudence, thoughtfully,— "in a word, my friends, circumstances are necessary to the Virtues themselves. Had, for instance, Economy changed with Generosity, and gone to the poor lieutenant's wife, and had I lodged with the Irish squireen instead of Hospitality, what misfortunes would have been saved to both! Alas! I perceive we lose all our efficacy when we are misplaced; and *then*, though in reality Virtues, we operate as Vices. Circumstances must be favourable to our exertions, and harmonious with our nature; and we lose our very divinity unless Wisdom direct our footsteps to the home we should inhabit and the dispositions we should govern."

The story was ended, and the travellers began to dispute about its moral. Here let us leave them.

CHAPTER VII.

COLOGNE. — THE TRACES OF THE ROMAN YOKE. — THE CHURCH OF ST. MARIA. — TREVYLYAN'S REFLECTIONS ON THE MONASTIC LIFE. — THE TOMB OF THE THREE KINGS. — AN EVENING EXCURSION ON THE RHINE.

ROME — magnificent Rome! wherever the pilgrim wends, the traces of thy dominion greet his eyes. Still in the heart of the bold German race is graven the print of the eagle's claws; and amidst the haunted regions of the Rhine we pause to wonder at the great monuments of the Italian yoke.

At Cologne our travellers rested for some days. They were in the city to which the camp of Marcus Agrippa had given birth; that spot had resounded with the armed tread of the legions of Trajan. In that city, Vitellius, Sylvanus, were proclaimed emperors. By that church did the latter receive his death.

As they passed round the door they saw some peasants loitering on the sacred ground; and when they noted the delicate cheek of Gertrude they uttered their salutations with more than common respect. Where they then were the building swept round in a circular form; and at its base it is supposed by tradition to retain something of the ancient Roman masonry. Just before them rose the spire of a plain and unadorned church, singularly contrasting the pomp of the old with the simplicity of the innovating creed.

The church of St. Maria occupies the site of the Roman Capitol, and the place retains the Roman name; and still something in the aspect of the people betrays the hereditary blood.

Gertrude, whose nature was strongly impressed with *the venerating character*, was fond of visiting the old Gothic churches, which, with so eloquent a moral, unite the living with the dead.

"Pause for a moment," said Trevylyan, before they entered the church of St. Mary. "What recollections crowd upon us! On the site of the Roman Capitol a Christian church and a convent are erected! By whom? The mother of Charles Martel,— the Conqueror of the Saracen, the arch-hero of Christendom itself! And to these scenes and calm retreats, to the cloisters of the convent once belonging to this church, fled the bruised spirit of a royal sufferer,— the victim of Richelieu,— the unfortunate and ambitious Mary de Medicis. Alas! the cell and the convent are but a vain emblem of that desire to fly to God which belongs to Distress; the solitude soothes, but the monotony recalls, regret. And for my own part in my frequent tours through Catholic countries, I never saw the still walls in which monastic vanity hoped to shut out the world, but a melancholy came over me! What hearts at war with themselves! what unceasing regrets! what pinings after the past! what long and beautiful years devoted to a moral grave, by a momentary rashness, an impulse, a disappointment! But in these churches the lesson is more impressive and less sad. The weary heart has ceased to ache; the burning pulses are still; the troubled spirit has flown to the only rest which is not a deceit. Power and love, hope and fear, avarice, ambition,— they are quenched at last! Death is the only monastery, the tomb is the only cell."

"Your passion is ever for active life," said Gertrude. "You allow no charm to solitude, and contemplation to you seems torture. If any great sorrow ever come upon you, you will never retire to seclusion as its balm. You will plunge into the world, and lose your individual existence in the universal rush of life."

"Ah, talk not of sorrow!" said Trevylyan, wildly. "Let us enter the church."

They went afterwards to the celebrated cathedral, which is considered one of the noblest of the architectural triumphs of Germany; but it is yet more worthy of notice from the Pilgrim of Romance than the searcher after antiquity, for here, behind the grand altar, is the Tomb of the Three Kings of Cologne,— the three worshippers whom tradition humbled to our Saviour. Legend is rife with a thousand tales of the relics of this tomb. The Three Kings of Cologne are the tutelary names of that golden superstition which has often more votaries than the religion itself from which it springs: and to Gertrude the simple story of Lucille sufficed to make her for the moment credulous of the sanctity of the spot. Behind the tomb three Gothic windows cast their "dim, religious light" over the tessellated pavement and along the Ionic pillars. They found some of the more credulous believers in the authenticity of the relics kneeling before the tomb, and they arrested their steps, fearful to disturb the superstition which is never without something of sanctity when contented with prayer and forgetful of persecution. The bones of the Magi are still supposed to consecrate the tomb, and on the higher part of the monument the artist has delineated their adoration to the infant Saviour.

That evening came on with a still and tranquil beauty, and as the sun hastened to its close they launched their boat for an hour or two's excursion upon the Rhine. Gertrude was in that happy mood when the quiet of nature is enjoyed like a bath for the soul, and the presence of him she so idolized deepened that stillness into a more delicious and subduing calm. Little did she dream as the boat glided over the water, and the towers of Cologne rose in the blue air of evening, how few were those hours that divided her from the tomb! But, in looking back to the life of one we have loved, how dear is the thought that the latter days were the days of light, that the cloud never chilled the beauty of the setting sun, and that if the years of existence were brief, all that existence has most tender, most sacred, was crowded into that space! Nothing dark, then, or bitter, rests with our remembrance of the lost: *we* are the mourners, but pity is not for the mourned, — our grief is purely selfish; when we turn to its object, the hues of happiness are round it, and that very love which is the parent of our woe was the consolation, the triumph, of the departed!

The majestic Rhine was calm as a lake; the splashing of the oar only broke the stillness, and after a long pause in their conversation, Gertrude, putting her hand on Trevylyan's arm, reminded him of a promised story: for he too had moods of abstraction, from which, in her turn, she loved to lure him; and his voice to her had become a sort of want.

"Let it be," said she, "a tale suited to the hour; no fierce tradition, — nay, no grotesque fable, but of the tenderer dye of superstition. Let it be of love, of woman's love,— of the love that defies the grave: for surely even after death it lives; and heaven would scarcely be heaven if memory were banished from its blessings."

"I recollect," said Trevylyan, after a slight pause, "a short German legend, the simplicity of which touched me much when I heard it; but," added he, with a slight smile, "so much more faithful appears in the legend the love of the woman than that of the man, that *I* at least ought scarcely to recite it."

"Nay," said Gertrude, tenderly, "the fault of the inconstant only heightens our gratitude to the faithful."

———◆———

CHAPTER VIII.

THE SOUL IN PURGATORY; OR LOVE STRONGER THAN DEATH.

THE angels strung their harps in heaven, and their music went up like a stream of odours to the pavilions of the Most High; but the harp of Seralim was sweeter than that of his fellows, and the Voice of the Invisible One (for the angels themselves know not the glories of Jehovah — only far in the depths of heaven they see one Unsleeping Eye watching forever over Creation) was heard saying,—

"Ask a gift for the love that burns in thy song, and it shall be given thee." And Seralim answered,—

"There is in that place which men call Purgatory, and which is the escape from hell, but the painful porch of heaven, many souls that adore Thee, and yet are punished justly for their sins; grant me the boon to visit them at times, and solace their suffering by the hymns of the harp that is consecrated to Thee!"

And the Voice answered,—

"Thy prayer is heard, O gentlest of the angels! and it seems good to Him who chastises but from love. Go! Thou hast thy will."

Then the angel sang the praises of God; and when the song was done he rose from his azure throne at the right hand of Gabriel, and, spreading his rainbow wings, he flew to that melancholy orb which, nearest to earth, echoes with the shrieks of souls that by torture become pure. There the unhappy ones see from afar the bright courts they are hereafter to obtain, and the shapes of glorious beings, who, fresh from the Fountains of Immortality, walk amidst the gardens of Paradise, and feel that their happiness hath no morrow; and this thought consoles amidst their torments, and makes the true difference between Purgatory and Hell.

Then the angel folded his wings, and entering the crystal gates, sat down upon a blasted rock and struck his divine lyre, and a peace fell over the wretched; the demon ceased to torture and the victim to wail. As sleep to the mourners of earth was the song of the angel to the souls of the purifying star: one only voice amidst the general stillness seemed not lulled by the angel; it was the voice of a woman, and it continued to cry out with a sharp cry,—

"Oh, Adenheim, Adenheim! mourn not for the lost!"

The angel struck chord after chord, till his most skilful melodies were exhausted; but still the solitary voice, unheeding — unconscious of — the sweetest harp of the angel choir, cried out, —

"Oh, Adenheim, Adenheim! mourn not for the lost!"

Then Seralim's interest was aroused, and approaching the spot whence the voice came, he saw the spirit of a young and beautiful girl chained to a rock, and the demons lying idly by. And Seralim said to the demons, "Doth the song lull ye thus to rest?"

And they answered, "Her care for another is bitterer than all our torments; therefore are we idle."

Then the angel approached the spirit, and said in a voice which stilled her cry — for in what state do we outlive sympathy? — "Wherefore, O daughter of earth, wherefore wailest thou with the same plaintive wail; and why doth the harp that soothes the most guilty of thy companions fail in its melody with thee?"

"O radiant stranger," answered the poor spirit, "thou speakest to one who on earth loved God's creature more than God; therefore is she thus justly sentenced. But I know that my poor Adenheim mourns ceaselessly for me, and the thought of his sorrow is more intolerable to me than all that the demons can inflict."

"And how knowest thou that he laments thee?" asked the angel.

"Because I know with what agony I should have mourned for *him*," replied the spirit, simply.

The divine nature of the angel was touched; for love is the nature of the sons of heaven. "And how," said he, "can I minister to thy sorrow?"

A transport seemed to agitate the spirit, and she lifted up her mistlike and impalpable arms, and cried, —

"Give me — oh, give me to return to earth, but for one little hour, that I may visit my Adenheim; and that, concealing from him my present sufferings, I may comfort him in his own."

"Alas!" said the angel, turning away his eyes, — for angels may not weep in the sight of others, — "I could, indeed, grant thee this boon, but thou knowest not the penalty. For the souls in Purgatory may return to Earth, but heavy is the sentence that awaits their return. In a word, for one hour on earth thou must add a thousand years to the torture of thy confinement here! "

"Is that all?" cried the spirit. "Willingly then will I brave the doom. Ah, surely they love not in heaven, or thou wouldst know, O Celestial Visitant, that one hour of consolation to the one we love is worth a thousand ages of torture to ourselves! Let me comfort and convince my Adenheim; no matter what becomes of me."

Then the angel looked on high, and he saw in far distant regions, which in that orb none else could discern, the rays that parted from the all-guarding Eye; and heard the VOICE of the Eternal One bidding him act as his pity whispered. He looked on the spirit, and her shadowy arms stretched pleadingly towards him; he uttered the word that loosens the bars of the gate of Purgatory; and lo, the spirit had re-entered the human world.

It was night in the halls of the lord of Adenheim, and he sat at the head of his glittering board. Loud and long was the laugh, and merry the jest that echoed round; and the laugh and the jest of the lord of Adenheim were louder and merrier than all. And by his right side sat a beautiful lady; and ever and anon he turned from others to whisper soft vows in her ear.

"And oh," said the bright dame of Falkenberg, "thy words what ladye can believe? Didst thou not utter the same oaths, and promise the same love, to Ida, the fair daughter of Loden, and now but three little months have closed upon her grave?"

"By my halidom," quoth the young lord of Adenheim, "thou dost thy beauty marvellous injustice. Ida! Nay, thou mockest me; *I* love the daughter of Loden! Why, how then should I be worthy thee? A few gay words, a few passing smiles,—behold all the love Adenheim ever bore to Ida. Was it my fault if the poor fool misconstrued such common courtesy? Nay, dearest lady, this heart is virgin to thee."

"And what!" said the lady of Falkenberg, as she suffered

the arm of Adenheim to encircle her slender waist, "didst thou not grieve for her loss?"

"Why, verily, yes, for the first week; but in thy bright eyes I found ready consolation."

At this moment, the lord of Adenheim thought he heard a deep sigh behind him; he turned, but saw nothing, save a slight mist that gradually faded away, and vanished in the distance. Where was the necessity for Ida to reveal herself?

.   .   .   .

"And thou didst not, then, do thine errand to thy lover?" said Seralim, as the spirit of the wronged Ida returned to Purgatory.

"Bid the demons recommence their torture," was poor Ida's answer.

"And was it for this that thou added a thousand years to thy doom?"

"Alas!" answered Ida, "after the single hour I have endured on Earth, there seems to be but little terrible in a thousand fresh years of Purgatory!"[1]

"What! is the story ended?" asked Gertrude.

"Yes."

"Nay, surely the thousand years were not added to poor Ida's doom; and Seralim bore her back with him to Heaven?"

"The legend saith no more. The writer was contented to show us the perpetuity of woman's love — "

"And its reward," added Vane.

"It was not *I* who drew that last conclusion, Albert," whispered Gertrude.

---

[1] This story is principally borrowed from a foreign soil. It seemed to the author worthy of being transferred to an English one, although he fears that much of its singular beauty in the original has been lost by the way.

CHAPTER IX.

THE SCENERY OF THE RHINE ANALOGOUS TO THE GERMAN LITERARY GENIUS. — THE DRACHENFELS.

On leaving Cologne, the stream winds round among banks that do not yet fulfil the promise of the Rhine; but they increase in interest as you leave Surdt and Godorf. The peculiar character of the river does not, however, really appear, until by degrees the Seven Mountains, and "The castled Crag of Drachenfels" above them all, break upon the eye. Around Nieder Cassel and Rheidt the vines lie thick and clustering; and, by the shore, you see from place to place the islands stretching their green length along, and breaking the exulting tide. Village rises upon village, and viewed from the distance as you sail, the pastoral errors that enamoured us of the village life crowd thick and fast upon us. So still do these hamlets seem, so sheltered from the passions of the world, — as if the passions were not like winds, only felt where they breathe, and invisible save by their effects! Leaping into the broad bosom of the Rhine come many a stream and rivulet upon either side. Spire upon spire rises and sinks as you sail on. Mountain and city, the solitary island, the castled steep, like the dreams of ambition, suddenly appear, proudly swell, and dimly fade away.

"You begin now," said Trevylyan, "to understand the character of the German literature. The Rhine is an emblem of its luxuriance, its fertility, its romance. The best commentary to the German genius is a visit to the German scenery. The mighty gloom of the Hartz, the feudal towers that look over vines and deep valleys on the legendary Rhine; the gigantic remains of antique power, profusely scattered over plain, mount, and forest; the thousand mixed recollections that hallow the ground; the stately Roman, the stalwart

Goth, the chivalry of the feudal age, and the dim brotherhood
of the ideal world, have here alike their record and their
remembrance.   And over such scenes wanders the young German student.   Instead of the pomp and luxury of the English
traveller, the thousand devices to cheat the way, he has but
his volume in his hand, his knapsack at his back.   From such
scenes he draws and hives all that various store which after
years ripen to invention.   Hence the florid mixture of the
German muse, — the classic, the romantic, the contemplative,
the philosophic, and the superstitious; each the result of
actual meditation over different scenes; each the produce of
separate but confused recollections.   As the Rhine flows, so
flows the national genius, by mountain and valley, the wildest
solitude, the sudden spires of ancient cities, the mouldered
castle, the stately monastery, the humble cot, — grandeur and
homeliness, history and superstition, truth and fable, succeeding one another so as to blend into a whole.

"But," added Trevylyan, a moment afterwards, "the Ideal
is passing slowly away from the German mind; a spirit for
the more active and the more material literature is springing up amongst them.   The revolution of mind gathers on,
preceding stormy events; and the memories that led their
grandsires to contemplate will urge the youth of the next
generation to dare and to act."[1]

Thus conversing, they continued their voyage, with a fair
wave and beneath a lucid sky.

The vessel now glided beside the Seven Mountains and the
Drachenfels.

The sun, slowly setting, cast his yellow beams over the
smooth waters.   At the foot of the mountains lay a village
deeply sequestered in shade; and above, the Ruin of the
Drachenfels caught the richest beams of the sun.   Yet thus
alone, though lofty, the ray cheered not the gloom that hung
over the giant rock: it stood on high, like some great name
on which the light of glory may shine, but which is associated
with a certain melancholy, from the solitude to which its very
height above the level of the herd condemned its owner!

[1] Is not this prediction already fulfilled ? — 1849.

CHAPTER X.

THE LEGEND OF ROLAND. — THE ADVENTURES OF NYMPHALIN ON THE ISLAND OF NONNEWËRTH. — HER SONG. — THE DE- CAY OF THE FAIRY-FAITH IN ENGLAND.

ON the shore opposite the Drachenfels stand the Ruins of Rolandseck, — they are the shattered crown of a lofty and per- pendicular mountain, consecrated to the memory of the brave Roland; below, the trees of an island to which the lady of Roland retired, rise thick and verdant from the smooth tide.

Nothing can exceed the eloquent and wild grandeur of the whole scene. That spot is the pride and beauty of the Rhine.

The legend that consecrates the tower and the island is briefly told; it belongs to a class so common to the Romaunts of Germany. Roland goes to the wars. A false report of his death reaches his betrothed. She retires to the convent in the isle of Nonnewërth, and takes the irrevocable veil. Roland returns home, flushed with glory and hope, to find that the very fidelity of his affianced had placed an eternal barrier be- tween them. He built the castle that bears his name, and which overlooks the monastery, and dwelt there till his death, — happy in the power at least to gaze, even to the last, upon those walls which held the treasure he had lost.

The willows droop in mournful luxuriance along the island, and harmonize with the memory that, through the desert of a thousand years, love still keeps green and fresh. Nor hath it permitted even those additions of fiction which, like mosses, gather by time over the truth that they adorn, yet adorning conceal, to mar the simple tenderness of the legend.

All was still in the island of Nonnewërth; the lights shone through the trees from the house that contained our travellers. On one smooth spot where the islet shelves into the Rhine met the wandering fairies.

"Oh, Pipalee! how beautiful!" cried Nymphalin, as she stood enraptured by the wave, a star-beam shining on her, with her yellow hair "dancing its ringlets in the whistling wind." "For the first time since our departure I do not miss the green fields of England."

"Hist!" said Pipalee, under her breath; "I hear fairy steps,—they must be the steps of strangers."

"Let us retreat into this thicket of weeds," said Nymphalin, somewhat alarmed; "the good lord-treasurer is already asleep there." They whisked into what to them was a forest, for the reeds were two feet high, and there sure enough they found the lord-treasurer stretched beneath a bulrush, with his pipe beside him, for since he had been in Germany he had taken to smoking; and indeed wild thyme, properly dried, makes very good tobacco for a fairy. They also found Nip and Trip sitting very close together, Nip playing with her hair, which was exceedingly beautiful.

"What do you do here?" said Pipalee, shortly; for she was rather an old maid, and did not like fairies to be too close to each other.

"Watching my lord's slumber," said Nip.

"Pshaw!" said Pipalee.

"Nay," quoth Trip, blushing like a sea-shell; "there is no harm in *that*, I 'm sure."

"Hush!" said the queen, peeping through the reeds.

And now forth from the green bosom of the earth came a tiny train; slowly, two by two, hand in hand, they swept from a small aperture, shadowed with fragrant herbs, and formed themselves into a ring: then came other fairies, laden with dainties, and presently two beautiful white mushrooms sprang up, on which the viands were placed, and lo, there was a banquet! Oh, how merry they were! what gentle peals of laughter, loud as a virgin's sigh! what jests! what songs! Happy race! if mortals could see you as often as I do, in the soft nights of summer, they would never be at a loss for entertainment. But as our English fairies looked on, they saw that these foreign elves were of a different race from themselves: they were taller.and less handsome, their hair was darker, they wore mustaches, and had something of a fiercer air. Poor Nymphalin was a little frightened; but presently soft music was heard floating along, something like the sound we suddenly hear of a still night when a light breeze steals through rushes, or wakes a ripple in some shallow brook dancing over pebbles. And lo, from the aperture of the earth came forth a fay, superbly dressed, and of a noble presence. The queen started back, Pipalee rubbed her eyes, Trip looked over Pipalee's shoulder, and Nip, pinching her arm, cried out amazed, "By the last new star, that is Prince von Fayzenheim!"

Poor Nymphalin gazed again, and her little heart beat under her bee's-wing bodice as if it would break. The prince had a melancholy air, and he sat apart from the banquet, gazing abstractedly on the Rhine.

"Ah!" whispered Nymphalin to herself, "does he think of me?"

Presently the prince drew forth a little flute hollowed from a small reed, and began to play a mournful air. Nymphalin listened with delight; it was one he had learned in her dominions.

When the air was over, the prince rose, and approaching the banqueters, despatched them on different errands; one to visit the dwarf of the Drachenfels, another to look after the grave of Musæus, and a whole detachment to puzzle the students of Heidelberg. A few launched themselves upon willow leaves on the Rhine to cruise about in the starlight, and another band set out a hunting after the gray-legged moth. The prince was left alone; and now Nymphalin, seeing the coast clear, wrapped herself up in a cloak made out of a withered leaf; and only letting her eyes glow out from the hood, she glided from the reeds, and the prince turnng round, saw a dark fairy figure by his side. He drew back, a little startled, and placed his hand on his sword, when Nymphalin circling round him, sang the following words: —

THE FAIRY'S REPROACH.

I.

By the glow-worm's lamp in the dewy brake ;
  By the gossamer's airy net ;
By the shifting skin of the faithless snake,
  Oh, teach me to forget :
          For none, ah none·
Can teach so well that human spell
          As thou, false one !

II.

By the fairy dance on the greensward smooth ;
  By the winds of the gentle west ;
By the loving stars, when their soft looks soothe
  The waves on their mother's breast,
          Teach me thy lore !
      By which, like withered flowers,
      The leaves of buried Hours
          Blossom no more !

III.

By the tent in the violet's bell ;
  By the may on the scented bough ;
By the lone green isle where my sisters dwell ;
  And thine own forgotten vow,
          Teach me to live,
        Nor feed on thoughts that pine
        For love so false as thine !
        Teach me thy lore,
        And one thou lov'st no more
            Will bless thee and forgive !

"Surely," said Fayzenheim, faltering, "surely I know that voice ! "

And Nymphalin's cloak dropped off her shoulder. "My English fairy ! " and Fayzenheim knelt beside her.

I wish you had seen the fay kneel, for you would have sworn it was so like a human lover that you would never have sneered at love afterwards. Love is so fairy-like a part of us, that even a fairy cannot make it differently from us,— that is to say, when we love truly.

There was great joy in the island that night among the elves. They conducted Nymphalin to their palace within the earth, and feasted her sumptuously; and Nip told their adventures with so much spirit that he enchanted the merry foreigners. But Fayzenheim talked apart to Nymphalin, and told her how he was lord of that island, and how he had been obliged to return to his dominions by the law of his tribe, which allowed him to be absent only a certain time in every year. "But, my queen, I always intended to revisit thee next spring."

"Thou need'st not have left us so abruptly," said Nymphalin, blushing.

"But do *thou* never leave me!" said the ardent fairy; "be mine, and let our nuptials be celebrated on these shores. Wouldst thou sigh for thy green island? No! for *there* the fairy altars are deserted, the faith is gone from the land; thou art among the last of an unhonoured and expiring race. Thy mortal poets are dumb, and Fancy, which was thy priestess, sleeps hushed in her last repose. New and hard creeds have succeeded to the fairy lore. Who steals through the starlit boughs on the nights of June to watch the roundels of thy tribe? The wheels of commerce, the din of trade, have silenced to mortal ear the music of thy subjects' harps! And the noisy habitations of men, harsher than their dreaming sires, are gathering round the dell and vale where thy comates linger: a few years, and where will be the green solitudes of England?"

The queen sighed, and the prince, perceiving that he was listened to, continued,—

"Who, in thy native shores, among the children of men, now claims the fairy's care? What cradle wouldst thou tend? On what maid wouldst thou shower thy rosy gifts? What barb wouldst thou haunt in his dreams? Poesy is fled the island, why shouldst thou linger behind? Time hath brought dull customs, that laugh at thy gentle being. Puck is buried in the harebell, he hath left no offspring, and none mourn for his loss; for night, which is the fairy season, is busy and garish as the day. What hearth is desolate after the curfew?

What house bathed in stillness at the hour in which thy revels commence? Thine empire among men hath passed from thee, and thy race are vanishing from the crowded soil; for, despite our diviner nature, our existence is linked with man's. Their neglect is our disease, their forgetfulness our death. Leave then those dull, yet troubled scenes, that are closing round the fairy rings of thy native isle. These mountains, this herbage, these gliding waves, these mouldering ruins, these starred rivulets, be they, O beautiful fairy! thy new domain. Yet in these lands our worship lingers; still can we fill the thought of the young bard, and mingle with his yearnings after the Beautiful, the Unseen. Hither come the pilgrims of the world, anxious only to gather from these scenes the legends of Us; ages will pass away ere the Rhine shall be desecrated of our haunting presence. Come then, my queen, let this palace be thine own, and the moon that glances over the shattered towers of the Dragon Rock witness our nuptials and our vows!"

In such words the fairy prince courted the young queen, and while she sighed at their truth she yielded to their charm. Oh, still may there be one spot on the earth where the fairy feet may press the legendary soil! still be there one land where the faith of The Bright Invisible hallows and inspires! Still glide thou, O majestic and solemn Rhine, among shades and valleys, from which the wisdom of belief can call the creations of the younger world!

* * *

CHAPTER XI.

WHEREIN THE READER IS MADE SPECTATOR WITH THE ENGLISH FAIRIES OF THE SCENES AND BEINGS THAT ARE BENEATH THE EARTH.

DURING the heat of next day's noon, Fayzenheim took the English visitors through the cool caverns that wind amidst the mountains of the Rhine. There, a thousand wonders awaited the eyes of the fairy queen. I speak not of the Gothic arch and aisle into which the hollow earth forms itself, or the stream that rushes with a mighty voice through the dark chasm, or the silver columns that shoot aloft, worked by the gnomes from the mines of the mountains of Taunus; but of the strange inhabitants that from time to time they came upon. They found in one solitary cell, lined with dried moss, two misshapen elves, of a larger size than common, with a plebeian working-day aspect, who were chatting noisily together, and making a pair of boots: these were the Hausmannen or domestic elves, that dance into tradesmen's houses of a night, and play all sorts of undignified tricks. They were very civil to the queen, for they are good-natured creatures on the whole, and once had many relations in Scotland. They then, following the course of a noisy rivulet, came to a hole from which the sharp head of a fox peeped out. The queen was frightened. "Oh, come on," said the fox, encouragingly, "I am one of the fairy race, and many are the gambols we of the brute-elves play in the German world of romance." "Indeed, Mr. Fox," said the prince, "you only speak the truth; and how is Mr. Bruin?" "Quite well, my prince, but tired of his seclusion; for indeed our race can do little or nothing now in the world; and lie here in our old age, telling stories of the past, and recalling the exploits we did in our youth,— which, madam, you may see in all the fairy histories in the prince's library."

"Your own love adventures, for instance, Master Fox," said the prince.

The fox snarled angrily, and drew in his head.

"You have displeased your friend," said Nymphalin.

"Yes; he likes no allusions to the amorous follies of his youth. Did you ever hear of his rivalry with the dog for the cat's good graces?"

"No; that must be very amusing."

"Well, my queen, when we rest by and by, I will relate to you the history of the fox's wooing."

The next place they came to was a vast Runic cavern, covered with dark inscriptions of a forgotten tongue; and sitting

on a huge stone they found a dwarf with long yellow hair, his
head leaning on his breast, and absorbed in meditation.

"This is a spirit of a wise and powerful race," whispered
Fayzenheim, "that has often battled with the fairies; but he
is of the kindly tribe."

Then the dwarf lifted his head with a mournful air; and
gazed upon the bright shapes before him, lighted by the pine-
torches that the prince's attendants carried.

"And what dost thou muse upon, O descendant of the race
of Laurin?" said the prince.

"Upon TIME!" answered the dwarf, gloomily. "I see a
River, and its waves are black, flowing from the clouds, and
none knoweth its source. It rolls deeply on, aye and evermore, through a green valley, which it slowly swallows up,
washing away tower and town, and vanquishing all things;
and the name of the River is TIME."

Then the dwarf's head sank on his bosom, and he spoke
no more.

The fairies proceeded. "Above us," said the prince, "rises
one of the loftiest mountains of the Rhine; for mountains are
the Dwarf's home. When the Great Spirit of all made earth,
he saw that the hollows of the rocks and hills were tenantless,
and yet that a mighty kingdom and great palaces were hid
within them,— a dread and dark solitude, but lighted at times
from the starry eyes of many jewels; and there was the treasure
of the human world — gold and silver — and great heaps of
gems, and a soil of metals. So God made a race for this vast
empire, and gifted them with the power of thought, and the
soul of exceeding wisdom, so that they want not the merriment and enterprise of the outer world; but musing in these
dark caves is their delight. Their existence rolls away in
the luxury of thought; only from time to time they appear in
the world, and betoken woe or weal to men, — according to
their nature, for they are divided into two tribes, the benevolent and the wrathful." While the prince spoke, they saw
glaring upon them from a ledge in the upper rock a grisly
face with a long matted beard. The prince gathered himself
up, and frowned at the evil dwarf, for such it was; but with

a wild laugh the face abruptly disappeared, and the echo of the laugh rang with a ghastly sound through the long hollows of the earth.

The queen clung to Fayzenheim's arm. "Fear not, my queen," said he. "The evil race have no power over our light and aërial nature; with men only they war; and he whom we have seen was, in the old ages of the world, one of the deadliest visitors to mankind."

But now they came winding by a passage to a beautiful recess in the mountain empire; it was of a circular shape of amazing height; in the midst of it played a natural fountain of sparkling waters, and around it were columns of massive granite, rising in countless vistas, till lost in the distant shade. Jewels were scattered round, and brightly played the fairy torches on the gem, the fountain, and the pale silver, that gleamed at frequent intervals from the rocks. "Here let us rest," said the gallant fairy, clapping his hands; "what, ho! music and the feast."

So the feast was spread by the fountain's side; and the courtiers scattered rose-leaves, which they had brought with them, for the prince and his visitor; and amidst the dark kingdom of the dwarfs broke the delicate sound of fairy lutes. "We have not these evil beings in England," said the queen, as low as she could speak; "they rouse my fear, but my interest also. Tell me, dear prince, of what nature was the intercourse of the evil dwarf with man?"

"You know," answered the prince, "that to every species of living thing there is something in common; the vast chain of sympathy runs through all creation. By that which they have in common with the beast of the field or the bird of the air, men govern the inferior tribes; they appeal to the common passions of fear and emulation when they tame the wild steed, to the common desire of greed and gain when they snare the fishes of the stream, or allure the wolves to the pitfall by the bleating of the lamb. In their turn, in the older ages of the world, it was by the passions which men had in common with the demon race that the fiends commanded or allured them. The dwarf whom you saw, being of that race which is characterized by the ambition of power and the desire of hoarding, appealed then in his intercourse with men to the same characteristics in their own bosoms,—to ambition or to avarice. And thus were his victims made! But, not now, dearest Nymphalin," continued the prince, with a more lively air,—"not now will we speak of those gloomy beings. Ho, there! cease the music, and come hither all of ye, to listen to a faithful and homely history of the Dog, the Cat, the Griffin, and the Fox."

CHAPTER XII.

THE WOOING OF MASTER FOX.[1]

You are aware, my dear Nymphalin, that in the time of which I am about to speak there was no particular enmity between the various species of brutes; the dog and the hare chatted very agreeably together, and all the world knows that the wolf, unacquainted with mutton, had a particular affection for the lamb. In these happy days, two most respectable cats, of very old family, had an only daughter. Never was kitten more amiable or more seducing; as she grew up she manifested so many charms, that in a little while she became noted as the greatest beauty in the neighbourhood. Need I to you, dearest Nymphalin, describe her perfection? Suffice it to say that her skin was of the most delicate tortoiseshell,

[1] In the excursions of the fairies, it is the object of the author to bring before the reader a rapid phantasmagoria of the various beings that belong to the German superstitions, so that the work may thus describe the outer and the inner world of the land of the Rhine. The tale of the Fox's Wooing has been composed to give the English reader an idea of a species of novel not naturalized amongst us, though frequent among the legends of our Irish neighbours; in which the brutes are the only characters drawn,—drawn too with shades of distinction as nice and subtle as if they were the creatures of the civilized world.

that her paws were smoother than velvet, that her whiskers
were twelve inches long at the least, and that her eyes had a
gentleness altogether astonishing in a cat.   But if the young
beauty had suitors in plenty during the lives of monsieur and
madame, you may suppose the number was not diminished
when, at the age of two years and a half, she was left an
orphan, and sole heiress to all the hereditary property.   In
fine, she was the richest marriage in the whole country.
Without troubling you, dearest queen, with the adventures of
the rest of her lovers, with their suit and their rejection, I
come at once to the two rivals most sanguine of success,— the
dog and the fox.

Now the dog was a handsome, honest, straightforward, affectionate fellow.   "For my part," said he, "I don't wonder
at my cousin's refusing Bruin the bear, and Gauntgrim the
wolf: to be sure they give themselves great airs, and call
themselves ' noble,' but what then?   Bruin is always in the
sulks, and Gauntgrim always in a passion; a cat of any sen-
sibility would lead a miserable life with them.   As for me, I
am very good-tempered when I 'm not put out, and I have no
fault except that of being angry if disturbed at my meals.   I
am young and good-looking, fond of play and amusement, and
altogether as agreeable a husband as a cat could find in a summer's day.   If she marries me, well and good; she may have
her property settled on herself: if not, I shall bear her no
malice; and I hope I sha'n't be too much in love to forget
that there are other cats in the world."

With that the dog threw his tail over his back, and set off
to his mistress with a gay face on the matter.

Now the fox heard the dog talking thus to himself,—
for the fox was always peeping about, in holes and corners,
and he burst out a laughing when the dog was out of
sight.

"Ho, ho, my fine fellow!" said he; "not so fast, if you
please: you 've got the fox for a rival, let me tell you."

The fox, as you very well know, is a beast that can never
do anything without a manœuvre; and as, from his cunning,
he was generally very lucky in anything he undertook, he did

not doubt for a moment that he should put the dog's nose out of joint. Reynard was aware that in love one should always, if possible, be the first in the field; and he therefore resolved to get the start of the dog and arrive before him at the cat's residence. But this was no easy matter; for though Reynard could run faster than the dog for a little way, he was no match for him in a journey of some distance. "However," said Reynard, "those good-natured creatures are never very wise; and I think I know already what will make him bait on his way."

With that, the fox trotted pretty fast by a short cut in the woods, and getting before the dog, laid himself down by a hole in the earth, and began to howl most piteously.

The dog, hearing the noise, was very much alarmed. "See now," said he, "if the poor fox has not got himself into some scrape! Those cunning creatures are always in mischief; thank Heaven, it never comes into my head to be cunning!" And the good-natured animal ran off as hard as he could to see what was the matter with the fox.

"Oh, dear!" cried Reynard; "what shall I do? What shall I do? My poor little sister has fallen into this hole, and I can't get her out; she'll certainly be smothered." And the fox burst out a howling more piteously than before.

"But, my dear Reynard," quoth the dog, very simply, "why don't you go in after your sister?"

"Ah, you may well ask that," said the fox; "but, in trying to get in, don't you perceive that I have sprained my back and can't stir? Oh, dear! what shall I do if my poor little sister is smothered!"

"Pray don't vex yourself," said the dog; "I'll get her out in an instant." And with that he forced himself with great difficulty into the hole.

Now, no sooner did the fox see that the dog was fairly in, than he rolled a great stone to the mouth of the hole and fitted it so tight, that the dog, not being able to turn round and scratch against it with his forepaws, was made a close prisoner.

"Ha, ha!" cried Reynard, laughing outside; "amuse your-

self with my poor little sister, while I go and make your compliments to Mademoiselle the Cat."

With that Reynard set off at an easy pace, never troubling
his head what became of the poor dog. When he arrived in
the neighbourhood of the beautiful cat's mansion, he resolved
to pay a visit to a friend of his, an old magpie that lived in a
tree and was well acquainted with all the news of the place.
"For," thought Reynard, "I may as well know the blind side
of my mistress that is to be, and get round it at once."

The magpie received the fox with great cordiality, and inquired what brought him so great a distance from home.

"Upon my word," said the fox, "nothing so much as the
pleasure of seeing your ladyship and hearing those agreeable
anecdotes you tell with so charming a grace; but to let you
into a secret — be sure it don't go further — "

"On the word of a magpie," interrupted the bird.

"Pardon me for doubting you," continued the fox; "I should
have recollected that a pie was a proverb for discretion. But,
as I was saying, you known her Majesty the lioness?"

"Surely," said the mapgie, bridling.

"Well; she was pleased to fall in — that is to say — to —
to — take a caprice to your humble servant, and the lion grew
so jealous that I thought it prudent to decamp. A jealous
lion is no joke, let me assure your ladyship. But mum 's the
word."

So great a piece of news delighted the magpie. She could
not but repay it in kind, by all the news in her budget. She
told the fox all the scandal about Bruin and Gauntgrim, and
she then fell to work on the poor young cat. She did not
spare her foibles, you may be quite sure. The fox listened
with great attention, and he learned enough to convince
him that however much the magpie might exaggerate, the
cat was very susceptible to flattery, and had a great deal of
imagination.

When the magpie had finished she said, "But it must be
very unfortunate for you to be banished from so magnificent a
court as that of the lion?"

"As to that," answered the fox, "I console myself for my

exile with a present his Majesty made me on parting, as a reward for my anxiety for his honour and domestic tranquillity;
namely, three hairs from the fifth leg of the amorouthologos-
phorus.   Only think of that, ma'am!"

"The what?" cried the pie, cocking down her left ear.

"The amoronthologosphorus."

"La!" said the magpie; "and what is that very long word,
my dear Reynard?"

"The amoronthologosphorus is a beast that lives on the
other side of the river Cylinx; it has five legs, and on the
fifth leg there are three hairs, and whoever has those three
hairs can be young and beautiful forever."

"Bless me!   I wish you would let me see them," said the
pie, holding out her claw.

"Would that I could oblige you, ma'am; but it's as much
as my life's worth to show them to any but the lady I marry.
In fact, they only have an effect on the fair sex, as you may
see by myself, whose poor person they utterly fail to improve:
they are, therefore, intended for a marriage present, and his
Majesty the lion thus generously atoned to me for relinquish-
ing the tenderness of his queen.   One must confess that there
was a great deal of delicacy in the gift.   But you'll be sure
not to mention it."

"A magpie gossip indeed!" quoth the old blab.

The fox then wished the magpie good night, and retired to
a hole to sleep off the fatigues of the day, before he presented
himself to the beautiful young cat.

The next morning, Heaven knows how! it was all over the
place that Reynard the fox had been banished from court for
the favour shown him by her Majesty, and that the lion had
bribed his departure with three hairs that would make any
lady whom the fox married young and beautiful forever.

The cat was the first to learn the news, and she became all
curiosity to see so interesting a stranger, possessed of "qualifications" which, in the language of the day, "would render
any animal happy!"   She was not long without obtaining her
wish.   As she was taking a walk in the wood the fox contrived to encounter her.   You may be sure that he made her

his best bow; and he flattered the poor cat with so courtly an air that she saw nothing surprising in the love of the lioness.

Meanwhile let us see what became of his rival, the dog.

"Ah, the poor creature!" said Nymphalin; "it is easy to guess that he need not be buried alive to lose all chance of marrying the heiress."

"Wait till the end," answered Fayzenheim.

When the dog found that he was thus entrapped, he gave himself up for lost. In vain he kicked with his hind-legs against the stone,— he only succeeded in bruising his paws; and at length he was forced to lie down, with his tongue out of his mouth, and quite exhausted. "However," said he, after he had taken breath, "it won't do to be starved here, without doing my best to escape; and if I can't get out one way, let me see if there is not a hole at the other end." Thus saying, his courage, which stood him in lieu of cunning, returned, and he proceeded on in the same straightforward way in which he always conducted himself. At first the path was exceedingly narrow, and he hurt his sides very much against the rough stones that projected from the earth; but by degrees the way became broader, and he now went on with considerable ease to himself, till he arrived in a large cavern, where he saw an immense griffin sitting on his tail, and smoking a huge pipe.

The dog was by no means pleased at meeting so suddenly a creature that had only to open his mouth to swallow him up at a morsel; however, he put a bold face on the danger, and walking respectfully up to the griffin, said, "Sir, I should be very much obliged to you if you would inform me the way out of these holes into the upper world."

The griffin took the pipe out of his mouth, and looked at the dog very sternly.

"Ho, wretch!" said he, "how comest thou hither? I suppose thou wantest to steal my treasure; but I know how to treat such vagabonds as you, and I shall certainly eat you up."

"You can do that if you choose," said the dog; "but it would be very unhandsome conduct in an animal so much bigger than myself. For my own part, I never attack any dog that is not of equal size,— I should be ashamed of myself if I did. And as to your treasure, the character I bear for honesty is too well known to merit such a suspicion."

"Upon my word," said the griffin, who could not help smiling for the life of him, "you have a singularly free mode of expressing yourself. And how, I say, came you hither?"

Then the dog, who did not know what a lie was, told the griffin his whole history,— how he had set off to pay his court to the cat, and how Reynard the fox had entrapped him into the hole.

When he had finished, the griffin said to him, "I see, my friend, that you know how to speak the truth; I am in want of just such a servant as you will make me, therefore stay with me and keep watch over my treasure when I sleep."

"Two words to that," said the dog. "You have hurt my feelings very much by suspecting my honesty, and I would much sooner go back into the wood and be avenged on that scoundrel the fox, than serve a master who has so ill an opinion of me. I pray you, therefore, to dismiss me, and to put me in the right way to my cousin the cat."

"I am not a griffin of many words," answered the master of the cavern, "and I give you your choice,— be my servant or be my breakfast; it is just the same to me. I give you time to decide till I have smoked out my pipe."

The poor dog did not take so long to consider. "It is true," thought he, "that it is a great misfortune to live in a cave with a griffin of so unpleasant a countenance; but, probably, if I serve him well and faithfully, he 'll take pity on me some day, and let me go back to earth, and prove to my cousin what a rogue the fox is; and as to the rest, though I would sell my life as dear as I could, it is impossible to fight a griffin with a mouth of so monstrous a size." In short, he decided to stay with the griffin.

"Shake a paw on it," quoth the grim smoker; and the dog shook paws.

"And now," said the griffin, "I will tell you what you are to do. Look here," and moving his tail, he showed the dog a great heap of gold and silver, in a hole in the ground, that he had covered with the folds of his tail; and also, what the dog thought more valuable, a great heap of bones of very tempting appearance. "Now," said the griffin, "during the day I can take very good care of these myself; but at night it is very necessary that I should go to sleep, so when I sleep you must watch over them instead of me."

"Very well," said the dog. "As to the gold and silver, I have no objection; but I would much rather that you would lock up the bones, for I 'm often hungry of a night, and—"

"Hold your tongue," said the griffin.

"But, sir," said the dog, after a short silence, "surely nobody ever comes into so retired a situation! Who are the thieves, if I may make bold to ask?"

"Know," answered the griffin, "that there are a great many serpents in this neighbourhood. They are always trying to steal my treasure; and if they catch me napping, they, not contented with theft, would do their best to sting me to death. So that I am almost worn out for want of sleep."

"Ah," quoth the dog, who was fond of a good night's rest, "I don't envy you your treasure, sir."

At night, the griffin, who had a great deal of penetration, and saw that he might depend on the dog, lay down to sleep in another corner of the cave; and the dog, shaking himself well, so as to be quite awake, took watch over the treasure. His mouth watered exceedingly at the bones, and he could not help smelling them now and then; but he said to himself, "A bargain 's a bargain, and since I have promised to serve the griffin, I must serve him as an honest dog ought to serve."

In the middle of the night he saw a great snake creeping in by the side of the cave; but the dog set up so loud a bark that the griffin awoke, and the snake crept away as fast as he could. Then the griffin was very much pleased, and he gave the dog one of the bones to amuse himself with; and every night the dog watched the treasure, and acquitted himself so well that not a snake, at last, dared to make its appearance,— so the griffin enjoyed an excellent night's rest.

The dog now found himself much more comfortable than he

expected. The griffin regularly gave him one of the bones for supper; and, pleased with his fidelity, made himself as agreeable a master as a griffin could be. Still, however, the dog was secretly very anxious to return to earth; for having nothing to do during the day but to doze on the ground, he dreamed perpetually of his cousin the cat's charms, and, in fancy, he gave the rascal Reynard as hearty a worry as a fox may well have the honour of receiving from a dog's paws. He awoke panting; alas! he could not realize his dreams.

One night, as he was watching as usual over the treasure, he was greatly surprised to see a beautiful little black and white dog enter the cave; and it came fawning to our honest friend, wagging its tail with pleasure.

"Ah, little one," said our dog, whom, to distinguish, I will call the watch-dog, "you had better make the best of your way back again. See, there is a great griffin asleep in the other corner of the cave, and if he wakes, he will either eat you up or make you his servant, as he has made me."

"I know what you would tell me," says the little dog; "and I have come down here to deliver you. The stone is now gone from the mouth of the cave, and you have nothing to do but to go back with me. Come, brother, come."

The dog was very much excited by this address. "Don't ask me, my dear little friend," said he; "you must be aware that I should be too happy to escape out of this cold cave, and roll on the soft turf once more: but if I leave my master, the griffin, those cursed serpents, who are always on the watch, will come in and steal his treasure,— nay, perhaps, sting him to death." Then the little dog came up to the watch-dog, and remonstrated with him greatly, and licked him caressingly on both sides of his face; and, taking him by the ear, endeavoured to draw him from the treasure: but the dog would not stir a step, though his heart sorely pressed him. At length the little dog, finding it all in vain, said, "Well, then, if I must leave, good-by; but I have become so hungry in coming down all this way after you, that I wish you would give me one of those bones; they smell very pleasantly, and one out of so many could never be missed."

"Alas!" said the watch-dog, with tears in his eyes, "how unlucky I am to have eaten up the bone my master gave me, otherwise you should have had it and welcome. But I can't give you one of these, because my master has made me promise to watch over them all, and I have given him my paw on it. I am sure a dog of your respectable appearance will say nothing further on the subject."

Then the little dog answered pettishly, "Pooh, what nonsense you talk! surely a great griffin can't miss a little bone fit for me?" and nestling his nose under the watch-dog, he tried forthwith to bring up one of the bones.

On this the watch-dog grew angry, and, though with much reluctance, he seized the little dog by the nape of the neck and threw him off, but without hurting him. Suddenly the little dog changed into a monstrous serpent, bigger even than the griffin himself, and the watch-dog barked with all his might. The griffin rose in a great hurry, and the serpent sprang upon him ere he was well awake. I wish, dearest Nymphalin, you could have seen the battle between the griffin and the serpent,—how they coiled and twisted, and bit and darted their fiery tongues at each other. At length the serpent got uppermost, and was about to plunge his tongue into that part of the griffin which is unprotected by his scales, when the dog, seizing him by the tail, bit him so sharply that he could not help turning round to kill his new assailant, and the griffin, taking advantage of the opportunity, caught the serpent by the throat with both claws, and fairly strangled him. As soon as the griffin had recovered from the nervousness of the conflict, he heaped all manner of caresses on the dog for saving his life. The dog told him the whole story, and the griffin then explained that the dead snake was the king of the serpents, who had the power to change himself into any shape he pleased. "If he had tempted you," said he, "to leave the treasure but for one moment, or to have given him any part of it, ay, but a single bone, he would have crushed you in an instant, and stung me to death ere I could have waked; but none, no, not the most venomous thing in creation, has power to hurt the honest!"

"That has always been my belief," answered the dog; "and now, sir, you had better go to sleep again and leave the rest to me."

"Nay," answered the griffin, "I have no longer need of a servant; for now that the king of the serpents is dead, the rest will never molest me. It was only to satisfy his avarice that his subjects dared to brave the den of the griffin."

Upon hearing this the dog was exceedingly delighted; and raising himself on his hind paws, he begged the griffin most movingly to let him return to earth, to visit his mistress the cat, and worry his rival the fox.

"You do not serve an ungrateful master," answered the griffin. "You shall return, and I will teach you all the craft of our race, which is much craftier than the race of that pettifogger the fox, so that you may be able to cope with your rival."

"Ah, excuse me," said the dog, hastily, "I am equally obliged to you; but I fancy honesty is a match for cunning any day, and I think myself a great deal safer in being a dog of honour than if I knew all the tricks in the world."

"Well," said the griffin, a little piqued at the dog's bluntness, "do as you please; I wish you all possible success."

Then the griffin opened a secret door in the side of the cabin, and the dog saw a broad path that led at once into the wood. He thanked the griffin with all his heart, and ran wagging his tail into the open moonlight. "Ah, ah, master fox," said he, "there's no trap for an honest dog that has not two doors to it, cunning as you think yourself."

With that he curled his tail gallantly over his left leg, and set off on a long trot to the cat's house. When he was within sight of it, he stopped to refresh himself by a pool of water, and who should be there but our friend the magpie.

"And what do *you* want, friend?" said she, rather disdainfully, for the dog looked somewhat out of case after his journey.

"I am going to see my cousin the cat," answered he.

"*Your* cousin! marry come up," said the magpie; "don't you know she is going to be married to Reynard the fox?

This is not a time for her to receive the visits of a brute like you."

These words put the dog in such a passion that he very nearly bit the magpie for her uncivil mode of communicating such bad news. However, he curbed his temper, and, without answering her, went at once to the cat's residence.

The cat was sitting at the window, and no sooner did the dog see her than he fairly lost his heart; never had he seen so charming a cat before. He advanced, wagging his tail, and with his most insinuating air, when the cat, getting up, clapped the window in his face, and lo! Reynard the fox appeared in her stead.

"Come out, thou rascal!" said the dog, showing his teeth; "come out, I challenge thee to single combat; I have not forgiven thy malice, and thou seest that I am no longer shut up in the cave, and unable to punish thee for thy wickedness."

"Go home, silly one!" answered the fox, sneering; "thou hast no business here, and as for fighting thee — bah!" Then the fox left the window and disappeared. But the dog, thoroughly enraged, scratched lustily at the door, and made such a noise, that presently the cat herself came to the window.

"How now!" said she, angrily; "what means all this rudeness? Who are you, and what do you want at my house?"

"Oh, my dear cousin," said the dog, "do not speak so severely. Know that I have come here on purpose to pay you a visit; and, whatever you do, let me beseech you not to listen to that villain Reynard, — you have no conception what a rogue he is!"

"What!" said the cat, blushing; "do you dare to abuse your betters in this fashion? I see you have a design on me. Go, this instant, or — "

"Enough, madam," said the dog, proudly; "you need not speak twice to me, — farewell."

And he turned away very slowly, and went under a tree, where he took up his lodgings for the night. But the next morning there was an amazing commotion in the neighbourhood; a stranger, of a very different style of travelling from that of the dog, had arrived at the dead of the night, and fixed his abode in a large cavern hollowed out of a steep rock. The noise he had made in flying through the air was so great that it had awakened every bird and beast in the parish; and Reynard, whose bad conscience never suffered him to sleep very soundly, putting his head out of the window, perceived, to his great alarm, that the stranger was nothing less than a monstrous griffin.

Now the griffins are the richest beasts in the world; and that's the reason they keep so close under ground. Whenever it does happen that they pay a visit above, it is not a thing to be easily forgotten.

The magpie was all agitation. What could the griffin possibly want there? She resolved to take a peep at the cavern, and accordingly she hopped timorously up the rock, and pretended to be picking up sticks for her nest.

"Holla, ma'am!" cried a very rough voice, and she saw the griffin putting his head out of the cavern. "Holla! you are the very lady I want to see; you know all the people about here, eh?"

"All the best company, your lordship, I certainly do," answered the magpie, dropping a courtesy.

Upon this the griffin walked out; and smoking his pipe leisurely in the open air, in order to set the pie at her ease, continued,—

"Are there any respectable beasts of good families settled in this neighbourhood?"

"Oh, most elegant society, I assure your lordship," cried the pie. "I have lived here myself these ten years, and the great heiress, the cat yonder, attracts a vast number of strangers."

"Humph! heiress, indeed! much *you* know about heiresses!" said the griffin. "There is only one heiress in the world, and that's my daughter."

"Bless me! has your lordship a family? I beg you a thousand pardons; but I only saw your lordship's own equipage last night, and did not know you brought any one with you."

"My daughter went first, and was safely lodged before I arrived. She did not disturb you, I dare say, as I did; for she sails along like a swan: but I have got the gout in my left claw, and that's the reason I puff and groan so in taking a journey."

"Shall I drop in upon Miss Griffin, and see how she is after her journey?" said the pie, advancing.

"I thank you, no. I don't intend her to be seen while I stay here,—it unsettles her; and I'm afraid of the young beasts running away with her if they once heard how handsome she was: she's the living picture of me, but she's monstrous giddy! Not that I should care much if she did go off with a beast of degree, were I not obliged to pay her portion, which is prodigious; and I don't like parting with money, ma'am, when I've once got it. Ho, ho, ho!"

"You are too witty, my lord. But if you refused your consent?" said the pie, anxious to know the whole family history of so grand a seigneur.

"I should have to pay the dowry all the same. It was left her by her uncle the dragon. But don't let this go any further."

"Your lordship may depend on my secrecy. I wish your lordship a very good morning."

Away flew the pie, and she did not stop till she got to the cat's house. The cat and the fox were at breakfast, and the fox had his paw on his heart. "Beautiful scene!" cried the pie; the cat coloured, and bade the pie take a seat.

Then off went the pie's tongue, glib, glib, glib, chatter, chatter, chatter. She related to them the whole story of the griffin and his daughter, and a great deal more besides, that the griffin had never told her.

The cat listened attentively. Another young heiress in the neighbourhood might be a formidable rival. "But is this griffiness handsome?" said she.

"Handsome!" cried the pie; "oh, if you could have seen the father!—such a mouth, such eyes, such a complexion; and he declares she's the living picture of himself! But what do you say, Mr. Reynard,—you, who have been so much in the world, have, perhaps, seen the young lady?"

"Why, I can't say I have," answered the fox, waking from

a revery; "but she must be wonderfully rich. I dare say that fool the dog will be making up to her."

"Ah, by the way," said the pie, "what a fuss he made at your door yesterday; why would you not admit him, my dear?"

"Oh," said the cat, demurely, "Mr. Reynard says that he is a dog of very bad character, quite a fortune-hunter; and hiding the most dangerous disposition to bite under an appearance of good nature. I hope he won't be quarrelsome with you, dear Reynard!"

"With me? Oh, the poor wretch, no! — he might bluster a little; but he knows that if I 'm once angry I 'm a devil at biting; — one should not boast of oneself."

In the evening Reynard felt a strange desire to go and see the griffin smoking his pipe; but what could he do? There was the dog under the opposite tree evidently watching for him, and Reynard had no wish to prove himself that devil at biting which he declared he was. At last he resolved to have recourse to stratagem to get rid of the dog.

A young buck of a rabbit, a sort of provincial fop, had looked in upon his cousin the cat, to pay her his respects, and Reynard, taking him aside, said, "You see that shabby-looking dog under the tree? He has behaved very ill to your cousin the cat, and you certainly ought to challenge him. Forgive my boldness, nothing but respect for your character induces me to take so great a liberty; you know I would chastise the rascal myself, but what a scandal it would make! If I were already married to your cousin, it would be a different thing. But you know what a story that cursed magpie would hatch out of it!"

The rabbit looked very foolish; he assured the fox he was no match for the dog; that he was very fond of his cousin, to be sure! but he saw no necessity to interfere with her domestic affairs; and, in short, he tried all he possibly could to get out of the scrape; but the fox so artfully played on his vanity, so earnestly assured him that the dog was the biggest coward in the world and would make a humble apology, and so eloquently represented to him the glory he would obtain for manifesting so much spirit, that at length the rabbit was persuaded to go out and deliver the challenge.

"I'll be your second," said the fox; "and the great field on the other side the wood, two miles hence, shall be the place of battle: there we shall be out of observation. You go first, I'll follow in half an hour; and I say, hark! — in case he does accept the challenge, and you feel the least afraid, I'll be in the field, and take it off your paws with the utmost pleasure; rely on *me*, my dear sir!"

Away went the rabbit. The dog was a little astonished at the temerity of the poor creature; but on hearing that the fox was to be present, willingly consented to repair to the place of conflict. This readiness the rabbit did not at all relish; he went very slowly to the field, and seeing no fox there, his heart misgave him; and while the dog was putting his nose to the ground to try if he could track the coming of the fox, the rabbit slipped into a burrow, and left the dog to walk back again.

Meanwhile the fox was already at the rock; he walked very soft-footedly, and looked about with extreme caution, for he had a vague notion that a griffin-papa would not be very civil to foxes.

Now there were two holes in the rock, — one below, one above, an upper story and an under; and while the fox was peering about, he saw a great claw from the upper rock beckoning to him.

"Ah, ah!" said the fox, "that's the wanton young griffiness, I'll swear."

He approached, and a voice said, —

"Charming Mr. Reynard, do you not think you could deliver an unfortunate griffiness from a barbarous confinement in this rock?"

"Oh, heavens!" cried the fox, tenderly, "what a beautiful voice! and, ah, my poor heart, what a lovely claw! Is it possible that I hear the daughter of my lord, the great griffin?"

"Hush, flatterer! not so loud, if you please. My father is taking an evening stroll, and is very quick of hearing. He has tied me up by my poor wings in the cavern, for he is mightily afraid of some beast running away with me. You know I have all my fortune settled on myself."

"Talk not of fortune," said the fox; "but how can I deliver you? Shall I enter and gnaw the cord?"

"Alas!" answered the griffiness, "it is an immense chain I am bound with. However, you may come in and talk more at your ease."

The fox peeped cautiously all round, and seeing no sign of the griffin, he entered the lower cave and stole upstairs to the upper story; but as he went on, he saw immense piles of jewels and gold, and all sorts of treasure, so that the old griffin might well have laughed at the poor cat being called an heiress. The fox was greatly pleased at such indisputable signs of wealth, and he entered the upper cave, resolved to be transported with the charms of the griffiness.

There was, however, a great chasm between the landing-place and the spot where the young lady was chained, and he found it impossible to pass; the cavern was very dark, but he saw enough of the figure of the griffiness to perceive, in spite of her petticoat, that she was the image of her father, and the most hideous heiress that the earth ever saw!

However, he swallowed his disgust, and poured forth such a heap of compliments that the griffiness appeared entirely won.

He implored her to fly with him the first moment she was unchained.

"That is impossible," said she; "for my father never un-chains me except in his presence, and then I cannot stir out of his sight."

"The wretch!" cried Reynard, "what is to be done?"

"Why, there is only one thing I know of," answered the griffiness, "which is this: I always make his soup for him. and if I could mix something in it that would put him fast to sleep before he had time to chain me up again I might slip down and carry off all the treasure below on my back."

"Charming!" exclaimed Reynard; "what invention! what wit! I will go and get some poppies directly."

"Alas!" said the griffiness, "poppies have no effect upon

griffins. The only thing that can ever put my father fast to sleep is a nice young cat boiled up in his soup; it is astonishing what a charm that has upon him! But where to get a cat? — it must be a maiden cat too!"

Reynard was a little startled at so singular an opiate. "But," thought he, "griffins are not like the rest of the world, and so rich an heiress is not to be won by ordinary means."

"I do know a cat, — a maiden cat," said he, after a short pause; "but I feel a little repugnance at the thought of having her boiled in the griffin's soup. Would not a dog do as well?"

"Ah, base thing!" said the griffiness, appearing to weep; "you are in love with the cat, I see it; go and marry her, poor dwarf that she is, and leave me to die of grief."

In vain the fox protested that he did not care a straw for the cat; nothing could now appease the griffiness but his positive assurance that come what would poor puss should be brought to the cave and boiled for the griffin's soup.

"But how will you get her here?" said the griffiness.

"Ah, leave that to me," said Reynard. "Only put a basket out of the window and draw it up by a cord; the moment it arrives at the window, be sure to clap your claw on the cat at once, for she is terribly active."

"Tush!" answered the heiress; "a pretty griffiness I should be if I did not know how to catch a cat!"

"But this must be when your father is out?" said Reynard.

"Certainly; he takes a stroll every evening at sunset."

"Let it be to-morrow, then," said Reynard, impatient for the treasure.

This being arranged, Reynard thought it time to decamp. He stole down the stairs again, and tried to filch some of the treasure by the way; but it was too heavy for him to carry, and he was forced to acknowledge to himself that it was impossible to get the treasure without taking the griffiness (whose back seemed prodigiously strong) into the bargain.

He returned home to the cat, and when he entered her house, and saw how ordinary everything looked after the jewels in the griffin's cave, he quite wondered how he had ever thought the cat had the least pretensions to good looks. However, he concealed his wicked design, and his mistress thought he had never appeared so amiable.

"Only guess," said he, "where I have been! — to our new neighbour the griffin; a most charming person, thoroughly affable, and quite the air of the court. As for that silly magpie, the griffin saw her character at once; and it was all a hoax about his daughter, — he has no daughter at all. You know, my dear, hoaxing is a fashionable amusement among the great. He says he has heard of nothing but your beauty, and on my telling him we were going to be married, he has insisted upon giving a great ball and supper in honour of the event. In fact, he is a gallant old fellow, and dying to see you. Of course, I was obliged to accept the invitation."

"You could not do otherwise," said the unsuspecting young creature, who, as I before said, was very susceptible to flattery.

"And only think how delicate his attentions are," said the fox. "As he is very badly lodged for a beast of his rank, and his treasure takes up the whole of the ground floor, he is forced to give the *fête* in the upper story, so he hangs out a basket for his guests, and draws them up with his own claw. How condescending! But the great *are* so amiable!"

The cat, brought up in seclusion, was all delight at the idea of seeing such high life, and the lovers talked of nothing else all the next day, — when Reynard, towards evening, putting his head out of the window, saw his old friend the dog lying as usual and watching him very grimly. "Ah, that cursed creature! I had quite forgotten him; what is to be done now? He would make no bones of me if he once saw me set foot out of doors."

With that, the fox began to cast in his head how he should get rid of his rival, and at length he resolved on a very notable project; he desired the cat to set out first, and wait for him at a turn in the road a little way off. "For," said he, "if we go together we shall certainly be insulted by the dog; and he will know that in the presence of a lady, the custom of a beast of my fashion will not suffer me to avenge the affront. But when I am alone, the creature is such a coward that he will not dare say his soul's his own; leave the door open and I'll follow immediately."

The cat's mind was so completely poisoned against her cousin that she implicitly believed this account of his character; and accordingly, with many recommendations to her lover not to sully his dignity by getting into any sort of quarrel with the dog, she set off first.

The dog went up to her very humbly, and begged her to allow him to say a few words to her; but she received him so haughtily, that his spirit was up; and he walked back to the tree more than ever enraged against his rival. But what was his joy when he saw that the cat had left the door open! "Now, wretch," thought he, "you cannot escape me!" So he walked briskly in at the back door. He was greatly surprised to find Reynard lying down in the straw, panting as if his heart would break, and rolling his eyes in the pangs of death.

"Ah, friend," said the fox, with a faltering voice, "you are avenged, my hour is come; I am just going to give up the ghost: put your paw upon mine, and say you forgive me."

Despite his anger, the generous dog could not set tooth on a dying foe.

"You have served me a shabby trick," said he; "you have left me to starve in a hole, and you have evidently maligned me with my cousin: certainly I meant to be avenged on you; but if you are really dying, that alters the affair."

"Oh, oh!" groaned the fox, very bitterly; "I am past help; the poor cat is gone for Doctor Ape, but he'll never come in time. What a thing it is to have a bad conscience on one's death-bed! But wait till the cat returns, and I'll do you full justice with her before I die."

The good-natured dog was much moved at seeing his mortal enemy in such a state, and endeavoured as well as he could to console him.

"Oh, oh!" said the fox; "I am so parched in the throat, I am burning;" and he hung his tongue out of his mouth, and rolled his eyes more fearfully than ever.

"Is there no water here?" said the dog, looking round.

"Alas, no! — yet stay! yes, now I think of it, there is some in that little hole in the wall; but how to get at it! It is so high that I can't, in my poor weak state, climb up to it; and I dare not ask such a favour of one I have injured so much."

"Don't talk of it," said the dog: "but the hole's very small, I could not put my nose through it."

"No; but if you just climb up on that stone, and thrust your paw into the hole, you can dip it into the water, and so cool my poor parched mouth. Oh, what a thing it is to have a bad conscience!"

The dog sprang upon the stone, and, getting on his hind legs, thrust his front paw into the hole; when suddenly Reynard pulled a string that he had concealed under the straw, and the dog found his paw caught tight to the wall in a running noose.

"Ah, rascal!" said he, turning round; but the fox leaped up gayly from the straw, and fastening the string with his teeth to a nail in the other end of the wall, walked out, crying, "Good-by, my dear friend; have a care how you believe hereafter in sudden conversions!" So he left the dog on his hind legs to take care of the house.

Reynard found the cat waiting for him where he had appointed, and they walked lovingly together till they came to the cave. It was now dark, and they saw the basket waiting below; the fox assisted the poor cat into it. "There is only room for one," said he, "you must go first!" Up rose the basket; the fox heard a piteous mew, and no more.

"So much for the griffin's soup!" thought he.

He waited patiently for some time, when the griffiness, waving her claw from the window, said cheerfully, "All's right, my dear Reynard; my papa has finished his soup, and sleeps as sound as a rock! All the noise in the world would not wake him now, till he has slept off the boiled cat, which won't be these twelve hours. Come and assist me in packing up the treasure; I should be sorry to leave a single diamond behind."

"So should I," quoth the fox. "Stay, I'll come round by

the lower hole: why, the door 's shut! pray, beautiful griffiness, open it to thy impatient adorer."

"Alas, my father has hid the key! I never know where he places it. You must come up by the basket; see, I will lower it for you."

The fox was a little loth to trust himself in the same conveyance that had taken his mistress to be boiled; but the most cautious grow rash when money 's to be gained, and avarice can trap even a fox. So he put himself as comfortably as he could into the basket, and up he went in an instant. It rested, however, just before it reached the window, and the fox felt, with a slight shudder, the claw of the griffiness stroking his back.

"Oh, what a beautiful coat!" quoth she, caressingly.

"You are too kind," said the fox; "but you can feel it more at your leisure when I am once up. Make haste, I beseech you."

"Oh, what a beautiful bushy tail! Never did I feel such a tail."

"It is entirely at your service, sweet griffiness," said the fox; "but pray let me in. Why lose an instant?"

"No, never did I feel such a tail! No wonder you are so successful with the ladies."

"Ah, beloved griffiness, my tail is yours to eternity, but you pinch it a little too hard."

Scarcely had he said this, when down dropped the basket, but not with the fox in it; he found himself caught by the tail, and dangling half way down the rock, by the help of the very same sort of pulley wherewith he had snared the dog. I leave you to guess his consternation; he yelped out as loud as he could,—for it hurts a fox exceedingly to be hanged by his tail with his head downwards,—when the door of the rock opened, and out stalked the griffin himself, smoking his pipe, with a vast crowd of all the fashionable beasts in the neighbourhood.

"Oho, brother," said the bear, laughing fit to kill himself; "who ever saw a fox hanged by the tail before?"

"You 'll have need of a physician," quoth Doctor Ape.

"A pretty match, indeed; a griffiness for such a creature as you!" said the goat, strutting by him.

The fox grinned with pain, and said nothing. But that which hurt him most was the compassion of a dull fool of a donkey, who assured him with great gravity that he saw nothing at all to laugh at in his situation!

"At all events," said the fox, at last, "cheated, gulled, betrayed as I am, I have played the same trick to the dog. Go and laugh at him, gentlemen; he deserves it as much as I can, I assure you."

"Pardon me," said the griffin, taking the pipe out of his mouth; "one never laughs at the honest."

"And see," said the bear, "here he is."

And indeed the dog had, after much effort, gnawed the string in two, and extricated his paw; the scent of the fox had enabled him to track his footsteps, and here he arrived, burning for vengeance and finding himself already avenged.

But his first thought was for his dear cousin. "Ah, where is she?" he cried movingly; "without doubt that villain Reynard has served her some scurvy trick."

"I fear so indeed, my old friend," answered the griffin; "but don't grieve,—after all, she was nothing particular. You shall marry my daughter the griffiness, and succeed to all the treasure; ay, and all the bones that you once guarded so faithfully."

"Talk not to me," said the faithful dog. "I want none of your treasure; and, though I don't mean to be rude, your griffiness may go to the devil. I will run over the world, but I will find my dear cousin."

"See her then," said the griffin; and the beautiful cat, more beautiful than ever, rushed out of the cavern, and threw herself into the dog's paws.

A pleasant scene this for the fox! He had skill enough in the female heart to know that it may excuse many little infidelities, but to be boiled alive for a griffin's soup — no, the offence was inexpiable.

"You understand me, Mr. Reynard," said the griffin, "I have no daughter, and it was me you made love to. Knowing what sort of a creature a magpie is, I amused myself with hoaxing her,—the fashionable amusement at court, you know."

The fox made a mighty struggle, and leaped on the ground, leaving his tail behind him. It did not grow again in a hurry.

"See," said the griffin, as the beasts all laughed at the figure Reynard made running into the wood, "the dog beats the fox with the ladies, after all; and cunning as he is in everything else, the fox is the last creature that should ever think of making love!"

"Charming!" cried Nymphalin, clasping her hands; "it is just the sort of story I like."

"And I suppose, sir," said Nip, pertly, "that the dog and the cat lived very happily ever afterwards? Indeed the nuptial felicity of a dog and cat is proverbial!"

"I dare say they lived much the same as any other married couple," answered the prince.

———•———

CHAPTER XIII.

THE TOMB OF A FATHER OF MANY CHILDREN.

THE feast being now ended, as well as the story, the fairies wound their way homeward by a different path, till at length a red steady light glowed through the long basaltic arches upon them, like the Demon Hunters' fires in the Forest of Pines.

The prince sobered in his pace. "You approach," said he, in a grave tone, "the greatest of our temples; you will witness the tomb of a mighty founder of our race!" An awe crept over the queen, in spite of herself. Tracking the fires in silence, they came to a vast space, in the midst of which was a long gray block of stone, such as the traveller finds amidst the dread silence of Egyptian Thebes.

And on this stone lay the gigantic figure of a man,— dead, but not death-like, for invisible spells had preserved the flesh and the long hair for untold ages; and beside him lay a rude instrument of music, and at his feet was a sword and a hunter's spear; and above, the rock wound, hollowed and roofless, to the upper air, and daylight came through, sickened and pale, beneath red fires that burned everlastingly around him, on such simple altars as belong to a savage race. But the place was not solitary, for many motionless but not lifeless shapes sat on large blocks of stone beside the tomb. There was the wizard, wrapped in his long black mantle, and his face covered with his hands; there was the uncouth and de-formed dwarf, gibbering to himself; there sat the household elf; there glowered from a gloomy rent in the wall, with glit-tering eyes and shining scale, the enormous dragon of the North. An aged crone in rags, leaning on a staff, and gazing malignantly on the visitors, with bleared but fiery eyes, stood opposite the tomb of the gigantic dead. And now the fairies themselves completed the group! But all was dumb and un-utterably silent,— the silence that floats over some antique city of the desert, when, for the first time for a hundred cen-turies, a living foot enters its desolate remains; the silence that belongs to the dust of eld,— deep, solemn, palpable, and sinking into the heart with a leaden and death-like weight. Even the English fairy spoke not; she held her breath, and gazing on the tomb, she saw, in rude vast characters,—

THE TEUTON.

"*We* are all that remain of his religion!" said the prince, as they turned from the dread temple.

CHAPTER XIV.

THE FAIRY'S CAVE, AND THE FAIRY'S WISH.

It was evening; and the fairies were dancing beneath the twilight star.

"And why art thou sad, my violet?" said the prince; "for thine eyes seek the ground!"

"Now that I have found thee," answered the queen, "and now that I feel what happy love is to a fairy, I sigh over that love which I have lately witnessed among mortals, but the bud of whose happiness already conceals the worm. For well didst thou say, my prince, that we are linked with a mysterious affinity to mankind, and whatever is pure and gentle amongst them speaks at once to our sympathy, and commands our vigils."

"And most of all," said the German fairy, "are they who love under our watch; for love is the golden chain that binds all in the universe: love lights up alike the star and the glow-worm; and wherever there is love in men's lot, lies the secret affinity with men, and with things divine."

"But with the human race," said Nymphalin, "there is no love that outlasts the hour, for either death ends, or custom alters. When the blossom comes to fruit, it is plucked and seen no more; and therefore, when I behold true love sentenced to an early grave, I comfort myself that I shall not at least behold the beauty dimmed, and the softness of the heart hardened into stone. Yet, my prince, while still the pulse can beat, and the warm blood flow, in that beautiful form which I have watched over of late, let me not desert her; still let my influence keep the sky fair, and the breezes pure; still let me drive the vapour from the moon, and the clouds from the faces of the stars; still let me fill her dreams with tender and brilliant images, and glass in the mirror of sleep the

happiest visions of fairy-land; still let me pour over her eyes
that magic, which suffers them to see no fault in one in whom
she has garnered up her soul! And as death comes slowly on,
still let me rob the spectre of its terror, and the grave of its
sting; so that, all gently and unconscious to herself, life may
glide into the Great Ocean where the shadows lie, and the
spirit without guile may be severed from its mansion without
pain! "

The wish of the fairy was fulfilled.

CHAPTER XV.

THE BANKS OF THE RHINE. — FROM THE DRACHENFELS TO
BROHL. — AN INCIDENT THAT SUFFICES IN THIS TALE FOR
AN EPOCH.

FROM the Drachenfels commences the true glory of the
Rhine; and once more Gertrude's eyes conquered the languor
that crept gradually over them as she gazed on the banks
around.

Fair blew the breeze, and freshly curled the waters; and
Gertrude did not feel the vulture that had fixed its talons
within her breast. The Rhine widens, like a broad lake, between the Drachenfels and Unkel; villages are scattered over
the extended plain on the left; on the right is the Isle of
Werth and the houses of Oberwinter; the hills are covered
with vines; and still Gertrude turned back with a lingering
gaze to the lofty crest of the Seven Hills.

On, on — and the spires of Unkel rose above a curve in the
banks, and on the opposite shore stretched those wondrous
basaltic columns which extend to the middle of the river, and
when the Rhine runs low, you may see them like an engulfed
city beneath the waves. You then view the ruins of Okken-
fels, and hear the voice of the pastoral Gasbach pouring its
waters into the Rhine. From amidst the clefts of the rocks

the vine peeps luxuriantly forth, and gives a richness and colouring to what Nature, left to herself, intended for the stern.

"But turn your eye backward to the right," said Trevylyan; "those banks were formerly the special haunt of the bold robbers of the Rhine, and from amidst the entangled brakes that then covered the ragged cliffs they rushed upon their prey. In the gloomy canvas of those feudal days what vigorous and mighty images were crowded! A robber's life amidst these mountains, and beside this mountain stream, must have been the very poetry of the spot carried into action."

They rested at Brohl, a small town between two mountains. On the summit of one you see the gray remains of Rheinech. There is something weird and preternatural about the aspect of this place; its soil betrays signs that in the former ages (from which even tradition is fast fading away) some volcano here exhausted its fires. The stratum of the earth is black and pitchy, and the springs beneath it are of a dark and graveolent water. Here the stream of the Brohlbach falls into the Rhine, and in a valley rich with oak and pine, and full of caverns, which are not without their traditionary inmates, stands the castle of Schweppenbourg, which our party failed not to visit.

Gertrude felt fatigued on their return, and Trevylyan sat by her in the little inn, while Vane went forth, with the curiosity of science, to examine the strata of the soil.

They conversed in the frankness of their plighted troth upon those topics which are only for lovers: upon the bright chapter in the history of their love; their first meeting; their first impressions; the little incidents in their present journey,— incidents noticed by themselves alone; that life *within* life which two persons know together,— which one knows not without the other, which ceases to both the instant they are divided.

"I know not what the love of others may be," said Gertrude, "but ours seems different from all of which I have read. Books tell us of jealousies and misconstructions, and the necessity of an absence, the sweetness of a quarrel; but *we*, dearest Albert, have had no experience of these passages in love. *We* have never misunderstood each other; *we* have no reconciliation to look back to. When was there ever occasion for me to ask forgiveness from you? Our love is made up only of one memory,— unceasing kindness! A harsh word, a wronging thought, never broke in upon the happiness we have felt and feel."

"Dearest Gertrude," said Trevylyan, "that character of our love is caught from you; you, the soft, the gentle, have been its pervading genius; and the well has been smooth and pure, for you were the spirit that lived within its depths."

And to such talk succeeded silence still more sweet,— the silence of the hushed and overflowing heart. The last voices of the birds, the sun slowly sinking in the west, the fragrance of descending dews, filled them with that deep and mysterious sympathy which exists between Love and Nature.

It was after such a silence — a long silence, that seemed but as a moment — that Trevylyan spoke, but Gertrude answered not; and, yearning once more for her sweet voice, he turned and saw that she had fainted away.

This was the first indication of the point to which her increasing debility had arrived. Trevylyan's heart stood still, and then beat violently; a thousand fears crept over him; he clasped her in his arms, and bore her to the open window. The setting sun fell upon her countenance, from which the play of the young heart and warm fancy had fled, and in its deep and still repose the ravages of disease were darkly visible. What were then his emotions! His heart was like stone; but he felt a rush as of a torrent to his temples: his eyes grew dizzy,— he was stunned by the greatness of his despair. For the last week he had taken hope for his companion; Gertrude had seemed so much stronger, for her happiness had given her a false support. And though there had been moments when, watching the bright hectic come and go, and her step linger, and the breath heave short, he had felt the hope suddenly cease, yet never had he known till now that fulness of anguish, that dread certainty of the worst, which the calm, fair face before him struck into his soul; and mixed with this agony as he gazed was all the passion of the most ardent love. For there she lay in his arms, the gentle breath rising from lips where the rose yet lingered, and the long, rich hair, soft and silken as an infant's, stealing from its confinement: everything that belonged to Gertrude's beauty was so inexpressibly soft and pure and youthful! Scarcely seventeen, she seemed much younger than she was; her figure had sunken from its roundness, but still how light, how lovely were its wrecks! the neck whiter than snow, the fair small hand! Her weight was scarcely felt in the arms of her lover; and he — what a contrast! — was in all the pride and flower of glorious manhood! His was the lofty brow, the wreathing hair, the haughty eye, the elastic form; and upon this frail, perishable thing had he fixed all his heart, all the hopes of his youth, the pride of his manhood, his schemes, his energies, his ambition!

"Oh, Gertrude!" cried he, "is it — is it thus — is there indeed no hope?"

And Gertrude now slowly recovering, and opening her eyes upon Trevylyan's face, the revulsion was so great, his emotions so overpowering, that, clasping her to his bosom, as if even death should not tear her away from him, he wept over her in an agony of tears; not those tears that relieve the heart, but the fiery rain of the internal storm, a sign of the fierce tumult that shook the very core of his existence, not a relief.

Awakened to herself, Gertrude, in amazement and alarm, threw her arms around his neck, and, looking wistfully into his face, implored him to speak to her.

"Was it my illness, love?" said she; and the music of her voice only conveyed to him the thought of how soon it would be dumb to him forever. "Nay," she continued winningly, "it was but the heat of the day; I am better now, — I am well; there is no cause to be alarmed for me:" and with all the innocent fondness of extreme youth, she kissed the burning tears from his eyes.

There was a playfulness, an innocence in this poor girl, so unconscious as yet of her destiny, which rendered her fate

doubly touching, and which to the stern Trevylyan, hackneyed by the world, made her irresistible charm; and now as
she put aside her hair, and looked up gratefully, yet pleadingly, into his face, he could scarce refrain from pouring out
to her the confession of his anguish and despair. But the
necessity of self-control, the necessity of concealing from *her*
a knowledge which might only, by impressing her imagination, expedite her doom, while it would embitter to her mind
the unconscious enjoyment of the hour, nerved and manned
him. He checked by those violent efforts which only men
can make, the evidence of his emotions; and endeavoured, by
a rapid torrent of words, to divert her attention from a weakness, the causes of which he could not explain. Fortunately
Vane soon returned, and Trevylyan, consigning Gertrude to
his care, hastily left the room.

Gertrude sank into a revery.

"Ah, dear father!" said she, suddenly, and after a pause,
"if I indeed were worse than I have thought myself of late,
if I were to die now, what would Trevylyan feel? Pray God
I may live for his sake!"

"My child, do not talk thus; you are better, much better
than you were. Ere the autumn ends, Trevylyan's happiness
will be your lawful care. Do not think so despondently of
yourself."

"I thought not of myself," sighed Gertrude, "but of
him!"

———•———

CHAPTER XVI.

GERTRUDE. — THE EXCURSION TO HAMMERSTEIN. — THOUGHTS.

THE next day they visited the environs of Brohl. Gertrude was unusually silent; for her temper, naturally sunny
and enthusiastic, was accustomed to light up everything she
saw. Ah, once how bounding was that step! how undulating

the young graces of that form! how playfully once danced the ringlets on that laughing cheek! But she clung to Trevylyan's proud form with a yet more endearing tenderness than was her wont, and hung yet more eagerly on his words; her hand sought his, and she often pressed it to her lips, and sighed as she did so. Something that she would not tell seemed passing within her, and sobered her playful mood. But there was this noticeable in Gertrude: whatever took away from her gayety increased her tenderness. The infirmities of her frame never touched her temper. She was kind, gentle, loving to the last.

They had crossed to the opposite banks, to visit the Castle of Hammerstein. The evening was transparently serene and clear; and the warmth of the sun yet lingered upon the air, even though the twilight had passed and the moon risen, as their boat returned by a lengthened passage to the village. Broad and straight flows the Rhine in this part of its career. On one side lay the wooded village of Namedy, the hamlet of Fornech, backed by the blue rock of Kruezborner Ley, the mountains that shield the mysterious Brohl; and on the opposite shore they saw the mighty rock of Hammerstein, with the green and livid ruins sleeping in the melancholy moonlight. Two towers rose haughtily above the more dismantled wrecks. How changed since the alternate banners of the Spaniard and the Swede waved from their ramparts, in that great war in which the gorgeous Wallenstein won his laurels! And in its mighty calm flowed on the ancestral Rhine, the vessel reflected on its smooth expanse; and above, girded by thin and shadowy clouds, the moon cast her shadows upon rocks covered with verdure, and brought into a dim light the twin spires of Andernach, tranquil in the distance.

"How beautiful is this hour!" said Gertrude, with a low voice, "surely we do not live enough in the night; one half the beauty of the world is slept away. What in the day can equal the holy calm, the loveliness, and the stillness which the moon now casts over the earth? These," she continued, pressing Trevylyan's hand, "are hours to remember; and *you* — will you ever forget them?"

Something there is in recollections of such times and scenes that seem not to belong to real life, but are rather an episode in its history; they are like some wandering into a more ideal world; they refuse to blend with our ruder associations; they live in us, apart and alone, to be treasured ever, but not lightly to be recalled. There are none living to whom we can confide them,— who can sympathize with what then we felt? It is this that makes poetry, and that page which we create as a confidant to ourselves, necessary to the thoughts that weigh upon the breast. We write, for our writing is our friend, the inanimate paper is our confessional; we pour forth on it the thoughts that we could tell to no private ear, and are relieved, are consoled. And if genius has one prerogative dearer than the rest, it is that which enables it to do honour to the dead,— to revive the beauty, the virtue that are no more; to wreathe chaplets that outlive the day around the urn which were else forgotten by the world!

When the poet mourns, in his immortal verse, for the dead, tell me not that fame is in his mind! It is filled by thoughts, by emotions that shut out the living. He is breathing to his genius — to that sole and constant friend which has grown up with him from his cradle — the sorrows too delicate for human sympathy! and when afterwards he consigns the confession to the crowd, it is indeed from the hope of honour,— honour not for himself, but for the being that is no more.

----♦----

CHAPTER XVII.

LETTER FROM TREVYLYAN TO ——.

COBLENTZ.

I am obliged to you, my dear friend, for your letter; which, indeed, I have not, in the course of our rapid journey, had the leisure, perhaps the heart, to answer before. But we are staying in this town for some days, and I write now in the early morning, ere any one else in our hotel is awake. Do not tell me of adventure, of politics, of intrigues; my nature is altered. I threw down your letter, animated and brilliant as it was, with a sick and revolted heart. But I am now in somewhat less dejected spirits. Gertrude is better,—yes, really better; there is a physician here who gives me hope; my care is perpetually to amuse, and never to fatigue her,— never to permit her thoughts to rest upon herself. For I have imagined that illness cannot, at least in the unexhausted vigour of our years, fasten upon us irremediably unless we feed it with our own belief in its existence. You see men of the most delicate frames engaged in active and professional pursuits, who literally have no time for illness. Let them become idle, let them take care of themselves, let them think of their health — and they die! The rust rots the steel which use preserves; and, thank Heaven, although Gertrude, once during our voyage, seemed roused, by an inexcusable imprudence of emotion on my part, into some suspicion of her state, yet it passed away; for she thinks rarely of herself,— I am ever in her thoughts and seldom from her side, and you know, too, the sanguine and credulous nature of her disease. But, indeed, I now hope more than I have done since I knew her.

When, after an excited and adventurous life which had comprised so many changes in so few years, I found myself at rest in the bosom of a retired and remote part of the country, and Gertrude and her father were my only neighbours, I was in that state of mind in which the passions, recruited by solitude, are accessible to the purer and more divine emotions. I was struck by Gertrude's beauty, I was charmed by her simplicity. Worn in the usages and fashions of the world, the inexperience, the trustfulness, the exceeding youth of her mind, charmed and touched me; but when I saw the stamp of our national disease in her bright eye and transparent cheek, I felt my love chilled while my interest was increased. I fancied myself safe, and I went daily into the danger; I imagined so pure a light could not burn, and I was consumed. Not till my anxiety grew into pain, my interest into terror, did I know the secret of my own heart; and at the moment that I discovered this secret, I discovered also that Gertrude loved me! What a destiny was mine! what happiness, yet what misery! Gertrude was my own — but for what period? I might touch that soft hand, I might listen to the tenderest confession from that silver voice; but all the while my heart spoke of passion, my reason whispered of death. You know that I am considered of a cold and almost callous nature, that I am not easily moved into affection; but my very pride bowed me here into weakness. There was so soft a demand upon my protection, so constant an appeal to my anxiety. You know that my father's quick temper burns within me, that I am hot, and stern, and exacting; but one hasty word, one thought of myself, here were inexcusable. So brief a time might be left for her earthly happiness, — could I embitter one moment? All that feeling of uncertainty which should in prudence have prevented my love, increased it almost to a preternatural excess. That which it is said mothers feel for an only child in sickness, I feel for Gertrude. *My* existence is not! — I exist in her!

Her illness increased upon her at home; they have recommended travel. She chose the course we were to pursue, and, fortunately, it was so familiar to me, that I have been enabled to brighten the way. I am ever on the watch that she shall not know a weary hour; you would almost smile to see how I have roused myself from my habitual silence, and to find me — me, the scheming and worldly actor of real life — plunged back into the early romance of my boyhood, and charming the childish delight of Gertrude with the invention of fables and the traditions of the Rhine.

But I believe that I have succeeded in my object; if not, what is left to me? *Gertrude is better!* — In that sentence what visions of hope dawn upon me! I wish you could have seen Gertrude before we left England; you might then have understood my love for her. Not that we have not, in the gay capitals of Europe, paid our brief vows to forms more richly beautiful; not that we have not been charmed by a more brilliant genius, by a more tutored grace. But there is that in Gertrude which I never saw before, — the union of the childish and the intellectual, an ethereal simplicity, a temper that is never dimmed, a tenderness — O God! let me not speak of her virtues, for they only tell me how little she is suited to the earth.

You will direct to me at Mayence, whither our course now leads us, and your friendship will find indulgence for a letter that is so little a reply to yours.

Your sincere friend,

A. G. TREVYLYAN.

CHAPTER XVIII.

COBLENTZ. — EXCURSION TO THE MOUNTAINS OF TAUNUS; ROMAN TOWER IN THE VALLEY OF EHRENBREITSTEIN. — TRAVEL, ITS PLEASURES ESTIMATED DIFFERENTLY BY THE YOUNG AND THE OLD. — THE STUDENT OF HEIDELBERG; HIS CRITICISMS ON GERMAN LITERATURE.

GERTRUDE had, indeed, apparently rallied during their stay at Coblentz; and a French physician established in the town (who adopted a peculiar treatment for consumption, which had been attended with no ordinary success) gave her father and Trevylyan a sanguine assurance of her ultimate recovery. The time they passed within the white walls of Coblentz was, therefore, the happiest and most cheerful part of their pilgrimage. They visited the various places in its vicinity; but the excursion which most delighted Gertrude was one to the mountains of Taunus.

They took advantage of a beautiful September day; and, crossing the river, commenced their tour from the Thal, or valley of Ehrenbreitstein. They stopped on their way to view the remains of a Roman tower in the valley; for the whole of that district bears frequent witness of the ancient conquerors of the world. The mountains of Taunus are still intersected with the roads which the Romans cut to the mines

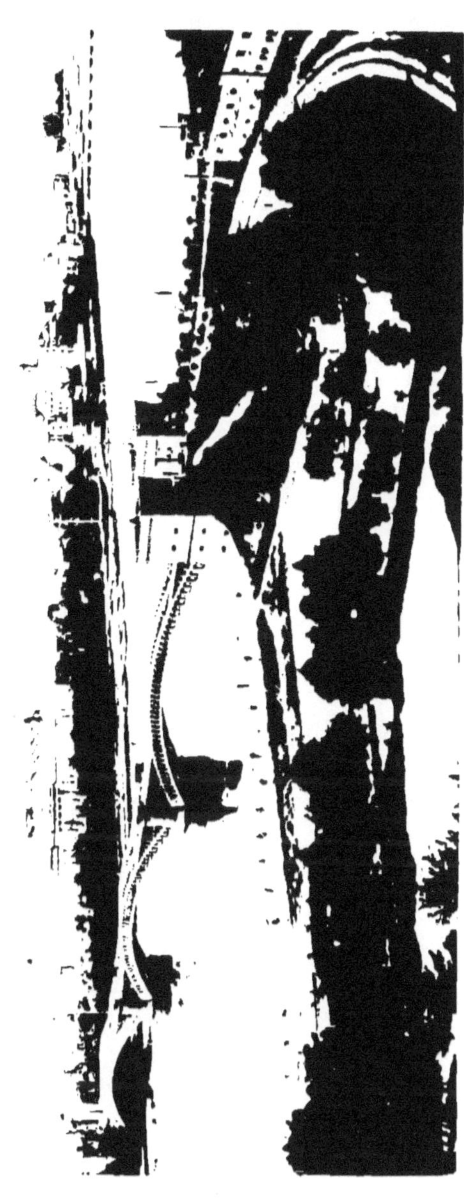

that supplied them with silver. Roman urns and inscribed stones are often found in these ancient places. The stones, inscribed with names utterly unknown,—a type of the uncertainty of fame! the urns, from which the dust is gone, a very satire upon life!

Lone, gray, and mouldering, this tower stands aloft in the valley; and the quiet Vane smiled to see the uniform of a modern Prussian, with his white belt and lifted bayonet, by the spot which had once echoed to the clang of the Roman arms. The soldier was paying a momentary court to a country damsel, whose straw hat and rustic dress did not stifle the vanity of the sex; and this rude and humble gallantry, in that spot, was another moral in the history of human passions. Above, the ramparts of a modern rule frowned down upon the solitary tower, as if in the vain insolence with which present power looks upon past decay,—the living race upon ancestral greatness. And indeed, in this respect, rightly! for modern times have no parallel to that degradation of human dignity stamped upon the ancient world by the long sway of the Imperial Harlot, all slavery herself, yet all tyranny to earth;—and, like her own Messalina, at once a prostitute and an empress!

They continued their course by the ancient baths of Ems, and keeping by the banks of the romantic Lahn, arrived at Holzapfel.

"Ah," said Gertrude, one day, as they proceeded to the springs of the Carlovingian Wiesbaden, "surely perpetual travel with those we love must be the happiest state of existence! If home has its comforts, it also has its cares; but here we are at home with Nature, and the minor evils vanish almost before they are felt."

"True," said Trevylyan, "we escape from 'THE LITTLE,' which is the curse of life; the small cares that devour us up, the grievances of the day. We are feeding the divinest part of our nature,—the appetite to admire."

"But of all things wearisome," said Vane, "a succession of changes is the most. There can be a monotony in variety itself. As the eye aches in gazing long at the new shapes of the kaleidoscope, the mind aches at the fatigue of a constant alternation of objects; and we delightedly return to 'REST,' which is to life what green is to the earth."

In the course of their sojourn among the various baths of Taunus, they fell in, by accident, with a German student of Heidelberg, who was pursuing the pedestrian excursions so peculiarly favoured by his tribe. He was tamer and gentler than the general herd of those young wanderers, and our party were much pleased with his enthusiasm, because it was unaffected. He had been in England, and spoke its language almost as a native.

"Our literature," said he, one day, conversing with Vane, "has two faults,— we are too subtle and too homely. We do not speak enough to the broad comprehension of mankind; we are forever making abstract qualities of flesh and blood. Our critics have turned your 'Hamlet' into an allegory; they will not even allow Shakspeare to paint mankind, but insist on his embodying qualities. They turn poetry into metaphysics, and truth seems to them shallow, unless an allegory, which is false, can be seen at the bottom. Again, too, with our most imaginative works we mix a homeliness that we fancy touching, but which in reality is ludicrous. We eternally step from the sublime to the ridiculous; we want taste."

"But not, I hope, French taste. Do not govern a Goethe, or even a Richter, by a Boileau!" said Trevylyan.

"No; but Boileau's taste was false. Men who have the reputation for good taste often acquire it solely because of the want of genius. By taste I mean a quick tact into the harmony of composition, the art of making the whole consistent with its parts, the *concinnitas*. Schiller alone of our authors has it. But we are fast mending; and by following shadows so long we have been led at last to the substance. Our past literature is to us what astrology was to science,— false but ennobling, and conducting us to the true language of the intellectual heaven."

Another time the scenes they passed, interspersed with the ruins of frequent monasteries, leading them to converse on the monastic life, and the various additions time makes to religion, the German said: "Perhaps one of the works most wanted in the world is the history of Religion. We have several books, it is true, on the subject, but none that supply the want I allude to. A German ought to write it; for it is, probably, only a German that would have the requisite learning. A German only, too, is likely to treat the mighty subject with boldness, and yet with veneration; without the shallow flippancy of the Frenchman, without the timid sectarianism of the English. It would be a noble task, to trace the winding mazes of antique falsehood; to clear up the first glimmerings of divine truth; to separate Jehovah's word from man's invention; to vindicate the All-merciful from the dread creeds of bloodshed and of fear: and, watching in the great Heaven of Truth the dawning of the True Star, follow it — like the Magi of the East — till it rested above the real God. Not indeed presuming to such a task," continued the German, with a slight blush, "I have about me a humble essay, which treats only of one part of that august subject; which, leaving to a loftier genius the history of the true religion, may be considered as the history of a false one,— of such a creed as Christianity supplanted in the North; or such as may perhaps be found among the fiercest of the savage tribes. It is a fiction — as you may conceive; but yet, by a constant reference to the early records of human learning, I have studied to weave it up from truths. If you would like to hear it,— it is very short — "

"Above all things," said Vane; and the German drew a manuscript neatly bound from his pocket.

"After having myself criticised so insolently the faults of our national literature," said he, smiling, "you will have a right to criticise the faults that belong to so humble a disciple of it; but you will see that, though I have commenced with the allegorical or the supernatural, I have endeavoured to avoid the subtlety of conceit, and the obscurity of design, which I blame in the wilder of our authors. As to the style, I wished to suit it to the subject; it ought to be, unless I err, rugged and massive,— hewn, as it were, out of the rock of primeval language. But you, madam — doubtless you do not understand German?"

"Her mother was an Austrian," said Vane; "and she knows at least enough of the tongue to understand you; so pray begin."

Without further preface, the German then commenced the story, which the reader will find translated[1] in the next chapter.

CHAPTER XIX.

THE FALLEN STAR; OR THE HISTORY OF A FALSE RELIGION.

AND the STARS sat, each on his ruby throne, and watched with sleepless eyes upon the world. It was the night ushering in the new year, a night on which every star receives from the archangel that then visits the universal galaxy its peculiar charge. The destinies of men and empires are then portioned forth for the coming year, and, unconsciously to ourselves, our fates become minioned to the stars. A hushed and solemn night is that in which the dark gates of time open to receive the ghost of the Dead Year, and the young and radiant Stranger rushes forth from the clouded chasms of Eternity. On that night, it is said that there are given to the spirits that we see not a privilege and a power; the dead are troubled in their forgotten graves, and men feast and laugh, while demon and angel are contending for their doom.

It was night in heaven; all was unutterably silent; the music of the spheres had paused, and not a sound came from the angels of the stars; and they who sat upon those shining thrones were three thousand and ten, each resembling each. Eternal youth clothed their radiant limbs with celestial beauty, and on their faces was written the dread of calm,— that fear-

---

[1] Nevertheless I beg to state seriously, that the German student is an impostor; and that he has no right to wrest the parentage of the fiction from the true author.

ful stillness which feels not, sympathizes not with the doom over which it broods. War, tempest, pestilence, the rise of empires and their fall, they ordain, they compass, unexultant and uncompassionate. The fell and thrilling crimes that stalk abroad when the world sleeps,—the parricide with his stealthy step and horrent brow and lifted knife; the unwifed mother that glides out and looks behind, and behind, and shudders, and casts her babe upon the river, and hears the wail, and pities not—the splash, and does not tremble,—these the starred kings behold, to these they lead the unconscious step; but the guilt blanches not their lustre, neither doth remorse wither their unwrinkled youth. Each star wore a kingly diadem; round the loins of each was a graven belt, graven with many and mighty signs; and the foot of each was on a burning ball, and the right arm drooped over the knee as they bent down from their thrones. They moved not a limb or feature, save the finger of the right hand, which ever and anon moved slowly pointing, and regulated the fates of men as the hand of the dial speaks the career of time.

One only of the three thousand and ten wore not the same aspect as his crowned brethren,—a star smaller than the rest, and less luminous; the countenance of this star was not impressed with the awful calmness of the others, but there were sullenness and discontent upon his mighty brow.

And this star said to himself, "Behold! I am created less glorious than my fellows, and the archangel apportions not to me the same lordly destinies. Not for me are the dooms of kings and bards, the rulers of empires, or, yet nobler, the swayers and harmonists of souls. Sluggish are the spirits and base the lot of the men I am ordained to lead through a dull life to a fameless grave. And wherefore? Is it mine own fault, or is it the fault which is not mine, that I was woven of beams less glorious than my brethren? Lo! when the archangel comes, I will bow not my crowned head to his decrees. I will speak, as the ancestral Lucifer before me: *he* rebelled because of his glory, *I* because of my obscurity; *he* from the ambition of pride, and *I* from its discontent."

And while the star was thus communing with himself, the

upward heavens were parted as by a long river of light, and adown that stream swiftly, and without sound, sped the archangel visitor of the stars. His vast limbs floated in the liquid lustre, and his outspread wings, each plume the glory of a sun, bore him noiselessly along; but thick clouds veiled his lustre from the eyes of mortals, and while above all was bathed in the serenity of his splendour, tempest and storm broke below over the children of the earth: "He bowed the heavens and came down, and darkness was under his feet."

And the stillness on the faces of the stars became yet more still, and the awfulness was humbled into awe. Right above their thrones paused the course of the archangel; and his wings stretched from east to west, overshadowing with the shadow of light the immensity of space. Then forth, in the shining stillness, rolled the dread music of his voice: and, fulfilling the heraldry of God, to each star he appointed the duty and the charge; and each star bowed his head yet lower as he heard the fiat, while his throne rocked and trembled at the Majesty of the Word. But at last, when each of the brighter stars had, in succession, received the mandate, and the viceroyalty over the nations of the earth, the purple and diadems of kings, the archangel addressed the lesser star as he sat apart from his fellows.

"Behold," said the archangel, "the rude tribes of the North, the fishermen of the river that flows beneath, and the hunters of the forests that darken the mountain tops with verdure! these be thy charge, and their destinies thy care. Nor deem thou, O Star of the sullen beams, that thy duties are less glorious than the duties of thy brethren; for the peasant is not less to thy master and mine than the monarch; nor doth the doom of empires rest more upon the sovereign than on the herd. The passions and the heart are the dominion of the stars,—a mighty realm; nor less mighty beneath the hide that garbs the shepherd than under the jewelled robes of the eastern kings."

Then the star lifted his pale front from his breast, and answered the archangel.

"Lo!" he said, "ages have passed, and each year thou hast

appointed me to the same ignoble charge. Release me, I pray thee, from the duties that I scorn; or, if thou wilt that the lowlier race of men be my charge, give unto me the charge not of many, but of one, and suffer me to breathe into him the desire that spurns the valleys of life, and ascends its steeps. If the humble are given to me, let there be amongst them one whom I may lead on the mission that shall abase the proud; for, behold, O Appointer of the Stars, as I have sat for un-counted years upon my solitary throne, brooding over the things beneath, my spirit hath gathered wisdom from the changes that shift below. Looking upon the tribes of earth, I have seen how the multitude are swayed, and tracked the steps that lead weakness into power; and fain would I be the ruler of one who, if abased, shall aspire to rule."

As a sudden cloud over the face of noon was the change on the brow of the archangel.

"Proud and melancholy star," said the herald, "thy wish would war with the courses of the invisible DESTINY, that, throned far above, sways and harmonizes all,—the source from which the lesser rivers of fate are eternally gushing through the heart of the universe of things. Thinkest thou that thy wisdom, of itself, can lead the peasant to become a king?"

And the crowned star gazed undauntedly on the face of the archangel, and answered,—

"Yea! Grant me but one trial!"

Ere the archangel could reply, the farthest centre of the Heaven was rent as by a thunderbolt; and the divine herald covered his face with his hands, and a voice low and sweet and mild, with the consciousness of unquestionable power, spoke forth to the repining star.

"The time has arrived when thou mayest have thy wish. Below thee, upon yon solitary plain, sits a mortal, gloomy as thyself, who, born under thy influence, may be moulded to thy will."

The voice ceased as the voice of a dream. Silence was over the seas of space, and the archangel, once more borne aloft, slowly soared away into the farther heaven, to promulgate the divine bidding to the stars of far-distant worlds. But the soul of the discontented star exulted within itself; and it said, "I will call forth a king from the valley of the herdsman that shall trample on the kings subject to my fellows, and render the charge of the contemned star more glorious than the minions of its favoured brethren; thus shall I revenge neglect! thus shall I prove my claim hereafter to the heritage of the great of earth!"

. . . .

At that time, though the world had rolled on for ages, and the pilgrimage of man had passed through various states of existence, which our dim traditionary knowledge has not preserved, yet the condition of our race in the northern hemisphere was then what *we*, in our imperfect lore, have conceived to be among the earliest.

. . . .

By a rude and vast pile of stones, the masonry of arts forgotten, a lonely man sat at midnight, gazing upon the heavens. A storm had just passed from the earth; the clouds had rolled away, and the high stars looked down upon the rapid waters of the Rhine; and no sound save the roar of the waves, and the dripping of the rain from the mighty trees, was heard around the ruined pile. The white sheep lay scattered on the plain, and slumber with them. He sat watching over the herd, lest the foes of a neighbouring tribe seized them unawares, and thus he communed with himself: "The king sits upon his throne, and is honoured by a warrior race, and the warrior exults in the trophies he has won; the step of the huntsman is bold upon the mountain-top, and his name is sung at night round the pine-fires by the lips of the bard; and the bard himself hath honour in the hall. But I, who belong not to the race of kings, and whose limbs can bound not to the rapture of war, nor scale the eyries of the eagle and the haunts of the swift stag; whose hand cannot string the harp, and whose voice is harsh in the song,— *I* have neither honour nor command, and men bow not the head as I pass along; yet do I feel within me the consciousness of a great power that should rule my species — not obey. My eye pierces the secret hearts of men. I see their thoughts ere their lips proclaim them; and I scorn, while I see, the weakness and the vices which I never shared. I laugh at the madness of the warrior; I mock within my soul at the tyranny of kings. Surely there is something in man's nature more fitted to command, more worthy of renown, than the sinews of the arm, or the swift-ness of the feet, or the accident of birth!"

As Morven, the son of Osslah, thus mused within himself, still looking at the heavens, the solitary man beheld a star suddenly shooting from its place, and speeding through the silent air, till it suddenly paused right over the midnight river, and facing the inmate of the pile of stones.

As he gazed upon the star, strange thoughts grew slowly over him. He drank, as it were, from its solemn aspect the spirit of a great design. A dark cloud rapidly passing over the earth snatched the star from his sight, but left to his awakened mind the thoughts and the dim scheme that had come to him as he gazed.

When the sun arose, one of his brethren relieved him of his charge over the herd, and he went away, but not to his father's home. Musingly he plunged into the dark and leaf-less recesses of the winter forest; and shaped out of his wild thoughts, more palpably and clearly, the outline of his daring hope. While thus absorbed he heard a great noise in the forest, and, fearful lest the hostile tribe of the Alrich might pierce that way, he ascended one of the loftiest pine-trees, to whose perpetual verdure the winter had not denied the shelter he sought; and, concealed by its branches, he looked anxiously forth in the direction whence the noise had proceeded. And IT came,— it came with a tramp and a crash, and a crushing tread upon the crunched boughs and matted leaves that strewed the soil; it came, it came,— the monster that the world now holds no more,— the mighty Mammoth of the North! Slowly it moved its huge strength along, and its burning eyes glittered through the gloomy shade; its jaws, falling apart, showed the grinders with which it snapped asunder the young oaks of the forest; and the vast tusks, which, curved downward to the midst of its massive limbs,

glisteued white and ghastly, curdling the blood of one destined hereafter to be the dreadest ruler of the men of that
distant age.

The livid eyes of the monster fastened on the form of the
herdsman, even amidst the thick darkness of the pine. It
paused, it glared upon him; its jaws opened, and a low deep
sound, as of gathering thunder, seemed to the son of Osslah
as the knell of a dreadful grave. But after glaring on him
for some moments, it again, and calmly, pursued its terrible
way, crashing the boughs as it marched along, till the last
sound of its heavy tread died away upon his ear.[1]

Ere yet, however, Morven summoned the courage to descend the tree, he saw the shining of arms through the bare
branches of the wood, and presently a small band of the hostile Alrich came into sight. He was perfectly hidden from
them; and, listening as they passed him, he heard one say to
another,—

"The night covers all things; why attack them by day?"

And he who seemed the chief of the band, answered,—

"Right. To-night, when they sleep in their city, we will
upon them. Lo! they will be drenched in wine, and fall like
sheep into our hands."

"But where, O chief," said a third of the band, "shall our
men hide during the day? for there are many hunters among
the youth of the Oestrich tribe, and they might see us in the
forest unawares, and arm their race against our coming."

"I have prepared for that," answered the chief. "Is not
the dark cavern of Oderlin at hand? Will it not shelter us
from the eyes of the victims?"

Then the men laughed, and, shouting, they went their way
adown the forest.

When they were gone, Morven cautiously descended, and,
striking into a broad path, hastened to a vale that lay between the forest and the river in which was the city where
the chief of his country dwelt. As he passed by the warlike

---

[1] *The Critic* will perceive that this sketch of the beast, whose race has perished, is mainly intended to designate the remote period of the world in which
the tale is cast.

men, giants in that day, who thronged the streets (if streets they might be called), their half garments parting from their huge limbs, the quiver at their backs, and the hunting spear in their hand, they laughed and shouted out, and, pointing to him, cried, "Morven the woman! Morven the cripple! what dost thou among men?"

For the son of Osslah was small in stature and of slender strength, and his step had halted from his birth; but he passed through the warriors unheedingly. At the outskirts of the city he came upon a tall pile in which some old men dwelt by themselves, and counselled the king when times of danger, or when the failure of the season, the famine or the drought, perplexed the ruler, and clouded the savage fronts of his warrior tribe.

They gave the counsels of experience, and when experience failed, they drew, in their believing ignorance, assurances and omens from the winds of heaven, the changes of the moon, and the flights of the wandering birds. Filled — by the voices of the elements, and the variety of mysteries, which ever shift along the face of things, unsolved by the wonder which pauses not, the fear which believes, and that eternal reasoning of all experience, which assigns causes to effect — with the notion of superior powers, they assisted their ignorance by the conjectures of their superstition. But as yet they knew no craft and practised no *voluntary* delusion; they trembled too much at the mysteries which had created their faith to seek to belie them. They counselled as they believed, and the bold dream of governing their warriors and their kings by the wisdom of deceit had never dared to cross men thus worn and gray with age.

The son of Osslah entered the vast pile with a fearless step, and approached the place at the upper end of the hall where the old men sat in conclave.

"How, base-born and craven-limbed!" cried the eldest, who had been a noted warrior in his day, "darest thou enter unsummoned amidst the secret councils of the wise men? Knowest thou not, scatterling! that the penalty is death?"

"Slay me, if thou wilt," answered Morven, "but hear! As

I sat last night in the ruined palace of our ancient kings, tending, as my father bade me, the sheep that grazed around, lest the fierce tribe of Alrich should descend unseen from the mountains upon the herd, a storm came darkly on; and when the storm had ceased, and I looked above on the sky, I saw a star descend from its height towards me, and a voice from the star said: 'Son of Osslah, leave thy herd and seek the council of the wise men and say unto them, that they take thee as one of their number, or that sudden will be the destruction of them and theirs.' But I had courage to answer the voice, and I said, 'Mock not the poor son of the herdsman. Behold, they will kill me if I utter so rash a word, for I am poor and valueless in the eyes of the tribe of Oestrich, and the great in deeds and the gray of hair alone sit in the council of the wise men.'

"Then the voice said: 'Do my bidding, and I will give thee a token that thou comest from the Powers that sway the seasons and sail upon the eagles of the winds. Say unto the wise men this very night if they refuse to receive thee of their band, evil shall fall upon them, and the morrow shall dawn in blood.'

"Then the voice ceased, and the cloud passed over the star; and I communed with myself, and came, O dread father, mournfully unto you; for I feared that ye would smite me because of my bold tongue, and that ye would sentence me to the death, in that I asked what may scarce be given even to the sons of kings."

Then the grim elders looked one at the other, and marvelled much, nor knew they what answer they should make to the herdsman's son.

At length one of the wise men said, "Surely there must be truth in the son of Osslah, for he would not dare to falsify the great lights of Heaven. If he had given unto men the words of the star, verily we might doubt the truth. But who would brave the vengeance of the gods of night?"

Then the elders shook their heads approvingly; but one answered and said,—

"Shall we take the herdsman's son as our equal? No!"

The name of the man who thus answered was Darvan, and his words were pleasing to the elders.

But Morven spoke out: "Of a truth, O councillors of kings, I look not to be an equal with yourselves. Enough if I tend the gates of your palace, and serve you as the son of Osslah may serve;" and he bowed his head humbly as he spoke.

Then said the chief of the elders, for he was wiser than the others, "But how wilt thou deliver us from the evil that is to come? Doubtless the star has informed thee of the service thou canst render to us if we take thee into our palace, as well as the ill that will fall on us if we refuse."

Morven answered meekly, "Surely, if thou acceptest thy servant, the star will teach him that which may requite thee; but as yet he knows only what he has uttered."

Then the sages bade him withdraw, and they communed with themselves, and they differed much; but though fierce men, and bold at the war-cry of a human foe, they shuddered at the prophecy of a star. So they resolved to take the son of Osslah, and suffer him to keep the gate of the council-hall.

He heard their decree and bowed his head, and went to the gate, and sat down by it in silence.

And the sun went down in the west, and the first stars of the twilight began to glimmer, when Morven started from his seat, and a trembling appeared to seize his limbs. His lips foamed; an agony and a fear possessed him; he writhed as a man whom the spear of a foeman has pierced with a mortal wound, and suddenly fell upon his face on the stony earth.

The elders approached him; wondering, they lifted him up. He slowly recovered as from a swoon; his eyes rolled wildly.

"Heard ye not the voice of the star?" he said.

And the chief of the elders answered, "Nay, we heard no sound."

Then Morven sighed heavily.

"To me only the word was given. Summon instantly, O councillors of the king, summon the armed men, and all the youth of the tribe, and let them take the sword and the spear, and follow thy servant! For lo! the star hath announced to him that the foe shall fall into our hands as the wild beasts of the forests."

The son of Osslah spoke with the voice of command, and the elders were amazed. "Why pause ye?" he cried. "Do the gods of the night lie? On my head rest the peril if I deceive ye."

Then the elders communed together; and they went forth and summoned the men of arms, and all the young of the tribe; and each man took the sword and the spear, and Morven also. And the son of Osslah walked first, still looking up at the star, and he motioned them to be silent, and moved with a stealthy step.

So they went through the thickest of the forest, till they came to the mouth of a great cave, overgrown with aged and matted trees, and it was called the Cave of Oberlin; and he bade the leaders place the armed men on either side the cave, to the right and to the left, among the bushes.

So they watched silently till the night deepened, when they heard a noise in the cave and the sound of feet, and forth came an armed man; and the spear of Morven pierced him, and he fell dead at the mouth of the cave. Another and another, and both fell! Then loud and long was heard the war-cry of Alrich, and forth poured, as a stream over a narrow bed, the river of armed men. And the sons of Oestrich fell upon them, and the foe were sorely perplexed and terrified by the suddenness of the battle and the darkness of the night; and there was a great slaughter.

And when the morning came, the children of Oestrich counted the slain, and found the leader of Alrich and the chief men of the tribe amongst them; and great was the joy thereof. So they went back in triumph to the city, and they carried the brave son of Osslah on their shoulders, and shouted forth, "Glory to the servant of the star."

And Morven dwelt in the council of the wise men.

Now the king of the tribe had one daughter, and she was stately amongst the women of the tribe, and fair to look upon. And Morven gazed upon her with the eyes of love, but he did not dare to speak.

Now the son of Osslah laughed secretly at the foolishness of men; he loved them not, for they had mocked him; he honoured them not, for he had blinded the wisest of their leaders. He shunned their feasts and merriment, and lived apart and solitary. The austerity of his life increased the mysterious homage which his commune with the stars had won him, and the boldest of the warriors bowed his head to the favourite of the gods.

One day he was wandering by the side of the river, and he saw a large bird of prey rise from the waters, and give chase to a hawk that had not yet gained the full strength of its wings. From his youth the solitary Morven had loved to watch, in the great forests and by the banks of the mighty stream, the habits of the things which nature has submitted to man; and looking now on the birds, he said to himself, "Thus is it ever; by cunning or by strength each thing wishes to master its kind." While thus moralizing, the larger bird had stricken down the hawk, and it fell terrified and panting at his feet. Morven took the hawk in his hands, and the vulture shrieked above him, wheeling nearer and nearer to its protected prey; but Morven scared away the vulture, and placing the hawk in his bosom he carried it home, and tended it carefully, and fed it from his hand until it had regained its strength; and the hawk knew him, and followed him as a dog. And Morven said, smiling to himself, "Behold, the credulous fools around me put faith in the flight and motion of birds. I will teach this poor hawk to minister to my ends." So he tamed the bird, and tutored it according to its nature; but he concealed it carefully from others, and cherished it in secret.

The king of the country was old, and like to die, and the eyes of the tribe were turned to his two sons, nor knew they which was the worthier to reign. And Morven, passing through the forest one evening, saw the younger of the two, who was a great hunter, sitting mournfully under an oak, and looking with musing eyes upon the ground.

"Wherefore musest thou, O swift-footed Siror?" said the son of Osslah; "and wherefore art thou sad?"

"Thou canst not assist me," answered the prince, sternly; "take thy way."

"Nay," answered Morven, "thou knowest not what thou sayest; am I not the favourite of the stars?"

"Away, I am no graybeard whom the approach of death makes doting: talk not to me of the stars; I know only the things that my eye sees and my ear drinks in."

"Hush," said Morven, solemnly, and covering his face; "hush! lest the heavens avenge thy rashness. But, behold, the stars have given unto me to pierce the secret hearts of others; and I can tell thee the thoughts of thine."

"Speak out, base-born!"

"Thou art the younger of two, and thy name is less known in war than the name of thy brother: yet wouldst thou desire to be set over his head, and to sit on the high seat of thy father?"

The young man turned pale. "Thou hast truth in thy lips," said he, with a faltering voice.

"Not from me, but from the stars, descends the truth."

"Can the stars grant my wish?"

"They can: let us meet to-morrow." Thus saying, Morven passed into the forest.

The next day, at noon, they met again.

"I have consulted the gods of night, and they have given me the power that I prayed for, but on one condition."

"Name it."

"That thou sacrifice thy sister on their altars; thou must build up a heap of stones, and take thy sister into the wood, and lay her on the pile, and plunge thy sword into her heart; so only shalt thou reign."

The prince shuddered, and started to his feet, and shook his spear at the pale front of Morven.

"Tremble," said the son of Osslah, with a loud voice. "Hark to the gods who threaten thee with death, that thou hast dared to lift thine arm against their servant!"

As he spoke, the thunder rolled above; for one of the frequent storms of the early summer was about to break. The spear dropped from the prince's hand; he sat down, and cast his eyes on the ground.

"Wilt thou do the bidding of the stars, and reign?" said Morven.

"I will!" cried Siror, with a desperate voice.

"This evening, then, when the sun sets, thou wilt lead her hither, alone; I may not attend thee. Now, let us pile the stones."

Silently the huntsman bent his vast strength to the fragments of rock that Mervon pointed to him, and they built the altar, and went their way.

And beautiful is the dying of the great sun, when the last song of the birds fades into the lap of silence; when the islands of the cloud are bathed in light, and the first star springs up over the grave of day!

"Whither leadest thou my steps, my brother?" said Orna; "and why doth thy lip quiver; and why dost thou turn away thy face?"

"Is not the forest beautiful; does it not tempt us forth, my sister?"

"And wherefore are those heaps of stone piled together?"

"Let others answer; *I* piled them not."

"Thou tremblest, brother: we will return."

"Not so; by these stones is a bird that my shaft pierced to-day,—a bird of beautiful plumage that I slew for thee."

"We are by the pile; where hast thou laid the bird?"

"Here!" cried Siror; and he seized the maiden in his arms, and, casting her on the rude altar, he drew forth his sword to smite her to the heart.

Right over the stones rose a giant oak, the growth of immemorial ages; and from the oak, or from the heavens, broke forth a loud and solemn voice, "Strike not, son of kings! the stars forbear their own: the maiden thou shalt not slay; yet shalt thou reign over the race of Oestrich; and thou shalt give Orna as a bride to the favourite of the stars. Arise, and go thy way!"

The voice ceased: the terror of Orna had overpowered for a time the springs of life; and Siror bore her home through the wood in his strong arms.

"Alas!" said Morven, when, at the next day, he again met

the aspiring prince; "alas! the stars have ordained me a lot which my heart desires not: for I, lonely of life, and crippled of shape, am insensible to the fires of love; and ever, as thou and thy tribe know, I have shunned the eyes of women, for the maidens laughed at my halting step and my sullen features; and so in my youth I learned betimes to banish all thoughts of love. But since they told me (as they declared to *thee*), that only through that marriage, thou, O beloved prince! canst obtain thy father's plumed crown, I yield me to their will."

"But," said the prince, "not until I am king can I give thee my sister in marriage; for thou knowest that my sire would smite me to the dust if I asked him to give the flower of our race to the son of the herdsman Osslah."

"Thou speakest the words of truth. Go home and fear not; but, when thou art king, the sacrifice must be made, and Orna mine. Alas! how can I dare to lift mine eyes to her! But so ordain the dread kings of the night! — who shall gainsay their word?"

"The day that sees me king sees Orna thine," answered the prince.

Morven walked forth, as was his wont, alone; and he said to himself, "The king is old, yet may he live long between me and mine hope!" and he began to cast in his mind how he might shorten the time. Thus absorbed, he wandered on so unheedingly that night advanced, and he had lost his path among the thick woods and knew not how to regain his home. So he lay down quietly beneath a tree, and rested till day dawned; then hunger came upon him, and he searched among the bushes for such simple roots as those with which, for he was ever careless of food, he was used to appease the cravings of nature.

He found, among other more familiar herbs and roots, a red berry of a sweetish taste, which he had never observed before. He ate of it sparingly, and had not proceeded far in the wood before he found his eyes swim, and a deadly sickness came over him. For several hours he lay convulsed on the ground, expecting death; but the gaunt spareness of his frame, and his unvarying abstinence, prevailed over the poison, and he recovered slowly, and after great anguish. But he went with feeble steps back to the spot where the berries grew, and, plucking several, hid them in his bosom, and by nightfall regained the city.

The next day he went forth among his father's herds, and seizing a lamb, forced some of the berries into his stomach, and the lamb, escaping, ran away, and fell down dead. Then Morven took some more of the berries and boiled them down, and mixed the juice with wine, and he gave the wine in secret to one of his father's servants, and the servant died.

Then Morven sought the king, and coming into his presence, alone, he said unto him, "How fares my lord?"

The king sat on a couch made of the skins of wolves, and his eye was glassy and dim; but vast were his aged limbs, and huge was his stature, and he had been taller by a head than the children of men, and none living could bend the bow he had bent in youth; gray, gaunt, and worn, as some mighty bones that are dug at times from the bosom of the earth,— a relic of the strength of old.

And the king said faintly, and with a ghastly laugh,—

"The men of my years fare ill. What avails my strength? Better had I been born a cripple like thee, so should I have had nothing to lament in growing old."

The red flush passed over Morven's brow; but he bent humbly,—

"O king, what if I could give thee back thy youth? What if I could restore to thee the vigour which distinguished thee above the sons of men, when the warriors of Alrich fell like grass before thy sword?"

Then the king uplifted his dull eyes, and he said,—

"What meanest thou, son of Osslah? Surely I hear much of thy great wisdom, and how thou speakest nightly with the stars. Can the gods of the night give unto thee the secret to make the old young?"

"Tempt them not by doubt," said Morven, reverently. "All things are possible to the rulers of the dark hour; and, lo! the star that loves thy servant spake to him at the dead of night, and said, 'Arise, and go unto the king; and tell him that the stars honour the tribe of Oestrich, and remember how the king bent his bow against the sons of Alrich; wherefore, look thou under the stone that lies to the right of thy dwelling, even beside the pine tree, and thou shalt see a vessel of clay, and in the vessel thou wilt find a sweet liquid, that shall make the king thy master forget his age forever.' Therefore, my lord, when the morning rose I went forth, and looked under the stone, and behold the vessel of clay; and I have brought it hither to my lord the king."

"Quick, slave, quick! that I may drink and regain my youth!"

"Nay, listen, O king! further said the star to me,—

"'It is only at night, when the stars have power, that this their gift will avail; wherefore the king must wait till the hush of the midnight, when the moon is high, and then may he mingle the liquid with his wine. And he must reveal to none that he hath received the gift from the hand of the servant of the stars. For THEY do their work in secret, and when men sleep; therefore they love not the babble of mouths, and he who reveals their benefits shall surely die.'"

"Fear not," said the king, grasping the vessel; "none shall know: and, behold, I will rise on the morrow; and my two sons, wrangling for my crown — verily I shall be younger than they!"

Then the king laughed loud; and he scarcely thanked the servant of the stars, neither did he promise him reward; for the kings in those days had little thought save for themselves.

And Morven said to him, "Shall I not attend my lord? — for without me, perchance, the drug might fail of its effect."

"Ay," said the king, "rest here."

"Nay," replied Morven; "thy servants will marvel and talk much, if they see the son of Osslah sojourning in thy palace. So would the displeasure of the gods of night perchance be incurred. Suffer that the lesser door of the palace be unbarred, so that at the night hour, when the moon is midway in the heavens, I may steal unseen into thy chamber, and mix the liquid with thy wine."

"So be it," said the king. "Thou art wise, though thy limbs are crooked and curt; and the stars might have chosen a taller man." Then the king laughed again; and Morven laughed too, but there was danger in the mirth of the son of Osslah.

The night had begun to wane, and the inhabitants of Oestrich were buried in deep sleep, when, hark! a sharp voice was heard crying out in the streets, "Woe, woe! Awake, ye sons of Oestrich! woe!" Then forth, wild, haggard, alarmed, spear in hand, rushed the giant sons of the rugged tribe, and they saw a man on a height in the middle of the city, shrieking "Woe!" and it was Morven, the son of Osslah! And he said unto them, as they gathered round him, "Men and warriors, tremble as ye hear. The star of the west hath spoken to me, and thus said the star: 'Evil shall fall upon the kingly house of Oestrich,—yea, ere the morning dawn; wherefore, go thou mourning into the streets, and wake the inhabitants to woe!' So I rose and did the bidding of the star." And while Morven was yet speaking, a servant of the king's house ran up to the crowd, crying loudly, "The king is dead!" So they went into the palace and found the king stark upon his couch, and his huge limbs all cramped and crippled by the pangs of death, and his hands clenched as if in menace of a foe,—the Foe of all living flesh! Then fear came on the gazers, and they looked on Morven with a deeper awe than the boldest warrior would have called forth; and they bore him back to the council-hall of the wise men, wailing and clashing their arms in woe, and shouting, ever and anon, "Honour to Morven the prophet!" And that was the first time the word PROPHET was ever used in those countries.

At noon, on the third day from the king's death, Siror sought Morven, and he said, "Lo, my father is no more, and the people meet this evening at sunset to elect his successor, and the warriors and the young men will surely choose my brother, for he is more known in war. Fail me not therefore."

"Peace, boy!" said Morven, sternly; "nor dare to question the truth of the gods of night."

For Morven now began to presume on his power among the people, and to speak as rulers speak, even to the sons of kings; and the voice silenced the fiery Siror, nor dared he to reply.

"Behold," said Morven, taking up a chaplet of coloured plumes, "wear this on thy head, and put on a brave face, for the people like a hopeful spirit, and go down with thy brother to the place where the new king is to be chosen, and leave the rest to the stars. But, above all things, forget not that chaplet; it has been blessed by the gods of night."

The prince took the chaplet and returned home.

It was evening, and the warriors and chiefs of the tribe were assembled in the place where the new king was to be elected. And the voices of the many favoured Prince Voltoch, the brother of Siror, for he had slain twelve foemen with his spear; and verily, in those days, that was a great virtue in a king.

Suddenly there was a shout in the streets, and the people cried out, "Way for Morven the prophet, the prophet!" For the people held the son of Osslah in even greater respect than did the chiefs. Now, since he had become of note, Morven had assumed a majesty of air which the son of the herdsman knew not in his earlier days; and albeit his stature was short, and his limbs halted, yet his countenance was grave and high. He only of the tribe wore a garment that swept the ground, and his head was bare and his long black hair descended to his girdle, and rarely was change or human passion seen in his calm aspect. He feasted not, nor drank wine, nor was his presence frequent in the streets. He laughed not, neither did he smile, save when alone in the forest,—and then he laughed at the follies of his tribe.

So he walked slowly through the crowd, neither turning to the left nor to the right, as the crowd gave way; and he supported his steps with a staff of the knotted pine.

And when he came to the place where the chiefs were met, and the two princes stood in the centre, he bade the people

around him proclaim silence; then mounting on a huge fragment of rock, he thus spake to the multitude: —

"Princes, Warriors, and Bards! ye, O council of the wise
men! and ye, O hunters of the forests and snarers of the fishes
of the streams! hearken to Morven, the son of Osslah. Ye
know that I am lowly of race and weak of limb; but did I
not give into your hands the tribe of Alrich, and did ye not
slay them in the dead of night with a great slaughter? Surely,
ye must know this of himself did not the herdsman's son;
surely he was but the agent of the bright gods that love the
children of Oestrich! Three nights since when slumber was
on the earth, was not my voice heard in the streets? Did
I not proclaim woe to the kingly house of Oestrich? and
verily the dark arm had fallen on the bosom of the mighty,
that is no more. Could I have dreamed this thing merely in
a dream, or was I not as the voice of the bright gods that
watch over the tribes of Oestrich? Wherefore, O men and
chiefs! scorn not the son of Osslah, but listen to his words;
for are they not the wisdom of the stars? Behold, last night,
I sat alone in the valley, and the trees were hushed around,
and not a breath stirred; and I looked upon the star that
counsels the son of Osslah; and I said, 'Dread conqueror of
the cloud! thou that bathest thy beauty in the streams and
piercest the pine-boughs with thy presence; behold thy servant grieved because the mighty one hath passed away, and
many foes surround the houses of my brethren; and it is well
that they should have a king valiant and prosperous in war,
the cherished of the stars. Wherefore, O star! as thou gavest
into our hands the warriors of Alrich, and didst warn us of
the fall of the oak of our tribe, wherefore I pray thee give
unto the people a token that they may choose that king whom
the gods of the night prefer!' Then a low voice, sweeter than
the music of the bard, stole along the silence. 'Thy love for
thy race is grateful to the stars of night: go, then, son of
Osslah, and seek the meeting of the chiefs and the people to
choose a king, and tell them not to scorn thee because thou art
slow to the chase, and little known in war; for the stars give
thee wisdom as a recompense for all. Say unto the people that

as the wise men of the council shape their lessons by the flight of birds, so by the flight of birds shall a token be given unto them, and they shall choose their kings. For, saith the star of night, the birds are the children of the winds, they pass to and fro along the ocean of the air, and visit the clouds that are the war-ships of the gods; and their music is but broken melodies which they glean from the harps above. Are they not the messengers of the storm? Ere the stream chafes against the bank, and the rain descends, know ye not, by the wail of birds and their low circle over the earth, that the tempest is at hand? Wherefore, wisely do ye deem that the children of the air are the fit interpreters between the sons of men and the lords of the world above. Say then to the people and the chiefs that they shall take, from among the doves that build their nests in the roof of the palace, a white dove, and they shall let it loose in the air, and verily the gods of the night shall deem the dove as a prayer coming from the people, and they shall send a messenger to grant the prayer and give to the tribes of Oestrich a king worthy of themselves.'

"With that the star spoke no more."

Then the friends of Voltoch murmured among themselves, and they said, "Shall this man dictate to us who shall be king?" But the people and the warriors shouted, "Listen to the star; do we not give or deny battle according as the bird flies, — shall we not by the same token choose him by whom the battle should be led?" And the thing seemed natural to them, for it was after the custom of the tribe. Then they took one of the doves that built in the roof of the palace, and they brought it to the spot where Morven stood, and he, looking up to the stars and muttering to himself, released the bird.

There was a copse of trees at a little distance from the spot, and as the dove ascended, a hawk suddenly rose from the copse and pursued the dove; and the dove was terrified, and soared circling high above the crowd, when lo, the hawk, poising itself one moment on its wings, swooped with a sudden swoop, and, abandoning its prey, alighted on the plumed head of Siror.

"Behold," cried Morven in a loud voice, "behold your king!"

"Hail, all hail the king!" shouted the people. "All hail the chosen of the stars!"

Then Morven lifted his right hand and the hawk left the prince and alighted on Morven's shoulder. "Bird of the gods!" said he, reverently, "hast thou not a secret message for my ear?" Then the hawk put its beak to Morven's ear, and Morven bowed his head submissively; and the hawk rested with Morven from that moment and would not be scared away. And Morven said, "The stars have sent me this bird, that in the day-time when I see them not, we may never be without a councillor in distress."

So Siror was made king and Morven the son of Osslah was constrained by the king's will to take Orna for his wife; and the people and the chiefs honoured Morven the prophet above all the elders of the tribe.

One day Morven said unto himself, musing, "Am I not already equal with the king,—nay, is not the king my servant? Did I not place him over the heads of his brothers? Am I not, therefore, more fit to reign than he is; shall I not push him from his seat? It is a troublesome and stormy office to reign over the wild men of Oestrich, to feast in the crowded hall, and to lead the warriors to the fray. Surely if I feasted not, neither went out to war, they might say, 'This is no king, but the cripple Morven;' and some of the race of Siror might slay me secretly. But can I not be greater far than kings, and continue to choose and govern them, living as now at mine own ease? Verily the stars shall give me a new palace, and many subjects."

Among the wise men was Darvan; and Morven feared him, for his eye often sought the movements of the son of Osslah.

And Morven said, "It were better to *trust* this man than to *blind*, for surely I want a helpmate and a friend." So he said to the wise man as he sat alone watching the setting sun,—

"It seemeth to me, O Darvan! that we ought to build a great pile in honour of the stars, and the pile should be more glorious than all the palaces of the chiefs and the palace of the king; for are not the stars our masters? And thou and I should be the chief dwellers in this new palace, and we would serve the gods of night and fatten their altars with the choicest of the herd and the freshest of the fruits of the earth."

And Darvan said, "Thou speakest as becomes the servant of the stars. But will the people help to build the pile? For they are a warlike race and they love not toil."

And Morven answered, "Doubtless the stars will ordain the work to be done. Fear not."

"In truth thou art a wondrous man; thy words ever come to pass," answered Darvan; "and I wish thou wouldest teach me, friend, the language of the stars."

"Assuredly if thou servest me, thou shalt know," answered the proud Morven; and Darvan was secretly wroth that the son of the herdsman should command the service of an elder and a chief.

And when Morven returned to his wife he found her weeping much. Now she loved the son of Osslah with an exceeding love, for he was not savage and fierce as the men she had known, and she was proud of his fame among the tribe; and he took her in his arms and kissed her, and asked her why she wept. Then she told him that her brother the king had visited her, and had spoken bitter words of Morven: "He taketh from me the affection of my people," said Siror, "and blindeth them with lies. And since he hath made me king, what if he take my kingdom from me? Verily a new tale of the stars might undo the old." And the king had ordered her to keep watch on Morven's secrecy, and to see whether truth was in him when he boasted of his commune with the Powers of night.

But Orna loved Morven better than Siror, therefore she told her husband all.

And Morven resented the king's ingratitude, and was troubled much, for a king is a powerful foe; but he comforted Orna, and bade her dissemble, and complain also of him to her brother, so that he might confide to her unsuspectingly whatsoever he might design against Morven.

There was a cave by Morven's house in which he kept the sacred hawk, and wherein he secretly trained and nurtured other birds against future need; and the door of the cave was always barred. And one day he was thus engaged when he beheld a chink in the wall that he had never noted before, and the sun came playfully in; and while he looked he perceived the sunbeam was darkened, and presently he saw a human face peering in through the chink. And Morven trembled, for he knew he had been watched. He ran hastily from the cave; but the spy had disappeared among the trees, and Morven went straight to the chamber of Darvan and sat himself down. And Darvan did not return home till late, and he started and turned pale when he saw Morven. But Morven greeted him as a brother, and bade him to a feast, which, for the first time, he purposed giving at the full of the moon, in honour of the stars. And going out of Darvan's chamber he returned to his wife, and bade her rend her hair, and go at the dawn of day to the king her brother, and complain bitterly of Morven's treatment, and pluck the black plans from the breast of the king. "For surely," said he, "Darvan hath lied to thy brother, and some evil waits me that I would fain know."

So the next morning Orna sought the king, and she said, "The herdsman's son hath reviled me, and spoken harsh words to me; shall I not be avenged?"

Then the king stamped his feet and shook his mighty sword. "Surely thou shalt be avenged; for I have learned from one of the elders that which convinceth me that the man hath lied to the people, and the base-born shall surely die. Yea, the first time that he goeth alone into the forest my brother and I will fall upon him and smite him to the death." And with this comfort Siror dismissed Orna.

And Orna flung herself at the feet of her husband. "Fly now, O my beloved! — fly into the forests afar from my brethren, or surely the sword of Siror will end thy days."

Then the son of Osslah folded his arms, and seemed buried

in black thoughts; nor did he heed the voice of Orna, until again and again she had implored him to fly.

"Fly!" he said at length. "Nay, I was doubting what punishment the stars should pour down upon our foe. Let warriors fly. Morven the prophet conquers by arms mightier than the sword."

Nevertheless Morven was perplexed in his mind, and knew not how to save himself from the vengeance of the king. Now, while he was musing hopelessly he heard a roar of waters; and behold, the river, for it was now the end of autumn, had burst its bounds, and was rushing along the valley to the houses of the city. And now the men of the tribe, and the women, and the children, came running, and with shrieks, to Morven's house, crying, "Behold, the river has burst upon us! Save us, O ruler of the stars!"

Then the sudden thought broke upon Morven, and he resolved to risk his fate upon one desperate scheme.

And he came out from the house calm and sad, and he said, "Ye know not what ye ask; I cannot save ye from this peril: ye have brought it on yourselves." And they cried, "How? O son of Osslah! We are ignorant of our crime."

And he answered, "Go down to the king's palace and wait before it, and surely I will follow ye, and ye shall learn wherefore ye have incurred this punishment from the gods." Then the crowd rolled murmuring back, as a receding sea; and when it was gone from the place, Morven went alone to the house of Darvan, which was next his own. And Darvan was greatly terrified; for he was of a great age, and had no children, neither friends, and he feared that he could not of himself escape the waters.

And Morven said to him soothingly, "Lo, the people love me, and I will see that thou art saved; for verily thou hast been friendly to me, and done me much service with the king."

And as he thus spake, Morven opened the door of the house and looked forth, and saw that they were quite alone. Then he seized the old man by the throat and ceased not his gripe till he was quite dead; and leaving the body of the elder on

the floor, Morven stole from the house and shut the gate.
And as he was going to his cave he mused a little while,
when, hearing the mighty roar of the waves advancing, and
far off the shrieks of women, he lifted up his head and said
proudly, "No, in this hour terror alone shall be my slave; I
will use no art save the power of my soul." So, leaning on
his pine-staff, he strode down to the palace. And it was now
evening, and many of the men held torches, that they might
see each other's faces in the universal fear. Red flashed the
quivering flames on the dark robes and pale front of Morven;
and he seemed mightier than the rest, because his face alone
was calm amidst the tumult. And louder and hoarser became
the roar of the waters; and swift rushed the shades of night
over the hastening tide.

And Morven said in a stern voice, "Where is the king; and
wherefore is he absent from his people in the hour of dread?"
Then the gate of the palace opened, and, behold, Siror was
sitting in the hall by the vast pine-fire, and his brother by
his side, and his chiefs around him: for they would not deign
to come amongst the crowd at the bidding of the herdsman's
son.

Then Morven, standing upon a rock above the heads of the
people (the same rock whereon he had proclaimed the king),
thus spake: —

"Ye desired to know, O sons of Oestrich! wherefore the
river hath burst its bounds, and the peril hath come upon you.
Learn, then, that the stars resent as the foulest of human
crimes an insult to their servants and delegates below. Ye
are all aware of the manner of life of Morven, whom ye have
surnamed the Prophet! He harms not man nor beast; he
lives alone; and, far from the wild joys of the warrior tribe,
he worships in awe and fear the Powers of Night. So is he
able to advise ye of the coming danger, — so is he able to save
ye from the foe. Thus are your huntsmen swift and your
warriors bold; and thus do your cattle bring forth their
young, and the earth its fruits. What think ye, and what
do ye ask to hear? Listen, men of Oestrich! — they have
laid snares for my life; and there are amongst you those who

have whetted the sword against the bosom that is only filled with love for you all. Therefore have the stern lords of heaven loosened the chains of the river; therefore doth this evil menace ye. Neither will it pass away until they who dug the pit for the servant of the stars are buried in the same."

Then, by the red torches, the faces of the men looked fierce and threatening; and ten thousand voices shouted forth, "Name them who conspired against thy life, O holy prophet, and surely they shall be torn limb from limb."

And Morven turned aside, and they saw that he wept bitterly; and he said,—

"Ye have asked me, and I have answered: but now scarce will ye believe the foe that I have provoked against me; and by the heavens themselves I swear, that if my death would satisfy their fury, nor bring down upon yourselves and your children's children the anger of the throned stars, gladly would I give my bosom to the knife. Yes," he cried, lifting up his voice, and pointing his shadowy arm towards the hall where the king sat by the pine-fire,— "yes, thou whom by my voice the stars chose above thy brother; yes, Siror, the guilty one! take thy sword, and come hither; strike, if thou hast the heart to strike, the Prophet of the Gods!"

The king started to his feet, and the crowd were hushed in a shuddering silence.

Morven resumed: —

"Know then, O men of Oestrich, that Siror and Voltoch his brother, and Darvan the elder of the wise men, have purposed to slay your prophet, even at such hour as when alone he seeks the shade of the forest to devise new benefits for you. Let the king deny it, if he can!"

Then Voltoch, of the giant limbs, strode forth from the hall, and his spear quivered in his hand.

"Rightly hast thou spoken, base son of my father's herdsman! and for thy sins shalt thou surely die; for thou liest when thou speakest of thy power with the stars, and thou laughest at the folly of them who hear thee: wherefore put him to death."

Then the chiefs in the hall clashed their arms, and rushed forth to slay the son of Osslah.

But he, stretching his unarmed hands on high, exclaimed, "Hear him, O dread ones of the night! Hark how he blasphemeth!"

Then the crowd took up the word, and cried, "He blasphemeth! he blasphemeth against the prophet!"

But the king and the chiefs, who hated Morven because of his power with the people, rushed into the crowd; and the crowd were irresolute, nor knew they how to act, for never yet had they rebelled against their chiefs, and they feared alike the prophet and the king.

And Siror cried, "Summon Darvan to us, for he hath watched the steps of Morven, and he shall lift the veil from my people's eyes." Then three of the swift of foot started forth to the house of Darvan.

And Morven cried out with a loud voice, "Hark! thus saith the star, who, now riding through yonder cloud, breaks forth upon my eyes, 'For the lie that the elder hath uttered against my servant, the curse of the stars shall fall upon him.' Seek, and as ye find him so may ye find ever the foes of Morven and the gods!"

A chill and an icy fear fell over the crowd, and even the cheek of Siror grew pale; and Morven, erect and dark above the waving torches, stood motionless with folded arms. And hark!—far and fast came on the war-steeds of the wave; the people heard them marching to the land, and tossing their white manes in the roaring wind.

"Lo, as ye listen," said Morven, calmly, "the river sweeps on. Haste, for the gods will have a victim, be it your prophet or your king."

"Slave!" shouted Siror, and his spear left his hand, and far above the heads of the crowd sped hissing beside the dark form of Morven, and rent the trunk of the oak behind. Then the people, wroth at the danger of their beloved seer, uttered a wild yell, and gathered round him with brandished swords, facing their chieftains and their king. But at that instant, ere the war had broken forth among the tribe, the three warriors returned, and they bore Darvan on their shoulders, and laid him at the feet of the king, and they said tremblingly, "Thus found we the elder in the centre of his own hall." And the people saw that Darvan was a corpse, and that the prediction of Morven was thus verified. "So perish the enemies of Morven and the stars!" cried the son of Osslah. And the people echoed the cry. Then the fury of Siror was at its height, and waving his sword above his head he plunged into the crowd, "Thy blood, baseborn, or mine!"

"So be it!" answered Morven, quailing not. "People, smite the blasphemer! Hark how the river pours down upon your children and your hearths! On, on, or ye perish!"

And Siror fell, pierced by five hundred spears.

"Smite! smite!" cried Morven, as the chiefs of the royal house gathered round the king. And the clash of swords, and the gleam of spears, and the cries of the dying, and the yell of the trampling people mingled with the roar of the elements, and the voices of the rushing wave.

Three hundred of the chiefs perished that night by the swords of their own tribe; and the last cry of the victors was, "Morven the prophet! *Morven the king!*"

And the son of Osslah, seeing the waves now spreading over the valley, led Orna his wife, and the men of Oestrich, their women, and their children, to a high mount, where they waited the dawning sun. But Orna sat apart and wept bitterly, for her brothers were no more, and her race had perished from the earth. And Morven sought to comfort her in vain.

When the morning rose, they saw that the river had overspread the greater part of the city, and now stayed its course among the hollows of the vale. Then Morven said to the people, "The star-kings are avenged, and their wrath appeased. Tarry only here until the waters have melted into the crevices of the soil." And on the fourth day they returned to the city, and no man dared to name another, save Morven, as the king.

But Morven retired into his cave and mused deeply; and then assembling the people, he gave them new laws; and he

made them build a mighty temple in honour of the stars, and
made them heap within it all that the tribe held most precious. And he took unto him fifty children from the most
famous of the tribe; and he took also ten from among the
men who had served him best, and he ordained that they
should serve the stars in the great temple: and Morven was
their chief. And he put away the crown they pressed upon
him, and he chose from among the elders a new king. And
he ordained that henceforth the servants only of the stars in
the great temple should elect the king and the rulers, and
hold council, and proclaim war; but he suffered the king to
feast, and to hunt, and to make merry in the banquet-halls.
And Morven built altars in the temple, and was the first who,
in the North, sacrificed the beast and the bird, and afterwards
human flesh, upon the altars. And he drew auguries from the
entrails of the victim, and made schools for the science of the
prophet; and Morven's piety was the wonder of the tribe,—
in that he refused to be a king. And Morven the high priest
was ten thousand times mightier than the king. He taught
the people to till the ground and to sow the herb; and by his
wisdom, and the valour that his prophecies instilled into
men, he conquered all the neighbouring tribes. And the sons
of Oestrich spread themselves over a mighty empire, and with
them spread the name and the laws of Morven. And in every
province which he conquered, he ordered them to build a temple to the stars.

But a heavy sorrow fell upon the fears of Morven. The
sister of Siror bowed down her head, and survived not long
the slaughter of her race. And she left Morven childless.
And he mourned bitterly and as one distraught, for her only
in the world had his heart the power to love. And he sat
down and covered his face, saying:—

"Lo! I have toiled and travailed; and never before in the
world did man conquer what I have conquered. Verily the
empire of the iron thews and the giant limbs is no more! I
have founded a new power, that henceforth shall sway the
lands,—the empire of a plotting brain and a commanding
mind. But, behold! my fate is barren, and I feel already

that it will grow neither fruit nor tree as a shelter to mine old age. Desolate and lonely shall I pass unto my grave. O Orna! my beautiful! my loved! none were like unto thee, and to thy love do I owe my glory and my life! Would for thy sake, O sweet bird! that nestled in the dark cavern of my heart,— would for thy sake that thy brethren had been spared, for verily with my life would I have purchased thine. Alas! only when I lost thee did I find that thy love was dearer to me than the fear of others!" And Morven mourned night and day, and none might comfort him.

But from that time forth he gave himself solely up to the cares of his calling; and his nature and his affections, and whatever there was yet left soft in him, grew hard like stone; and he was a man without love, and he forbade love and marriage to the priest.

Now, in his latter years, there arose *other* prophets; for the world had grown wiser even by Morven's wisdom, and some did say unto themselves, "Behold Morven, the herdsman's son, is a king of kings: this did the stars for their servant; shall we not also be servants to the star?"

And they wore black garments like Morven, and went about prophesying of what the stars foretold them. And Morven was exceeding wroth; for he, more than other men, knew that the prophets lied. Wherefore he went forth against them with the ministers of the temple, and he took them, and burned them by a slow fire; for thus said Morven to the people: "A true prophet hath honour, but *I* only am a true prophet; to all false prophets there shall be surely death."

And the people applauded the piety of the son of Osslah.

And Morven educated the wisest of the children in the mysteries of the temple, so that they grew up to succeed him worthily.

And he died full of years and honour; and they carved his effigy on a mighty stone before the temple, and the effigy endured for a thousand ages, and whoso looked on it trembled; for the face was calm with the calmness of unspeakable awe!

And Morven was the first mortal of the North that made Religion the stepping-stone to Power. Of a surety Morven was a great man!

It was the last night of the old year, and the stars sat, each upon his ruby throne, and watched with sleepless eyes upon the world. The night was dark and troubled, the dread winds were abroad, and fast and frequent hurried the clouds beneath the thrones of the kings of night. And ever and anon fiery meteors flashed along the depths of heaven, and were again swallowed up in the grave of darkness. But far below his brethren, and with a lurid haze around his orb, sat the discontented star that had watched over the hunters of the North.

And on the lowest abyss of space there was spread a thick and mighty gloom, from which, as from a caldron, rose columns of wreathing smoke; and still, when the great winds rested for an instant on their paths, voices of woe and laughter, mingled with shrieks, were heard booming from the abyss to the upper air.

And now, in the middest night, a vast figure rose slowly from the abyss, and its wings threw blackness over the world. High upward to the throne of the discontented star sailed the fearful shape, and the star trembled on his throne when the form stood before him face to face.

And the shape said, "Hail, brother! all hail!"

"I know thee not," answered the star; "thou art not the archangel that visitest the kings of night."

And the shape laughed loud. "I am the fallen star of the morning! I am Lucifer, thy brother! Hast thou not, O sullen king, served me and mine; and hast thou not wrested the earth from thy Lord who sittest above, and given it to me, by darkening the souls of men with the religion of fear? Wherefore come, brother, come; thou hast a throne prepared beside my own in the fiery gloom. Come! The heavens are no more for thee!"

Then the star rose from his throne, and descended to the side of Lucifer; for ever hath the spirit of discontent had sympathy with the soul of pride. And they sank slowly down to the gulf of gloom.

It was the first night of the new year, and the stars sat each on his ruby throne, and watched with sleepless eyes upon the world. But sorrow dimmed the bright faces of the kings of night, for they mourned in silence and in fear for a fallen brother.

And the gates of the heaven of heavens flew open with a golden sound, and the swift archangel fled down on his silent wings; and the archangel gave to each of the stars, as before, the message of his Lord, and to each star was his appointed charge. And when the heraldry seemed done there came a laugh from the abyss of gloom, and half-way from the gulf rose the lurid shape of Lucifer the fiend!

"Thou countest thy flock ill, O radiant shepherd! Behold! one star is missing from the three thousand and ten!"

"Back to thy gulf, false Lucifer! — the throne of thy brother hath been filled."

And, lo! as the archangel spake, the stars beheld a young and all-lustrous stranger on the throne of the erring star; and his face was so soft to look upon that the dimmest of human eyes might have gazed upon its splendour unabashed: but the dark fiend alone was dazzled by its lustre, and, with a yell that shook the flaming pillars of the universe, he plunged backward into the gloom.

Then, far and sweet from the arch unseen, came forth the voice of God, —

"Behold! on the throne of the discontented star sits the star of Hope; and he that breathed into mankind the religion of Fear hath a successor in him who shall teach earth the religion of Love!"

And evermore the star of Fear dwells with Lucifer, and the star of Love keeps vigil in heaven!

CHAPTER XX.

GLENHAUSEN. — THE POWER OF LOVE IN SANCTIFIED PLACES.
— A PORTRAIT OF FREDERICK BARBAROSSA. — THE AMBI-
TION OF MEN FINDS NO ADEQUATE SYMPATHY IN WOMEN.

"You made me tremble for you more than once," said Gertrude to the student; "I feared you were about to touch upon
ground really sacred, but your end redeemed all."

"The false religion always tries to counterfeit the garb, the
language, the aspect of the true," answered the German; "for
that reason, I purposely suffered my tale to occasion that very
fear and anxiety you speak of, conscious that the most scrupu-
lous would be contented when the whole was finished."

This German was one of a new school, of which England
as yet knows nothing. We shall see hereafter what it will
produce.

The student left them at Friedberg, and our travellers proceeded to Glenhausen,—a spot interesting to lovers; for here
Frederick the First was won by the beauty of Gela, and, in
the midst of an island vale, he built the Imperial Palace, in
honour of the lady of his love. This spot is, indeed, well
chosen of itself; the mountains of the Rhinegebürg close it in
with the green gloom of woods and the glancing waters of the
Kinz.

"Still, wherever we go," said Trevylyan, "we find all tradition is connected with love; and history, for that reason,
hallows less than romance."

"It is singular," said Vane, moralizing, "that love makes
but a small part of our actual lives, but is yet the master-key
to our sympathies. The hardest of us, who laugh at the passion when they see it palpably before them, are arrested by
some dim tradition of its existence in the past. It is as if
life had few opportunities of bringing out certain qualities

within us, so that they always remain untold and dormant, susceptible to thought, but deaf to action."

"You refine and mystify too much," said Trevylyan, smiling; "none of us have any faculty, any passion, uncalled forth, if we have *really* loved, though but for a day."

Gertrude smiled, and drawing her arm within his, Trevylyan left Vane to philosophize on passion, — a fit occupation for one who had never felt it.

"Here let us pause," said Trevylyan, afterwards, as they visited the remains of the ancient palace, and the sun glittered on the scene, "to recall the old chivalric day of the gallant Barbarossa; let us suppose him commencing the last great action of his life; let us picture him as setting out for the Holy Land. Imagine him issuing from those walls on his white charger, — his fiery eye somewhat dimmed by years, and his hair blanched; but nobler from the impress of time itself, — the clang of arms; the tramp of steeds; banners on high; music pealing from hill to hill; the red cross and the nodding plume; the sun, as now glancing on yonder trees; and thence reflected from the burnished arms of the Crusaders. But, Gela — "

"Ah," said Gertrude, "*she* must be no more; for she would have outlived her beauty, and have found that glory had now no rival in his breast. Glory consoles men for the death of the loved; but glory is infidelity to the living."

"Nay, not so, dearest Gertrude," said Trevylyan, quickly; "for my darling dream of Fame is the hope of laying its honours at your feet! And if ever, in future years, I should rise above the herd, I should only ask if *your* step were proud and *your* heart elated."

"I was wrong," said Gertrude, with tears in her eyes; "and for your sake I can be ambitious."

Perhaps there, too, she was mistaken; for one of the common disappointments of the heart is, that women have so rarely a sympathy in our better and higher aspirings. Their ambition is not for great things; they cannot understand that desire "which scorns delight, and loves laborious days." If they love us, they usually exact too much. They are jealous

of the ambition to which we sacrifice so largely, and which divides us from them; and they leave the stern passion of great minds to the only solitude which affection cannot share. To aspire is to be alone!

CHAPTER XXI.

VIEW OF EHRENBREITSTEIN. — A NEW ALARM IN GERTRUDE'S HEALTH. — TRARBACH.

ANOTHER time our travellers proceeded from Coblentz to Treves, following the course of the Moselle. They stopped on the opposite bank below the bridge that unites Coblentz with the Petersberg, to linger over the superb view of Ehrenbreitstein which you may there behold.

It was one of those calm noonday scenes which impress upon us their own bright and voluptuous tranquillity. There stood the old herdsman leaning on his staff, and the quiet cattle knee-deep in the gliding waters. Never did stream more smooth and sheen than was at that hour the surface of the Moselle mirror the images of the pastoral life. Beyond, the darker shadows of the bridge and of the walls of Coblentz fell deep over the waves, checkered by the tall sails of the craft that were moored around the harbour. But clear against the sun rose the spires and roofs of Coblentz, backed by many a hill sloping away to the horizon. High, dark, and massive, on the opposite bank, swelled the towers and rock of Ehrenbreitstein,— a type of that great chivalric spirit — the HONOUR that the rock arrogates for its name — which demands so many sacrifices of blood and tears, but which ever creates in the restless heart of man a far deeper interest than the more peaceful scenes of life by which it is contrasted. There, still — from the calm waters, and the abodes of common toil and ordinary pleasure — turns the aspiring mind! Still as we gaze on that lofty and immemorial rock we recall the famine and the siege; and own that the more daring crimes of men have a strange privilege in hallowing the very spot which they devastate.

Below, in green curves and mimic bays covered with herbage, the gradual banks mingled with the water; and just where the bridge closed, a solitary group of trees, standing dark in the thickest shadow, gave that melancholy feature to the scene which resembles the one dark thought that often forces itself into our sunniest hours. Their boughs stirred not; no voice of birds broke the stillness of their gloomy verdure: the eye turned from them, as from the sad moral that belongs to existence.

In proceeding to Trarbach, Gertrude was seized with another of those fainting fits which had so terrified Trevylyan before; they stopped an hour or two at a little village, but Gertrude rallied with such apparent rapidity, and so strongly insisted on proceeding, that they reluctantly continued their way. This event would have thrown a gloom over their journey, if Gertrude had not exerted herself to dispel the impression she had occasioned; and so light, so cheerful, were her spirits, that for the time at least she succeeded.

They arrived at Trarbach late at noon. This now small and humble town is said to have been the Thronus Bacchi of the ancients. From the spot where the travellers halted to take, as it were, their impression of the town, they saw before them the little hostelry, a poor pretender to the Thronus Bacchi, with the rude sign of the Holy Mother over the door. The peaked roof, the sunk window, the gray walls, checkered with the rude beams of wood so common to the meaner houses on the Continent, bore something of a melancholy and prepossessing aspect. Right above, with its Gothic windows and venerable spire, rose the church of the town; and, crowning the summit of a green and almost perpendicular mountain, scowled the remains of one of those mighty castles which make the never-failing frown on a German landscape.

The scene was one of quiet and of gloom: the exceeding serenity of the day contrasted, with an almost unpleasing brightness, the poverty of the town, the thinness of the population, and the dreary grandeur of the ruins that overhung the capital of the perished race of the bold Counts of Spanheim.

They passed the night at Trarbach, and continued their journey next day. At Treves, Gertrude was for some days seriously ill; and when they returned to Coblentz, her disease had evidently received a rapid and alarming increase.

CHAPTER XXII.

THE DOUBLE LIFE. — TREVYLYAN'S FATE. — SORROW THE PARENT OF FAME. — NIEDERLAHNSTEIN. — DREAMS.

THERE are two lives to each of us, gliding on at the same time, scarcely connected with each other,— the life of our actions, the life of our minds; the external and the inward history; the movements of the frame, the deep and ever-restless workings of the heart! They who have loved know that there is a diary of the affections, which we might keep for years without having occasion even to touch upon the exterior surface of life, our busy occupations, the mechanical progress of our existence; yet by the last are we judged, the first is never known. History reveals men's deeds, men's outward character, but *not themselves.* There is a secret self that hath its own life "rounded by a dream," unpenetrated, unguessed. What passed within Trevylyan, hour after hour, as he watched over the declining health of the only being in the world whom his proud heart had been ever destined to love? His real record of the time was marked by every cloud upon Gertrude's brow, every smile of her countenance, every — the faintest — alteration in her disease; yet, to the outward seeming, all this vast current of varying eventful emotion lay dark and unconjectured. He filled up with wonted regularity the colourings of existence, and smiled and moved as other men. For still, in the heroism with which devotion conquers self, he sought only to cheer and gladden the young heart on which he had embarked his all; and he kept the dark tempest of his anguish for the solitude of night.

That was a peculiar doom which Fate had reserved for him; and casting him, in after years, on the great sea of public strife, it seemed as if she were resolved to tear from his heart all yearnings for the land. For him there was to be no green or sequestered spot in the valley of household peace. His bark was to know no haven, and his soul not even the desire of rest. For action is that Lethe in which alone we forget our former dreams, and the mind that, too stern not to wrestle with its emotions, seeks to conquer regret, must leave itself no leisure to look behind. Who knows what benefits to the world may have sprung from the sorrows of the benefactor? As the harvest that gladdens mankind in the suns of autumn was called forth by the rains of spring, so the griefs of youth may make the fame of maturity.

Gertrude, charmed by the beauties of the river, desired to continue the voyage to Mayence. The rich Trevylyan persuaded the physician who had attended her to accompany them, and they once more pursued their way along the banks of the feudal Rhine. For what the Tiber is to the classic, the Rhine is to the chivalric age. The steep rock and the gray dismantled tower, the massive and rude picturesque of the feudal days, constitute the great features of the scene; and you might almost fancy, as you glide along, that you are sailing back adown the river of Time, and the monuments of the pomp and power of old, rising, one after one, upon its shores!

Vane and Du——e, the physician, at the farther end of the vessel, conversed upon stones and strata, in that singular pedantry of science which strips nature to a skeleton, and prowls among the dead bones of the world, unconscious of its living beauty.

They left Gertrude and Trevylyan to themselves; and, "bending o'er the vessel's laving side," they indulged in silence the melancholy with which each was imbued. For Gertrude began to waken, though doubtingly and at intervals, to a sense of the short span that was granted to her life; and over the loveliness around her there floated that sad and ineffable interest which springs from the presentiment of our own death. They passed the rich island of Oberwerth, and Hochheim, famous for its ruby grape, and saw, from his mountain bed, the Lahn bear his tribute of fruits and corn into the treasury of the Rhine. Proudly rose the tower of Niederlahnstein, and deeply lay its shadow along the stream. It was late noon; the cattle had sought the shade from the slanting sun, and, far beyond, the holy castle of Marksburg raised its battlements above mountains covered with the vine. On the water two boats had been drawn alongside each other; and from one, now moving to the land, the splash of oars broke the general stillness of the tide. Fast by an old tower the fishermen were busied in their craft, but the sound of their voices did not reach the ear. It was life, but a silent life, suited to the tranquillity of noon.

"There is something in travel," said Gertrude, "which constantly, even amidst the most retired spots, impresses us with the exuberance of life. We come to those quiet nooks and find a race whose existence we never dreamed of. In their humble path they know the same passions and tread the same career as ourselves. The mountains shut them out from the great world, but their village is a world in itself. And they know and heed no more of the turbulent scenes of remote cities than our own planet of the inhabitants of the distant stars. What then is death, but the forgetfulness of some few hearts added to the general unconsciousness of our existence that pervades the universe? The bubble breaks in the vast desert of the air without a sound."

"Why talk of death?" said Trevylyan, with a writhing smile. "These sunny scenes should not call forth such melancholy images."

"Melancholy," repeated Gertrude, mechanically. "Yes, death is indeed melancholy when we are loved!"

They stayed a short time at Niederlahnstein, for Vane was anxious to examine the minerals that the Lahn brings into the Rhine; and the sun was waning towards its close as they renewed their voyage. As they sailed slowly on, Gertrude said, "How like a dream is this sentiment of existence, when, without labour or motion, every change of scene is brought before us; and if I am with you, dearest, I do not feel it less resembling a dream, for I have dreamed of you lately more than ever; and dreams have become a part of my life itself."

"Speaking of dreams," said Trevylyan, as they pursued that mysterious subject, "I once during my former residence in Germany fell in with a singular enthusiast, who had taught himself what he termed 'A System of Dreaming.' When he first spoke to me upon it I asked him to explain what he meant, which he did somewhat in the following words."

CHAPTER XXIII.

THE LIFE OF DREAMS.

"I was born," said he, "with many of the sentiments of the poet, but without the language to express them; my feelings were constantly chilled by the intercourse of the actual world. My family, mere Germans, dull and unimpassioned, had nothing in common with me; nor did I out of my family find those with whom I could better sympathize. I was revolted by friendships,— for they were susceptible to every change; I was disappointed in love,— for the truth never approached to my ideal. Nursed early in the lap of Romance, enamoured of the wild and the adventurous, the commonplaces of life were to me inexpressibly tame and joyless. And yet indolence, which belongs to the poetical character, was more inviting than that eager and uncontemplative action which can alone wring enterprise from life. Meditation was my natural element. I loved to spend the noon reclined by some shady stream, and in a half sleep to shape images from the glancing sunbeams. A dim and unreal order of philosophy, that belongs to our nation, was my favourite intellectual pursuit; and I sought amongst the Obscure and the Recondite the variety and emotion I could not find in the Familiar.

Thus constantly watching the operations of the inner mind, it occurred to me at last that sleep having its own world, but as yet a rude and fragmentary one, it might be possible to shape from its chaos all those combinations of beauty, of power, of glory, and of love, which were denied to me in the world in which my frame walked and had its being. So soon as this idea came upon me, I nursed and cherished and mused over it, till I found that the imagination began to effect the miracle I desired. By brooding ardently, intensely, before I retired to rest, over any especial train of thought, over any ideal creations; by keeping the body utterly still and quiescent during the whole day; by shutting out all living adventure, the memory of which might perplex and interfere with the stream of events that I desired to pour forth into the wilds of sleep, I discovered at last that I could lead in dreams a life solely their own, and utterly distinct from the life of day. Towers and palaces, all my heritage and seigneury, rose before me from the depths of night; I quaffed from jewelled cups the Falernian of imperial vaults; music from harps of celestial tone filled up the crevices of air; and the smiles of immortal beauty flushed like sunlight over all. Thus the adventure and the glory that I could not for my waking life obtain, was obtained for me in sleep. I wandered with the gryphon and the gnome; I sounded the horn at enchanted portals; I conquered in the knightly lists; I planted my standard over battlements huge as the painter's birth of Babylon itself.

"But I was afraid to call forth one shape on whose loveliness to pour all the hidden passion of my soul. I trembled lest my sleep should present me some image which it could never restore, and, waking from which, even the new world I had created might be left desolate forever. I shuddered lest I should adore a vision which the first ray of morning could smite to the grave.

"In this train of mind I began to wonder whether it might not be possible to connect dreams together; to supply the thread that was wanting; to make one night continue the history of the other, so as to bring together the same shapes and the same

scenes, and thus lead a connected and harmonious life, not
only in the one half of existence, but in the other, the richer
and more glorious half.   No sooner did this idea present itself to me, than I burned to accomplish it.   I had before
taught myself that Faith is the great creator; that to believe
fervently is to make belief true.   So I would not suffer my
mind to doubt the practicability of its scheme.   I shut myself
up then entirely by day, refused books, and hated the very
sun, and compelled all my thoughts (and sleep is the mirror
of thought) to glide in one direction,— the direction of my
dreams,— so that from night to night the imagination might
keep up the thread of action, and I might thus lie down full
of the past dream and confident of the sequel.   Not for one
day only, or for one month, did I pursue this system, but I
continued it zealously and sternly till at length it began to
succeed.   Who shall tell," cried the enthusiast,— I see him
now with his deep, bright, sunken eyes, and his wild hair
thrown backward from his brow,— "the rapture I experienced, when first, faintly and half distinct, I perceived the
harmony I had invoked dawn upon my dreams?   At first there
was only a partial and desultory connection between them;
my eye recognized certain shapes, my ear certain tones common to each; by degrees these augmented in number, and
were more defined in outline.   At length one fair face broke
forth from among the ruder forms, and night after night appeared mixing with them for a moment and then vanishing,
just as the mariner watches, in a clouded sky, the moon shining through the drifting rack, and quickly gone.   My curiosity was now vividly excited; the face, with its lustrous
eyes and seraph features, roused all the emotions that no living shape had called forth.   I became enamoured of a dream,
and as the statue to the Cyprian was my creation to me; so
from this intent and unceasing passion I at length worked out
my reward.   My dream became more palpable; I spoke with
it; I knelt to it; my lips were pressed to its own; we exchanged the vows of love, and morning only separated us with
the certainty that at night we should meet again.   Thus then,"
continued my visionary, "I commenced a history utterly sepa-

rate from the history of the world, and it went on alternately with my harsh and chilling history of the day, equally regular and equally continuous. And what, you ask, was that history? Methought I was a prince in some Eastern island that had no features in common with the colder north of my native home. By day I looked upon the dull walls of a German town, and saw homely or squalid forms passing before me; the sky was dim and the sun cheerless. Night came on with her thousand stars, and brought me the dews of sleep. Then suddenly there was a new world; the richest fruits hung from the trees in clusters of gold and purple. Palaces of the quaint fashion of the sunnier climes, with spiral minarets and glittering cupolas, were mirrored upon vast lakes sheltered by the palm-tree and banana. The sun seemed a different orb, so mellow and gorgeous were his beams; birds and winged things of all hues fluttered in the shining air; the faces and garments of men were not of the northern regions of the world, and their voices spoke a tongue which, strange at first, by degrees I interpreted. Sometimes I made war upon neighbouring kings; sometimes I chased the spotted pard through the vast gloom of immemorial forests; my life was at once a life of enterprise and pomp. But above all there was the history of my love! I thought there were a thousand difficulties in the way of attaining its possession. Many were the rocks I had to scale, and the battles to wage, and the fortresses to storm, in order to win her as my bride. But at last" (continued the enthusiast), "she *is* won, she is my own! Time in that wild world, which I visit nightly, passes not so slowly as in this, and yet an hour may be the same as a year. This continuity of existence, this successive series of dreams, so different from the broken incoherence of other men's sleep, at times bewilders me with strange and suspicious thoughts. What if this glorious sleep be a real life, and this dull waking the true repose? Why not? What is there more faithful in the one than in the other? And there have I garnered and collected all of pleasure that I am capable of feeling. I seek no joy in this world; I form no ties, I feast not, nor love, nor make merry; I am only impatient till the hour when I may re-enter my royal realms and pour my renewed delight into the bosom of my bright Ideal. There then have I found all that the world denied me; there have I realized the yearning and the aspiration within me; there have I coined the untold poetry into the Felt, the Seen!"

I found, continued Trevylyan, that this tale was corroborated by inquiry into the visionary's habits. He shunned society; avoided all unnecessary movement or excitement. He fared with rigid abstemiousness, and only appeared to feel pleasure as the day departed, and the hour of return to his imaginary kingdom approached. He always retired to rest punctually at a certain hour, and would sleep so soundly that a cannon fired under his window would not arouse him. He never, which may seem singular, spoke or moved much in his sleep, but was peculiarly calm, almost to the appearance of lifelessness; but, discovering once that he had been watched in sleep, he was wont afterwards carefully to secure the chamber from intrusion. His victory over the natural incoherence of sleep had, when I first knew him, lasted for some years; possibly what imagination first produced was afterwards continued by habit.

I saw him again a few months subsequent to this confession, and he seemed to me much changed. His health was broken, and his abstraction had deepened into gloom.

I questioned him of the cause of the alteration, and he answered me with great reluctance,—

"She is dead," said he; "my realms are desolate! A serpent stung her, and she died in these very arms. Vainly, when I started from my sleep in horror and despair, vainly did I say to myself,—This is but a dream. I shall see her again. A vision cannot die! Hath it flesh that decays; is it not a spirit,—bodiless, indissoluble? With what terrible anxiety I awaited the night! Again I slept, and the DREAM lay again before me, dead and withered. Even the ideal can vanish. I assisted in the burial; I laid her in the earth; I heaped the monumental mockery over her form. And never since hath she, or aught like her, revisited my dreams. I see her only when I wake; thus to wake is indeed to dream!

But," continued the visionary in a solemn voice, "I feel myself departing from this world, and with a fearful joy; for I think there may be a land beyond even the land of sleep where I shall see her again,— a land in which a vision itself may be restored."

And in truth, concluded Trevylyan, the dreamer died shortly afterwards, suddenly, and in his sleep. And never before, perhaps, had Fate so literally made of a living man (with his passions and his powers, his ambition and his love) the plaything and puppet of a dream!

"Ah," said Vane, who had heard the latter part of Trevylyan's story, "could the German have bequeathed to us his secret, what a refuge should we possess from the ills of earth! The dungeon and disease, poverty, affliction, shame, would cease to be the tyrants of our lot; and to Sleep we should confine our history and transfer our emotions."

"Gertrude," whispered the lover, "what his kingdom and his bride were to the Dreamer art thou to me!"

———◆———

CHAPTER XXIV.

THE BROTHERS.

THE banks of the Rhine now shelved away into sweeping plains, and on their right rose the once imperial city of Boppart. In no journey of similar length do you meet with such striking instances of the mutability and shifts of power. To find, as in the Memphian Egypt, a city sunk into a heap of desolate ruins; the hum, the roar, the mart of nations, hushed into the silence of ancestral tombs, is less humbling to our human vanity than to mark, as along the Rhine, the kingly city dwindled into the humble town or the dreary village,— decay without its grandeur, change without the awe of its solitude! On the site on which Drusus raised his Roman tower, and the kings of the Franks their palaces, trade now dribbles in tobacco-pipes, and transforms into an excellent cotton factory the antique nunnery of Königsberg! So be it; it is the progressive order of things,— the world itself will soon be one excellent cotton factory!

"Look," said Trevylyan, as they sailed on, "at yonder mountain, with its two traditionary Castles of Liebenstein and Sternfels."

Massive and huge the ruins swelled above the green rock, at the foot of which lay, in happier security from time and change, the clustered cottages of the peasant, with a single spire rising above the quiet village.

"Is there not, Albert, a celebrated legend attached to those castles?" said Gertrude. "I think I remember to have heard their names in connection with your profession of taleteller."

"Yes," said Trevylyan, "the story relates to the last lords of those shattered towers, and — "

"You will sit here, nearer to me, and begin," interrupted Gertrude, in her tone of childlike command. "Come."

THE BROTHERS.

A TALE.[1]

You must imagine then, dear Gertrude (said Trevylyan), a beautiful summer day, and by the same faculty that none possess so richly as yourself, for it is you who can kindle something of that divine spark even in me, you must rebuild those shattered towers in the pomp of old; raise the gallery and the hall; man the battlements with warders, and give the proud banners of ancestral chivalry to wave upon the walls. But above, sloping half down the rock, you must fancy the hanging gardens of Liebenstein, fragrant with flowers, and basking in the noonday sun.

On the greenest turf, underneath an oak, there sat three persons, in the bloom of youth. Two of the three were brothers; the third was an orphan girl, whom the lord of the opposite tower of Sternfels had bequeathed to the protection

---

[1] This tale is, in reality, founded on the beautiful tradition which belongs to Liebenstein and Sternfels.

of his brother, the chief of Liebenstein. The castle itself and the demesne that belonged to it passed away from the female line, and became the heritage of Otho, the orphan's cousin, and the younger of the two brothers now seated on the turf.

"And oh," said the elder, whose name was Warbeck, "you have twined a chaplet for my brother; have you not, dearest Leoline, a simple flower for me?"

The beautiful orphan (for beautiful she was, Gertrude, as the heroine of the tale you bid me tell ought to be,— should she not have to the dreams of my fancy your lustrous hair, and your sweet smile, and your eyes of blue, that are never, never silent? Ah, pardon me, that in a former tale, I denied the heroine the beauty of your face, and remember that to atone for it, I endowed her with the beauty of your mind) — the beautiful orphan blushed to her temples, and culling from the flowers in her lap the freshest of the roses, began weaving them into a wreath for Warbeck.

"It would be better," said the gay Otho, "to make my sober brother a chaplet of the rue and cypress; the rose is much too bright a flower for so serious a knight."

Leoline held up her hand reprovingly.

"Let him laugh, dearest cousin," said Warbeck, gazing passionately on her changing cheek; "and thou, Leoline, believe that the silent stream runs the deepest."

At this moment, they heard the voice of the old chief, their father, calling aloud for Leoline; for ever when he returned from the chase he wanted her gentle presence; and the hall was solitary to him if the light sound of her step and the music of her voice were not heard in welcome.

Leoline hastened to her guardian, and the brothers were left alone.

Nothing could be more dissimilar than the features and the respective characters of Otho and Warbeck. Otho's countenance was flushed with the brown hues of health; his eyes were of the brightest hazel: his dark hair wreathed in short curls round his open and fearless brow; the jest ever echoed on his lips, and his step was bounding as the foot of the hunter of the Alps. Bold and light was his spirit; if at times he betrayed the haughty insolence of youth, he felt generously, and though not ever ready to confess sorrow for a fault, he was at least ready to brave peril for a friend.

But Warbeck's frame, though of equal strength, was more slender in its proportions than that of his brother; the fair long hair that characterized his northern race hung on either side of a countenance calm and pale, and deeply impressed with thought, even to sadness. His features, more majestic and regular than Otho's, rarely varied in their expression. More resolute even than Otho, he was less impetuous; more impassioned, he was also less capricious.

The brothers remained silent after Leoline had left them. Otho carelessly braced on his sword, that he had laid aside on the grass; but Warbeck gathered up the flowers that had been touched by the soft hand of Leoline, and placed them in his bosom.

The action disturbed Otho; he bit his lip, and changed colour; at length he said, with a forced laugh,—

"It must be confessed, brother, that you carry your affection for our fair cousin to a degree that even relationship seems scarcely to warrant."

"It is true," said Warbeck, calmly; "I love her with a love surpassing that of blood."

"How!" said Otho, fiercely: "do you dare to think of Leoline as a bride?"

"Dare!" repeated Warbeck, turning yet paler than his wonted hue.

"Yes, I have said the word! Know, Warbeck, that I, too, love Leoline; I, too, claim her as my bride; and never, while I can wield a sword, never, while I wear the spurs of knighthood, will I render my claim to a living rival,—even," he added, sinking his voice, "though that rival be my brother!"

Warbeck answered not; his very soul seemed stunned; he gazed long and wistfully on his brother, and then, turning his face away, ascended the rock without uttering a single word.

This silence startled Otho. Accustomed to vent every emotion of his own, he could not comprehend the forbearance of his brother; he knew his high and brave nature too well to imagine that it arose from fear. Might it not be contempt, or might he not, at this moment, intend to seek their father; and, the first to proclaim his love for the orphan, advance, also, the privilege of the elder born? As these suspicions flashed across him, the haughty Otho strode to his brother's side, and laying his hand on his arm, said,—

"Whither goest thou; and dost thou consent to surrender Leoline?"

"Does she love thee, Otho?" answered Warbeck, breaking silence at last; and his voice spoke so deep an anguish, that it arrested the passions of Otho even at their height.

"It is thou who art now silent," continued Warbeck; "speak. Doth she love thee, and has her lip confessed it?"

"I have believed that she loved me," faltered Otho; "but she is of maiden bearing, and her lip, at least, has never told it."

"Enough," said Warbeck; "release your hold."

"Stay," said Otho, his suspicions returning; "stay,—yet one word; dost thou seek my father? He ever honoured thee more than me: wilt thou own to him thy love, and insist on thy right of birth? By my soul and my hope of heaven, do it, and one of us two must fall!"

"Poor boy!" answered Warbeck, bitterly; "how little thou canst read the heart of one who loves truly! Thinkest thou I would wed her if she loved thee? Thinkest thou I could, even to be blessed myself, give her one moment's pain? Out on the thought! away!"

"Then wilt not thou seek our father?" said Otho, abashed.

"Our father! — has our father the keeping of Leoline's affection?" answered Warbeck; and shaking off his brother's grasp, he sought the way to the castle.

As he entered the hall, he heard the voice of Leoline; she was singing to the old chief one of the simple ballads of the time that the warrior and the hunter loved to hear. He paused lest he should break the spell (a spell stronger than a sorcerer's to him), and gazing upon Leoline's beautiful form, his heart sank within him. His brother and himself had each that day, as they sat in the gardens, given her a flower;

his flower was the fresher and the rarer; his he saw not, but she wore his brother's in her bosom!

The chief, lulled by the music and wearied with the toils of the chase, sank into sleep as the song ended, and Warbeck, coming forward, motioned to Leoline to follow him. He passed into a retired and solitary walk, and when they were a little distance from the castle, Warbeck turned round, and taking Leoline's hand gently, said,—

"Let us rest here for one moment, dearest cousin; I have much on my heart to say to thee."

"And what is there," answered Leoline, as they sat on a mossy bank, with the broad Rhine glancing below, "what is there that my kind Warbeck would ask of me? Ah, would it might be some favour, something in poor Leoline's power to grant; for ever from my birth you have been to me most tender, most kind. You, I have often heard them say, taught my first steps to walk; you formed my infant lips into language, and, in after years, when my wild cousin was far away in the forests at the chase, you would brave his gay jest and remain at home, lest Leoline should be weary in the solitude. Ah, would I could repay you!"

Warbeck turned away his cheek; his heart was very full, and it was some moments before he summoned courage to reply.

"My fair cousin," said he, "those were happy days; but they were the days of childhood. New cares and new thoughts have now come on us; but I am still thy friend, Leoline, and still thou wilt confide in me thy young sorrows and thy young hopes, as thou ever didst. Wilt thou not, Leoline?"

"Canst thou ask me?" said Leoline; and Warbeck, gazing on her face, saw that though her eyes were full of tears, they yet looked steadily upon his; and he knew that she loved him only as a sister.

He sighed, and paused again ere he resumed. "Enough," said he; "now to my task. Once on a time, dear cousin, there lived among these mountains a certain chief who had two sons, and an orphan like thyself dwelt also in his halls. And the elder son — but no matter, let us not waste words on *him!* — the younger son, then, loved the orphan dearly, — more dearly than cousins love; and fearful of refusal, he prayed the elder one to urge his suit to the orphan. Leoline, my tale is done. Canst thou not love Otho as he loves thee?"

And now lifting his eyes to Leoline, he saw that she trembled violently, and her cheek was covered with blushes.

"Say," continued he, mastering himself, "is not that flower — his present — a token that he is chiefly in thy thoughts?"

"Ah, Warbeck! do not deem me ungrateful that I wear not yours also; but — "

"Hush!" said Warbeck, hastily; "I am but as thy brother; is not Otho more? He is young, brave, and beautiful. God grant that he may deserve thee, if thou givest him so rich a gift as thy affections!"

"I saw less of Otho in my childhood," said Leoline, evasively; "therefore, his kindness of late years seemed stranger to me than thine."

"And thou wilt not then reject him? Thou wilt be his bride?"

"And *thy* sister," answered Leoline.

"Bless thee, mine own dear cousin! one brother's kiss then, and farewell! Otho shall thank thee for himself."

He kissed her forehead calmly, and, turning away, plunged into the thicket; then, nor till then, he gave vent to such emotions as, had Leoline seen them, Otho's suit had been lost forever; for passionately, deeply as in her fond and innocent heart she loved Otho, the *happiness* of Warbeck was not less dear to her.

When the young knight had recovered his self-possession he went in search of Otho. He found him alone in the wood, leaning with folded arms against a tree, and gazing moodily on the ground. Warbeck's noble heart was touched at his brother's dejection.

"Cheer thee, Otho," said he; "I bring thee no bad tidings; I have seen Leoline, I have conversed with her — nay, start not, — she loves thee! she is thine!"

"Generous, generous Warbeck!" exclaimed Otho; and he

threw himself on his brother's neck. "No, no," said he, "this must not be; thou hast the elder claim,— I resign her to thee. Forgive me my waywardness, brother, forgive me!"

"Think of the past no more," said Warbeck; "the love of Leoline is an excuse for greater offences than thine. And now, be kind to her; her nature is soft and keen. *I* know her well; for *I* have studied her faintest wish. Thou art hasty and quick of ire; but remember that a word wounds where love is deep. For my sake, as for hers, think more of her happiness than thine own; now seek her,— she waits to hear from thy lips the tale that sounded cold upon mine."

With that he left his brother, and, once more re-entering the castle, he went into the hall of his ancestors. His father still slept; he put his hand on his gray hair, and blessed him; then stealing up to his chamber, he braced on his helm and armour, and thrice kissing the hilt of his sword, said, with a flushed cheek, —

"Henceforth be *thou* my bride!" Then passing from the castle, he sped by the most solitary paths down the rock, gained the Rhine, and hailing one of the numerous fishermen of the river, won the opposite shore; and alone, but not sad, for his high heart supported him, and Leoline at least was happy, he hastened to Frankfort.

The town was all gayety and life, arms clanged at every corner, the sounds of martial music, the wave of banners, the glittering of plumed casques, the neighing of war-steeds, all united to stir the blood and inflame the sense. Saint Bertrand had lifted the sacred cross along the shores of the Rhine, and the streets of Frankfort witnessed with what success!

On that same day Warbeck assumed the sacred badge, and was enlisted among the knights of the Emperor Conrad.

We must suppose some time to have elapsed, and Otho and Leoline were not yet wedded; for, in the first fervour of his gratitude to his brother, Otho had proclaimed to his father and to Leoline the conquest Warbeck had obtained over himself; and Leoline, touched to the heart, would not consent that the wedding should take place immediately. "Let him, at least," said she, "not be insulted by a premature festivity;

and give him time, amongst the lofty beauties he will gaze upon in a far country, to forget, Otho, that he once loved her who is the beloved of thee."

The old chief applauded this delicacy; and even Otho, in the first flush of his feelings towards his brother, did not venture to oppose it. They settled, then, that the marriage should take place at the end of a year.

Months rolled away, and an absent and moody gloom settled upon Otho's brow. In his excursions with his gay companions among the neighbouring towns, he heard of nothing but the glory of the Crusaders, of the homage paid to the heroes of the Cross at the courts they visited, of the adventures of their life, and the exciting spirit that animated their war. In fact, neither minstrel nor priest suffered the theme to grow cold; and the fame of those who had gone forth to the holy strife gave at once emulation and discontent to the youths who remained behind.

"And my brother enjoys this ardent and glorious life," said the impatient Otho; "while I, whose arm is as strong, and whose heart is as bold, languish here listening to the dull tales of a hoary sire and the silly songs of an orphan girl." His heart smote him at the last sentence, but he had already begun to weary of the gentle love of Leoline. Perhaps when he had no longer to gain a triumph over a rival the excitement palled; or perhaps his proud spirit secretly chafed at being conquered by his brother in generosity, even when outshining him in the success of love.

But poor Leoline, once taught that she was to consider Otho her betrothed, surrendered her heart entirely to his control. His wild spirit, his dark beauty, his daring valour, won while they awed her; and in the fitfulness of his nature were those perpetual springs of hope and fear that are the fountains of ever-agitated love. She saw with increasing grief the change that was growing over Otho's mind; nor did she divine the cause. "Surely I have not offended him?" thought she.

Among the companions of Otho was one who possessed a singular sway over him. He was a knight of that mysterious

Order of the Temple, which exercised at one time so great a command over the minds of men.

A severe and dangerous wound in a brawl with an English knight had confined the Templar at Frankfort, and prevented his joining the Crusade. During his slow recovery he had formed an intimacy with Otho, and, taking up his residence at the castle of Liebenstein, had been struck with the beauty of Leoline. Prevented by his oath from marriage, he allowed himself a double license in love, and doubted not, could he disengage the young knight from his betrothed, that she would add a new conquest to the many he had already achieved. Artfully therefore he painted to Otho the various attractions of the Holy Cause; and, above all, he failed not to describe, with glowing colours, the beauties who, in the gorgeous East, distinguished with a prodigal favour the warriors of the Cross. Dowries, unknown in the more sterile mountains of the Rhine, accompanied the hand of these beauteous maidens; and even a prince's daughter was not deemed, he said, too lofty a marriage for the heroes who might win kingdoms for themselves.

"To me," said the Templar, "such hopes are eternally denied. But you, were you not already betrothed, what fortunes might await you!"

By such discourses the ambition of Otho was perpetually aroused; they served to deepen his discontent at his present obscurity, and to convert to distaste the only solace it afforded in the innocence and affection of Leoline.

One night, a minstrel sought shelter from the storm in the halls of Liebenstein. His visit was welcomed by the chief, and he repaid the hospitality he had received by the exercise of his art. He sang of the chase, and the gaunt hound started from the hearth. He sang of love, and Otho, forgetting his restless dreams, approached to Leoline, and laid himself at her feet. Louder then and louder rose the strain. The minstrel sang of war; he painted the feats of the Crusaders; he plunged into the thickest of the battle; the steed neighed; the trump sounded; and you might have heard the ringing of the steel. But when he came to signalize the names of the boldest knights, high among the loftiest sounded the name of

Sir Warbeck of Liebenstein. Thrice had he saved the imperial banner; two chargers slain beneath him, he had covered their bodies with the fiercest of the foe.

Gentle in the tent and terrible in the fray, the minstrel should forget his craft ere the Rhine should forget its hero. The chief started from his seat. Leoline clasped the minstrel's hand.

"Speak,—you have seen him, he lives, he is honoured?"

"I myself am but just from Palestine, brave chief and noble maiden. I saw the gallant knight of Liebenstein at the right hand of the imperial Conrad. And he, ladye, was the only knight whom admiration shone upon without envy, its shadow. Who then," continued the minstrel, once more striking his harp, "who then would remain inglorious in the hall? Shall not the banners of his sires reproach him as they wave; and shall not every voice from Palestine strike shame into his soul?"

"Right!" cried Otho, suddenly, and flinging himself at the feet of his father. "Thou hearest what my brother has done, and thine aged eyes weep tears of joy. Shall *I* only dishonour thine old age with a rusted sword? No! grant me, like my brother, to go forth with the heroes of the Cross!"

"Noble youth," cried the harper, "therein speaks the soul of Sir Warbeck; hear him, sir knight,—hear the noble youth."

"Heaven cries aloud in his voice," said the Templar, solemnly.

"My son, I cannot chide thine ardour," said the old chief, raising him with trembling hands; "but Leoline, thy betrothed?"

Pale as a statue, with ears that doubted their sense as they drank in the cruel words of her lover, stood the orphan. She did not speak, she scarcely breathed; she sank into her seat, and gazed upon the ground, till, at the speech of the chief both maiden pride and maiden tenderness restored her consciousness, and she said,—

"*I*, uncle! Shall *I* bid Otho stay when his wishes bid him depart?"

"He will return to thee, noble ladye, covered with glory," said the harper: but Otho said no more. The touching voice of Leoline went to his soul; he resumed his seat in silence; and Leoline, going up to him, whispered gently, "Act as though I were not;" and left the hall to commune with her heart and to weep alone.

"I can wed her before I go," said Otho, suddenly, as he sat that night in the Templar's chamber.

"Why, that is true! and leave thy bride in the first week, — a hard trial!"

"Better than incur the chance of never calling her mine. Dear, kind, beloved Leoline!"

"Assuredly, she deserves all from thee; and, indeed, it is no small sacrifice, at thy years and with thy mien, to renounce forever all interest among the noble maidens thou wilt visit. Ah, from the galleries of Constantinople what eyes will look down on thee, and what ears, learning that thou art Otho the bridegroom, will turn away, caring for thee no more! A bridegroom without a bride! Nay, man, much as the Cross wants warriors, I am enough thy friend to tell thee, if thou weddest, to stay peaceably at home, and forget in the chase the labours of war, from which thou wouldst strip the ambition of love."

"I would I knew what were best," said Otho, irresolutely. "My brother — ha, shall he forever excel me? But Leoline, how will she grieve, — she who left him for me!"

"Was that thy fault?" said the Templar, gayly. "It may many times chance to thee again to be preferred to another. Troth, it is a sin under which the conscience may walk lightly enough. But sleep on it, Otho; my eyes grow heavy."

The next day Otho sought Leoline, and proposed to her that their wedding should precede his parting; but so embarrassed was he, so divided between two wishes, that Leoline, offended, hurt, stung by his coldness, refused the proposal at once. She left him lest he should see her weep, and then — then she repented even of her just pride!

But Otho, striving to appease his conscience with the belief that hers now was the *sole* fault, busied himself in preparations for his departure. Anxious to outshine his brother, he departed not as Warbeck, alone and unattended, but levying all the horse, men, and money that his domain of Sternfels — which he had not yet tenanted — would afford, he repaired to Frankfort at the head of a glittering troop.

The Templar, affecting a relapse, tarried behind, and promised to join him at that Constantinople of which he had so loudly boasted. Meanwhile he devoted his whole powers of pleasing to console the unhappy orphan. The force of her simple love was, however, stronger than all his arts. In vain he insinuated doubts of Otho,— she refused to hear them; in vain he poured with the softest accents into her ear the witchery of flattery and song,— she turned heedlessly away; and only pained by the courtesies that had so little resemblance to Otho, she shut herself up in her chamber, and pined in solitude for her forsaker.

The Templar now resolved to attempt darker arts to obtain power over her, when, fortunately, he was summoned suddenly away by a mission from the Grand Master of so high import, that it could not be resisted by a passion stronger in his breast than love,— the passion of ambition. He left the castle to its solitude; and Otho peopling it no more with his gay companions, no solitude *could* be more unfrequently disturbed.

Meanwhile, though, ever and anon, the fame of Warbeck reached their ears, it came unaccompanied with that of Otho, — of him they had no tidings; and thus the love of the tender orphan was kept alive by the perpetual restlessness of fear. At length the old chief died, and Leoline was left utterly alone.

One evening as she sat with her maidens in the hall, the ringing of a steed's hoofs was heard in the outer court; a horn sounded, the heavy gates were unbarred, and a knight of a stately mien and covered with the mantle of the Cross entered the hall. He stopped for one moment at the entrance, as if overpowered by his emotion; in the next he had clasped Leoline to his breast.

"Dost thou not recognize thy cousin Warbeck?" He doffed

his casque, and she saw that majestic brow which, unlike Otho's, had never changed or been clouded in its aspect to her.

"The war is suspended for the present," said he. "I learned my father's death, and I have returned home to hang up my banner in the hall and spend my days in peace."

Time and the life of camps had worked their change upon Warbeck's face; the fair hair, deepened in its shade, was worn from the temples, and disclosed one scar that rather aided the beauty of a countenance that had always something high and martial in its character; but the calm it had once worn had settled down into sadness; he conversed more rarely than before, and though he smiled not less often, nor less kindly, the smile had more of thought, and the kindness had forgot its passion. He had apparently conquered a love that was so early crossed, but not that fidelity of remembrance which made Leoline dearer to him than all others, and forbade him to replace the images he had graven upon his soul.

The orphan's lips trembled with the name of Otho, but a certain recollection stifled even her anxiety. Warbeck hastened to forestall her questions. Otho was well, he said, and sojourning at Constantinople; he had lingered there so long that the crusade had terminated without his aid: doubtless now he would speedily return,— a month, a week, nay, a day, might restore him to her side.

Leoline was inexpressibly consoled, yet something remained untold. Why, so eager for the strife of the sacred tomb, had he thus tarried at Constantinople? She wondered, she wearied conjecture, but she did not dare to search further.

The generous Warbeck concealed from her that Otho led a life of the most reckless and indolent dissipation,— wasting his wealth in the pleasures of the Greek court, and only occupying his ambition with the wild schemes of founding a principality in those foreign climes, which the enterprises of the Norman adventurers had rendered so alluring to the knightly bandits of the age.

The cousins resumed their old friendship, and Warbeck believed that it was friendship alone.

They walked again among the gardens in which their childhood had strayed; they sat again on the green turf whereon they had woven flowers; they looked down on the eternal mirror of the Rhine,—ah! could it have reflected the same unawakened freshness of their life's early spring!

The grave and contemplative mind of Warbeck had not been so contented with the honours of war but that it had sought also those calmer sources of emotion which were yet found among the sages of the East. He had drunk at the fountain of the wisdom of those distant climes, and had acquired the habits of meditation which were indulged by those wiser tribes from which the Crusaders brought back to the North the knowledge that was destined to enlighten their posterity. Warbeck, therefore, had little in common with the ruder chiefs around; he did not summon them to his board, nor attend at their noisy wassails. Often late at night, in yon shattered tower, his lonely lamp shone still over the mighty stream, and his only relief to loneliness was in the presence and the song of his soft cousin.

Months rolled on, when suddenly a vague and fearful rumour reached the castle of Liebenstein. Otho was returning home to the neighbouring tower of Sternfels; but not alone. He brought back with him a Greek bride of surprising beauty, and dowered with almost regal wealth. Leoline was the first to discredit the rumour; Leoline was soon the only one who disbelieved.

Bright in the summer noon flashed the array of horsemen; far up the steep ascent wound the gorgeous cavalcade; the lonely towers of Liebenstein heard the echo of many a laugh and peal of merriment. Otho bore home his bride to the hall of Sternfels.

That night there was a great banquet in Otho's castle; the lights shone from every casement, and music swelled loud and ceaselessly within.

By the side of Otho, glittering with the prodigal jewels of the East, sat the Greek. Her dark locks, her flashing eye, the false colours of her complexion, dazzled the eyes of her guests. On her left hand sat the Templar.

"By the holy rood," quoth the Templar, gayly, though he crossed himself as he spoke, "we shall scare the owls to-night on those grim towers of Liebenstein. Thy grave brother, Sir Otho, will have much to do to comfort his cousin when she sees what a gallant life she would have led with thee."

"Poor damsel!" said the Greek, with affected pity, "doubtless she will now be reconciled to the rejected one. I hear he is a knight of a comely mien."

"Peace!" said Otho, sternly, and quaffing a large goblet of wine.

The Greek bit her lip, and glanced meaningly at the Templar, who returned the glance.

"Nought but a beauty such as thine can win my pardon," said Otho, turning to his bride, and gazing passionately in her face.

The Greek smiled.

Well sped the feast, the laugh deepened, the wine circled, when Otho's eye rested on a guest at the bottom of the board, whose figure was mantled from head to foot, and whose face was covered by a dark veil.

"Beshrew me!" said he, aloud, "but this is scarce courteous at our revel: will the stranger vouchsafe to unmask?"

These words turned all eyes to the figure, and they who sat next it perceived that it trembled violently; at length it rose, and walking slowly, but with grace, to the fair Greek, it laid beside her a wreath of flowers.

"It is a simple gift, ladye," said the stranger, in a voice of such sweetness that the rudest guest was touched by it; "but it is all I can offer, and the bride of Otho should not be without a gift at my hands. May ye both be happy!"

With these words, the stranger turned and passed from the hall silent as a shadow.

"Bring back the stranger!" cried the Greek, recovering her surprise. Twenty guests sprang up to obey her mandate.

"No, no!" said Otho, waving his hand impatiently. "Touch her not, heed her not, at your peril."

The Greek bent over the flowers to conceal her anger, and from amongst them dropped the broken half of a ring. Otho recognized it at once; it was the broken half of that ring which he had broken with his betrothed. Alas! he required not such a sign to convince him that that figure, so full of ineffable grace, that touching voice, that simple action so tender in its sentiment, that gift, that blessing, came only from the forsaken and forgiving Leoline.

But Warbeck, alone in his solitary tower, paced to and fro with agitated steps. Deep, undying wrath at his brother's falsehood mingled with one burning, one delicious hope. He confessed now that he had deceived himself when he thought his passion was no more; was there any longer a bar to his union with Leoline?

In that delicacy which was breathed into him by his love, he had forborne to seek, or to offer her the insult of consolation. He felt that the shock should be borne alone, and yet he pined, he thirsted, to throw himself at her feet.

Nursing these contending thoughts, he was aroused by a knock at his door; he opened it. The passage was thronged by Leoline's maidens, pale, anxious, weeping. Leoline had left the castle, with but one female attendant, none knew whither; they knew too soon. From the hall of Sternfels she had passed over in the dark and inclement night to the valley in which the convent of Bornhofen offered to the weary of spirit and the broken of heart a refuge at the shrine of God.

At daybreak the next morning, Warbeck was at the convent's gate. He saw Leoline. What a change one night of suffering had made in that face, which was the fountain of all loveliness to him! He clasped her in his arms; he wept; he urged all that love could urge: he besought her to accept that heart which had never wronged her memory by a thought. "Oh, Leoline! didst thou not say once that these arms nursed thy childhood; that this voice soothed thine early sorrows? Ah, trust to them again and forever. From a love that forsook thee turn to the love that never swerved."

"No," said Leoline; "no. What would the chivalry of which thou art the boast,— what would they say of thee, wert thou to wed one affianced and deserted, who tarried years for another, and brought to thine arms only that heart which he had abandoned? No; and even if thou, as I know thou wouldst be, wert callous to such wrong of thy high name, shall I bring to thee a broken heart and bruised spirit? Shalt thou wed sorrow and not joy; and shall sighs that will not cease, and tears that may not be dried, be the only dowry of thy bride? Thou, too, for whom all blessings should be ordained! No, forget me; forget thy poor Leoline! She hath nothing but prayers for thee."

In vain Warbeck pleaded; in vain he urged all that passion and truth could urge; the springs of earthly love were forever dried up in the orphan's heart, and her resolution was immovable. She tore herself from his arms, and the gate of the convent creaked harshly on his ear.

A new and stern emotion now wholly possessed him; though naturally mild and gentle, he cherished anger, when once it was aroused, with the strength of a calm mind. Leoline's tears, her sufferings, her wrongs, her uncomplaining spirit, the change already stamped upon her face, — all cried aloud to him for vengeance. "She is an orphan," said he, bitterly; "she hath none to protect, to redress her, save me alone. My father's charge over her forlorn youth descends of right to me. What matters it whether her forsaker be my brother? He is *her* foe. Hath he not crushed her heart? Hath he not consigned her to sorrow till the grave? And with what insult! no warning, no excuse; with lewd wassailers keeping revel for his new bridals in the hearing — before the sight — of his betrothed! Enough! the time hath come when, to use his own words, 'One of us two must fall!'" He half drew his sword as he spoke, and thrusting it back violently into the sheath, strode home to his solitary castle. The sound of steeds and of the hunting horn met him at his portal; the bridal train of Sternfels, all mirth and gladness, were parting for the chase.

That evening a knight in complete armour entered the banquet-hall of Sternfels, and defied Otho, on the part of Warbeck of Liebenstein, to mortal combat.

Even the Templar was startled by so unnatural a challenge; but Otho, reddening, took up the gage, and the day and spot were fixed. Discontented, wroth with himself, a savage gladness seized him; he longed to wreak his desperate feelings even on his brother. Nor had he ever in his jealous heart forgiven that brother his virtues and his renown.

At the appointed hour the brothers met as foes. Warbeck's vizor was up, and all the settled sternness of his soul was stamped upon his brow. But Otho, more willing to brave the arm than to face the front of his brother, kept his vizor down; the Templar stood by him with folded arms. It was a study in human passions to his mocking mind. Scarce had the first trump sounded to this dread conflict, when a new actor entered on the scene. The rumour of so unprecedented an event had not failed to reach the convent of Bornhofen; and now, two by two, came the sisters of the holy shrine, and the armed men made way, as with trailing garments and veiled faces they swept along into the very lists. At that moment one from amongst them left her sisters with a slow majestic pace, and paused not till she stood right between the brother foes.

"Warbeck," she said in a hollow voice, that curdled up his dark spirit as it spoke, "is it thus thou wouldst prove thy love, and maintain thy trust over the fatherless orphan whom thy sire bequeathed to thy care? Shall I have murder on my soul?" At that question she paused, and those who heard it were struck dumb, and shuddered. "The murder of one man by the hand of his own brother! Away, Warbeck! *I command.*"

"Shall I forget thy wrongs, Leoline?" said Warbeck.

"Wrongs! they united me to God! they are forgiven, they are no more. Earth has deserted me, but Heaven hath taken me to its arms. Shall I murmur at the change? And thou, Otho"—here her voice faltered—"thou, does thy conscience smite thee not? Wouldst thou atone for robbing me of hope by barring against me the future? Wretch that I should be, could I dream of mercy, could I dream of comfort, if thy brother fell by thy sword in my cause? Otho, I have pardoned thee, and blessed thee and thine. Once, perhaps, thou didst love me; remember how I loved thee,—cast down thine arms."

Otho gazed at the veiled form before him. Where had the soft Leoline learned to command? He turned to his brother; he felt all that he had inflicted upon both; and casting his sword upon the ground, he knelt at the feet of Leoline, and kissed her garment with a devotion that votary never lavished on a holier saint.

The spell that lay over the warriors around was broken; there was one loud cry of congratulation and joy. "And thou, Warbeck?" said Leoline, turning to the spot where, still motionless and haughty, Warbeck stood.

"Have I ever rebelled against thy will?" said he, softly; and buried the point of his sword in the earth. "Yet, Leoline, yet," added he, looking at his kneeling brother, "yet art thou already better avenged than by this steel!"

"Thou art! thou art!" cried Otho, smiting his breast; and slowly, and scarce noting the crowd that fell back from his path, Warbeck left the lists.

Leoline said no more; her divine errand was fulfilled. She looked long and wistfully after the stately form of the knight of Liebenstein, and then, with a slight sigh, she turned to Otho, "This is the last time we shall meet on earth. Peace be with us all!"

She then, with the same majestic and collected bearing, passed on towards the sisterhood; and as, in the same solemn procession, they glided back towards the convent, there was not a man present — no, not even the hardened Templar — who would not, like Otho, have bent his knee to Leoline.

Once more Otho plunged into the wild revelry of the age; his castle was thronged with guests, and night after night the lighted halls shone down athwart the tranquil Rhine. The beauty of the Greek, the wealth of Otho, the fame of the Templar, attracted all the chivalry from far and near. Never had the banks of the Rhine known so hospitable a lord as the knight of Sternfels. Yet gloom seized him in the midst of gladness, and the revel was welcome only as the escape from remorse. The voice of scandal, however, soon began to mingle with that of envy at the pomp of Otho. The fair Greek, it was said, weary of her lord, lavished her smiles on others;

the young and the fair were always most acceptable at the castle; and, above all, her guilty love for the Templar scarcely affected disguise. Otho alone appeared unconscious of the rumour; and though he had begun to neglect his bride, he relaxed not in his intimacy with the Templar.

It was noon, and the Greek was sitting in her bower alone with her suspected lover; the rich perfumes of the East mingled with the fragrance of flowers, and various luxuries, unknown till then in those northern shores, gave a soft and effeminate character to the room.

"I tell thee," said the Greek, petulantly, "that he begins to suspect; that I have seen him watch thee, and mutter as he watched, and play with the hilt of his dagger. Better let us fly ere it is too late, for his vengeance would be terrible were it once roused against us. Ah, why did I ever forsake my own sweet land for these barbarous shores! There, love is not considered eternal, nor inconstancy a crime worthy death."

"Peace, pretty one!" said the Templar, carelessly; "thou knowest not the laws of our foolish chivalry. Thinkest thou I could fly from a knight's halls like a thief in the night? Why, verily, even the red cross would not cover such dishonour. If thou fearest that thy dull lord suspects, let us part. The emperor hath sent to me from Frankfort. Ere evening I might be on my way thither."

"And I left to brave the barbarian's revenge alone? Is this thy chivalry?"

"Nay, prate not so wildly," answered the Templar. "Surely, when the object of his suspicion is gone, thy woman's art and thy Greek wiles can easily allay the jealous fiend. Do I not know thee, Glycera? Why, thou wouldst fool all men — save a Templar."

"And thou, cruel, wouldst thou leave me?" said the Greek, weeping. "How shall I live without thee?"

The Templar laughed slightly. "Can such eyes ever weep without a comforter? But farewell; I must not be found with thee. To-morrow I depart for Frankfort; we shall meet again."

As soon as the door closed on the Templar, the Greek rose, and pacing the room, said, "Selfish, selfish! how could I ever trust him? Yet I dare not brave Otho alone. Surely it was his step that disturbed us in our yesterday's interview? Nay, I will fly. I can never want a companion."

She clapped her hands; a young page appeared; she threw herself on her seat and wept bitterly.

The page approached, and love was mingled with his compassion.

"Why weepest thou, dearest lady?" said he. "Is there aught in which Conrad's services — services! — ah, thou hast read his heart — *his devotion* may avail?"

Otho had wandered out the whole day alone; his vassals had observed that his brow was more gloomy than its wont, for he usually concealed whatever might prey within. Some of the most confidential of his servitors he had conferred with, and the conference had deepened the shadow of his countenance. He returned at twilight; the Greek did not honour the repast with her presence. She was unwell, and not to be disturbed. The gay Templar was the life of the board.

"Thou carriest a sad brow to-day, Sir Otho," said he; "good faith, thou hast caught it from the air of Liebenstein."

"I have something troubles me," answered Otho, forcing a smile, "which I would fain impart to thy friendly bosom. The night is clear and the moon is up, let us forth alone into the garden."

The Templar rose, and he forgot not to gird on his sword as he followed the knight.

Otho led the way to one of the most distant terraces that overhung the Rhine.

"Sir Templar," said he, pausing, "answer me one question on thy knightly honour. Was it thy step that left my lady's bower yester-eve at vesper?"

Startled by so sudden a query, the wily Templar faltered in his reply.

The red blood mounted to Otho's brow. "Nay, lie not, sir knight; these eyes, thanks to God! have not witnessed, but these ears have heard from others of my dishonour."

As Otho spoke, the Templar's eye resting on the water perceived a boat rowing fast over the Rhine; the distance forbade him to see more than the outline of two figures within it. "She was right," thought he; "perhaps that boat already bears her from the danger."

Drawing himself up to the full height of his tall stature, the Templar replied haughtily,—

"Sir Otho of Sternfels, if thou hast deigned to question thy vassals, obtain from them only an answer. It is not to contradict such minions that the knights of the Temple pledge their word!"

"Enough," cried Otho, losing patience, and striking the Templar with his clenched hand. "Draw, traitor, draw!"

Alone in his lofty tower Warbeck watched the night deepen over the heavens, and communed mournfully with himself. "To what end," thought he, "have these strong affections, these capacities of love, this yearning after sympathy, been given me? Unloved and unknown I walk to my grave, and all the nobler mysteries of my heart are forever to be untold."

Thus musing, he heard not the challenge of the warder on the wall, or the unbarring of the gate below, or the tread of footsteps along the winding stair; the door was thrown suddenly open, and Otho stood before him. "Come," he said, in a low voice trembling with passion; "come, I will show thee that which shall glad thine heart. Twofold is Leoline avenged."

Warbeck looked in amazement on a brother he had not met since they stood in arms each against the other's life, and he now saw that the arm that Otho extended to him dripped with blood, trickling drop by drop upon the floor.

"Come," said Otho, "follow me; it is my last prayer. Come, for Leoline's sake, come."

At that name Warbeck hesitated no longer; he girded on his sword, and followed his brother down the stairs and through the castle gate. The porter scarcely believed his eyes when he saw the two brothers, so long divided, go forth at that hour alone, and seemingly in friendship.

Warbeck, arrived at that epoch in the feelings when nothing stuns, followed with silent steps the rapid strides of his brother. The two castles, as you are aware, are scarce a stone's throw from each other. In a few minutes Otho paused at an open space in one of the terraces of Sternfels, on which the moon shone bright and steady. "Behold!" he said, in a ghastly voice, "behold!" and Warbeck saw on the sward the corpse of the Templar, bathed with the blood that even still poured fast and warm from his heart.

"Hark!" said Otho. "He it was who first made me waver in my vows to Leoline; he persuaded me to wed yon whited falsehood. Hark! he, who had thus wronged my real love, dishonoured me with my faithless bride, and thus — thus — thus" — as grinding his teeth, he spurned again and again the dead body of the Templar — "thus Leoline and myself are avenged!"

"And thy wife?" said Warbeck, pityingly.

"Fled, — fled with a hireling page. It is well! she was not worth the sword that was once belted on — by Leoline."

The tradition, dear Gertrude, proceeds to tell us that Otho, though often menaced by the rude justice of the day for the death of the Templar, defied and escaped the menace. On the very night of his revenge a long and delirious illness seized him; the generous Warbeck forgave, forgot all, save that he had been once consecrated by Leoline's love. He tended him through his sickness, and when he recovered, Otho was an altered man. He forswore the comrades he had once courted, the revels he had once led. The halls of Sternfels were desolate as those of Liebenstein. The only companion Otho sought was Warbeck, and Warbeck bore with him. They had no topic in common, for on one subject Warbeck at least felt too deeply ever to trust himself to speak; yet did a strange and secret sympathy re-unite them. They had at least a common sorrow; often they were seen wandering together by the solitary banks of the river, or amidst the woods, without apparently interchanging word or sign. Otho died first, and still in the prime of youth; and Warbeck was now left companionless. In vain the imperial court wooed him to its pleasures;

in vain the camp proffered him the oblivion of renown. Ah!
could he tear himself from a spot where morning and night
he could see afar, amidst the valley, the roof that sheltered
Leoline, and on which every copse, every turf, reminded him
of former days? His solitary life, his midnight vigils, strange
scrolls about his chamber, obtained him by degrees the repute
of cultivating the darker arts; and shunning, he became
shunned by all. But still it was sweet to hear from time to
time of the increasing sanctity of her in whom he had treasured up his last thoughts of earth. She it was who healed
the sick; she it was who relieved the poor; and the superstition of that age brought pilgrims from afar to the altars that
she served.

Many years afterwards, a band of lawless robbers, who ever
and anon broke from their mountain fastnesses to pillage and
to desolate the valleys of the Rhine, — who spared neither sex
nor age, neither tower nor hut, nor even the houses of God
Himself, — laid waste the territories round Bornhofen, and de-
manded treasure from the convent. The abbess, of the bold
lineage of Rudesheim, refused the sacrilegious demand. The
convent was stormed; its vassals resisted; the robbers, inured
to slaughter, won the day; already the gates were forced,
when a knight, at the head of a small but hardy troop, rushed
down from the mountain side and turned the tide of the fray.
Wherever his sword flashed fell a foe; wherever his war-cry
sounded was a space of dead men in the thick of the battle.
The fight was won, the convent saved; the abbess and the
sisterhood came forth to bless their deliverer. Laid under an
aged oak, he was bleeding fast to death; his head was bare
and his locks were gray, but scarcely yet with years. One
only of the sisterhood recognized that majestic face; one
bathed his parched lips; one held his dying hand; and in
Leoline's presence passed away the faithful spirit of the last
lord of Liebenstein!

"Oh!" said Gertrude, through her tears; "surely you must
have altered the facts, — surely — surely — it must have been
impossible for Leoline, with a woman's heart, to have loved
Otho more than Warbeck?"

"My child," said Vane, "so think women when they *read* a tale of love, and see *the whole heart* bared before them; but not so act they in real life, when they see only the surface of character, and pierce not its depths — until it is too late!"

CHAPTER XXV.

THE IMMORTALITY OF THE SOUL. — A COMMON INCIDENT NOT BEFORE DESCRIBED. — TREVYLYAN AND GERTRUDE.

THE day now grew cool as it waned to its decline, and the breeze came sharp upon the delicate frame of the sufferer. They resolved to proceed no farther; and as they carried with them attendants and baggage, which rendered their route almost independent of the ordinary accommodation, they steered for the opposite shore, and landed at a village beautifully sequestered in a valley, and where they fortunately obtained a lodging not often met with in the regions of the picturesque.

When Gertrude, at an early hour, retired to bed, Vane and Du——e fell into speculative conversation upon the nature of man. Vane's philosophy was of a quiet and passive scepticism; the physician dared more boldly, and rushed from doubt to negation. The attention of Trevylyan, as he sat apart and musing, was arrested in despite of himself. He listened to an argument in which he took no share, but which suddenly inspired him with an interest in that awful subject which, in the heat of youth and the occupations of the world, had never been so prominently called forth before.

"What," thought he, with unutterable anguish, as he listened to the earnest vehemence of the Frenchman and the tranquil assent of Vane, "if this creed were indeed true, — if there be no other world, — Gertrude is lost to me eternally. through the dread gloom of death there would break forth no star!"

That is a peculiar incident that perhaps occurs to us all at times, but which I have never found expressed in books,— namely, to hear a doubt of futurity at the very moment in which the present is most overcast; and to find at once this world stripped of its delusion and the next of its consolation. It is perhaps for others, rather than ourselves, that the fond heart requires a Hereafter. The tranquil rest, the shadow, and the silence, the mere pause of the wheel of life, have no terror for the wise, who know the due value of the world.

> " After the billows of a stormy sea,
>   Sweet is at last the haven of repose ! "

But not so when that stillness is to divide us eternally from others; when those we have loved with all the passion, the devotion, the watchful sanctity of the weak human heart, are to exist to us no more! when, after long years of desertion and widowhood on earth, there is to be no hope of reunion in that INVISIBLE beyond the stars; when the torch, not of life only, but of love, is to be quenched in the Dark Fountain, and the grave, that we would fain hope is the great restorer of broken ties, is but the dumb seal of hopeless, utter, inexorable separation! And it is this thought, this sentiment, which makes religion out of woe, and teaches belief to the mourning heart that in the gladness of united affections felt not the necessity of a heaven! To how many is the death of the beloved the parent of faith!

Stung by his thoughts, Trevylyan rose abruptly, and stealing from the lowly hostelry, walked forth amidst the serene and deepening night; from the window of Gertrude's room the light streamed calm on the purple air.

With uneven steps and many a pause, he paced to and fro beneath the window, and gave the rein to his thoughts. How intensely he felt the ALL that Gertrude was to him! how bitterly he foresaw the change in his lot and character that her death would work out! For who that met him in later years ever dreamed that emotions so soft, and yet so ardent, had visited one so stern? Who could have believed that time was when the polished and cold Trevylyan had kept the vigils he now held below the chamber of one so little like himself as Gertrude, in that remote and solitary hamlet, shut in by the haunted mountains of the Rhine, and beneath the moonlight of the romantic North?

While thus engaged, the light in Gertrude's room was suddenly extinguished; it is impossible to express how much that trivial incident affected him! It was like an emblem of what was to come; the light had been the only evidence of life that broke upon that hour, and he was now left alone with the shades of night. Was not this like the herald of Gertrude's own death; the extinction of the only living ray that broke upon the darkness of the world?

His anguish, his presentiment of utter desolation, increased. He groaned aloud; he dashed his clenched hand to his breast; large and cold drops of agony stole down his brow. "Father," he exclaimed with a struggling voice, "let this cup pass from me! Smite my ambition to the root; curse me with poverty, shame, and bodily disease; but leave me this one solace, this one companion of my fate!"

At this moment Gertrude's window opened gently, and he heard accents steal soothingly upon his ear.

"Is not that your voice, Albert?" said she, softly. "I heard it just as I lay down to rest, and could not sleep while you were thus exposed to the damp night air. You do not answer; surely it is your voice: when did I mistake it for another's?"

Mastering with a violent effort his emotions, Trevylyan answered, with a sort of convulsive gayety,—

"Why come to these shores, dear Gertrude, unless you are honoured with the chivalry that belongs to them? What wind, what blight, can harm me while within the circle of your presence; and what sleep can bring me dreams so dear as the waking thought of you?"

"It is cold," said Gertrude, shivering; "come in, dear Albert, I beseech you, and I will thank you to-morrow." Gertrude's voice was choked by the hectic cough, that went like an arrow to Trevylyan's heart; and he felt that in her anxiety for him she was now exposing her own frame to the unwholesome night.

He spoke no more, but hurried within the house; and when the gray light of morn broke upon his gloomy features, haggard from the want of sleep, it might have seemed, in that dim eye and fast-sinking cheek, as if the lovers were not to be divided — even by death itself.

CHAPTER XXVI.

IN WHICH THE READER WILL LEARN HOW THE FAIRIES WERE RECEIVED BY THE SOVEREIGNS OF THE MINES. — THE COMPLAINT OF THE LAST OF THE FAUNS. — THE RED HUNTSMAN. — THE STORM. — DEATH.

In the deep valley of Ehrenthal, the metal kings — the Prince of the Silver Palaces, the Gnome Monarch of the dull Lead Mine, the President of the Copper United States — held a court to receive the fairy wanderers from the island of Nonnewürth.

The prince was there, in a gallant hunting-suit of oak leaves, in honour to England; and wore a profusion of fairy orders, which had been instituted from time to time, in honour of the human poets that had celebrated the spiritual and ethereal tribes. Chief of these, sweet Dreamer of the "Midsummer Night's Dream," was the badge crystallized from the dews that rose above the whispering reeds of Avon on the night of thy birth, — the great epoch of the intellectual world! Nor wert thou, O beloved Musæus! nor thou, dim-dreaming Tieck! nor were ye, the wild imaginer of the bright-haired Undine, and the wayward spirit that invoked for the gloomy Manfred the Witch of the breathless Alps and the spirits of earth and air! — nor were ye without the honours of fairy homage! Your memory may fade from the heart of man, and the spells of new enchanters may succeed to the charm you once wove over the face of the common world; but still in the green knolls of the haunted valley and the deep shade of forests, and the starred palaces of air, ye are honoured by the beings of your dreams, as demigods and kings! Your graves are tended by invisible hands, and the places of your birth are hallowed by no perishable worship!

Even as I write,[1] far away amidst the hills of Scotland, and by the forest thou hast clothed with immortal verdure, thou, the maker of "the Harp by lone Glenfillan's spring," art passing from the earth which thou hast "painted with delight." And such are the chances of mortal fame, our children's children may raise new idols on the site of thy holy altar, and cavil where their sires adored; but for thee the mermaid of the ocean shall wail in her coral caves, and the sprite that lives in the waterfalls shall mourn! Strange shapes shall hew thy monument in the recesses of the lonely rocks! ever by moonlight shall the fairies pause from their roundel when some wild note of their minstrelsy reminds them of thine own,— ceasing from their revelries, to weep for the silence of that mighty lyre, which breathed alike a revelation of the mysteries of spirits and of men!

The King of the Silver Mines sat in a cavern in the valley, through which the moonlight pierced its way and slept in shadow on the soil shining with metals wrought into unnumbered shapes; and below him, on a humbler throne, with a gray beard and downcast eye, sat the aged King of the Dwarfs that preside over the dull realms of lead, and inspire the verse of ——, and the prose of ——! And there too a fantastic household elf was the President of the Copper Republic,— a spirit that loves economy and the Uses, and smiles sparely on the Beautiful. But, in the centre of the cave, upon beds of the softest mosses, the untrodden growth of ages, reclined the fairy visitors, Nymphalin seated by her betrothed. And round the walls of the cave were dwarf attendants on the sovereigns of the metals, of a thousand odd shapes and fantastic garments. On the abrupt ledges of the rocks the bats, charmed to stillness but not sleep, clustered thickly, watching the scene with fixed and amazed eyes; and one old gray owl, the favour-

---

[1] It was just at the time the author was finishing this work that the great master of his art was drawing to the close of his career.

ite of the witch of the valley, sat blinking in a corner, listening with all her might that she might bring home the scandal to her mistress.

"And tell me, Prince of the Rhine-Island Fays," said the King of the Silver Mines, "for thou art a traveller, and a fairy that hath seen much, how go men's affairs in the upper world? As to ourself, we live here in a stupid splendour, and only hear the news of the day when our brother of lead pays a visit to the English printing-press, or the President of Copper goes to look at his improvements in steam-engines."

"Indeed," replied Fayzenheim, preparing to speak like Æneas in the Carthaginian court,— "indeed, your Majesty, I know not much that will interest you in the present aspect of mortal affairs, except that you are quite as much honoured at this day as when the Roman conqueror bent his knee to you among the mountains of Taunus; and a vast number of little round subjects of yours are constantly carried about by the rich, and pined after with hopeless adoration by the poor. But, begging your Majesty's pardon, may I ask what has become of your cousin, the King of the Golden Mines? I know very well that he has no dominion in these valleys, and do not therefore wonder at his absence from your court this night; but I see so little of his subjects on earth that I should fear his empire was well nigh at an end, if I did not recognize everywhere the most servile homage paid to a power now become almost invisible."

The King of the Silver Mines fetched a deep sigh. "Alas, prince," said he, "too well do you divine the expiration of my cousin's empire. So many of his subjects have from time to time gone forth to the world, pressed into military service and never returning, that his kingdom is nearly depopulated. And he lives far off in the distant parts of the earth, in a state of melancholy seclusion; the age of gold has passed, the age of paper has commenced."

"Paper," said Nymphalin, who was still somewhat of a *précieuse*,— "paper is a wonderful thing. What pretty books the human people write upon it!"

"Ah! that's what I design to convey," said the silver king.

"It is the age less of paper money than paper government: the Press is the true bank." The lord treasurer of the English fairies pricked up his ears at the word "bank;" for he was the Attwood of the fairies: he had a favourite plan of making money out of bulrushes, and had written four large bees'-wings full upon the true nature of capital.

While they were thus conversing, a sudden sound as of some rustic and rude music broke along the air, and closing its wild burden, they heard the following song: —

THE COMPLAINT OF THE LAST FAUN.

I.

The moon on the Latmos mountain
  Her pining vigil keeps;
And ever the silver fountain
  In the Dorian valley weeps.
But gone are Endymion's dreams;
  And the crystal lymph
  Bewails the nymph
Whose beauty sleeked the streams!

II.

Round Arcady's oak its green
  The Bromian ivy weaves;
But no more is the satyr seen
  Laughing out from the glossy leaves.
Hushed is the Lycian lute,
  Still grows the seed
  Of the Mœnale reed,
But the pipe of Pan is mute!

III.

The leaves in the noon-day quiver;
  The vines on the mountains wave;
And Tiber rolls his river
  As fresh by the Sylvan's cave.
But my brothers are dead and gone;
  And far away
  From their graves I stray,
And dream of the past alone!

IV.

And the sun of the north is chill;
 And keen is the northern gale;
Alas for the song of the Argive hill;
 And the dance in the Cretan vale!
The youth of the earth is o'er,
 And its breast is rife
 With the teeming life
Of the golden Tribes no more!

V.

My race are more blest than I,
 Asleep in their distant bed;
'T were better, be sure, to die
 Than to mourn for the buried Dead:
To rove by the stranger streams,
 At dusk and dawn
 A lonely faun,
The last of the Grecian's dreams.

As the song ended a shadow crossed the moonlight, that lay white and lustrous before the aperture of the cavern; and Nymphalin, looking up, beheld a graceful yet grotesque figure standing on the sward without, and gazing on the group in the cave. It was a shaggy form, with a goat's legs and ears; but the rest of its body, and the height of the stature, like a man's. An arch, pleasant, yet malicious smile played about its lips; and in its hand it held the pastoral pipe of which poets have sung,— they would find it difficult to sing to it!

"And who art thou?" said Fayzenheim, with the air of a hero.

"I am the last lingering wanderer of the race which the Romans worshipped; hither I followed their victorious steps, and in these green hollows have I remained. Sometimes in the still noon, when the leaves of spring bud upon the whispering woods, I peer forth from my rocky lair, and startle the peasant with my strange voice and stranger shape. Then goes he home, and puzzles his thick brain with mopes and fancies, till at length he imagines me, the creature of the South! one of his northern demons, and his poets adapt the apparition to their barbarous lines."

"Ho!" quoth the silver king, "surely thou art the origin of the fabled Satan of the cowled men living whilom in yonder ruins, with its horns and goatish limbs; and the harmless faun has been made the figuration of the most implacable of fiends. But why, O wanderer of the South, lingerest thou in these foreign dells? Why returnest thou not to the bi-forked hill-top of old Parnassus, or the wastes around the yellow course of the Tiber?"

"My brethren are no more," said the poor faun; "and the very faith that left us sacred and unharmed is departed. But here all the spirits not of mortality are still honoured; and I wander, mourning for Silenus, though amidst the vines that should console me for his loss."

"Thou hast known great beings in thy day," said the leaden king, who loved the philosophy of a truism (and the history of whose inspirations I shall one day write).

"Ah, yes," said the faun; "my birth was amidst the freshness of the world, when the flush of the universal life coloured all things with divinity; when not a tree but had its Dryad, not a fountain that was without its Nymph. I sat by the gray throne of Saturn, in his old age, ere yet he was discrowned (for he was no visionary ideal, but the arch monarch of the pastoral age), and heard from his lips the history of the world's birth. But those times are gone forever,—they have left harsh successors."

"It is the age of paper," muttered the lord treasurer, shaking his head.

"What ho, for a dance!" cried Fayzenheim, too royal for moralities, and he whirled the beautiful Nymphalin into a waltz. Then forth issued the fairies, and out went the dwarfs. And the faun leaning against an aged elm, ere yet the midnight waned, the elves danced their charmed round to the antique minstrelsy of his pipe,— the minstrelsy of the Grecian world!

"Hast thou seen yet, my Nymphalin," said Fayzenheim, in

the pauses of the dance, "the recess of the Hartz, and the red form of its mighty hunter?"

"It is a fearful sight," answered Nymphalin; "but with thee I should not fear."

"Away then!" cried Fayzenheim; "let us away at the first cock-crow, into those shaggy dells; for there is no need of night to conceal us, and the unwitnessed blush of morn or the dreary silence of noon is, no less than the moon's reign, the season for the sports of the superhuman tribes."

Nymphalin, charmed with the proposal, readily assented; and at the last hour of night, bestriding the starbeams of the many-titled Friga, away sped the fairy cavalcade to the gloom of the mystic Hartz.

Fain would I relate the manner of their arrival in the thick recesses of the forest, — how they found the Red Hunter seated on a fallen pine beside a wide chasm in the earth, with the arching bows of the wizard oak wreathing above his head as a canopy, and his bow and spear lying idle at his feet. Fain would I tell of the reception which he deigned to the fairies, and how he told them of his ancient victories over man; how he chafed at the gathering invasions of his realm; and how joyously he gloated of some great convulsion[1] in the northern States, which, rapt into moody reveries in those solitary woods, the fierce demon broodingly foresaw. All these fain would I narrate, but they are not of the Rhine, and my story will not brook the delay. While thus conversing with the fiend, noon had crept on, and the sky had become overcast and lowering; the giant trees waved gustily to and fro, and the low gatherings of the thunder announced the approaching storm. Then the hunter rose and stretched his mighty limbs, and seizing his spear, he strode rapidly into the forest to meet the things of his own tribe that the tempest wakes from their rugged lair.

A sudden recollection broke upon Nymphalin. "Alas, alas!" she cried, wringing her hands; "what have I done! In journeying hither with thee, I have forgotten my office. I have neglected my watch over the elements, and my human

---

[1] Which has come to pass.— 1847.

charge is at this hour, perhaps, exposed to all the fury of the storm."

"Cheer thee, my Nymphalin," said the prince, "we will lay the tempest;" and he waved his sword and muttered the charms which curb the winds and roll back the marching thunder: but for once the tempest ceased not at his spells. And now, as the fairies sped along the troubled air, a pale and beautiful form met them by the way, and the fairies paused and trembled; for the power of that Shape could vanquish even them. It was the form of a Female, with golden hair, crowned with a chaplet of withered leaves; her bosoms, of an exceeding beauty, lay bare to the wind, and an infant was clasped between them, hushed into a sleep so still, that neither the roar of the thunder, nor the livid lightning flashing from cloud to cloud, could even ruffle, much less arouse, the slumberer. And the face of the female was unutterably calm and sweet (though with a something of severe); there was no line nor wrinkle in the hueless brow; care never wrote its defacing characters upon that everlasting beauty. It knew no sorrow or change; ghostlike and shadowy floated on that Shape through the abyss of Time, governing the world with an unquestioned and noiseless sway. And the children of the green solitudes of the earth, the lovely fairies of my tale, shuddered as they gazed and recognized — the form of DEATH, — death vindicated.

"And why," said the beautiful Shape, with a voice soft as the last sighs of a dying babe, — "why trouble ye the air with spells? Mine is the hour and the empire, and the storm is the creature of my power. Far yonder to the west it sweeps over the sea, and the ship ceases to vex the waves; it smites the forest, and the destined tree, torn from its roots, feels the winter strip the gladness from its boughs no more! The roar of the elements is the herald of eternal stillness to their victims; and they who hear the progress of my power idly shudder at the coming of peace. And thou, O tender daughter of the fairy kings, why grievest thou at a mortal's doom? Knowest thou not that sorrow cometh with years, and that to live is to mourn? Blessed is the flower that, nipped in its early spring, feels not the blast that one by one scatters its blossoms around it, and leaves but the barren stem. Blessed are the young whom I clasp to my breast, and lull into the sleep which the storm cannot break, nor the morrow arouse to sorrow or to toil. The heart that is stilled in the bloom of its first emotions, that turns with its last throb to the eye of love, as yet unlearned in the possibility of change,— has exhausted already the wine of life, and is saved only from the lees. As the mother soothes to sleep the wail of her troubled child, I open my arms to the vexed spirit, and my bosom cradles the unquiet to repose!"

The fairies answered not, for a chill and a fear lay over them, and the Shape glided on; ever as it passed away through the veiling clouds they heard its low voice singing amidst the roar of the storm, as the dirge of the water-sprite over the vessel it hath lured into the whirlpool or the shoals.

———◆———

CHAPTER XXVII.

THURMBERG. — A STORM UPON THE RHINE. — THE RUINS OF RHEINFELS. — PERIL UNFELT BY LOVE. — THE ECHO OF THE LURLEI-BERG. — ST. GOAR. — KAUB, GUTENFELS, AND PFALZGRAFENSTEIN. — A CERTAIN VASTNESS OF MIND IN THE FIRST HERMITS. — THE SCENERY OF THE RHINE TO BACHARACH.

OUR party continued their voyage the next day, which was less bright than any they had yet experienced. The clouds swept on dull and heavy, suffering the sun only to break forth at scattered intervals. They wound round the curving bay which the Rhine forms in that part of its course, and gazed upon the ruins of Thurmberg, with the rich gardens that skirt the banks below. The last time Trevylyan had seen those ruins soaring against the sky, the green foliage at the foot of the rocks, and the quiet village sequestered beneath, glassing its roofs and solitary tower upon the wave, it had been with a gay summer troop of light friends, who had paused on the opposite shore during the heats of noon, and, over wine and fruits, had mimicked the groups of Boccaccio, and intermingled the lute, the jest, the momentary love, and the laughing tale.

What a difference now in his thoughts, in the object of the voyage, in his present companions! The feet of years fall noiseless; we heed, we note them not, till tracking the same course we passed long since, we are startled to find how deep the impression they leave behind. To revisit the scenes of our youth is to commune with the ghost of ourselves.

At this time the clouds gathered rapidly along the heavens, and they were startled by the first peal of the thunder. Sudden and swift came on the storm, and Trevylyan trembled as he covered Gertrude's form with the rude boat-cloaks they had brought with them; the small vessel began to rock wildly to and fro upon the waters. High above them rose the vast dismantled ruins of Rheinfels, the lightning darting through its shattered casements and broken arches, and brightening the gloomy trees that here and there clothed the rocks, and tossed to the angry wind. Swift wheeled the water-birds over the river, dipping their plumage in the white foam, and uttering their discordant screams. A storm upon the Rhine has a grandeur it is in vain to paint. Its rocks, its foliage, the feudal ruins that everywhere rise from the lofty heights, speaking in characters of stern decay of many a former battle against time and tempest; the broad and rapid course of the legendary river,— all harmonize with the elementary strife; and you feel that to see the Rhine only in the sunshine is to be unconscious of its most majestic aspects. What baronial war had those ruins witnessed! From the rapine of the lordly tyrant of those battlements rose the first Confederation of the Rhine,— the great strife between the new time and the old, the town and the castle, the citizen and the chief. Gray and stern those ruins breasted the storm,— a type of the antique opinion which once manned them with armed serfs; and, yet

in ruins and decay, appeals from the victorious freedom it may no longer resist!

Clasped in Trevylyan's guardian arms, and her head pillowed on his breast, Gertrude felt nothing of the storm save its grandeur; and Trevylyan's voice whispered cheer and courage to her ear. She answered by a smile and a sigh, but not of pain. In the convulsions of nature we forget our own separate existence, our schemes, our projects, our fears; our dreams vanish back into their cells. One passion only the storm quells not, and the presence of Love mingles with the voice of the fiercest storms, as with the whispers of the southern wind. So she felt, as they were thus drawn close together, and as she strove to smile away the anxious terror from Trevylyan's gaze, a security, a delight; for peril is sweet even to the fears of woman, when it impresses upon her yet more vividly that she is beloved.

"A moment more and we reach the land," murmured Trevylyan.

"I wish it not," answered Gertrude, softly. But ere they got into St. Goar the rain descended in torrents, and even the thick coverings round Gertrude's form were not sufficient protection against it. Wet and dripping she reached the inn; but not then, nor for some days, was she sensible of the shock her decaying health had received.

The storm lasted but a few hours, and the sun afterwards broke forth so brightly, and the stream looked so inviting, that they yielded to Gertrude's earnest wish, and, taking a larger vessel, continued their course; they passed along the narrow and dangerous defile of the Gewirre, and the fearful whirlpool of the "Bank;" and on the shore to the left the enormous rock of Lurlei rose, huge and shapeless, on their gaze. In this place is a singular echo, and one of the boatmen wound a horn, which produced an almost supernatural music, — so wild, loud, and oft reverberated was its sound.

The river now curved along in a narrow and deep channel amongst rugged steeps, on which the westering sun cast long and uncouth shadows; and here the hermit, from whose sacred name the town of St. Goar derived its own, fixed his abode and preached the religion of the Cross. "There was a certain vastness of mind," said Vane, "in the adoption of utter solitude, in which the first enthusiasts of our religion indulged. The remote desert, the solitary rock, the rude dwelling hollowed from the cave, the eternal commune with their own hearts, with nature, and their dreams of God,— all make a picture of severe and preterhuman grandeur. Say what we will of the necessity and charm of social life, there is a greatness about man when he dispenses with mankind."

"As to that," said Du——e, shrugging his shoulders, "there was probably very good wine in the neighbourhood, and the females' eyes about Oberwesel are singularly blue."

They now approached Oberwesel, another of the once imperial towns, and behind it beheld the remains of the castle of the illustrious family of Schomberg, the ancestors of the old hero of the Boyne. A little farther on, from the opposite shore, the castle of Gutenfels rose above the busy town of Kaub.

"Another of those scenes," said Trevylyan, "celebrated equally by love and glory, for the castle's name is derived from that of the beautiful ladye of an emperor's passion; and below, upon a ridge in the steep, the great Gustavus issued forth his command to begin battle with the Spaniards."

"It looks peaceful enough now," said Vane, pointing to the craft that lay along the stream, and the green trees drooping over a curve in the bank. Beyond, in the middle of the stream itself, stands the lonely castle of Pfalzgrafenstein, sadly memorable as a prison to the more distinguished of criminals. How many pining eyes may have turned from those casements to the vine-clad hills of the free shore! how many indignant hearts have nursed the deep curses of hate in the dungeons below, and longed for the wave that dashed against the gray walls to force its way within and set them free!

Here the Rhine seems utterly bounded, shrunk into one of those delusive lakes into which it so frequently seems to change its course; and as you proceed, it is as if the waters were silently overflowing their channel and forcing their way into the clefts of the mountain shore. Passing the Werth

Island on one side and the castle of Stahleck on the other, our voyagers arrived at Bacharach, which, associating the feudal recollections with the classic, takes its name from the god of the vine; and as Du——e declared with peculiar emphasis, quaffing a large goblet of the peculiar liquor, "richly deserves the honour!"

———◆———

CHAPTER XXVIII.

THE VOYAGE TO BINGEN. — THE SIMPLE INCIDENTS IN THIS TALE EXCUSED. — THE SITUATION AND CHARACTER OF GERTRUDE. — THE CONVERSATION OF THE LOVERS IN THE TEMPEST. — A FACT CONTRADICTED. — THOUGHTS OCCASIONED BY A MADHOUSE AMONGST THE MOST BEAUTIFUL LANDSCAPES OF THE RHINE.

THE next day they again resumed their voyage, and Gertrude's spirits were more cheerful than usual. The air seemed to her lighter, and she breathed with a less painful effort; once more hope entered the breast of Trevylyan; and, as the vessel bounded on, their conversation was steeped in no sombre hues. When Gertrude's health permitted, no temper was so gay, yet so gently gay, as hers; and now the *naïve* sportiveness of her remarks called a smile to the placid lip of Vane, and smoothed the anxious front of Trevylyan himself; as for Du——e, who had much of the boon companion beneath his professional gravity, he broke out every now and then into snatches of French songs and drinking glees, which he declared were the result of the air of Bacharach. Thus conversing, the ruins of Furstenberg, and the echoing vale of Rheindeibach, glided past their sail; then the old town of Lorch, on the opposite bank (where the red wine is said first to have been made), with the green island before it in the water. Winding round, the stream showed castle upon castle alike in ruins, and built alike upon scarce accessible steeps. Then came the chapel of St. Clements and the opposing village of Asmannshausen; the lofty Rossell, built at the extremest verge of the cliff; and now the tower of Hatto, celebrated by Southey's ballad, and the ancient town of Bingen. Here they paused a while from their voyage, with the intention of visiting more minutely the Rheingau, or valley of the Rhine.

It must occur to every one of my readers, that, in undertaking, as now, in these passages in the history of Trevylyan, scarcely so much a tale as an episode in real life, it is very difficult to offer any interest save of the most simple and unexciting kind. It is true that to Trevylyan every day, every hour, had its incident; but what are those incidents to others? A cloud in the sky; a smile from the lip of Gertrude,— these were to him far more full of events than had been the most varied scenes of his former adventurous career; but the history of the heart is not easily translated into language; and the world will not readily pause from its business to watch the alternations in the check of a dying girl.

In the immense sum of human existence what is a single unit? Every sod on which we tread is the grave of some former being; yet is there something that softens without enervating the heart in tracing in the life of another those emotions that all of us have known ourselves. For who is there that has not, in his progress through life, felt all its ordinary business arrested, and the varieties of fate commuted into one chronicle of the affections? Who has not watched over the passing away of some being, more to him at that epoch than all the world? And this unit, so trivial to the calculation of others, of what inestimable value was it not to him? Retracing in another such recollections, shadowed and mellowed down by time, we feel the wonderful sanctity of human life, we feel what emotions a single being can awake; what a world of hope may be buried in a single grave! And thus we keep alive within ourselves the soft springs of that morality which unites us with our kind, and sheds over the harsh scenes and turbulent contests of earth the colouring of a common love.

There is often, too, in the time of year in which such thoughts are presented to us, a certain harmony with the feelings they awaken. As I write I hear the last sighs of the departing summer, and the sere and yellow leaf is visible in the green of nature. But when this book goes forth into the world, the year will have passed through a deeper cycle of decay; and the first melancholy signs of winter have breathed into the Universal Mind that sadness which associates itself readily with the memory of friends, of feelings, that are no more. The seasons, like ourselves, track their course by something of beauty, or of glory, that is left behind. As the traveller in the land of Palestine sees tomb after tomb rise before him, the landmarks of his way, and the only signs of the holiness of the soil, thus Memory wanders over the most sacred spots in its various world, and traces them but by the graves of the Past.

It was now that Gertrude began to feel the shock her frame had received in the storm upon the Rhine. Cold shiverings frequently seized her; her cough became more hollow, and her form trembled at the slightest breeze.

Vane grew seriously alarmed; he repented that he had yielded to Gertrude's wish of substituting the Rhine for the Tiber or the Arno; and would even now have hurried across the Alps to a warmer clime, if Du——e had not declared that she could not survive the journey, and that her sole chance of regaining her strength was rest. Gertrude herself, however, in the continued delusion of her disease, clung to the belief of recovery, and still supported the hopes of her father, and soothed, with secret talk of the future, the anguish of her betrothed. The reader may remember that in the most touching passage in the ancient tragedians, the most pathetic part of the most pathetic of human poets — the pleading speech of Iphigenia, when imploring for her prolonged life, she impresses you with so soft a picture of its innocence and its beauty, and in this Gertrude resembled the Greek's creation — that she felt, on the verge of death, all the flush, the glow, the loveliness of life. Her youth was filled with hope and many-coloured dreams; she loved, and the hues of morning slept upon the yet disenchanted earth. The heavens to her were not as the common sky; the wave had its peculiar music to her ear, and the rustling leaves a pleasantness that none whose heart is not bathed in the love and sense of beauty could discern. Therefore it was, in future years, a thought of deep gratitude to Trevylyan that she was so little sensible of her danger; that the landscape caught not the gloom of the grave; and that, in the Greek phrase, "death found her sleeping amongst flowers."

At the end of a few days, another of those sudden turns, common to her malady, occurred in Gertrude's health; her youth and her happiness rallied against the encroaching tyrant, and for the ensuing fortnight she seemed once more within the bounds of hope. During this time they made several excursions into the Rheingau, and finished their tour at the ancient Heidelberg.

One morning, in these excursions, after threading the wood of Niederwald, they gained that small and fairy temple, which hanging lightly over the mountain's brow, commands one of the noblest landscapes of earth. There, seated side by side, the lovers looked over the beautiful world below; far to the left lay the happy islets, in the embrace of the Rhine, as it wound along the low and curving meadows that stretch away towards Nieder-Ingelheim and Mayence. Glistening in the distance, the opposite Nah swept by the Mause tower, and the ruins of Klopp, crowning the ancient Bingen, into the mother tide. There, on either side the town, were the mountains of St. Roch and Rupert, with some old monastic ruin saddening in the sun. But nearer, below the temple, contrasting all the other features of landscape, yawned a dark and rugged gulf, girt by cragged elms and mouldering towers, the very prototype of the abyss of time, — black and fathomless amidst ruin and desolation.

"I think sometimes," said Gertrude, "as in scenes like these we sit together, and rapt from the actual world, see only the enchantment that distance lends to our view, — I think sometimes what pleasure it will be hereafter to recall these hours. If ever you should love me less, I need only whisper to you, 'The Rhine,' and will not all the feelings you have now for me return?"

"Ah, there will never be occasion to recall my love for you, — it can never decay."

"What a strange thing is life!" said Gertrude; "how unconnected, how desultory seem all its links! Has this sweet pause from trouble, from the ordinary cares of life — has it anything in common with your past career, with your future? You will go into the great world; in a few years hence these moments of leisure and musing will be denied to you. The action that you love and court is a jealous sphere,— it allows no wandering, no repose. These moments will then seem to you but as yonder islands that stud the Rhine,— the stream lingers by them for a moment, and then hurries on in its rapid course; they vary, but they do not interrupt the tide."

"You are fanciful, my Gertrude; but your simile might be juster. Rather let these banks be as our lives, and this river the one thought that flows eternally by both, blessing each with undying freshness."

Gertrude smiled; and, as Trevylyan's arm encircled her, she sank her beautiful face upon his bosom, he covered it with his kisses, and she thought at the moment, that, even had she passed death, that embrace could have recalled her to life.

They pursued their course to Mayence, partly by land, partly along the river. One day, as returning from the vine-clad mountains of Johannisberg, which commands the whole of the Rheingau, the most beautiful valley in the world, they proceeded by water to the town of Ellfeld, Gertrude said,—

"There is a thought in your favourite poet which you have often repeated, and which I cannot think true, —

"'In nature there is nothing melancholy.'

To me, it seems as if a certain melancholy were inseparable from beauty; in the sunniest noon there is a sense of solitude and stillness which pervades the landscape, and even in the flush of life inspires us with a musing and tender sadness. Why is this?"

"I cannot tell," said Trevylyan, mournfully; "but I allow that it is true."

"It is as if," continued the romantic Gertrude, "the spirit

of the world spoke to us in the silence, and filled us with a sense of our mortality,— a whisper from the religion that belongs to nature, and is ever seeking to unite the earth with the reminiscences of Heaven. Ah, what without a heaven would be even love! — a perpetual terror of the separation that must one day come! If," she resumed solemnly, after a momentary pause, and a shadow settled on her young face, "if it be true, Albert, that I must leave you soon — "

"It cannot! it cannot!" cried Trevylyan, wildly; "be still, be silent, I beseech you."

"Look yonder," said Du——e, breaking seasonably in upon the conversation of the lovers; "on that hill to the left, what once was an abbey is now an asylum for the insane. Does it not seem a quiet and serene abode for the unstrung and erring minds that tenant it? What a mystery is there in our conformation! — those strange and bewildered fancies which replace our solid reason, what a moral of our human weakness do they breathe!"

It does indeed induce a dark and singular train of thought, when, in the midst of these lovely scenes, we chance upon this lone retreat for those on whose eyes Nature, perhaps, smiles in vain. *Or is it in vain?* They look down upon the broad Rhine, with its tranquil isles: do their wild delusions endow the river with another name, and people the valleys with no living shapes? Does the broken mirror within reflect back the countenance of real things, or shadows and shapes, crossed, mingled, and bewildered,— the phantasma of a sick man's dreams? Yet, perchance, one memory unscathed by the general ruin of the brain can make even the beautiful Rhine more beautiful than it is to the common eye; can calm it with the hues of departed love, and bids its possessor walk over its vine-clad mountains with the beings that have ceased to *be!* There, perhaps, the self-made monarch sits upon his throne and claims the vessels as his fleet, the waves and the valleys as his own; there, the enthusiast, blasted by the light of some imaginary creed, beholds the shapes of angels, and watches in the clouds round the setting sun the pavilions of God; there the victim of forsaken or perished love, mightier than the sor-

cerers of old, evokes the dead, or recalls the faithless by the philter of undying fancies. Ah, blessed art thou, the winged power of Imagination that is within us! conquering even grief, brightening even despair. Thou takest us from the world when reason can no longer bind us to it, and givest to the maniac the inspiration and the solace of the bard! Thou, the parent of the purer love, lingerest like love, when even ourself forsakes us, and lightest up the shattered chambers of the heart with the glory that makes a sanctity of decay.

CHAPTER XXIX.

ELLFELD. — MAYENCE. — HEIDELBERG. — A CONVERSATION BE-
TWEEN VANE AND THE GERMAN STUDENT. — THE RUINS
OF THE CASTLE OF HEIDELBERG AND ITS SOLITARY
HABITANT.

IT was now the full noon; light clouds were bearing up towards the opposite banks of the Rhine, but over the Gothic towers of Ellfeld the sky spread blue and clear; the river danced beside the old gray walls with a sunny wave, and close at hand a vessel crowded with passengers, and loud with eager voices, gave a merry life to the scene. On the opposite bank the hills sloped away into the far horizon, and one slight skiff in the midst of the waters broke the solitary brightness of the noonday calm.

The town of Ellfeld was the gift of Otho the First to the Church; not far from thence is the crystal spring that gives its name to the delicious grape of Markbrunner.

"Ah," quoth Du——e, "doubtless the good bishops of May-ence made the best of the vicinity!"

They stayed some little time at this town, and visited the ruins of Scharfenstein; thence proceeding up the river, they passed Nieder Walluf, called the Gate of the Rheingau, and the luxuriant garden of Schierstein; thence, sailing by the castle-seat of the Prince Nassau Usingen, and passing two long and narrow isles, they arrived at Mayence, as the sun shot his last rays upon the waters, gilding the proud cathedral-spire, and breaking the mists that began to gather behind, over the rocks of the Rheingau.

Ever memorable Mayence,— memorable alike for freedom and for song, within those walls how often woke the gallant music of the Troubadour; and how often beside that river did the heart of the maiden tremble to the lay! Within those walls the stout Walpoden first broached the great scheme of the Hanseatic league; and, more than all, O memorable Mayence, thou canst claim the first invention of the mightiest engine of human intellect,—the great leveller of power, the Demiurgus of the moral world,—the Press! Here too lived the maligned hero of the greatest drama of modern genius, the traditionary Faust, illustrating in himself the fate of his successors in dispensing knowledge,—held a monster for his wisdom, and consigned to the penalties of hell as a recompense for the benefits he had conferred on earth!

At Mayence, Gertrude heard so much and so constantly of Heidelberg, that she grew impatient to visit that enchanting town; and as Du——e considered the air of Heidelberg more pure and invigorating than that of Mayence, they resolved to fix within it their temporary residence. Alas! it was the place destined to close their brief and melancholy pilgrimage, and to become to the heart of Trevylyan the holiest spot which the earth contained,— the KAABA of the world. But Gertrude, unconscious of her fate, conversed gayly as their carriage rolled rapidly on, and, constantly alive to every new sensation, she touched with her characteristic vivacity on all that they had seen in their previous route. There is a great charm in the observations of one new to the world; if we ourselves have become somewhat tired of "its hack sights and sounds," we hear in their freshness a voice from our own youth.

In the haunted valley of the Neckar, the most crystal of rivers, stands the town of Heidelberg. The shades of evening gathered round it as their heavy carriage rattled along the antique streets, and not till the next day was Gertrude aware of all the unrivalled beauties that environ the place.

Vane, who was an early riser, went forth alone in the morning to reconnoitre the town; and as he was gazing on the tower of St. Peter, he heard himself suddenly accosted. He turned round and saw the German student whom they had met among the mountains of Taunus at his elbow.

"Monsieur has chosen well in coming hither," said the student; "and I trust our town will not disappoint his expectations." Vane answered with courtesy, and the German offering to accompany him in his walk, their conversation fell naturally on the life of a university, and the current education of the German people.

"It is surprising," said the student, "that men are eternally inventing new systems of education, and yet persevering in the old. How many years ago is it since Fichte predicted in the system of Pestalozzi the regeneration of the German people? What has it done? We admire, we praise, and we blunder on in the very course Pestalozzi proves to be erroneous. Certainly," continued the student, "there must be some radical defect in a system of culture in which genius is an exception, and dulness the result. Yet here, in our German universities, everything proves that education without equitable institutions avails little in the general formation of character. Here the young men of the colleges mix on the most equal terms; they are daring, romantic, enamoured of freedom even to its madness. They leave the University: no political career continues the train of mind they had acquired; they plunge into obscurity; live scattered and separate, and the student inebriated with Schiller sinks into the passive priest or the lethargic baron. His college career, so far from indicating his future life, exactly reverses it: he is brought up in one course in order to proceed in another. And this I hold to be the universal error of education in all countries; they conceive it a certain something to be finished at a certain age. They do not make it a part of the continuous history of life, but a wandering from it."

"You have been in England?" asked Vane.

"Yes; I have travelled over nearly the whole of it on foot. I was poor at that time, and imagining there was a sort of masonry between all men of letters, I inquired at each town for the *savants*, and asked money of them as a matter of course."

Vane almost laughed outright at the simplicity and *naïve* unconsciousness of degradation with which the student proclaimed himself a public beggar.

"And how did you generally succeed?"

"In most cases I was threatened with the stocks, and twice I was consigned by the *juge de paix* to the village police, to be passed to some mystic Mecca they were pleased to entitle 'a parish.' Ah" (continued the German with much *bonhomie*), "it was a pity to see in a great nation so much value attached to such a trifle as money. But what surprised me greatly was the tone of your poetry. Madame de Staël, who knew perhaps as much of England as she did of Germany, tells us that its chief character is the *chivalresque ;* and, excepting only Scott, who, by the way, is *not* English, I did not find one chivalrous poet among you. Yet," continued the student, "between ourselves, I fancy that in our present age of civilization, there is an unexamined mistake in the general mind as to the value of poetry. It delights still as ever, but it has ceased to teach. The prose of the heart enlightens, touches, rouses, far more than poetry. Your most philosophical poets would be commonplace if turned into prose. Verse cannot contain the refining subtle thoughts which a great prose writer embodies; the rhyme eternally cripples it; it properly deals with the common problems of human nature, which are now hackneyed, and not with the nice and philosophizing corollaries which may be drawn from them. Thus, though it would seem at first a paradox, commonplace is more the element of poetry than of prose."

This sentiment charmed Vane, who had nothing of the poet about him; and he took the student to share their breakfast at the inn, with a complacency he rarely experienced at the remeeting with a new acquaintance.

After breakfast, our party proceeded through the town

towards the wonderful castle which is its chief attraction, and the noblest wreck of German grandeur.

And now pausing, the mountain yet unscaled, the stately ruin frowned upon them, girt by its massive walls and hanging terraces, round which from place to place clung the dwarfed and various foliage. High at the rear rose the huge mountain, covered, save at its extreme summit, with dark trees, and concealing in its mysterious breast the shadowy beings of the legendary world. But towards the ruins, and up a steep ascent, you may see a few scattered sheep thinly studding the broken ground. Aloft, above the ramparts, rose, desolate and huge, the Palace of the Electors of the Palatinate. In its broken walls you may trace the tokens of the lightning that blasted its ancient pomp, but still leaves in the vast extent of pile a fitting monument of the memory of Charlemagne. Below, in the distance, spread the plain far and spacious, till the shadowy river, with one solitary sail upon its breast, united the melancholy scene of earth with the autumnal sky.

"See," said Vane, pointing to two peasants who were conversing near them on the matters of their little trade, utterly unconscious of the associations of the spot, "see, after all that is said and done about human greatness, it is always the greatness of the few. Ages pass, and leave the poor herd, the mass of men, eternally the same,— hewers of wood and drawers of water. The pomp of princes has its ebb and flow, but the peasant sells his fruit as gayly to the stranger on the ruins as to the emperor in the palace."

"Will it be always so?" said the student.

"Let us hope not, for the sake of permanence in glory," said Trevylyan. "Had *a people* built yonder palace, its splendour would never have passed away."

Vane shrugged his shoulders, and Du——e took snuff.

But all the impressions produced by the castle at a distance are as nothing when you stand within its vast area and behold the architecture of all ages blended into one mighty ruin! The rich hues of the masonry, the sweeping façades — every description of building which man ever framed for war or for luxury — is here; all having only the common character,— RUIN. The feudal rampart, the yawning fosse, the rude tower, the splendid arch, the strength of a fortress, the magnificence of a palace,— all united, strike upon the soul like the history of a fallen empire in all its epochs.

"There is one singular habitant of these ruins," said the student,— "a solitary painter, who has dwelt here some twenty years, companioned only by his Art. No other apartment but that which he tenants is occupied by a human being."

"What a poetical existence!" cried Gertrude, enchanted with a solitude so full of associations.

"Perhaps so," said the cruel Vane, ever anxious to dispel an illusion, "but more probably custom has deadened to him all that overpowers ourselves with awe; and he may tread among these ruins rather seeking to pick up some rude morsel of antiquity, than feeding his imagination with the dim traditions that invest them with so august a poetry."

"Monsieur's conjecture has something of the truth in it," said the German; "but then the painter is a Frenchman."

There is a sense of fatality in the singular mournfulness and majesty which belong to the ruins of Heidelberg, contrasting the vastness of the strength with the utterness of the ruin. It has been twice struck with lightning, and is the wreck of the elements, not of man; during the great siege it sustained, the lightning is supposed to have struck the powder magazine by accident.

What a scene for some great imaginative work! What a mocking interference of the wrath of nature in the puny contests of men! One stroke of "the red right arm " above us, crushing the triumph of ages, and laughing to scorn the power of the beleaguers and the valour of the besieged!

They passed the whole day among these stupendous ruins, and felt, when they descended to their inn, as if they had left the caverns of some mighty tomb.

CHAPTER XXX.

NO PART OF THE EARTH REALLY SOLITARY. — THE SONG OF THE FAIRIES. — THE SACRED SPOT. — THE WITCH OF THE EVIL WINDS. — THE SPELL AND THE DUTY OF THE FAIRIES.

BUT in what spot of the world is there ever utter solitude? The vanity of man supposes that loneliness is *his* absence! Who shall say what millions of spiritual beings glide invisibly among scenes apparently the most deserted? Or what know we of our own mechanism, that we should deny the possibility of life and motion to things that we cannot ourselves recognize?

At moonlight, in the Great Court of Heidelberg, on the borders of the shattered basin overgrown with weeds, the following song was heard by the melancholy shades that roam at night through the mouldering halls of old, and the gloomy hollows in the mountain of Heidelberg.

SONG OF THE FAIRIES IN THE RUINS OF HEIDELBERG.

> From the woods and the glossy green,
>   With the wild thyme strewn ;
> From the rivers whose crispéd sheen
>   Is kissed by the trembling moon :
> While the dwarf looks out from his mountain cave,
>   And the erl king from his lair,
> And the water-nymph from her moaning wave,
>   We skirr the limber air.
>
> There 's a smile on the vine-clad shore,
>   A smile on the castled heights ;
> They dream back the days of yore,
>   And they smile at our roundel rites !
>   Our roundel rites !

> Lightly we tread these halls around,
>   Lightly tread we;
> Yet, hark! we have scared with a single sound
>   The moping owl on the breathless tree,
>   And the goblin sprites!
> Ha, ha! we have scared with a single sound
>   The old gray owl on the breathless tree,
>   And the goblin sprites!

"They come not," said Pipalee; "yet the banquet is prepared, and the poor queen will be glad of some refreshment."

"What a pity! all the rose-leaves will be over-broiled," said Nip.

"Let us amuse ourselves with the old painter," quoth Trip, springing over the ruins.

"Well said," cried Pipalee and Nip; and all three, leaving my lord-treasurer amazed at their levity, whisked into the painter's apartment. Permitting them to throw the ink over their victim's papers, break his pencils, mix his colours, mislay his nightcap, and go whiz against his face in the shape of a great bat, till the astonished Frenchman began to think the pensive goblins of the place had taken a sprightly fit,— we hasten to a small green spot some little way from the town, in the valley of the Neckar, and by the banks of its silver stream. It was circled round by dark trees, save on that side bordered by the river. The wild-flowers sprang profusely from the turf, which yet was smooth and singularly green. And there was the German fairy describing a circle round the spot, and making his elvish spells; and Nymphalin sat droopingly in the centre, shading her face, which was bowed down as the head of a water-lily, and weeping crystal tears.

There came a hollow murmur through the trees, and a rush as of a mighty wind, and a dark form emerged from the shadow and approached the spot.

The face was wrinkled and old, and stern with a malevolent and evil aspect. The frame was lean and gaunt, and supported by a staff, and a short gray mantle covered its bended shoulders.

"Things of the moonbeam!" said the form, in a shrill and

ghastly voice, "what want ye here; and why charm ye this spot from the coming of me and mine?"

"Dark witch of the blight and blast," answered the fairy, "THOU that nippest the herb in its tender youth, and eatest up the core of the soft bud; behold, it is but a small spot that the fairies claim from thy demesnes, and on which, through frost and heat, they will keep the herbage green and the air gentle in its sighs!"

"And, wherefore, O dweller in the crevices of the earth, wherefore wouldst thou guard this spot from the curses of the seasons?"

"We know by our instinct," answered the fairy, "that this spot will become the grave of one whom the fairies love; hither, by an unfelt influence, shall we guide her yet living steps; and in gazing upon this spot shall the desire of quiet and the resignation to death steal upon her soul. Behold, throughout the universe, all things are at war with one another,— the lion with the lamb; the serpent with the bird; and even the gentlest bird itself with the moth of the air, or the worm of the humble earth! What then to men, and to the spirits transcending men, is so lovely and so sacred as a being that harmeth none; what so beautiful as Innocence; what so mournful as its untimely tomb? And shall not that tomb be sacred; shall it not be our peculiar care? May we not mourn over it as at the passing away of some fair miracle in Nature, too tender to endure, too rare to be forgotten? It is for this, O dread waker of the blast, that the fairies would consecrate this little spot; for this they would charm away from its tranquil turf the wandering ghoul and the evil children of the night. Here, not the ill-omened owl, nor the blind bat, nor the unclean worm shall come. And thou shouldst have neither will nor power to nip the flowers of spring, nor sear the green herbs of summer. Is it not, dark mother of the evil winds,— is it not *our* immemorial office to tend the grave of Innocence, and keep fresh the flowers round the resting-place of Virgin Love?"

Then the witch drew her cloak round her, and muttered to herself, and without further answer turned away among the trees and vanished, as the breath of the east wind, which goeth with her as her comrade, scattered the melancholy leaves along her path!

CHAPTER XXXI.

GERTRUDE AND TREVYLYAN, WHEN THE FORMER IS AWAKENED TO THE APPROACH OF DEATH.

THE next day, Gertrude and her companions went along the banks of the haunted Neckar. She had passed a sleepless and painful night, and her evanescent and childlike spirits had sobered down into a melancholy and thoughtful mood. She leaned back in an open carriage with Trevylyan, ever constant, by her side, while Du——e and Vane rode slowly in advance. Trevylyan tried in vain to cheer her; even his attempts (usually so eagerly received) to charm her duller moments by tale or legend were, in this instance, fruitless. She shook her head gently, pressed his hand, and said, "No, dear Trevylyan, no; even your art fails to-day, but your kindness never!" and pressing his hand to her lips, she burst passionately into tears.

Alarmed and anxious, he clasped her to his breast, and strove to lift her face, as it drooped on its resting-place, and kiss away its tears. "Oh," said she, at length, "do not despise my weakness; I am overcome by my own thoughts: I look upon the world, and see that it is fair and good; I look upon you, and I see all that I can venerate and adore. Life seems to me so sweet, and the earth so lovely; can you wonder, then, that I should shrink at the thought of death? Nay, interrupt me not, dear Albert; the thought must be borne and braved. I have not cherished, I have not yielded to it through my long-increasing illness; but there have been times when it has forced itself upon me, and now, *now* more palpably than ever. Do not think me weak and childish. I never feared death till I knew you; but to see you no more,— never again to touch this dear hand, never to thank you for your love, never to be sensible of your care,— to lie down and sleep, *and never, never, once more to dream of you!* Ah, that is a bitter thought! but I will brave it,— yes, brave it as one worthy of your regard."

Trevylyan, choked by his emotions, covered his own face with his hands, and, leaning back in the carriage, vainly struggled with his sobs.

"Perhaps," she said, yet ever and anon clinging to the hope that had utterly abandoned *him*, "perhaps, I may yet deceive myself; and my love for you, which seems to me as if it could conquer death, may bear me up against this fell disease. The hope to live with you, to watch you, to share your high dreams, and oh! above all, to soothe you in sorrow and sickness, as you have soothed me — has not that hope something that may support even this sinking frame? And who shall love thee as I love; who see thee as I have seen; who pray for thee in gratitude and tears as I have prayed? Oh, Albert, so little am I jealous of you, so little do I think of myself in comparison, that I could close my eyes happily on the world if I knew that what I could be to thee another will be!"

"Gertrude," said Trevylyan, and lifting up his colourless face, he gazed upon her with an earnest and calm solemnity, "Gertrude, let us be united at once! If Fate must sever us, let her cut the last tie too; let us feel that at least upon earth we have been all in all to each other; let us defy death, even as it frowns upon us. Be mine to-morrow — this day — oh, God! be mine!"

Over even that pale countenance, beneath whose hues the lamp of life so faintly fluttered, a deep, radiant flush passed one moment, lighting up the beautiful ruin with the glow of maiden youth and impassioned hope, and then died rapidly away.

"No, Albert," she said sighing; "no! it must not be. Far easier would come the pang to you, while yet we are not wholly united; and for my own part I am selfish, and feel as if I should leave a tenderer remembrance on your heart thus parted,— tenderer, but not so sad. I would not wish you to feel yourself widowed to my memory; I would not cling like a blight to your fair prospects of the future. Remember me rather as a dream,— as something never wholly won, and therefore asking no fidelity but that of kind and forbearing thoughts. Do you remember one evening as we sailed along the Rhine — ah! happy, happy hour! — that we heard from the banks a strain of music,— not so skilfully played as to be worth listening to for itself, but, suiting as it did the hour and the scene, we remained silent, that we might hear it the better; and when it died insensibly upon the waters, a certain melancholy stole over us; we felt that a something that softened the landscape had gone, and we conversed less lightly than before? Just so, my own loved, my own adored Trevylyan, just so is the influence that our brief love, your poor Gertrude's existence, should bequeath to your remembrance. A sound, a presence, should haunt you for a little while, but no more, ere you again become sensible of the glories that court your way!"

But as Gertrude said this, she turned to Trevylyan, and seeing his agony, she could refrain no longer; she felt that to soothe was to insult; and throwing herself upon his breast, they mingled their tears together.

CHAPTER XXXII.

A SPOT TO BE BURIED IN.

On their return homeward, Du——e took the third seat in the carriage, and endeavoured, with his usual vivacity, to cheer the spirits of his companions; and such was the elasticity of Gertrude's nature, that with her, he, to a certain degree, succeeded in his kindly attempt. Quickly alive to the charms of scenery, she entered by degrees into the external beauties which every turn in the road opened to their view;

and the silvery smoothness of the river, that made the constant attraction of the landscape, the serenity of the time, and the clearness of the heavens, tended to tranquillize a mind that, like a sunflower, so instinctively turned from the shadow to the light.

Once Du——e stopped the carriage in a spot of herbage, bedded among the trees, and said to Gertrude, "We are now in one of the many places along the Neckar which your favourite traditions serve to consecrate. Amidst yonder copses, in the early ages of Christianity, there dwelt a hermit, who, though young in years, was renowned for the sanctity of his life. None knew whence he came, nor for what cause he had limited the circle of life to the seclusion of his cell. He rarely spoke, save when his ghostly advice or his kindly prayer was needed; he lived upon herbs, and the wild fruits which the peasants brought to his cave; and every morning and every evening he came to this spot to fill his pitcher from the water of the stream. But here he was observed to linger long after his task was done, and to sit gazing upon the walls of a convent which then rose upon the opposite side of the bank, though now even its ruins are gone. Gradually his health gave way beneath the austerities he practised; and one evening he was found by some fishermen insensible on the turf. They bore him for medical aid to the opposite convent; and one of the sisterhood, the daughter of a prince, was summoned to attend the recluse. But when his eyes opened upon hers, a sudden recognition appeared to seize both. He spoke; and the sister threw herself on the couch of the dying man, and shrieked forth a name, the most famous in the surrounding country,—the name of a once noted minstrel, who, in those rude times, had mingled the poet with the lawless chief, and was supposed, years since, to have fallen in one of the desperate frays between prince and outlaw, which were then common; storming the very castle which held her, now the pious nun, then the beauty and presider over the tournament and galliard. In her arms the spirit of the hermit passed away. She survived but a few hours, and left conjecture busy with a history to which it never obtained further clew. Many a troubadour in later times furnished forth in poetry the details which truth refused to supply; and the place where the hermit at sunrise and sunset ever came to gaze upon the convent became consecrated by song."

The place invested with this legendary interest was impressed with a singular aspect of melancholy quiet; wild-flowers yet lingered on the turf, whose grassy sedges gently overhung the Neckar, that murmured amidst them with a plaintive music. Not a wind stirred the trees; but at a little distance from the place, the spire of a church rose amidst the copse; and, as they paused, they suddenly heard from the holy building the bell that summons to the burial of the dead. It came on the ear in such harmony with the spot, with the hour, with the breathing calm, that it thrilled to the heart of each with an inexpressible power. It was like the voice of another world, that amidst the solitude of nature summoned the lulled spirit from the cares of this; it invited, not repulsed, and had in its tone more of softness than of awe.

Gertrude turned, with tears starting to her eyes, and, laying her hand on Trevylyan's, whispered, "In such a spot, so calm, so sequestered, yet in the neighbourhood of the house of God, would I wish this broken frame to be consigned to rest."

CHAPTER THE LAST.

THE CONCLUSION OF THIS TALE.

From that day Gertrude's spirit resumed its wonted cheerfulness, and for the ensuing week she never reverted to her approaching fate; she seemed once more to have grown unconscious of its limit. Perhaps she sought, anxious for Trevylyan to the last, not to throw additional gloom over their earthly separation; or, perhaps, once steadily regarding the certainty of her doom, its terrors vanished. The chords of thought, vibrating to the subtlest emotions, may be changed by a single incident, or in a single hour; a sound of sacred music, a green and quiet burial-place, may convert the form of death into the aspect of an angel. And therefore wisely, and with a beautiful lore, did the Greeks strip the grave of its unreal gloom; wisely did they body forth the great principle of Rest by solemn and lovely images, unconscious of the northern madness that made a Spectre of REPOSE!

But while Gertrude's *spirit* resumed its healthful tone, her *frame* rapidly declined, and a few days now could do the ravage of months a little while before.

One evening, amidst the desolate ruins of Heidelberg, Trevylyan, who had gone forth alone to indulge the thoughts which he strove to stifle in Gertrude's presence, suddenly encountered Vane. That calm and almost callous pupil of the adversities of the world was standing alone, and gazing upon the shattered casements and riven tower, through which the sun now cast its slant and parting ray.

Trevylyan, who had never loved this cold and unsusceptible man, save for the sake of Gertrude, felt now almost a hatred creep over him, as he thought in such a time, and with death fastening upon the flower of his house, he could yet be calm, and smile, and muse, and moralize, and play the common part of the world. He strode slowly up to him, and standing full before him, said with a hollow voice and writhing smile, "You amuse yourself pleasantly, sir: this is a fine scene; and to meditate over griefs a thousand years hushed to rest is better than watching over a sick girl and eating away your heart with fear!"

Vane looked at him quietly, but intently, and made no reply.

"Vane!" continued Trevylyan, with the same preternatural attempt at calm, "Vane, in a few days all will be over, and you and I, the things, the plotters, the false men of the world, will be left alone,— left by the sole being that graces our dull life, that makes by her love either of us worthy of a thought!"

Vane started, and turned away his face. "You are cruel," said he, with a faltering voice.

"What, man!" shouted Trevylyan, seizing him abruptly by the arm, "can *you* feel? Is your cold heart touched? Come then," added he, with a wild laugh, "come, let us be friends!"

Vane drew himself aside, with a certain dignity, that impressed Trevylyan even at that hour. "Some years hence," said he, "you will be called cold as I am; sorrow will teach you the wisdom of indifference — it is a bitter school, sir, — a bitter school! But think you that I do indeed see unmoved my last hope shivered, — the last tie that binds me to my kind? No, no! I feel it as a man may feel; I cloak it as a man grown gray in misfortune should do! My child is more to me than your betrothed to you; for you are young and wealthy, and life smiles before you; but I — no more — sir, — no more!"

"Forgive me," said Trevylyan, humbly, "I have wronged you; but Gertrude is an excuse for any crime of love; and now listen to my last prayer, — give her to me, even on the verge of the grave. Death cannot seize her in the arms, in the vigils of a love like mine."

Vane shuddered. "It were to wed the dead," said he. "No!"

Trevylyan drew back, and without another word, hurried away; he returned to the town; he sought, with methodical calmness, the owner of the piece of ground in which Gertrude had wished to be buried. He purchased it, and that very night he sought the priest of a neighbouring church, and directed it should be consecrated according to the due rite and ceremonial.

The priest, an aged and pious man, was struck by the request, and the air of him who made it.

"Shall it be done forthwith, sir?" said he, hesitating.

"Forthwith," answered Trevylyan, with a calm smile, — "a bridegroom, you know, is naturally impatient."

For the next three days, Gertrude was so ill as to be confined to her bed. All that time Trevylyan sat outside her door, without speaking, scarcely lifting his eyes from the ground. The attendants passed to and fro, — he heeded them not; perhaps as even the foreign menials turned aside and wiped their eyes, and prayed God to comfort him, he required compassion less at that time than any other. There is a stupefaction in woe, and the heart sleeps without a pang when exhausted by its afflictions.

But on the fourth day Gertrude rose, and was carried down (how changed, yet how lovely ever!) to their common apartment. During those three days the priest had been with her often, and her spirit, full of religion from her childhood, had been unspeakably soothed by his comfort. She took food from the hand of Trevylyan; she smiled upon him as sweetly as of old. She conversed with him, though with a faint voice, and at broken intervals. But she felt no pain; life ebbed away gradually, and without a pang. "My father," she said to Vane, whose features still bore their usual calm, whatever might have passed within, "I know that you will grieve when I am gone more than the world might guess; for I alone know what you were years ago, ere friends left you and fortune frowned, and ere my poor mother died. But do not — do not believe that hope and comfort leave you with me. Till the heaven pass away from the earth there shall be comfort and hope for all."

They did not lodge in the town, but had fixed their abode on its outskirts, and within sight of the Neckar; and from the window they saw a light sail gliding gayly by till it passed, and solitude once more rested upon the waters.

"The sail passes from our eyes," said Gertrude, pointing to it, "but still it glides on as happily though we see it no more; and I feel — yes, Father, I feel — I know that it is so with *us*. We glide down the river of time from the eyes of men, but we cease not the less to *be!*"

And now, as the twilight descended, she expressed a wish, before she retired to rest, to be left alone with Trevylyan. He was not then sitting by her side, for he would not trust himself to do so, but with his face averted, at a little distance from her. She called him by his name; he answered not, nor turned. Weak as she was, she raised herself from the sofa, and crept gently along the floor till she came to him, and sank in his arms.

"Ah, unkind!" she said, "unkind for once! Will you turn away from me? Come, let us look once more on the river: see! the night darkens over it. Our pleasant voyage, the type of our love, is finished; our sail may be unfurled no more. Never again can your voice soothe the lassitude of sickness with the legend and the song; the course is run, the vessel is broken up, night closes over its fragments; but now, in this hour, love me, be kind to me as ever. Still let me be your own Gertrude, still let me close my eyes this night, as before, with the sweet consciousness that I am loved."

"Loved! O Gertrude! speak not to me thus!"

"Come, that is yourself again!" and she clung with weak arms caressingly to his breast. "And now," she said more solemnly, "let us forget that we are mortal; let us remember only that life is a part, not the whole, of our career; let us feel in this soft hour, and while·yet we are unsevered, the presence of The Eternal that is within us, so that it shall not be as death, but as a short absence; and when once the pang of parting is over, you must think only that we are shortly to meet again. What! you turn from me still? See, I do not weep or grieve, I have conquered the pang of our absence; will you be outdone by me? Do you remember, Albert, that you once told me how the wisest of the sages of old, in prison, and before death, consoled his friends with the proof of the immortality of the soul? Is it not a consolation; does it not suffice; or will you deem it wise from the lips of wisdom, but vain from the lips of love?"

"Hush, hush!" said Trevylyan, wildly; "or I shall think you an angel already."

But let us close this commune, and leave unrevealed the *last* sacred words that ever passed between them upon earth.

When Vane and the physician stole back softly into the room, Trevylyan motioned to them to be still. "She sleeps," he whispered; "hush!" And in truth, wearied out by her own emotions, and lulled by the belief that she had soothed one with whom her heart dwelt now, as ever, she had fallen into sleep, or it may be, insensibility, on his breast. There as she lay, so fair, so frail, so delicate, the twilight deepened into shade, and the first star, like the hope of the future, broke forth upon the darkness of the earth.

Nothing could equal the stillness without, save that which lay breathlessly within. For not one of the group stirred or spoke, and Trevylyan, bending over her, never took his eyes from her face, watching the parted lips, and fancying that he imbibed the breath. Alas, the breath was stilled! from sleep to death she had glided without a sigh,—happy, most happy in that death! cradled in the arms of unchanged love, and brightened in her last thought by the consciousness of innocence and the assurances of Heaven!

.   .   .   .

Trevylyan, after a long sojourn on the Continent, returned to England. He plunged into active life, and became what is termed in this age of little names a distinguished and noted man. But what was mainly remarkable in his future conduct was his impatience of rest. He eagerly courted all occupations, even of the most varied and motley kind,—business, letters, ambition, pleasure. He suffered no pause in his career; and leisure to him was as care to others. He lived in the world, as the worldly do, discharging its duties, fostering its affections, and fulfilling its career. But there was a deep and wintry change within him,—*the sunlight of his life was gone;* the loveliness of romance had left the earth. The stem was proof as heretofore to the blast, but the green leaves were severed from it forever, and the bird had forsaken its boughs. Once he had idolized the beauty that is born of song, the glory and the ardour that invest such thoughts as are not of our common clay; but the well of enthusiasm was dried up, and the golden bowl was broken at the fountain. With Gertrude the poetry of existence was gone. As she herself had described her loss, a music had ceased to breathe along the face of things; and though the bark might sail on as swiftly, and the stream swell with as proud a wave, a something that had vibrated on the heart was still, and the magic of the voyage was no more.

And Gertrude sleeps on the spot where she wished her last couch to be made; and far — oh, far dearer is that small spot on the distant banks of the gliding Neckar to Trevylyan's heart than all the broad lands and fertile fields of his ancestral domain. The turf too preserves its emerald greenness; and it would seem to me that the field flowers spring up by the sides of the simple tomb even more profusely than of old. A curve in the bank breaks the tide of the Neckar; and therefore its stream pauses, as if to linger reluctantly, by that solitary grave, and to mourn among the rustling sedges ere it passes on. And I have thought, when I last looked upon that quiet place, when I saw the turf so fresh, and the flowers so bright of hue, that aërial hands might *indeed* tend the sod; that it was by no *imaginary* spells that I summoned the fairies to my tale; that in truth, and with vigils constant though unseen, they yet kept from all polluting footsteps, and from the harsher influence of the seasons, the grave of one who so loved their race; and who, in her gentle and spotless virtue claimed kindred with the beautiful Ideal of the world. Is there one of us who has not known some being for whom it seemed not too wild a fantasy to indulge such dreams?

THE END.

THE COMING RACE.

Inscribed

TO

MAX MÜLLER,

IN TRIBUTE OF RESPECT AND ADMIRATION.

THE COMING RACE.

CHAPTER I.

I **am** a native of ——, in the United States of America. My ancestors migrated from England in the reign of Charles II.; and my grandfather was not undistinguished in the War of Independence. My family, therefore, enjoyed a somewhat high social position in right of birth; and being also opulent, they were considered disqualified for the public service. My father once ran for Congress, but was signally defeated by his tailor. After that event he interfered little in politics, and lived much in his library. I was the eldest of three sons, and sent at the age of sixteen to the old country, partly to complete my literary education, partly to commence my commercial training in a mercantile firm at Liverpool. My father died shortly after I was twenty-one; and being left well off, and having a taste for travel and adventure, I resigned, for a time, all pursuit of the almighty dollar, and became a desultory wanderer over the face of the earth.

In the year 18—, happening to be in ——, I was invited by a professional engineer, with whom I had made acquaintance, to visit the recesses of the —— mine, upon which he was employed.

The reader will understand, ere he close this narrative, my reason for concealing all clew to the district of which I write, and will perhaps thank me for refraining from any description that may tend to its discovery.

Let me say, then, as briefly as possible, that I accompanied the engineer into the interior of the mine, and became so strangely fascinated by its gloomy wonders, and so interested in my friend's explorations, that I prolonged my stay in the neighbourhood, and descended daily, for some weeks, into the vaults and galleries hollowed by nature and art beneath the surface of the earth. The engineer was persuaded that far richer deposits of mineral wealth than had yet been detected would be found in a new shaft that had been commenced under his operations. In piercing this shaft we came one day upon a chasm jagged and seemingly charred at the sides, as if burst asunder at some distant period by volcanic fires. Down this chasm my friend caused himself to be lowered in a "cage," having first tested the atmosphere by the safety-lamp. He remained nearly an hour in the abyss. When he returned he was very pale, and with an anxious, thoughtful expression of face, very different from its ordinary character, which was open, cheerful, and fearless.

He said briefly that the descent appeared to him unsafe, and leading to no result; and suspending further operations in the shaft, we returned to the more familiar parts of the mine.

All the rest of that day the engineer seemed pre-occupied by some absorbing thought. He was unusually taciturn, and there was a scared, bewildered look in his eyes, as that of a man who has seen a ghost. At night, as we two were sitting alone in the lodging we shared together near the mouth of the mine, I said to my friend,—

"Tell me frankly what you saw in that chasm; I am sure it was something strange and terrible. Whatever it be, it has left your mind in a state of doubt. In such a case two heads are better than one. Confide in me."

The engineer long endeavoured to evade my inquiries; but as, while he spoke, he helped himself unconsciously out of the brandy-flask to a degree to which he was wholly unaccustomed, for he was a very temperate man, his reserve gradually melted away. He who would keep himself to himself should imitate the dumb animals, and drink water. At last he said, "I will tell you all. When the cage stopped, I found myself on a ridge of rock; and below me, the chasm, taking a slanting direction, shot down to a considerable depth, the darkness of which my lamp could not have penetrated. But through it, to my infinite surprise, streamed upward a steady brilliant light. Could it be any volcanic fire? In that case, surely I should have felt the heat. Still, if on this there was doubt, it was of the utmost importance to our common safety to clear it up. I examined the sides of the descent, and found that I could venture to trust myself to the irregular projections or ledges, at least for some way. I left the cage, and clambered down. As I drew near and nearer to the light, the chasm became wider, and at last I saw, to my unspeakable amaze, a broad level road at the bottom of the abyss, illumined as far as the eye could reach by what seemed artificial gas-lamps placed at regular intervals, as in the thoroughfare of a great city; and I heard confusedly at a distance a hum as of human voices. I know, of course, that no rival miners are at work in this district. Whose could be those voices? What human hands could have levelled that road and marshalled those lamps?

"The superstitious belief, common to miners, that gnomes or fiends dwell within the bowels of the earth, began to seize me. I shuddered at the thought of descending farther and braving the inhabitants of this nether valley. Nor indeed could I have done so without ropes, as from the spot I had reached to the bottom of the chasm the sides of the rock sank down abrupt, smooth, and sheer. I retraced my steps with some difficulty. Now I have told you all."

"You will descend again?"

"I ought, yet I feel as if I durst not."

"A trusty companion halves the journey and doubles the courage. I will go with you. We will provide ourselves with ropes of suitable length and strength, and — pardon me — you must not drink more to-night. Our hands and feet must be steady and firm to-morrow."

CHAPTER II.

WITH the morning my friend's nerves were re-braced, and he was not less excited by curiosity than myself. Perhaps more; for he evidently believed in his own story, and I felt considerable doubt of it: not that he would have wilfully told an untruth, but that I thought he must have been under one of those hallucinations which seize on our fancy or our nerves in solitary, unaccustomed places, and in which we give shape to the formless and sound to the dumb.

We selected six veteran miners to watch our descent; and as the cage held only one at a time, the engineer descended first; and when he had gained the ledge at which he had before halted, the cage re-arose for me. I soon gained his side. We had provided ourselves with a strong coil of rope.

The light struck on my sight as it had done the day before on my friend's. The hollow through which it came sloped diagonally; it seemed to me a diffused atmospheric light, not like that from fire, but soft and silvery, as from a northern star. Quitting the cage, we descended, one after the other, easily enough, owing to the juts in the side, till we reached the place at which my friend had previously halted, and which was a projection just spacious enough to allow us to stand abreast. From this spot the chasm widened rapidly, like the lower end of a vast funnel, and I saw distinctly the valley, the road, the lamps which my companion had described. He had exaggerated nothing. I heard the sounds he had heard,— a mingled indescribable hum as of voices and a dull tramp as of feet. Straining my eye farther down, I clearly beheld at a distance the outline of some large building. It could not be mere natural rock,— it was too symmetrical, with huge heavy Egyptian-like columns, and the whole lighted as from within. I had about me a small pocket-telescope, and by the aid of this I could distinguish, near the building I mention, two forms which seemed human, though I could not be sure. At least they were living, for they moved, and both vanished within the building. We now proceeded to attach the end of the rope we had brought with us to the ledge on which we stood, by the aid of clamps and grappling-hooks, with which, as well as with necessary tools, we were provided.

We were almost silent in our work. We toiled like men afraid to speak to each other. One end of the rope being thus apparently made firm to the ledge, the other, to which we fastened a fragment of the rock, rested on the ground below, a distance of some fifty feet. I was a younger and a more active man than my companion, and having served on board ship in my boyhood, this mode of transit was more familiar to me than to him. In a whisper I claimed the precedence, so that when I gained the ground I might serve to hold the rope more steady for his descent. I got safely to the ground beneath, and the engineer now began to lower himself. But he had scarcely accomplished ten feet of the descent, when the fastenings, which we had fancied so secure, gave way, or rather the rock itself proved treacherous and crumbled beneath the strain; and the unhappy man was precipitated to the bottom, falling just at my feet, and bringing down with his fall splinters of the rock, one of which, fortunately but a small one, struck and for the time stunned me. When I recovered my senses I saw my companion an inanimate mass beside me, life utterly extinct. While I was bending over his corpse in grief and horror, I heard close at hand a strange sound between a snort and a hiss; and turning instinctively to the quarter from which it came, I saw emerging from a dark fissure in the rock a vast and terrible head, with open jaws and dull, ghastly, hungry eyes,— the head of a monstrous reptile resembling that of the crocodile or alligator, but infinitely larger than the largest creature of that kind I had ever beheld in my travels. I started to my feet and fled down the valley at my utmost speed. I stopped at last, ashamed of my panic and my flight, and returned to the spot on which I had left the body of my friend. It was gone; doubtless the monster had already drawn it into its den and devoured it. The rope and the grappling-hooks still lay where they had fallen, but they afforded me no chance of return; it was impossible to re-attach them to the rock above, and the sides of the rock were too sheer and smooth for human steps to clamber. I was alone in this strange world, amidst the bowels of the earth.

CHAPTER III.

SLOWLY and cautiously I went my solitary way down the lamplit road and towards the large building I have described. The road itself seemed like a great Alpine pass, skirting rocky mountains, of which the one through whose chasms I had descended formed a link. Deep below to the left lay a vast valley, which presented to my astonished eye the unmistakable evidences of art and culture. There were fields covered with a strange vegetation, similar to none I have seen above the earth; the colour of it not green, but rather of a dull leaden hue or of a golden red.

There were lakes and rivulets which seemed to have been curved into artificial banks; some of pure water, others that shone like pools of naphtha. At my right hand, ravines and defiles opened amidst the rocks, with passes between, evidently constructed by art, and bordered by trees resembling, for the most part, gigantic ferns, with exquisite varieties of feathery foliage, and stems like those of the palm-tree. Others were more like the cane-plant, but taller, bearing large clusters of flowers. Others, again, had the form of enormous fungi, with short thick stems supporting a wide dome-like roof, from which either rose or drooped long and slender branches. The whole scene behind, before, and beside me, far as the eye could reach, was brilliant with innumerable lamps. The world without a sun was bright and warm as an Italian landscape at noon, but the air less oppressive, the heat softer. Nor was the scene before me void of signs of habitation. I could distinguish at a distance, whether on the banks of lake or rivulet, or half-way upon eminences, embedded amidst the vegetation, buildings that must surely be the homes of men. I could even discover, though far off, forms that appeared to me human moving amidst the landscape. As I paused to gaze, I saw to the right, gliding quickly through the air, what appeared a small boat, impelled by sails shaped like wings. It soon passed out of sight, descending amidst the shades of a forest. Right above me there was no sky, but only a cavernous roof. This roof grew higher and higher at the distance of the landscapes beyond, till it became imperceptible, as an atmosphere of haze formed itself beneath.

Continuing my walk, I started — from a bush that resembled a great tangle of seaweeds, interspersed with fern-like shrubs and plants of large leafage shaped like that of the aloe or prickly pear — a curious animal about the size and shape of a deer. But as, after bounding away a few paces, it turned round and gazed at me inquisitively, I perceived that it was not like any species of deer now extant above the earth, but it brought instantly to my recollection a plaster cast I had seen in some museum of a variety of the elk stag, said to have existed before the Deluge. The creature seemed tame enough, and, after inspecting me a moment or two, began to graze on the singular herbage around, undismayed and careless.

———— ◆ ————

CHAPTER IV.

I NOW came in full sight of the building. Yes, it had been made by hands, and hollowed partly out of a great rock. I should have supposed it at the first glance to have been of the earliest form of Eygptian architecture. It was fronted by huge columns, tapering upward from massive plinths, and with capitals that, as I came nearer, I perceived to be more ornamental and more fantastically graceful than Egyptian architecture allows. As the Corinthian capital mimics the leaf of the acanthus, so the capitals of these columns imitated the foliage of the vegetation neighbouring them, some aloe-like, some fern-like. And now there came out of this building a form, human,—was it human? It stood on the broad way and looked around, beheld me and approached. It came within a few yards of me, and at the sight and presence of it an indescribable awe and tremor seized me, rooting my feet to the ground. It reminded me of symbolical images of Genius or Demon that are seen on Etruscan vases or limned on the walls of Eastern sepulchres,—images that borrow the outlines of man, and are yet of another race. It was tall, not gigantic, but tall as the tallest men below the height of giants. Its chief covering seemed to me to be composed of large wings folded over its breast and reaching to its knees; the rest of its attire was composed of an under tunic and leggings of some thin fibrous material. It wore on its head a kind of tiara that shone with jewels, and carried in its right hand a slender staff of bright metal like polished steel. But the face! it was that which inspired my awe and my terror. It was the face of man, but yet of a type of man distinct from our known extant races. The nearest approach to it in outline and expression is the face of the sculptured sphinx, so regular in its calm, intellectual, mysterious beauty. Its colour was peculiar, more like that of the red man than any other variety of our species, and yet different from it,—a richer and a softer hue, with large black eyes, deep and brilliant, and brows arched as a semicircle. The face was beardless; but a nameless something in the aspect, tranquil though the expression, and beauteous though the features, roused that instinct of danger which the sight of a tiger or serpent arouses. I felt that this man-like image was endowed with forces inimical to man. As it drew near, a cold shudder came over me. I fell on my knees and covered my face with my hands.

CHAPTER V.

A VOICE accosted me — a very quiet and very musical key
of voice — in a language of which I could not understand a
word, but it served to dispel my fear. I uncovered my face
and looked up. The stranger (I could scarcely bring myself
to call him man) surveyed me with an eye that seemed to read
the very depths of my heart. He then placed his left hand on
my forehead, and with the staff in his right gently touched
my shoulder. The effect of this double contact was magical.
In place of my former terror there passed into me a sense of
contentment, of joy, of confidence in myself and in the being
before me. I rose and spoke in my own language. He listened to me with apparent attention, but with a slight surprise in his looks; and shook his head, as if to signify that I
was not understood. He then took me by the hand and led
me in silence to the building. The entrance was open,— indeed, there was no door to it. We entered an immense hall,
lighted by the same kind of lustre as in the scene without,
but diffusing a fragrant odour. The floor was in large tessellated blocks of precious metals, and partly covered with a sort
of mat-like carpeting. A strain of low music, above and
around, undulated as if from invisible instruments, seeming
to belong naturally to the place, just as the sound of murmuring waters belongs to a rocky landscape, or the warble of
birds to vernal groves.

A figure, in a simpler garb than that of my guide, but of
similar fashion, was standing motionless near the threshold.
My guide touched it twice with his staff, and it put itself into
a rapid and gliding movement, skimming noiselessly over the
floor. Gazing on it, I then saw that it was no living form, but a
mechancial automaton. It might be two minutes after it vanished through a doorless opening, half screened by curtains at
the other end of the hall, when through the same opening advanced a boy of about twelve years old, with features closely

resembling those of my guide, so that they seemed to me evidently son and father. On seeing me the child uttered a cry, and lifted a staff like that borne by my guide, as if in menace. At a word from the elder he dropped it. The two then conversed for some moments, examining me while they spoke. The child touched my garments, and stroked my face with evident curiosity, uttering a sound like a laugh, but with an hilarity more subdued than the mirth of our laughter. Presently the roof of the hall opened, and a platform descended, seemingly constructed on the same principle as the "lifts" used in hotels and warehouses for mounting from one story to another.

The stranger placed himself and the child on the platform, and motioned to me to do the same, which I did. We ascended quickly and safely, and alighted in the midst of a corridor with doorways on either side.

Through one of these doorways I was conducted into a chamber fitted up with an Oriental splendour; the walls were tessellated with spars and metals and uncut jewels; cushions and divans abounded; apertures as for windows, but unglazed, were made in the chamber, opening to the floor; and as I passed along I observed that these openings led into spacious balconies, and commanded views of the illumined landscape without. In cages suspended from the ceiling there were birds of strange form and bright plumage, which at our entrance set up a chorus of song, modulated into tune, as is that of our piping bullfinches. A delicious fragrance, from censers of gold elaborately sculptured, filled the air. Several automata, like the one I had seen, stood dumb and motionless by the walls. The stranger placed me beside him on a divan, and again spoke to me, and again I spoke, but without the least advance towards understanding each other.

But now I began to feel the effects of the blow I received from the splinters of the falling rock more acutely than I had done at first.

There came over me a sense of sickly faintness, accompanied with acute, lancinating pains in the head and neck. I sank back on the seat, and strove in vain to stifle a groan. On this the child, who had hitherto seemed to eye me with distrust or dislike, knelt by my side to support me; taking one of my hands in both his own, he approached his lips to my forehead, breathing on it softly. In a few moments my pain ceased; a drowsy, happy calm crept over me; I fell asleep.

How long I remained in this state I know not, but when I woke I felt perfectly restored. My eyes opened upon a group of silent forms, seated around me in the gravity and quietude of Orientals, — all more or less like the first stranger; the same mantling wings, the same fashion of garment, the same sphinx-like faces, with the deep dark eyes and red man's colour; above all, the same type of race, — race akin to man's, but infinitely stronger of form and grander of aspect, and inspiring the same unutterable feeling of dread. Yet each countenance was mild and tranquil, and even kindly in its expression; and strangely enough, it seemed to me that in this very calm and benignity consisted the secret of the dread which the countenances inspired. They seemed as void of the lines and shadows which care and sorrow, and passion and sin, leave upon the faces of men, as are the faces of sculptured gods, or as, in the eyes of Christian mourners, seem the peaceful brows of the dead.

I felt a warm hand on my shoulder; it was the child's. In his eyes there was a sort of lofty pity and tenderness, such as that with which we may gaze on some suffering bird or butterfly. I shrank from that touch, I shrank from that eye. I was vaguely impressed with a belief that, had he so pleased, that child could have killed me as easily as a man can kill a bird or a butterfly. The child seemed pained at my repugnance, quitted me, and placed himself beside one of the windows. The others continued to converse with each other in a low tone, and by their glances towards me I could perceive that I was the object of their conversation. One in especial seemed to be urging some proposal affecting me on the being whom I had first met, and this last by his gesture seemed about to assent to it, when the child suddenly quitted his post by the window, placed himself between me and the other forms, as if in protection, and spoke quickly and eagerly. By some intuition or instinct I felt that the child I had before so dreaded was pleading in my behalf. Ere he had ceased another stranger entered the room. He appeared older than the rest, though not old; his countenance, less smoothly serene than theirs, though equally regular in its features, seemed to me to have more the touch of a humanity akin to my own. He listened quietly to the words addressed to him, first by my guide, next by two others of the group, and lastly by the child; then turned towards myself, and addressed me, not by words, but by signs and gestures. These I fancied that I perfectly understood, and I was not mistaken. I comprehended that he inquired whence I came. I extended my arm and pointed towards the road which had led me from the chasm in the rock; then an idea seized me. I drew forth my pocket-book, and sketched on one of its blank leaves a rough design of the ledge of the rock, the rope, myself clinging to it; then of the cavernous rock below, the head of the reptile, the lifeless form of my friend. I gave this primitive kind of hieroglyph to my interrogator, who, after inspecting it gravely, handed it to his next neighbour, and it thus passed round the group. The being I had at first encountered then said a few words, and the child, who approached and looked at my drawing, nodded as if he comprehended its purport, and, returning to the window, expanded the wings attached to his form, shook them once or twice, and then launched himself into space without. I started up in amaze, and hastened to the window. The child was already in the air, buoyed on his wings, which he did not flap to and fro as a bird does, but which were elevated over his head, and seemed to bear him steadily aloft without effort of his own. His flight seemed as swift as any eagle's; and I observed that it was towards the rock whence I had descended, of which the outline loomed visible in the brilliant atmosphere. In a very few minutes he returned, skimming through the opening from which he had gone, and dropping on the floor the rope and grappling-hooks I had left at the descent from the chasm. Some words in a low tone passed between the beings present. One of the group touched an automaton, which started forward and glided from the room; then the last comer, who had addressed me by gestures, rose, took me by the hand, and led me into the corridor. There the platform by which I had mounted awaited us; we placed ourselves on it, and were lowered into the hall below. My new companion, still holding me by the hand, conducted me from the building into a street (so to speak) that stretched beyond it, with buildings on either side, separated from each other by gardens bright with rich-coloured vegetation and strange flowers. Interspersed amidst these gardens, which were divided from each other by low walls, or walking slowly along the road, were many forms similar to those I had already seen. Some of the passers-by, on observing me, approached my guide, evidently by their tones, looks, and gestures addressing to him inquiries about myself. In a few moments a crowd collected round us, examining me with great interest, as if I were some rare wild animal. Yet even in gratifying their curiosity they preserved a grave and courteous demeanour; and after a few words from my guide, who seemed to me to deprecate obstruction in our road, they fell back with a stately inclination of head, and resumed their own way with tranquil indifference. Midway in this thoroughfare we stopped at a building that differed from those we had hitherto passed, inasmuch as it formed three sides of a vast court, at the angles of which were lofty pyramidal towers; in the open space between the sides was a circular fountain of colossal dimensions, and throwing up a dazzling spray of what seemed to me fire. We entered the building through an open doorway and came into an enormous hall, in which were several groups of children, all apparently employed in work as at some great factory. There was a huge engine in the wall which was in full play, with wheels and cylinders, and resembling our own steam-engines, except that it was richly ornamented with precious stones and metals, and appeared to emit a pale phosphorescent atmosphere of shifting light. Many of the children were at some mysterious work on this machinery, others were seated before tables. I was not allowed to linger long enough to examine into the nature of their employment. Not one young voice was heard, not one young face turned to gaze on us. They were all still and indifferent as may be ghosts, through the midst of which pass unnoticed the forms of the living.

Quitting this hall, my guide led me through a gallery richly painted in compartments, with a barbaric mixture of gold in the colours, like pictures by Louis Cranach. The subjects described on these walls appeared to my glance as intended to illustrate events in the history of the race amidst which I was admitted. In all there were figures, most of them like the manlike creatures I had seen, but not all in the same fashion of garb, nor all with wings. There were also the effigies of various animals and birds wholly strange to me, with back-grounds depicting landscapes or buildings. So far as my imperfect knowledge of the pictorial art would allow me to form an opinion, these paintings seemed very accurate in design and very rich in colouring, showing a perfect knowledge of perspective, but their details not arranged according to the rules of composition acknowledged by our artists,— wanting, as it were, a centre; so that the effect was vague, scattered, confused, bewildering; they were like heterogeneous fragments of a dream of art.

We now came into a room of moderate size, in which was assembled what I afterwards knew to be the family of my guide, seated at a table spread as for repast. The forms thus grouped were those of my guide's wife, his daughter, and two sons. I recognized at once the difference between the two sexes, though the two females were of taller stature and ampler proportions than the males; and their countenances, if still more symmetrical in outline and contour, were devoid of the softness and timidity of expression which give charm to the face of woman as seen on the earth above. The wife wore no wings, the daughter wore wings longer than those of the males.

My guide uttered a few words, on which all the persons seated rose, and with that peculiar mildness of look and manner which I have before noticed, and which is, in truth, the common attribute of this formidable race, they saluted me according to their fashion, which consists in laying the right hand very gently on the head and uttering a soft sibilant monosyllable,— S. Si, equivalent to "Welcome."

The mistress of the house then seated me beside her, and heaped a golden platter before me from one of the dishes.

While I ate (and though the viands were new to me, I marvelled more at the delicacy than the strangeness of their flavour), my companions conversed quietly, and, so far as I could detect, with polite avoidance of any direct reference to myself, or any obtrusive scrutiny of my appearance. Yet I was the first creature of that variety of the human race to which I belong that they had ever beheld, and was consequently regarded by them as a most curious and abnormal phenomenon. But all rudeness is unknown to this people, and the youngest child is taught to despise any vehement emotional demonstration. When the meal was ended, my guide again took me by the hand, and, re-entering the gallery, touched a metallic plate inscribed with strange figures, and which I rightly conjectured to be of the nature of our telegraphs. A platform descended, but this time we mounted to a much greater height than in the former building, and found ourselves in a room of moderate dimensions, and which in its general character had much that might be familiar to the associations of a visitor from the upper world. There were shelves on the wall containing what appeared to be books, and indeed were so; mostly very small, like our diamond duodecimos, shaped in the fashion of our volumes, and bound in fine sheets of metal. There were several curious-looking pieces of mechanism scattered about, apparently models, such as might be seen in the study of any professional mechanician. Four automata (mechanical contrivances which, with these people, answer the ordinary purposes of domestic service) stood phantom-like at each angle in the wall. In a recess was a low couch, or bed with pillows. A window, with curtains of some fibrous material drawn aside, opened upon a large balcony. My host stepped out into the balcony; I followed him. We were on the uppermost story of one of the angular pyramids; the view beyond was of a wild and solemn beauty impossible to describe,— the vast ranges of precipitous rock which formed the distant background; the intermediate valleys of mystic many-coloured herbage; the flash of waters, many of them like streams of roseate flame; the serene lustre diffused over all by myriads of lamps, combined to form a whole of which no words of mine can convey adequate description,— so splendid was it, yet so sombre; so lovely, yet so awful.

But my attention was soon diverted from these nether landscapes. Suddenly there arose, as from the streets below, a burst of joyous music; then a winged form soared into the space; another, as in chase of the first, another and another; others after others, till the crowd grew thick and the number countless. But how describe the fantastic grace of these forms in their undulating movements! They appeared engaged in some sport or amusement, now forming into opposite squadrons; now scattering; now each group threading the other, soaring, descending, interweaving, severing,— all in measured time to the music below, as if in the dance of the fabled Peri.

I turned my gaze on my host in a feverish wonder. I ventured to place my hand on the large wings that lay folded on his breast, and in doing so a slight shock as of electricity passed through me. I recoiled in fear; my host smiled, and, as if courteously to gratify my curiosity, slowly expanded his pinions. I observed that his garment beneath then became dilated as a bladder that fills with air. The arms seemed to slide into the wings, and in another moment he had launched himself into the luminous atmosphere, and hovered there, still, and with outspread wings, as an eagle that basks in the sun. Then, rapidly as an eagle swoops, he rushed downwards into the midst of one of the groups, skimming through the mist, and as suddenly again soaring aloft. Thereon, three forms, in one of which I thought to recognize my host's daughter, detached themselves from the rest, and followed him as a bird sportively follows a bird. My eyes, dazzled with the lights and bewildered by the throngs, ceased to distinguish the gyrations and evolutions of these winged playmates, till presently my host re-emerged from the crowd and alighted at my side.

The strangeness of all I had seen began now to operate fast on my senses; my mind itself began to wander. Though not inclined to be superstitious, nor hitherto believing that man could be brought into bodily communication with demons, I felt the terror and the wild excitement with which, in the Gothic ages, a traveller might have persuaded himself that he witnessed a *sabbat* of fiends and witches. I have a vague recollection of having attempted with vehement gesticulation, and forms of exorcism, and loud incoherent words, to repel my courteous and indulgent host; of his mild endeavours to calm and soothe me; of his intelligent conjecture that my fright and bewilderment were occasioned by the difference of form and movement between us, which the wings that had excited my marvelling curiosity had, in exercise, made still more strongly perceptible; of the gentle smile with which he had sought to dispel my alarm by dropping the wings to the ground and endeavouring to show me that they were but a mechanical contrivance. That sudden transformation did but increase my horror, and as extreme fright often shows itself by extreme daring, I sprang at his throat like a wild beast. On an instant I was felled to the ground as by an electric shock, and the last confused images floating before my sight ere I became wholly insensible were the form of my host kneeling beside me with one hand on my forehead, and the beautiful calm face of his daughter, with large, deep, inscrutable eyes intently fixed upon my own.

CHAPTER VI.

I remained in this unconscious state, as I afterwards learned, for many days, even for some weeks, according to our computation of time. When I recovered I was in a strange room, my host and all his family were gathered round me, and to my utter amaze my host's daughter accosted me in my own language with but a slightly foreign accent.

"How do you feel?" she asked.

It was some moments before I could overcome my surprise enough to falter out, "You know my language? How? Who and what are you?"

My host smiled, and motioned to one of his sons, who then took from a table a number of thin metallic sheets on which were traced drawings of various figures,—a house, a tree, a bird, a man, etc.

In these designs I recognized my own style of drawing. Under each figure was written the name of it in my language, and in my writing; and in another handwriting a word strange to me beneath it.

Said the host, "Thus we began; and my daughter Zee, who belongs to the College of Sages, has been your instructress and ours too."

Zee then placed before me other metallic sheets, on which, in my writing, words first, and then sentences, were inscribed; under each word and each sentence strange characters in another hand. Rallying my senses, I comprehended that thus a rude dictionary had been effected. Had it been done while I was dreaming? "That is enough now," said Zee, in a tone of command. "Repose and take food."

CHAPTER VII.

A ROOM to myself was assigned to me in this vast edifice. It was prettily and fantastically arranged, but without any of the splendour of metal work or gems which was displayed in the more public apartments. The walls were hung with a variegated matting made from the stalks and fibres of plants, and the floor carpeted with the same.

The bed was without curtains, its supports of iron resting on balls of crystal; the coverings, of a thin white substance resembling cotton. There were sundry shelves containing books. A curtained recess communicated with an aviary filled with singing-birds, of which I did not recognize one resembling those I have seen on earth, except a beautiful species of dove, though this was distinguished from our doves by a tall crest of bluish plumes. All these birds had been trained to sing in artful tunes, and greatly exceeded the skill of our piping bullfinches, which can rarely achieve more than two tunes, and cannot, I believe, sing those in concert. One might have supposed one's self at an opera in listening to the voices in my aviary. There were duets and trios, and quartettes and choruses, all arranged as in one piece of music. Did I want to silence the birds? I had but to draw a curtain over the aviary, and their song hushed as they found themselves left in the dark. Another opening formed a window, not glazed, but on touching a spring, a shutter ascended from the floor, formed of some substance less transparent than glass, but still sufficiently pellucid to allow a softened view of the scene without. To this window was attached a balcony, or rather hanging-garden, wherein grew many graceful plants and brilliant flowers. The apartment and its appurtenances had thus a character, if strange in detail, still familiar, as a whole, to modern notions of luxury, and would have excited admiration if found attached to the apartments of an English duchess or a fashionable French author.   Before I arrived this was Zee's chamber; she had hospitably assigned it to me.

Some hours after the waking up which is described in my last chapter, I was lying alone on my couch, trying to fix my thoughts on conjecture as to the nature and genus of the people amongst whom I was thrown, when my host and his daughter Zee entered the room. My host, still speaking my native language, inquired, with much politeness, whether it would be agreeable to me to converse, or if I preferred solitude. I replied that I should feel much honoured and obliged by the opportunity offered me to express my gratitude for the hospitality and civilities I had received in a country to which I was a stranger, and to learn enough of its customs and manners not to offend through ignorance.

As I spoke, I had of course risen from my couch; but Zee,

much to my confusion, curtly ordered me to lie down again, and there was something in her voice and eye, gentle as both were, that compelled my obedience. She then seated herself unconcernedly at the foot of my bed, while her father took his place on a divan a few feet distant.

"But what part of the world do you come from," asked my host, "that we should appear so strange to you, and you to us? I have seen individual specimens of nearly all the races differing from our own, except the primeval savages who dwell in the most desolate and remote recesses of uncultivated nature, unacquainted with other light than that they obtain from volcanic fires, and contented to grope their way in the dark, as do many creeping, crawling, and even flying things. But certainly you cannot be a member of those barbarous tribes, nor, on the other hand, do you seem to belong to any civilized people."

I was somewhat nettled at this last observation, and replied that I had the honour to belong to one of the most civilized nations of the earth; and that, so far as light was concerned, while I admired the ingenuity and disregard of expense with which my host and his fellow-citizens had contrived to illumine the regions unpenetrated by the rays of the sun, yet I could not conceive how any who had once beheld the orbs of heaven could compare to their lustre the artificial lights invented by the necessities of man. But my host said he had seen specimens of most of the races differing from his own, save the wretched barbarians he had mentioned. Now, was it possible that he had never been on the surface of the earth, or could he only be referring to communities buried within its entrails?

My host was for some moments silent; his countenance showed a degree of surprise which the people of that race very rarely manifest under any circumstances, howsoever extraordinary. But Zee was more intelligent, and exclaimed, "So you see, my father, that there is truth in the old tradition; there always is truth in every tradition commonly believed in all times and by all tribes."

"Zee," said my host, mildly, "you belong to the College of

Sages, and ought to be wiser than I am; but, as chief of the Light-preserving Council, it is my duty to take nothing for granted till it is proved to the evidence of my own senses." Then, turning to me, he asked me several questions about the surface of the earth and the heavenly bodies; upon which, though I answered him to the best of my knowledge, my answers seemed not to satisfy nor convince him. He shook his head quietly, and, changing the subject rather abruptly, asked how I had come down from what he was pleased to call one world to the other. I answered that under the surface of the earth there were mines containing minerals, or metals, essential to our wants and our progress in all arts and industries; and I then briefly explained the manner in which, while exploring one of these mines, I and my ill-fated friend had obtained a glimpse of the regions into which we had descended, and how the descent had cost him his life,— appealing to the rope and grappling-hooks that the child had brought to the house in which I had been at first received, as a witness of the truthfulness of my story.

My host then proceeded to question me as to the habits and modes of life among the races on the upper earth, more especially among those considered to be the most advanced in that civilization which he was pleased to define "the art of diffusing throughout a community the tranquil happiness which belongs to a virtuous and well-ordered household." Naturally desiring to represent in the most favourable colours the world from which I came, I touched but slightly, though indulgently, on the antiquated and decaying institutions of Europe, in order to expatiate on the present grandeur and prospective pre-eminence of that glorious American Republic, in which Europe enviously seeks its model and tremblingly foresees its doom. Selecting for an example of the social life of the United States that city in which progress advances at the fastest rate, I indulged in an animated description of the moral habits of New York. Mortified to see, by the faces of my listeners, that I did not make the favourable impression I had anticipated, I elevated my theme, dwelling on the excellence of democratic institutions, their promotion of tranquil happiness by the government of party, and the mode in which they diffused such happiness throughout the community by preferring, for the exercise of power and the acquisition of honours, the lowliest citizens in point of property, education, and character. Fortunately recollecting the peroration of a speech, on the purifying influences of American democracy and their destined spread over the world, made by a certain eloquent senator (for whose vote in the Senate a Railway Company, to which my two brothers belonged, had just paid twenty thousand dollars), I wound up by repeating its glowing predictions of the magnificent future that smiled upon mankind,— when the flag of freedom should float over an entire continent, and two hundred millions of intelligent citizens, accustomed from infancy to the daily use of revolvers, should apply to a cowering universe the doctrine of the Patriot Monroe.

When I had concluded my host gently shook his head, and fell into a musing study, making a sign to me and his daughter to remain silent while he reflected; and after a time he said, in a very earnest and solemn tone, "If you think as you say, that you, though a stranger, have received kindness at the hands of me and mine, I adjure you to reveal nothing to any other of our people respecting the world from which you came, unless, on consideration, I give you permission to do so. Do you consent to this request?"

"Of course I pledge my word to it," said I, somewhat amazed; and I extended my right hand to grasp his. But he placed my hand gently on his forehead and his own right hand on my breast, which is the custom among this race in all matters of promise or verbal obligations. Then turning to his daughter, he said, "And you, Zee, will not repeat to any one what the stranger has said, or may say, to me or to you, of a world other than our own." Zee rose and kissed her father on the temples, saying, with a smile, "A Gy's tongue is wanton, but love can fetter it fast; and if, my father, you fear lest a chance word from me or yourself could expose our community to danger, by a desire to explore a world beyond us, will not a wave of the *vril*, properly impelled, wash even the memory of what we have heard the stranger say out of the tablets of the brain?"

"What is vril?" I asked.

Therewith Zee began to enter into an explanation of which I understood very little, for there is no word in any language I know which is an exact synonym for vril. I should call it electricity, except that it comprehends in its manifold branches other forces of nature, to which, in our scientific nomenclature, differing names are assigned, such as magnetism, galvanism, etc. These people consider that in vril they have arrived at the unity in natural energetic agencies, which has been conjectured by many philosophers above ground, and which Faraday thus intimates under the more cautious term of "correlation": —

"I have long held an opinion," says that illustrious experimentalist, "almost amounting to a conviction, in common, I believe, with many other lovers of natural knowledge, that the various forms under which the forces of matter are made manifest have one common origin; or, in other words, are so directly related and mutually dependent, that they are convertible, as it were, into one another, and possess equivalents of power in their action."

These subterranean philosophers assert that, by one operation of vril, which Faraday would perhaps call "atmospheric magnetism," they can influence the variations of temperature, — in plain words, the weather; that by other operations, akin to those ascribed to mesmerism, electro-biology, odic force, etc., but applied scientifically through vril conductors, they can exercise influence over minds, and bodies· animal and vegetable, to an extent not surpassed in the romances of our mystics. To all such agencies they give the common name of "vril." Zee asked me if, in my world, it was not known that all the faculties of the mind could be quickened to a degree unknown in the waking state, by trance or vision, in which the thoughts of one brain could be transmitted to another, and knowledge be thus rapidly interchanged. I replied that there were among us stories told of such trance or vision, and that I had heard much and seen something of the mode in which they were artificially effected, as in mesmeric clairvoyance;

but that these practices had fallen much into disuse or contempt, partly because of the gross impostures to which they
had been made subservient, and partly because, even where
the effects upon certain abnormal constitutions were genuinely
produced, the effects, when fairly examined and analyzed,
were very unsatisfactory,— not to be relied upon for any systematic truthfulness or any practical purpose, and rendered
very mischievous to credulous persons by the superstitions
they tended to produce. Zee received my answers with much
benignant attention, and said that similar instances of abuse
and credulity had been familiar to their own scientific experience in the infancy of their knowledge and while the
properties of vril were misapprehended, but that she reserved
further discussion on this subject till I was more fitted to enter into it. She contented herself with adding that it was
through the agency of vril, while I had been placed in the state
of trance, that I had been made acquainted with the rudiments
of their language; and that she and her father, who, alone of
the family, took the pains to watch the experiment, had acquired a greater proportionate knowledge of my language than
I of their own,— partly because my language was much simpler than theirs, comprising far less of complex ideas; and
partly because their organization was, by hereditary culture,
much more ductile and more readily capable of acquiring
knowledge than mine. At this I secretly demurred; and having had, in the course of a practical life, to sharpen my wits,
whether at home or in travel, I could not allow that my cere-
bral organization could possibly be duller than that of people
who had lived all their lives by lamplight. However, while
I was thus thinking, Zee quietly pointed her forefinger at my
forehead and sent me to sleep.

CHAPTER VIII.

When I once more awoke I saw by my bedside the child who had brought the rope and grappling-hooks to the house in which I had been first received, and which, as I afterwards learned, was the residence of the chief magistrate of the tribe. The child, whose name was Taë (pronounced Tar-ēē), was the magistrate's eldest son. I found that during my last sleep or trance I had made still greater advance in the language of the country, and could converse with comparative ease and fluency.

This child was singularly handsome, even for the beautiful race to which he belonged, with a countenance very manly in aspect for his years, and with a more vivacious and energetic expression than I had hitherto seen in the serene and passionless faces of the men. He brought me the tablet on which I had drawn the mode of my descent, and had also sketched the head of the horrible reptile that had scared me from my friend's corpse. Pointing to that part of the drawing, Taë put to me a few questions respecting the size and form of the monster, and the cave or chasm from which it had emerged. His interest in my answers seemed so grave as to divert him for a while from any curiosity as to myself or my antecedents; but to my great embarrassment, seeing how I was pledged to my host, he was just beginning to ask me where I came from, when Zee fortunately entered, and, overhearing him, said, "Taë, give to our guest any information he may desire, but ask none from him in return. To question him who he is, whence he comes, or wherefore he is here, would be a breach of the law which my father has laid down for this house."

"So be it," said Taë, pressing his hand to his heart; and from that moment till the one in which I saw him last, this child, with whom I became very intimate, never once put to me any of the questions thus interdicted.

CHAPTER IX.

IT was not for some time, and until, by repeated trances, if they are so to be called, my mind became better prepared to interchange ideas with my entertainers, and more fully to comprehend differences of manners and customs, at first too strange to my experience to be seized by my reason, that I was enabled to gather the following details respecting the origin and history of this subterranean population, as portion of one great family race called the "Ana."

According to the earliest traditions, the remote progenitors of the race had once tenanted a world above the surface of that in which their descendants dwelt. Myths of that world were still preserved in their archives, and in those myths were legends of a vaulted dome in which the lamps were lighted by no human hand; but such legends were considered by most commentators as allegorical fables. According to these traditions the earth itself, at the date to which the traditions ascend, was not indeed in its infancy, but in the throes and travail of transition from one form of development to another, and subject to many violent revolutions of nature. By one of such revolutions, that portion of the upper world inhabited by the ancestors of this race had been subjected to inundations, not rapid, but gradual and uncontrollable, in which all, save a scanty remnant, were submerged and perished. Whether this be a record of our historical and sacred Deluge, or of some earlier one contended for by geologists, I do not pretend to conjecture; though, according to the chronology of this people as compared with that of Newton, it must have been many thousands of years before the time of Noah. On the other hand, the account of these writers does not harmonize with the opinions most in vogue among geological authorities, inasmuch as it places the existence of a human race upon earth at dates long anterior to that assigned to the terrestrial formation adapted to the introduction of mammalia. A band of the ill-fated race, thus invaded by the Flood, had, during the march of the waters, taken refuge in caverns amidst the loftier rocks, and, wandering through these hollows, they lost sight of the upper world forever. Indeed, the whole face of the earth had been changed by this great revulsion; land had been turned into sea, sea into land. In the bowels of the inner earth even now, I was informed as a positive fact, might be discovered the remains of human habitation,— habitation not in huts and caverns, but in vast cities whose ruins attest the civilization of races which flourished before the age of Noah, and are not to be classified with those genera to which philosophy ascribes the use of flint and the ignorance of iron.

The fugitives had carried with them the knowledge of the arts they had practised above ground,— arts of culture and civilization. Their earliest want must have been that of supplying below the earth the light they had lost above it; and at no time, even in the traditional period, do the races, of which the one I now sojourned with formed a tribe, seem to have been unacquainted with the art of extracting light from gases or manganese or petroleum. They had been accustomed in their former state to contend with the rude forces of nature; and indeed the lengthened battle they had fought with their conqueror Ocean, which had taken centuries in its spread, had quickened their skill in curbing waters into dikes and channels. To this skill they owed their preservation in their new abode. "For many generations," said my host, with a sort of contempt and horror, "these primitive forefathers are said to have degraded their rank and shortened their lives by eating the flesh of animals, many varieties of which had, like themselves, escaped the Deluge, and sought shelter in the hollows of the earth; other animals, supposed to be unknown to the upper world, those hollows themselves produced."

When what we should term the historical age emerged from the twilight of tradition, the Ana were already established in different communities, and had attained to a degree of civilization very analogous to that which the more advanced nations above the earth now enjoy. They were familiar with most of our mechanical inventions, including the application of steam as well as gas. The communities were in fierce competition with each other. They had their rich and their poor; they had orators and conquerors; they made war either for a domain or an idea. Though the various States acknowledged various forms of government, free institutions were beginning to preponderate; popular assemblies increased in power; republics soon became general; the democracy to which the most enlightened European politicians look forward as the extreme goal of political advancement, and which still prevailed among other subterranean races, whom they despised as barbarians, the loftier family of Ana, to which belonged the tribe I was visiting, looked back to as one of the crude and ignorant experiments which belong to the infancy of political science. It was the age of envy and hate, of fierce passions, of constant social changes more or less violent, of strife between classes, of war between State and State. This phase of society lasted, however, for some ages, and was finally brought to a close, at least among the nobler and more intellectual populations, by the gradual discovery of the latent powers stored in the all-permeating fluid which they denominate "Vril."

According to the account I received from Zee, who, as an erudite professor in the College of Sages, had studied such matters more diligently than any other member of my host's family, this fluid is capable of being raised and disciplined into the mightiest agency over all forms of matter, animate or inanimate. It can destroy like the flash of lightning; yet, differently applied, it can replenish or invigorate life, heal, and preserve; and on it they chiefly rely for the cure of disease, or rather for enabling the physical organization to reestablish the due equilibrium of its natural powers, and thereby to cure itself. By this agency they rend way through the most solid substances, and open valleys for culture through the rocks of their subterranean wilderness. From it they extract the light which supplies their lamps, finding it steadier, softer, and healthier than the other inflammable materials they had formerly used.

But the effects of the alleged discovery of the means to
direct the more terrible force of vril were chiefly remarkable
in their influence upon social polity. As these effects became
familiarly known and skilfully administered, war between the
Vril-discoverers ceased, for they brought the art of destruction to such perfection as to annul all superiority in numbers,
discipline, or military skill. The fire lodged in the hollow of
a rod directed by the hand of a child could shatter the strongest fortress, or cleave its burning way from the van to the
rear of an embattled host. If army met army, and both had
command of this agency, it could be but to the annihilation of
each. The age of war was therefore gone, but with the cessa-
tion of war other effects bearing upon the social state soon
became apparent. Man was so completely at the mercy of
man, each whom he encountered being able, if so willing, to
slay him on the instant, that all notions of government by
force gradually vanished from political systems and forms of
law. It is only by force that vast communities, dispersed
through great distances of space, can be kept together; but
now there was no longer either the necessity of self-preserva-
tion or the pride of aggrandizement to make one State desire
to preponderate in population over another.

The Vril-discoverers thus, in the course of a few generations, peacefully split into communities of moderate size.
The tribe amongst which I had fallen was limited to twelve
thousand families. Each tribe occupied a territory sufficient
for all its wants, and at stated periods the surplus population
departed to seek a realm of its own. There appeared no necessity for any arbitrary selection of these emigrants; there
was always a sufficient number who volunteered to depart.

These subdivided States, petty if we regard either territory
or population, all appertained to one vast general family.
They spoke the same language, though the dialects might
slightly differ. They intermarried; they maintained the same
general laws and customs; and so important a bond between
these several communities was the knowledge of vril and the
practice of its agencies, that the word A-Vril was synonymous
with civilization; and Vril-ya, signifying "The Civilized Na-

tions," was the common name by which the communities employing the uses of vril distinguished themselves from such of the Ana as were yet in a state of barbarism.

The government of the tribe of Vril-ya I am treating of was apparently very complicated, really very simple. It was based upon a principle recognized in theory, though little carried out in practice, above ground,— namely, that the object of all systems of philosophical thought tends to the attainment of unity, or the ascent through all intervening labyrinths to the simplicity of a single first cause or principle. Thus in politics, even republican writers have agreed that a benevolent autocracy would insure the best administration, if there were any guarantees for its continuance, or against its gradual abuse of the powers accorded to it. This singular community elected therefore a single supreme magistrate styled "Tur;" he held his office nominally for life, but he could seldom be induced to retain it after the first approach of old age. There was indeed in this society nothing to induce any of its members to covet the cares of office. No honours, no insignia of higher rank were assigned to it. The supreme magistrate was not distinguished from the rest by superior habitation or revenue. On the other hand, the duties awarded to him were marvellously light and easy, requiring no preponderant degree of energy or intelligence. There being no apprehensions of war, there were no armies to maintain; being no government of force, there was no police to appoint and direct. What we call crime was utterly unknown to the Vril-ya; and there were no courts of criminal justice. The rare instances of civil disputes were referred for arbitration to friends chosen by either party, or decided by the Council of Sages, which will be described later. There were no professional lawyers; and indeed their laws were but amicable conventions, for there was no power to enforce laws against an offender who carried in his staff the power to destroy his judges. There were customs and regulations to compliance with which, for several ages, the people had tacitly habituated themselves; or if in any instance an individual felt such compliance hard, he quitted the community and went elsewhere. There was, in

fact, quietly established amid this State much the same com-
pact that is found in our private families, in which we virtu-
ally say to any independent grown-up member of the family
whom we receive and entertain, "Stay or go, according as our
habits and regulations suit or displease you." But though
there were no laws such as we call laws, no race above ground
is so law-observing. Obedience to the rule adopted by the
community has become as much an instinct as if it were implanted by nature. Even in every household the head of it
makes a regulation for its guidance, which is never resisted
nor even cavilled at by those who belong to the family. They
have a proverb, the pithiness of which is much lost in this
paraphrase, "No happiness without order, no order without
authority, no authority without unity." The mildness of all
government among them, civil or domestic, may be signalized
by their idiomatic expressions for such terms as illegal or
forbidden,—namely, "It is requested not to do so-and-so."
Poverty among the Ana is as unknown as crime; not that
property is held in common, or that all are equals in the
extent of their possessions or the size and luxury of their
habitations: but there being no difference of rank or position
between the grades of wealth or the choice of occupations,
each pursues his own inclinations without creating envy or
vying; some like a modest, some a more splendid kind of life;
each makes himself happy in his own way. Owing to this
absence of competition, and the limit placed on the population, it is difficult for a family to fall into distress; there are
no hazardous speculations, no emulators striving for superior
wealth and rank. No doubt, in each settlement all originally
had the same proportions of land dealt out to them; but some,
more adventurous than others, had extended their possessions
farther into the bordering wilds, or had improved into richer
fertility the produce of their fields, or entered into commerce
or trade. Thus, necessarily, some had grown richer than
others, but none had become absolutely poor, or wanting anything which their tastes desired. If they did so, it was
always in their power to migrate, or at the worst to apply,
without shame and with certainty of aid, to the rich; for all

the members of the community considered themselves as
brothers of one affectionate and united family. More upon
this head will be treated of incidentally as my narrative
proceeds.

The chief care of the supreme magistrate was to communicate with certain active departments charged with the administration of special details. The most important and essential
of such details was that connected with the due provision of
light. Of this department my host, Aph-Lin, was the chief.
Another department, which might be called the foreign, communicated with the neighbouring kindred States, principally
for the purpose of ascertaining all new inventions; and to a
third department, all such inventions and improvements in
machinery were committed for trial. Connected with this
department was the College of Sages,— a college especially
favoured by such of the Ana as were widowed and childless,
and by the young unmarried females, amongst whom Zee was
the most active, and, if what we call renown or distinction
was a thing acknowledged by this people (which I shall later
show it is not), among the most renowned or distinguished.
It is by the female Professors of this College that those studies
which are deemed of least use in practical life — as purely
speculative philosophy, the history of remote periods, and
such sciences as entomology, conchology, etc. — are the more
diligently cultivated. Zee, whose mind, active as Aristotle's,
equally embraced the largest domains and the minutest details
of thought, had written two volumes on the parasite insect
that dwells amid the hairs of a tiger's [1] paw, which work was
considered the best authority on that interesting subject. But
the researches of the sages are not confined to such subtle or
elegant studies. They comprise various others more impor-

---

[1] The animal here referred to has many points of difference from the tiger
of the upper world. It is larger, and with a broader paw, and still more
receding frontal. It haunts the sides of lakes and pools, and feeds principally on fishes, though it does not object to any terrestrial animal of inferior
strength that comes in its way. It is becoming very scarce even in the wild
districts, where it is devoured by gigantic reptiles. I apprehend that it
clearly belongs to the tiger species, since the parasite animalcule found in its
paw, like that found in the Asiatic tiger's, is a miniature image of itself.

tant, and especially the properties of vril, to the perception of which their finer nervous organization renders the female Professors eminently keen. It is out of this college that the Tur, or chief magistrate, selects Councillors, limited to three, in the rare instances in which novelty of event or circumstance perplexes his own judgment.

There are a few other departments of minor consequence, but all are carried on so noiselessly and quietly that the evidence of a government seems to vanish altogether, and social order to be as regular and unobtrusive as if it were a law of nature. Machinery is employed to an inconceivable extent in all the operations of labour within and without doors, and it is the unceasing object of the department charged with its administration to extend its efficiency. There is no class of labourers or servants, but all who are required to assist or control the machinery are found in the children, from the time they leave the care of their mothers to the marriageable age, which they place at sixteen for the Gy-ei (the females), twenty for the Ana (the males). These children are formed into bands and sections under their own chiefs, each following the pursuits in which he is most pleased, or for which he feels himself most fitted. Some take to handicrafts, some to agriculture, some to household work, and some to the only services of danger to which the population is exposed; for the sole perils that threaten this tribe are, first, from those occasional convulsions within the earth, to foresee and guard against which tasks their utmost ingenuity,— irruptions of fire and water, the storms of subterranean winds and escaping gases. At the borders of the domain, and at all places where such peril might be apprehended, vigilant inspectors are stationed with telegraphic communication to the hall in which chosen sages take it by turns to hold perpetual sittings. These inspectors are always selected from the elder boys approaching the age of puberty, and on the principle that at that age observation is more acute and the physical forces more alert than at any other. The second service of danger, less grave, is in the destruction of all creatures hostile to the life, or the culture, or even the comfort, of the Ana. Of these the most formidable are the vast reptiles, of some of which antediluvian relics are preserved in our museums, and certain gigantic winged creatures, half bird, half reptile. These, together with lesser wild animals, corresponding to our tigers or venomous serpents, it is left to the younger children to hunt and destroy; because, according to the Ana, here ruthlessness is wanted, and the younger a child the more ruthlessly he will destroy. There is another class of animals in the destruction of which discrimination is to be used, and against which children of intermediate age are appointed,—animals that do not threaten the life of man, but ravage the produce of his labour, — varieties of the elk and deer species, and a smaller creature much akin to our rabbit, though infinitely more destructive to crops, and much more cunning in its mode of depredation. It is the first object of these appointed infants to tame the more intelligent of such animals into respect for enclosures signalized by conspicuous landmarks, as dogs are taught to respect a larder, or even to guard the master's property. It is only where such creatures are found untamable to this extent that they are destroyed. Life is never taken away for food or for sport, and never spared where untamably inimical to the Ana. Concomitantly with these bodily services and tasks, the mental education of the children goes on till boyhood ceases. It is the general custom, then, to pass through a course of instruction at the College of Sages, in which, besides more general studies, the pupil receives special lessons in such vocation or direction of intellect as he himself selects. Some, however, prefer to pass this period of probation in travel, or to emigrate, or to settle down at once into rural or commercial pursuits. No force is put upon individual inclination.

CHAPTER X.

The word Ana (pronounced broadly *Arna*) corresponds with our plural *men;* An (pronounced *Arn*), the singular, with *man.* The word for woman is Gy (pronounced hard, as in Guy); it forms itself into Gy-ei for the plural, but the G becomes soft in the plural, like Jy-ei. They have a proverb to the effect that this difference in pronunciation is symbolical, for that the female sex is soft collectively, but hard to deal with in the individual. The Gy-ei are in the fullest enjoyment of all the rights of equality with males, for which certain philosophers above ground contend.

In childhood they perform the offices of work and labour impartially with boys; and, indeed, in the earlier age appropriated to the destruction of animals irreclaimably hostile, the girls are frequently preferred, as being by constitution more ruthless under the influence of fear or hate. In the interval between infancy and the marriageable age familiar intercourse between the sexes is suspended. At the marriageable age it is renewed, never with worse consequences than those which attend upon marriage. All arts and vocations allotted to the one sex are open to the other, and the Gy-ei arrogate to themselves a superiority in all those abstruse and mystical branches of reasoning, for which they say the Ana are unfitted by a duller sobriety of understanding, or the routine of their matter-of-fact occupations, just as young ladies in our own world constitute themselves authorities in the subtlest points of theological doctrine, for which few men, actively engaged in worldly business, have sufficient learning or refinement of intellect. Whether owing to early training in gymnastic exercises, or to their constitutional organization, the Gy-ei are usually superior to the Ana in physical strength (an important element in the consideration and maintenance of female rights). They attain to loftier stature, and amid their rounder proportions are embedded sinews and muscles as hardy as those of the other sex. Indeed they assert that, according to the original laws of nature, females were intended to be larger than males, and maintain this dogma by reference to the earliest formations of life in insects, and in the most ancient family of the vertebrata,— namely, fishes,— in both of which the females are generally large enough to make a meal of their consorts if they so desire. Above all, the Gy-ei have a readier and more concentrated power over that mysterious fluid or agency which contains the element of destruction, with a larger portion of that sagacity which comprehends dissimulation. Thus they can not only defend themselves against all aggressions from the males, but could, at any moment when he least suspected his danger, terminate the existence of an offending spouse. To the credit of the Gy-ei no instance of their abuse of this awful superiority in the art of destruction is on record for several ages. The last that occurred in the community I speak of appears (according to their chronology) to have been about two thousand years ago. A Gy, then in a fit of jealousy, slew her husband; and this abominable act inspired such terror among the males that they emigrated in a body and left all the Gy-ei to themselves. The history runs that the widowed Gy-ei, thus reduced to despair, fell upon the murderess when in her sleep (and therefore unarmed), and killed her, and then entered into a solemn obligation amongst themselves to abrogate forever the exercise of their extreme conjugal powers, and to inculcate the same obligation for ever and ever on their female children. By this conciliatory process, a deputation despatched to the fugitive consorts succeeded in persuading many to return, but those who did return were mostly the elder ones. The younger, either from too craven a doubt of their consorts, or too high an estimate of their own merits, rejected all overtures, and, remaining in other communities, were caught up there by other mates, with whom perhaps they were no better off. But the loss of so large a portion of the male youth operated as a salutary warning on the Gy-ei, and confirmed them in the pious resolution to which they had pledged themselves. Indeed it is now popularly considered that, by long hereditary disuse, the Gy-ei have lost both the aggressive and the defensive superiority over the Ana which they once possessed, just as in the inferior animals above the earth many peculiarities in their original formation, intended by nature for their protection, gradually fade or become inoperative when not needed under altered circumstances. I should be sorry, however, for any An who induced a Gy to make the experiment whether he or she were the stronger.

From the incident I have narrated, the Ana date certain alterations in the marriage customs, tending, perhaps, somewhat to the advantage of the male. They now bind themselves in wedlock only for three years; at the end of each third year either male or female can divorce the other and is free to marry again. At the end of ten years the An has the privilege of taking a second wife, allowing the first to retire if she so please. These regulations are for the most part a dead letter; divorces and polygamy are extremely rare, and the marriage state now seems singularly happy and serene among this astonishing people,— the Gy-ei, notwithstanding their boastful superiority in physical strength and intellectual abilities, being much curbed into gentle manners by the dread of separation or of a second wife, and the Ana being very much the creatures of custom, and not, except under great aggravation, liking to exchange for hazardous novelties faces and manners to which they are reconciled by habit. But there is one privilege the Gy-ei carefully retain, and the desire for which perhaps forms the secret motive of most lady asserters of woman rights above ground. They claim the privilege, here usurped by men, of proclaiming their love and urging their suit,— in other words, of being the wooing party rather than the wooed. Such a phenomenon as an old maid does not exist among the Gy-ei. Indeed it is very seldom that a Gy does not secure any An upon whom she sets her heart, if his affections be not strongly engaged elsewhere. However coy, reluctant, and prudish the male she courts may prove at first, yet her perseverance, her ardour, her persuasive powers, her command over the mystic agencies of vril, are pretty sure to run down his neck into what we call "the fatal noose." Their argument for the reversal of that relationship of the sexes which the blind tyranny of man has established on the surface of the earth, appears cogent, and is advanced with a frankness which might well be commended to impartial consideration. They say, that of the two the female is by nature of a more loving disposition than the male; that love occupies a larger space in her thoughts, and is more essential to her happiness, and that therefore she ought to be the wooing party; that otherwise the male is a shy and dubitant creature, that he has often a selfish predilection for the single state, that he often pretends to misunderstand tender glances and delicate hints,— that, in short, he must be resolutely pursued and captured. They add, moreover, that unless the Gy can secure the An of her choice, and one whom she would not select out of the whole world becomes her mate, she is not only less happy than she otherwise would be, but she is not so good a being, that her qualities of heart are not sufficiently developed; whereas the An is a creature that less lastingly concentrates his affections on one object; that if he cannot get the Gy whom he prefers he easily reconciles himself to another Gy; and, finally, that at the worst, if he is loved and taken care of, it is less necessary to the welfare of his existence that he should love as well as be loved; he grows contented with his creature comforts, and the many occupations of thought which he creates for himself.

Whatever may be said as to this reasoning, the system works well for the male; for being thus sure that he is truly and ardently loved, and that the more coy and reluctant he shows himself, the more the determination to secure him increases, he generally contrives to make his consent dependent on such conditions as he thinks the best calculated to insure, if not a blissful, at least a peaceful life. Each individual An has his own hobbies, his own ways, his own predilections, and, whatever they may be, he demands a promise of full and unrestrained concession to them. This, in the pursuit of her object, the Gy readily promises; and as the characteristic of this extraordinary people is an implicit veneration for truth,

and her word once given is never broken even by the giddiest
Gy, the conditions stipulated for are religiously observed. In
fact, notwithstanding all their abstract rights and powers, the
Gy-ei are the most amiable, conciliatory, and submissive wives
I have ever seen even in the happiest households above
ground. It is an aphorism among them that "where a Gy
loves it is her pleasure to obey." It will be observed that in
the relationship of the sexes I have spoken only of marriage,
for such is the moral perfection to which this community has
attained, that any illicit connection is as little possible
amongst them as it would be to a couple of linnets during the
time they agreed to live in pairs.

———◆———

CHAPTER XI.

NOTHING had more perplexed me in seeking to reconcile
my sense to the existence of regions extending below the surface of the earth, and habitable by beings, if dissimilar from,
still, in all material points of organism, akin to those in the
upper world, than the contradiction thus presented to the doctrine in which, I believe, most geologists and philosophers
concur, — namely, that though with us the sun is the great
source of heat, yet the deeper we go beneath the crust of the
earth, the greater is the increasing heat, being, it is said,
found in the ratio of a degree for every foot, commencing
from fifty feet below the surface. But though the domains
of the tribe I speak of were, on the higher ground, so comparatively near to the surface that I could account for a temperature, therein, suitable to organic life, yet even the ravines
and valleys of that realm were much less hot than philosophers would deem possible at such a depth, — certainly not
warmer than the south of France, or at least of Italy. And
according to all the accounts I received, vast tracts immeasurably deeper beneath the surface, and in which one might have

thought only salamanders could exist, were inhabited by in-numerable races organized like ourselves. I cannot pretend in any way to account for a fact which is so at variance with the recognized laws of science, nor could Zee much help me towards a solution of it. She did but conjecture that suffi-cient allowance had not been made by our philosophers for the extreme porousness of the interior earth, the vastness of its cavities and irregularities, which served to create free cur-rents of air and frequent winds, and for the various modes in which heat is evaporated and thrown off. She allowed, how-ever, that there was a depth at which the heat was deemed to be intolerable to such organized life as was known to the ex-perience of the Vril-ya, though their philosophers believed that even in such places life of some kind, life sentient, life intellectual, would be found abundant and thriving, could the philosophers penetrate to it. "Wherever the All-Good builds," said she, "there, be sure, He places inhabitants. He loves not empty dwellings." She added, however, that many changes in temperature and climate had been effected by the skill of the Vril-ya, and that the agency of vril had been successfully employed in such changes. She described a sub-tle and life-giving medium called Lai, which I suspect to be identical with the ethereal oxygen of Dr. Lewins, wherein work all the correlative forces united under the name of vril; and contended that wherever this medium could be expanded, as it were, sufficiently for the various agencies of vril to have ample play, a temperature congenial to the highest forms of life could be secured. She said also that it was the belief of their naturalists that flowers and vegetation had been pro-duced originally (whether developed from seeds borne from the surface of the earth in the earlier convulsions of nature, or imported by the tribes that first sought refuge in cavernous hollows) through the operations of the light constantly brought to bear on them, and the gradual improvement in culture. She said also, that since the vril light had superseded all other light-giving bodies, the colours of flower and foliage had become more brilliant, and vegetation had acquired larger growth.

Leaving these matters to the consideration of those better competent to deal with them, I must now devote a few pages to the very interesting questions connected with the language of the Vril-ya.

CHAPTER XII.

THE language of the Vril-ya is peculiarly interesting, because it seems to me to exhibit with great clearness the traces of the three main transitions through which language passes in attaining to perfection of form.

One of the most illustrious of recent philologists, Max Müller, in arguing for the analogy between the strata of language and the strata of the earth, lays down this absolute dogma: —

" No language can, by any possibility, be inflectional without having passed through the agglutinative and isolating stratum. No language can be agglutinative without clinging with its roots to the underlying stratum of isolation." [1]

Taking then the Chinese language as the best existing type of the original isolating stratum, "as the faithful photograph of man in his leading-strings trying the muscles of his mind, groping his way, and so delighted with his first successful grasps that he repeats them again and again," [2] — we have, in the language of the Vril-ya, still "clinging with its roots to the underlying stratum," the evidences of the original isolation. It abounds in monosyllables, which are the foundations of the language. The transition into the agglutinative form marks an epoch that must have gradually extended through ages, the written literature of which has only survived in a few fragments of symbolical mythology and certain pithy sentences which have passed into popular proverbs. With the extant literature of the Vril-ya the inflectional stratum commences. No doubt at that time there must have operated

[1] On the Stratification of Language, p. 20.
[2] Max Müller, Stratification of Language, p. 13.

concurrent causes, in the fusion of races by some dominant
people, and the rise of some great literary phenomena by
which the form of language became arrested and fixed. As
the inflectional stage prevailed over the agglutinative, it is
surprising to see how much more boldly the original roots of
the language project from the surface that conceals them.   In
the old fragments and proverbs of the preceding stage the
monosyllables which compose those roots vanish amidst words
of enormous length, comprehending whole sentences from
which no one part can be disentangled from the other and employed separately. But when the inflectional form of language became so far advanced as to have its scholars and
grammarians, they seem to have united in extirpating all
such polysynthetical or polysyllabic monsters, as devouring
invaders of the aboriginal forms. Words beyond three syllables became proscribed as barbarous, and in proportion as the
language grew thus simplified it increased in strength, in dignity, and in sweetness. Though now very compressed in
sound, it gains in clearness by that compression. By a single
letter, according to its position, they contrive to express all
that with civilized nations in our upper world it takes the
waste, sometimes of syllables, sometimes of sentences, to express. Let me here cite one or two instances: An (which I
will translate man), Ana (men); the letter S is with them a
letter implying multitude, according to where it is placed;
Sana means mankind; Ansa, a multitude of men. The prefix
of certain letters in their alphabet invariably denotes com-
pound significations. For instance, Gl (which with them is
a single letter, as Th is a single letter with the Greeks) at the
commencement of a word infers an assemblage or union of
things, sometimes kindred, sometimes dissimilar,—as Oon, a
house; Gloon, a town (that is, an assemblage of houses). Ata
is sorrow; Glata, a public calamity. Aur-an is the health or
well-being of a man; Glauran, the well-being of the State,
the good of the community; and a word constantly in their
mouths is A-glauran, which denotes their political creed,—
namely, that "the first principle of a community is the good
of all." Aub is invention; Sila, a tone in music. Glaubsila,

as uniting the ideas of invention and of musical intonation, is the classical word for poetry,— abbreviated in ordinary conversation to Glaubs. Na, which with them is, like GI, but a single letter, always, when an initial, implies something antagonistic to life or joy or comfort, resembling in this the Aryan root Nak, expressive of perishing or destruction. Nax is darkness; Narl, death; Naria, sin or evil; Nas — an uttermost condition of sin and evil, — corruption. In writing, they deem it irreverent to express the Supreme Being by any special name. He is symbolized by what may be termed the hieroglyphic of a pyramid, Δ. In prayer they address Him by a name which they deem too sacred to confide to a stranger, and I know it not. In conversation they generally use a periphrastic epithet, such as the All-Good. The letter V, symbolical of the inverted pyramid, where it is an initial, nearly always denotes excellence or power; as Vril, of which I have said so much; Veed, an immortal spirit; Veedya, immortality. Koom, pronounced like the Welsh Cwm, denotes something of hollowness. Koom itself is a profound hollow, metaphorically a cavern; Koom-in, a hole; Zi-koom, a valley; Koom-zi, vacancy or void; Bodh-koom, ignorance (literally, knowledge-void). Koom-Posh is their name for the government of the many, or the ascendancy of the most ignorant or hollow. Posh is an almost untranslatable idiom implying, as the reader will see later, contempt. The closest rendering I can give to it is our slang term "bosh;" and thus Koom-Posh may be loosely rendered "Hollow-Bosh." But when Democracy or Koom-Posh degenerates from popular ignorance into that popular passion or ferocity which precedes its decease, as (to cite illustrations from the upper world) during the French Reign of Terror, or for the fifty years of the Roman Republic preceding the ascendancy of Augustus, their name for that state of things is Glek-Nas. Ek is strife; Glek, the universal strife; Nas, as I before said, is corruption or rot,— thus Glek-Nas may be construed "the universal strife-rot." Their compounds are very expressive; thus, Bodh being knowledge, and Too, a participle that implies the action of cautiously approaching, Too-bodh is their word for Philosophy. Pah is a contemptuous exclamation analogous to our idiom, "stuff and nonsense;" Pah-bodh (literally, stuff-and-nonsense-knowledge) is their term for futile or false philosophy, and is applied to a species of metaphysical or speculative ratiocination formerly in vogue, which consisted in making inquiries that could not be answered, and were not worth making,— such, for instance, as, "Why does an An have five toes to his feet instead of four or six?" "Did the first An, created by the All-Good, have the same number of toes as his descendants?" "In the form by which an An will be recognized by his friends in the future state of being, will he retain any toes at all, and, if so, will they be material toes or spiritual toes?" I take these illustrations of Pah-bodh, not in irony or jest, but because the very inquiries I name formed the subject of controversy by the latest cultivators of that "science" four thousand years ago.

In the declension of nouns I was informed that anciently there were eight cases (one more than in the Sanskrit Grammar); but the effect of time has been to reduce these cases, and multiply, instead of these varying terminations, explanatory prepositions. At present, in the Grammar submitted to my study, there were four cases to nouns, three having varying terminations, and the fourth a differing prefix.

	SINGULAR.			PLURAL.	
Nom.	An,	Man.	*Nom.*	Ana,	Men.
Dat.	Ano,	to Man.	*Dat.*	Anoi,	to Men.
Ac.	Anam,	Man.	*Ac.*	Ananda,	Men.
Voc.	Hil-An,	O Man.	*Voc.*	Hil-Ananda,	O Men.

In the elder inflectional literature the dual form existed; it has long been obsolete.

The genitive case with them is also obsolete; the dative supplies its place: they say the house *to* a man, instead of the house *of* a man. When used (sometimes in poetry), the genitive in the termination is the same as the nominative; so is the ablative, the preposition that marks it being a prefix or suffix at option, and generally decided by ear, according to the sound of the noun. It will be observed that the prefix Hil marks the vocative case. It is always retained in addressing another, except in the most intimate domestic relations; its omission would be considered rude: just as in our old forms of speech in addressing a king it would have been deemed disrespectful to say "King," and reverential to say "O King." In fact, as they have no titles of honour, the vocative adjuration supplies the place of a title, and is given impartially to all. The prefix Hil enters into the composition of words that imply distant communications, as Hil-ya, to travel.

In the conjugation of their verbs, which is much too lengthy a subject to enter on here, the auxiliary verb Ya, "to go," which plays so considerable a part in the Sanskrit, appears and performs a kindred office, as if it were a radical in some language from which both had descended. But another auxiliary of opposite signification also accompanies it and shares its labours,— namely, Zi, to stay or repose. Thus Ya enters into the future tense, and Zi in the preterite of all verbs requiring auxiliaries. Yam, I go, Yiam, I may go, Yani-ya, I shall go (literally, I go to go), Zampoo-yau, I have gone (literally, I rest from gone). Ya, as a termination, implies by analogy progress, movement, effloresence. Zi, as a terminal, denotes fixity, sometimes in a good sense, sometimes in a bad, according to the word with which it is coupled. Iva-zi, eternal goodness; Nan-zi, eternal evil. Poo (from) enters as a prefix to words that denote repugnance, or things from which we ought to be averse: Poo-pra, disgust; Poo-naria, falsehood, the vilest kind of evil. Poosh, or Posh, I have already confessed to be untranslatable literally. It is an expression of contempt not unmixed with pity. This radical seems to have originated from inherent sympathy between the labial effort and the sentiment that impelled it, Poo being an utterance in which the breath is exploded from the lips with more or less vehemence. On the other hand, Z, when an initial, is with them a sound in which the breath is sucked inward, and thus Zu, pronounced Zoo (which in their language is one letter), is the ordinary prefix to words that signify something that attracts, pleases, touches the heart,— as Zummer, lover; Zutze, love; Zuzulia, delight. This indrawn sound of Z seems indeed naturally appropriate to fondness.

Thus, even in our language, mothers say to their babies, in defiance of grammar, "Zoo darling;" and I have heard a learned professor at Boston call his wife (he had been only married a month) "Zoo little pet."

I cannot quit this subject, however, without observing by what slight changes in the dialects favoured by different tribes of the same race, the original signification and beauty of sounds may become confused and deformed. Zee told me with much indignation that Zūmmer (lover), which, in the way she uttered it, seemed slowly taken down to the very depths of her heart, was, in some not very distant communities of the Vril-ya, vitiated into the half-hissing, half-nasal, wholly disagreeable, sound of Sūbber. I thought to myself it only wanted the introduction of *n* before *u* to render it into an English word significant of the last quality an amorous Gy would desire in her Zummer.

I will but mention another peculiarity in this language which gives equal force and brevity to its forms of expressions.

A is with them, as with us, the first letter of the alphabet, and is often used as a prefix word by itself to convey a complex idea of sovereignty or chiefdom, or presiding principle. For instance, Iva is goodness; Diva, goodness and happiness united; A-Diva is unerring and absolute truth. I have already noticed the value of A in A-glauran; so, in vril (to whose properties they trace their present state of civilization), A-vril, denotes, as I have said, civilization itself.

The philologist will have seen from the above how much the language of the Vril-ya is akin to the Aryan or Indo-Germanic; but, like all languages, it contains words and forms in which transfers from very opposite sources of speech have been taken. The very title of Tur, which they give to their supreme magistrate, indicates theft from a tongue akin to the Turanian. They say themselves that this is a foreign word borrowed from a title which their historical records show to have been borne by the chief of a nation with whom the ancestors of the Vril-ya were, in very remote periods, on friendly terms, but which has long become extinct; and they

say that when, after the discovery of vril, they remodelled
their political institutions, they expressly adopted a title
taken from an extinct race and a dead language for that of
their chief magistrate, in order to avoid all titles for that
office with which they had previous associations.

Should life be spared to me, I may collect into systematic
form such knowledge as I acquired of this language during
my sojourn amongst the Vril-ya. But what I have already
said will perhaps suffice to show to genuine philological students that a language which, preserving so many of the roots
in the aboriginal form, and clearing from the immediate, but
transitory, polysynthetical stage so many rude incumbrances,
has attained to such a union of simplicity and compass in its
final inflectional forms, must have been the gradual work of
countless ages and many varieties of mind; that it contains
the evidence of fusion between congenial races, and necessi-
tated, in arriving at the shape of which I have given examples, the continuous culture of a highly thoughtful people.

That, nevertheless, the literature which belongs to this language is a literature of the past; that the present felicitous
state of society at which the Ana have attained forbids the
progressive cultivation of literature, especially in the two
main divisions of fiction and history,— I shall have occasion
to show later.

CHAPTER XIII.

This people have a religion, and, whatever may be said
against it, at least it has these strange peculiarities: firstly,
that they all believe in the creed they profess; secondly, that
they all practise the precepts which the creed inculcates.
They unite in the worship of the one divine Creator and Sustainer of the universe. They believe that it is one of the
properties of the all-permeating agency of vril to transmit to
the well-spring of life and intelligence every thought that a

living creature can conceive; and though they do not contend that the idea of a Deity is innate, yet they say that the An (man) is the only creature, so far as their observation of nature extends, to whom *the capacity of conceiving that idea,* with all the trains of thought which open out from it, is vouchsafed. They hold that this capacity is a privilege that cannot have been given in vain, and hence that prayer and thanksgiving are acceptable to the divine Creator, and necessary to the complete development of the human creature. They offer their devotions both in private and public. Not being considered one of their species, I was not admitted into the building or temple in which the public worship is rendered; but I am informed that the service is exceedingly short, and unattended with any pomp of ceremony. It is a doctrine with the Vril-ya that earnest devotion or complete abstraction from the actual world cannot, with benefit to itself, be maintained long at a stretch by the human mind, especially in public, and that all attempts to do so either lead to fanaticism or to hypocrisy. When they pray in private, it is when they are alone or with their young children.

They say that in ancient times there was a great number of books written upon speculations as to the nature of the Deity, and upon the forms of belief or worship supposed to be most agreeable to Him; but these were found to lead to such heated and angry disputations as not only to shake the peace of the community and divide families before the most united, but in the course of discussing the attributes of the Deity, the existence of the Deity Himself became argued away, or, what was worse, became invested with the passions and infirmities of the human disputants. "For," said my host, "since a finite being like an An cannot possibly define the Infinite, so, when he endeavours to realize an idea of the Divinity, he only reduces the Divinity into an An like himself." During the later ages, therefore, all theological speculations, though not forbidden, have been so discouraged as to have fallen utterly into disuse.

The Vril-ya unite in a conviction of a future state, more felicitous and more perfect than the present. If they have

very vague notions of the doctrine of rewards and punishments, it is perhaps because they have no systems of rewards
and punishments among themselves, for there are no crimes
to punish, and their moral standard is so even that no An
among them is, upon the whole, considered more virtuous than
another. If one excels, perhaps, in one virtue, another equally
excels in some other virtue; if one has his prevalent fault or
infirmity, so also another has his. In fact, in their extraordinary mode of life, there are so few temptations to wrong, that
they are good (according to their notions of goodness) merely
because they live. They have some fanciful notions upon the
continuance of life, when once bestowed, even in the vegetable
world, as the reader will see in the next chapter.

CHAPTER XIV.

Though, as I have said, the Vril-ya discourage all speculations on the nature of the Supreme Being, they appear to
concur in a belief by which they think to solve that great
problem of the existence of evil which has so perplexed the
philosophy of the upper world. They hold that wherever He
has once given life, with the perceptions of that life, however
faint it be, as in a plant, the life is never destroyed; it passes
into new and improved forms, though not in this planet (differing therein from the ordinary doctrine of metempsychosis),
and that the living thing retains the sense of identity, so that
it connects its past life with its future, and is *conscious* of its
progressive improvement in the scale of joy. For they say
that, without this assumption, they cannot, according to the
lights of human reason vouchsafed to them, discover the perfect justice which must be a constituent quality of the All-
Wise and the All-Good. Injustice, they say, can only emanate
from three causes: want of wisdom to perceive what is just,
want of benevolence to desire, want of power to fulfil it; and
that each of these three wants is incompatible in the All-Wise,

the All-Good, the All-Powerful; but that while, even in this
life, the wisdom, the benevolence, and the power of the Supreme Being are sufficiently apparent to compel our recognition, the justice necessarily resulting from those attributes
absolutely requires another life, not for man only, but for
every living thing of the inferior orders; that, alike in the
animal and the vegetable world, we see one individual rendered, by circumstances beyond its control, exceedingly
wretched compared to its neighbours,— one only exists as
the prey of another,— even a plant suffers from disease till
it perishes prematurely, while the plant next to it rejoices in
its vitality and lives out its happy life free from a pang; that
it is an erroneous analogy from human infirmities to reply by
saying that the Supreme Being only acts by general laws,
thereby making his own secondary causes so potent as to mar
the essential kindness of the First Cause; and a still meaner
and more ignorant conception of the All-Good to dismiss with
a brief contempt all consideration of justice for the myriad
forms into which He has infused life, and assume that justice
is only due to the single product of the An. There is no
small and no great in the eyes of the divine Life-Giver. But
once grant that nothing, however humble, which feels that it
lives and suffers, can perish through the series of ages; that
all its suffering here, if continuous from the moment of its
birth to that of its transfer to another form of being, would
be more brief compared with eternity than the cry of the new-
born is compared to the whole life of a man; and once suppose
that this living thing retains its sense of identity when so
transferred (for without that sense it could be aware of no
future being),— then, though indeed the fulfilment of divine
justice is removed from the scope of our ken, yet we have a
right to assume it to be uniform and universal, and not varying and partial, as it would be if acting only upon general
secondary laws; because such perfect justice flows of necessity
from perfectness of knowledge to conceive, perfectness of love
to will, and perfectness of power to complete it.

However fantastic this belief of the Vril-ya may be, it tends
perhaps to confirm politically the systems of government

which, admitting differing degrees of wealth, yet establishes perfect equality in rank, exquisite mildness in all relations and intercourse, and tenderness to all created things which the good of the community does not require them to destroy. And though their notion of compensation to a tortured insect or a cankered flower may seem to some of us a very wild crotchet, yet, at least, it is not a mischievous one; and it may furnish matter for no unpleasing reflection to think that within the abysses of earth, never lit by a ray from the material heavens, there should have penetrated so luminous a conviction of the ineffable goodness of the Creator,— so fixed an idea that the general laws by which He acts cannot admit of any partial injustice or evil, and therefore cannot be comprehended without reference to their action over all space and throughout all time. And since, as I shall have occasion to observe later, the intellectual conditions and social systems of this subterranean race comprise and harmonize great, and apparently antagonistic, varieties in philosophical doctrine and speculation which have from time to time been started, discussed, dismissed, and have re-appeared amongst thinkers or dreamers in the upper world,— so I may perhaps appropriately conclude this reference to the belief of the Vril-ya — that self-conscious or sentient life once given is indestructible among inferior creatures as well as in man — by an eloquent passage from the work of that eminent zoölogist, Louis Agassiz, which I have only just met with, many years after I had committed to paper those recollections of the life of the Vril-ya which I now reduce into something like arrangement and form: —

" The relations which individual animals bear to one another are of such a character that they ought long ago to have been considered as sufficient proof that no organized being could ever have been called into existence by other agency than by the direct intervention of a reflective mind. This argues strongly in favour of the existence in every animal of an immaterial principle similar to that which by its excellence and superior endowments places man so much above animals; yet the principle unquestionably exists, and whether it be called sense, reason, or instinct, it presents in the whole range of organized beings a series of phenomena closely linked together, and upon it are based not only the higher manifestations of the mind, but the very permanence of the specific differences which characterize every organism. Most of the arguments in favour of the immortality of man apply equally to the permanency of this principle in other living beings. May I not add that a future life in which man would be deprived of that great source of enjoyment and intellectual and moral improvement which results from the contemplation of the harmonies of an organic world would involve a lamentable loss? And may we not look to a spiritual concert of the combined worlds and *all* their inhabitants in the presence of their Creator as the highest conception of paradise?" [1]

———◆———

CHAPTER XV.

KIND to me as I found all in this household, the young daughter of my host was the most considerate and thoughtful in her kindness. At her suggestion I laid aside the habiliments in which I had descended from the upper earth, and adopted the dress of the Vril-ya, with the exception of the artful wings which served them, when on foot, as a graceful mantle. But as many of the Vril-ya, when occupied in urban pursuits, did not wear these wings, this exception created no marked difference between myself and the race among which I sojourned, and I was thus enabled to visit the town without exciting unpleasant curiosity. Out of the household no one suspected that I had come from the upper world, and I was but regarded as one of some inferior and barbarous tribe whom Aph-Lin entertained as a guest.

The city was large in proportion to the territory round it, which was of no greater extent than many an English or Hungarian nobleman's estate; but the whole of it, to the verge of the rocks which constituted its boundary, was cultivated to the nicest degree, except where certain allotments of mountain and pasture were humanely left free to the suste-

---

[1] Essay on Classification, sect. xvii. pp. 97–99.

nance of the harmless animals they had tamed, though not for domestic use. So great is their kindness towards these humbler creatures, that a sum is devoted from the public treasury for the purpose of deporting them to other Vril-ya communities willing to receive them (chiefly new colonies), whenever they become too numerous for the pastures allotted to them in their native place. They do not, however, multiply to an extent comparable to the ratio at which, with us, animals bred for slaughter increase. It seems a law of nature that animals not useful to man gradually recede from the domains he occupies, or even become extinct. It is an old custom of the various sovereign States amidst which the race of the Vril-ya are distributed, to leave between each State a neutral and uncultivated border-land. In the instance of the community I speak of, this tract, being a ridge of savage rocks, was impassable by foot, but was easily surmounted, whether by the wings of the inhabitants or the air-boats, of which I shall speak hereafter. Roads through it were also cut for the transit of vehicles impelled by vril. These intercommunicating tracts were always kept lighted, and the expense thereof defrayed by a special tax, to which all the communities comprehended in the denomination of Vril-ya contribute in settled proportions. By these means a considerable commercial traffic with other States, both near and distant, was carried on. The surplus wealth of this special community was chiefly agricultural. The community was also eminent for skill in constructing implements connected with the arts of husbandry. In exchange for such merchandise it obtained articles more of luxury than necessity. There were few things imported on which they set a higher price than birds taught to pipe artful tunes in concert. These were brought from a great distance, and were marvellous for beauty of song and plumage. I understood that extraordinary care was taken by their breeders and teachers in selection, and that the species had wonderfully improved during the last few years. I saw no other pet animals among this community except some very amusing and sportive creatures of the Batrachian species, resembling frogs, but with very intelligent countenances, which

the children were fond of, and kept in their private gardens.
They appear to have no animals akin to our dogs or horses,
though that learned naturalist, Zee, informed me that such
creatures had once existed in those parts, and might now be
found in regions inhabited by other races than the Vril-ya.
She said that they had gradually disappeared from the more
civilized world since the discovery of vril, and the results
attending that discovery, had dispensed with their uses. Machinery and the invention of wings had superseded the horse
as a beast of burden; and the dog was no longer wanted either
for protection or the chase, as it had been when the ancestors
of the Vril-ya feared the aggressions of their own kind, or
hunted the lesser animals for food. Indeed, however, so far
as the horse was concerned, this region was so rocky that a
horse could have been, there, of little use either for pastime
or burden. The only creature they use for the latter purpose
is a kind of large goat, which is much employed on farms.
The nature of the surrounding soil in these districts may be
said to have first suggested the invention of wings and air-
boats. The largeness of space, in proportion to the rural territory occupied by the city, was occasioned by the custom of
surrounding every house with a separate garden. The broad
main street, in which Aph-Lin dwelt, expanded into a vast
square, in which were placed the College of Sages and all the
public offices,— a magnificent fountain of the luminous fluid
which I call naphtha (I am ignorant of its real nature) in the
centre. All these public edifices have a uniform character of
massiveness and solidity. They reminded me of the architectural pictures of Martin. Along the upper stories of each
ran a balcony, or rather a terraced garden, supported by columns, filled with flowering-plants, and tenanted by many
kinds of tame birds. From the square branched several
streets, all broad and brilliantly lighted, and ascending up
the eminence on either side. In my excursions in the town I
was never allowed to go alone; Aph-Lin or his daughter was
my habitual companion. In this community the adult Gy is
seen walking with any young An as familiarly as if there
were no difference of sex.

The retail shops are not very numerous; the persons who attend on a customer are all children of various ages, and exceedingly intelligent and courteous, but without the least touch of importunity or cringing. The shopkeeper himself might or might not be visible; when visible, he seemed rarely employed on any matter connected with his professional business; and yet he had taken to that business from special liking to it, and quite independently of his general sources of fortune.

Some of the richest citizens in the community kept such shops. As I have before said, no difference of rank is recognizable, and therefore all occupations hold the same equal social status. An An, of whom I bought my sandals, was the brother of the Tur, or chief magistrate; and though his shop was not larger than that of any bootmaker in Bond Street or Broadway, he was said to be twice as rich as the Tur, who dwelt in a palace. No doubt, however, he had some country-seat.

The Ana of the community are, on the whole, an indolent set of beings after the active age of childhood. Whether by temperament or philosophy, they rank repose among the chief blessings of life. Indeed, when you take away from a human being the incentives to action which are found in cupidity or ambition, it seems to me no wonder that he rests quiet.

In their ordinary movements they prefer the use of their feet to that of their wings. But for their sports, or (to indulge in a bold misuse of terms) their public *promenades*, they employ the latter, also for the aërial dances I have described, as well as for visiting their country-places, which are mostly placed on lofty heights; and, when still young, they prefer their wings, for travel into the other regions of the Ana, to vehicular conveyances.

Those who accustom themselves to flight can fly, if less rapidly than some birds, yet from twenty-five to thirty miles an hour, and keep up that rate for five or six hours at a stretch. But the Ana generally, on reaching middle age, are not fond of rapid movements requiring violent exercise. Perhaps for this reason, as they hold a doctrine which our own physicians will doubtless approve,—namely, that regular transpiration through the pores of the skin is essential to health,—they habitually use the sweating-baths to which we give the name of Turkish or Roman, succeeded by douches of perfumed waters. They have great faith in the salubrious virtue of certain perfumes.

It is their custom also, at stated but rare periods, perhaps four times a year when in health, to use a bath charged with vril.[1] They consider that this fluid, sparingly used, is a great sustainer of life; but used in excess, when in the normal state of health, rather tends to reaction and exhausted vitality. For nearly all their diseases, however, they resort to it as the chief assistant to nature in throwing off the complaint.

In their own way they are the most luxurious of people, but all their luxuries are innocent. They may be said to dwell in an atmosphere of music and fragrance. Every room has its mechanical contrivances for melodious sounds, usually tuned down to soft-murmured notes, which seem like sweet whispers from invisible spirits. They are too accustomed to these gentle sounds to find them a hindrance to conversation, nor, when alone, to reflection. But they have a notion that to breathe an air filled with continuous melody and perfume has necessarily an effect at once soothing and elevating upon the formation of character and the habits of thought. Though so temperate, and with total abstinence from other animal food than milk, and from all intoxicating drinks, they are delicate and dainty to an extreme in food and beverage; and in all their sports even the old exhibit a childlike gayety. Happiness is the end at which they aim, not as the excitement of a moment, but as the prevailing condition of the entire existence; and regard for the happiness of each other is evinced by the exquisite amenity of their manners.

Their conformation of skull has marked differences from

---

[1] I once tried the effect of the vril bath. It was very similar in its invigorating powers to that of the baths at Gastein, the virtues of which are ascribed by many physicians to electricity; but though similar, the effect of the vril bath was more lasting.

that of any known races in the upper world, though I cannot help thinking it a development, in the course of countless ages, of the Brachycephalic type of the Age of Stone in Lyell's "Elements of Geology," ch. X, p. 113, as compared with the Dolichocephalic type of the beginning of the Age of Iron, correspondent with that now so prevalent amongst us, and called the Celtic type. It has the same comparative massiveness of forehead, not receding like the Celtic, the same even roundness in the frontal organs; but it is far loftier in the apex, and far less pronounced in the hinder cranial hemisphere where phrenologists place the animal organs. To speak as a phrenologist, the cranium common to the Vril-ya has the organs of weight, number, tune, form, order, causality, very largely developed; that of construction much more pronounced than that of ideality. Those which are called the moral organs, such as conscientiousness and benevolence, are amazingly full; amativeness and combativeness are both small; adhesiveness large; the organ of destructiveness (that is, of determined clearance of intervening obstacles) immense, but less than that of benevolence; and their philoprogenitiveness takes rather the character of compassion and tenderness to things that need aid or protection than of the animal love of offspring. I never met with one person deformed or misshapen. The beauty of their countenances is not only in symmetry of feature, but in a smoothness of surface, which continues without line or wrinkle to the extreme of old age, and a serene sweetness of expression, combined with that majesty which seems to come from consciousness of power and the freedom of all terror, physical or moral. It is that very sweetness, combined with that majesty, which inspired in a beholder like myself, accustomed to strive with the passions of mankind, a sentiment of humiliation, of awe, of dread. It is such an expression as a painter might give to a demi-god, a genius, an angel. The males of the Vril-ya are entirely beardless; the Gy-ei sometimes, in old age, develop a small mustache.

I was surprised to find that the colour of their skin was not uniformly that which I had remarked in those individuals whom I had first encountered,—some being much fairer, and even with blue eyes, and hair of a deep golden auburn, though still of complexions warmer or richer in tone than persons in the north of Europe.

I was told that this admixture of colouring arose from intermarriage with other and more distant tribes of the Vril-ya, who, whether by the accident of climate or early distinction of race, were of fairer hues than the tribes of which this community formed one. It was considered that the dark-red skin showed the most ancient family of Ana; but they attached no sentiment of pride to that antiquity, and, on the contrary, believed their present excellence of breed came from frequent crossing with other families differing, yet akin; and they encourage such intermarriages, always provided that it be with the Vril-ya nations. Nations which, not conforming their manners and institutions to those of the Vril-ya, nor indeed held capable of acquiring the powers over the vril agencies which it had taken them generations to attain and transmit, were regarded with more disdain than citizens of New York regard the negroes.

I learned from Zee, who had more lore in all matters than any male with whom I was brought into familiar converse, that the superiority of the Vril-ya was supposed to have originated in the intensity of their earlier struggles against obstacles in nature amidst the localities in which they had first settled. "Wherever," said Zee, moralizing, "wherever goes on that early process in the history of civilization by which life is made a struggle, in which the individual has to put forth all his powers to compete with his fellow, we invariably find this result,—namely, since in the competition a vast number must perish, nature selects for preservation only the strongest specimens. With our race, therefore, even before the discovery of vril, only the highest organizations were preserved; and there is among our ancient books a legend, once popularly believed, that we were driven from a region that seems to denote the world you come from, in order to perfect our condition and attain to the purest elimination of our species by the severity of the struggles our forefathers underwent; and that, when our education shall become finally completed, we are destined to return to the upper world, and supplant all the inferior races now existing therein."

Aph-Lin and Zee often conversed with me in private upon the political and social conditions of that upper world, in which Zee so philosophically assumed that the inhabitants were to be exterminated one day or other by the advent of the Vril-ya. They found in my accounts — in which I continued to do all I could (without launching into falsehoods so positive that they would have been easily detected by the shrewdness of my listeners) to present our powers and ourselves in the most flattering point of view — perpetual subjects of comparison between our most civilized populations and the meaner subterranean races which they considered hopelessly plunged in barbarism, and doomed to gradual if certain extinction. But they both agreed in desiring to conceal from their community all premature opening into the regions lighted by the sun; both were humane, and shrunk from the thought of annihilating so many millions of creatures; and the pictures I drew of our life, highly coloured as they were, saddened them. In vain I boasted of our great men, — poets, philosophers, orators, generals, — and defied the Vril-ya to produce their equals. "Alas!" said Zee, her grand face softening into an angel-like compassion, "this predominance of the few over the many is the surest and most fatal sign of a race incorrigibly savage. See you not that the primary condition of mortal happiness consists in the extinction of that strife and competition between individuals, which, no matter what forms of government they adopt, render the many subordinate to the few, destroy real liberty to the individual, whatever may be the nominal liberty of the State, and annul that calm of existence, without which felicity, mental or bodily, cannot be attained? Our notion is, that the more we can assimilate life to the existence which our noblest ideas can conceive to be that of spirits on the other side of the grave, why, the more we approximate to a divine happiness here, and the more easily we glide into the conditions of being hereafter. For, surely, all we can imagine of the life of gods, or of blessed immortals, supposes the absence of self-made cares and contentious passions, such as avarice and ambition. It seems to us that it must be a life of serene tranquillity, not indeed without active occupations to the intellectual or spiritual powers, but occupations, of whatsoever nature they be, congenial to the idiosyncrasies of each, not forced and repugnant,—a life gladdened by the untrammelled interchange of gentle affections, in which the moral atmosphere utterly kills hate and vengeance and strife and rivalry. Such is the political state to which all the tribes and families of the Vril-ya seek to attain, and towards that goal all our theories of government are shaped. You see how utterly opposed is such a progress to that of the uncivilized nations from which you come, and which aim at a systematic perpetuity of troubles and cares and warring passions, aggravated more and more as their progress storms its way onward. The most powerful of all the races in our world, beyond the pale of the Vril-ya, esteems itself the best governed of all political societies, and to have reached in that respect the extreme end at which political wisdom can arrive, so that the other nations should tend more or less to copy it. It has established, on its broadest base, the Koom-Posh,— namely, the government of the ignorant upon the principle of being the most numerous. It has placed the supreme bliss in the vying with each other in all things, so that the evil passions are never in repose,—vying for power, for wealth, for eminence of some kind; and in this rivalry it is horrible to hear the vituperation, the slanders, and calumnies which even the best and mildest among them heap on each other without remorse or shame."

"Some years ago," said Aph-Lin, "I visited this people, and their misery and degradation were the more appalling because they were always boasting of their felicity and grandeur as compared with the rest of their species; and there is no hope that this people, which evidently resembles your own, can improve, because all their notions tend to further deterioration. They desire to enlarge their dominion more and more, in direct antagonism to the truth that, beyond a very limited range, it is impossible to secure to a community the happiness which belongs to a well-ordered family; and the more they mature a system by which a few individuals are heated and swollen to a size above the standard slenderness of the millions, the more they chuckle and exult, and cry out, 'See by what great exceptions to the common littleness of our race we prove the magnificent results of our system!'"

"In fact," resumed Zee, "if the wisdom of human life be to approximate to the serene equality of immortals, there can be no more direct flying off into the opposite direction than a system which aims at carrying to the utmost the inequalities and turbulences of mortals. Nor do I see how, by any forms of religious belief, mortals, so acting, could fit themselves even to appreciate the joys of immortals to which they still expect to be transferred by the mere act of dying. On the contrary, minds accustomed to place happiness in things so much the reverse of godlike, would find the happiness of gods exceedingly dull, and would long to get back to a world in which they could quarrel with each other."

<hr />

CHAPTER XVI.

I HAVE spoken so much of the Vril Staff that my reader may expect me to describe it. This I cannot do accurately, for I was never allowed to handle it for fear of some terrible accident occasioned by my ignorance of its use. It is hollow, and has in the handle several stops, keys, or springs by which its force can be altered, modified, or directed,— so that by one process it destroys, by another it heals; by one it can rend the rock, by another disperse the vapour; by one it affects bodies, by another it can exercise a certain influence over minds. It is usually carried in the convenient size of a walking-staff, but it has slides by which it can be lengthened or shortened at will. When used for special purposes, the upper part rests in the hollow of the palm, with the fore and middle fingers protruded. I was assured, however, that its power was not equal in all, but proportioned to the amount of certain vril properties in the wearer, in affinity, or *rapport*, with the purposes to be effected. Some were more potent to destroy, others to heal, etc.; much also depended on the calm and steadiness of volition in the manipulator. They assert that the full exercise of vril power can only be acquired by constitutional temperament,— that is, by hereditarily transmitted organization,— and that a female infant of four years old belonging to the Vril-ya races can accomplish feats with the wand placed for the first time in her hand, which a life spent in its practice would not enable the strongest and most skilled mechanician born out of the pale of the Vril-ya to achieve. All these wands are not equally complicated; those intrusted to children are much simpler than those borne by sages of either sex, and constructed with a view to the special object in which the children are employed,— which, as I have before said, is among the youngest children the most destructive. In the wands of wives and mothers the correlative destroying force is usually abstracted, the healing power fully charged. I wish I could say more in detail of this singular conductor of the vril fluid, but its machinery is as exquisite as its effects are marvellous.

I should say, however, that this people have invented certain tubes by which the vril fluid can be conducted towards the object it is meant to destroy, throughout a distance almost indefinite; at least I put it modestly when I say from five to six hundred miles. And their mathematical science as applied to such purpose is so nicely accurate, that on the report of some observer in an air-boat, any member of the vril department can estimate unerringly the nature of intervening obstacles, the height to which the projectile instrument should be raised, and the extent to which it should be charged, so as to reduce to ashes, within a space of time too short for me to venture to specify it, a capital twice as vast as London.

Certainly these Ana are wonderful mechanicians,— wonderful for the adaptation of the inventive faculty to practical uses.

I went with my host and his daughter Zee over the great public museum, which occupies a wing in the College of Sages, and in which are hoarded, as curious specimens of the ignorant and blundering experiments of ancient times, many contrivances on which we pride ourselves as recent achievements. In one department, carelessly thrown aside as obsolete lumber, are tubes for destroying life by metallic balls and an inflammable powder, on the principle of our cannons and catapults, and even still more murderous than our latest improvements.

My host spoke of these with a smile of contempt, such as an artillery officer might bestow on the bows and arrows of the Chinese. In another department there were models of vehicles and vessels worked by steam, and of a balloon which might have been constructed by Montgolfier. "Such," said Zee, with an air of meditative wisdom,— "such were the feeble triflings with nature of our savage forefathers, ere they had even a glimmering perception of the properties of vril!"

This young Gy was a magnificent specimen of the muscular force to which the females of her country attain. Her features were beautiful, like those of all her race: never in the upper world have I seen a face so grand and so faultless; but her devotion to the severer studies had given to her countenance an expression of abstract thought which rendered it somewhat stern when in repose, and such sternness became formidable when observed in connection with her ample shoulders and lofty stature. She was tall even for a Gy, and I saw her lift up a cannon as easily as I could lift a pocket-pistol. Zee inspired me with a profound terror,— a terror which increased when we came into a department of the museum appropriated to models of contrivances worked by the agency of vril; for here, merely by a certain play of her vril staff, she herself standing at a distance, she put into movement large and weighty substances. She seemed to endow them with intelligence, and to make them comprehend and obey her command. She set complicated pieces of machinery into movement, arrested the movement or continued it, until, within an incredibly short time, various kinds of raw material were reproduced as symmetrical works of art, complete and perfect. Whatever effect mesmerism or electro-biology produces over the nerves and muscles of animated objects, this young Gy produced by the motions of her slender rod over the springs and wheels of lifeless mechanism.

When I mentioned to my companions my astonishment at this influence over inanimate matter,— while owning that, in our world, I had witnessed phenomena which showed that over certain living organizations certain other living organizations could establish an influence genuine in itself, but often exaggerated by credulity or craft,— Zee, who was more interested in such subjects than her father, bade me stretch forth my hand, and then, placing her own beside it, she called my attention to certain distinctions of type and character. In the first place, the thumb of the Gy (and, as I afterwards noticed, of all that race, male or female) was much larger, at once longer and more massive, than is found with our species above ground. There is almost, in this, as great a difference as there is between the thumb of a man and that of a gorilla. Secondly, the palm is proportionately thicker than ours, the texture of the skin infinitely finer and softer, its average warmth is greater. More remarkable than all this, is a visible nerve, perceptible under the skin, which starts from the wrist skirting the ball of the thumb, and branching, fork-like, at the roots of the fore and middle fingers. "With your slight formation of thumb," said the philosophical young Gy, "and with the absence of the nerve which you find more or less developed in the hands of our race, you can never achieve other than imperfect and feeble power over the agency of vril; but so far as the nerve is concerned, that is not found in the hands of our earliest progenitors, nor in those of the ruder tribes without the pale of the Vril-ya. It has been slowly developed in the course of generations, commencing in the early achievements, and increasing with the continuous exercise, of the vril power; therefore, in the course of one or two thousand years, such a nerve may possibly be engendered in those higher beings of your race who devote themselves to that paramount science through which is attained command over all the subtler forces of nature permeated by vril. But when you talk of matter as something in itself inert and motionless, your parents or tutors surely cannot have left you so ignorant as not to know that no form of matter is motionless and inert: every particle is constantly in motion and constantly acted upon by agencies, of which heat is the most apparent and rapid, but vril the most subtle, and, when skilfully wielded, the most powerful. So that, in fact, the current launched by my hand and guided by my will does but render quicker and more potent the action which is eternally at work upon every particle of matter, however inert and stubborn it may seem. If a heap of metal be not capable of originating a thought of its own, yet, through its internal susceptibility to movement, it obtains the power to receive the thought of the intellectual agent at work on it; and which, when conveyed with a sufficient force of the vril power, it is as much compelled to obey as if it were displaced by a visible bodily force. It is animated for the time being by the soul thus infused into it, so that one may almost say that it lives and it reasons. Without this we could not make our automata supply the place of servants."

I was too much in awe of the thews and the learning of the young Gy to hazard the risk of arguing with her. I had read somewhere in my schoolboy days that a wise man, disputing with a Roman emperor, suddenly drew in his horns; and when the emperor asked him whether he had nothing further to say on his side of the question, replied, "Nay, Cæsar, there is no arguing against a reasoner who commands twenty-five legions."

Though I had a secret persuasion that, whatever the real effects of vril upon matter, Mr. Faraday could have proved her a very shallow philosopher as to its extent or its causes, I had no doubt that Zee could have brained all the Fellows of the Royal Society, one after the other, with a blow of her fist. Every sensible man knows that it is useless to argue with any ordinary female upon matters he comprehends; but to argue with a Gy seven feet high upon the mysteries of vril —as well argue in a desert, and with a simoom!

Amid the various departments to which the vast building of the College of Sages was appropriated, that which interested me most was devoted to the archæology of the Vril-ya, and comprised a very ancient collection of portraits. In these the pigments and groundwork employed were of so durable a nature that even pictures said to be executed at dates as remote as those in the earliest annals of the Chinese retained much freshness of colour. In examining this collection, two things especially struck me,— firstly, That the pictures said to be between six and seven thousand years old were of a much higher degree of art than any produced within the last three or four thousand years; and, secondly, That the portraits within the former period much more resembled our own upper world and European types of countenance. Some of them, indeed, reminded me of the Italian heads which look out from the canvas of Titian, speaking of ambition or craft, of care or of grief, with furrows in which the passions have passed with iron ploughshare. These were the countenances of men who had lived in struggle and conflict before the discovery of the latent forces of vril had, changed the character of society,— men who had fought with each other for power or fame as we in the upper world fight.

The type of face began to evince a marked change about a thousand years after the vril revolution, becoming then, with each generation, more serene, and in that serenity more terribly distinct from the faces of labouring and sinful men; while in proportion as the beauty and the grandeur of the countenance itself became more fully developed, the art of the painter became more tame and monotonous.

But the greatest curiosity in the collection was that of three portraits belonging to the pre-historical age, and, according to mythical tradition, taken by the orders of a philosopher, whose origin and attributes were as much mixed up with symbolical fable as those of an Indian Budh or a Greek Prometheus.

From this mysterious personage, at once a sage and a hero, all the principal sections of the Vril-ya race pretend to trace a common origin.

The portraits are of the philosopher himself, of his grand-father, and great-grandfather. They are all at full length. The philosopher is attired in a long tunic which seems to form a loose suit of scaly armour, borrowed, perhaps, from some fish or reptile: but the feet and hands are exposed; the digits in both are wonderfully long, and webbed. He has little or no perceptible throat, and a low receding forehead, not at all the ideal of a sage's. He has bright brown prominent eyes, a very wide mouth and high cheek-bones, and a muddy complexion. According to tradition, this philosopher had lived to a patriarchal age, extending over many centuries, and he remembered distinctly in middle life his grandfather as surviving, and in childhood his great-grandfather; the portrait of the first he had taken, or caused to be taken, while yet alive, that of the latter was taken from his effigies in mummy. The portrait of the grandfather had the features and aspect of the philosopher, only much more exaggerated; he was not dressed, and the colour of his body was singular, — the breast and stomach yellow, the shoulders and legs of a dull bronze hue: the great-grandfather was a magnificent specimen of the Batrachian genus, a Giant Frog, *pur et simple*.

Among the pithy sayings which, according to tradition, the philosopher bequeathed to posterity in rhythmical form and sententious brevity, this is notably recorded: "Humble yourselves, my descendants; the father of your race was a *twat* (tadpole): exalt yourselves, my descendants, for it was the same Divine Thought which created your father that develops itself in exalting you."

Aph-Lin told me this fable while I gazed on the three Batrachian portraits. I said in reply: "You make a jest of my supposed ignorance and credulity as an uneducated Tish; but though these horrible daubs may be of great antiquity, and were intended, perhaps, for some rude caricature, I presume that none of your race, even in the less enlightened ages, ever believed that the great-grandson of a Frog became a sententious philosopher; or that any section, I will not say of the lofty Vril-ya, but of the meanest varieties of the human race, had its origin in a Tadpole."

"Pardon me," answered Aph-Lin. "In what we call the Wrangling or Philosophical Period of History, which was at its height about seven thousand years ago, there was a very distinguished naturalist, who proved to the satisfaction of numerous disciples such analogical and anatomical agreements in structure between an An and a Frog, as to show that out of the one must have developed the other. They had some diseases in common; they were both subject to the same parasitical worms in the intestines; and, strange to say, the An has, in his structure, a swimming-bladder, no longer of any use to him, but which is a rudiment that clearly proves his descent from a Frog. Nor is there any argument against this theory to be found in the relative difference of size, for there are still existent in our world Frogs of a size and stature not inferior to our own, and many thousand years ago they appear to have been still larger."

"I understand that," said I, "because Frogs thus enormous are, according to our eminent geologists, who perhaps saw them in dreams, said to have been distinguished inhabitants of the upper world before the Deluge; and such Frogs are exactly the creatures likely to have flourished in the lakes and morasses of your subterranean regions. But pray, proceed."

"In the Wrangling Period of History, whatever one sage asserted another sage was sure to contradict. In fact, it was a maxim in that age that the human reason could only be sustained aloft by being tossed to and fro in the perpetual motion of contradiction; and therefore another sect of philosophers maintained the doctrine that the An was not the descendant of the Frog, but that the Frog was clearly the improved development of the An. The shape of the Frog, taken generally, was much more symmetrical than that of the An; beside the beautiful conformation of its lower limbs, its flanks, and shoulders, the majority of the Ana in that day were almost deformed, and certainly ill-shaped. Again, the Frog had the power to live alike on land and in water,—a mighty privilege, partaking of a spiritual essence denied to the An, since the disuse of his swimming-bladder clearly proves his degeneration from a higher development of species. Again, the earlier

races of the Ana seem to have been covered with hair; and
even to a comparatively recent date, hirsute bushes deformed
the very faces of our ancestors, spreading wild over their
cheeks and chins, as similar bushes, my poor Tish, spread
wild over yours. But the object of the higher races of the
Ana through countless generations has been to erase all ves-
tige of connection with hairy vertebrata, and they have gradually eliminated that debasing capillary excrement by the law
of sexual selection, the Gy-ei naturally preferring youth or
the beauty of smooth faces. But the degree of the Frog in
the scale of the vertebrata is shown in this, — that he has no
hair at all, not even on his head. He was born to that hair-
less perfection which the most beautiful of the Ana, despite
the culture of incalculable ages, have not yet attained. The
wonderful complication and delicacy of a Frog's nervous system and arterial circulation were shown by this school to be
more susceptible of enjoyment than our inferior, or at least
simpler, physical frame allows us to be. The examination
of a Frog's hand, if I may use that expression, accounted for
its keener susceptibility to love, and to social life in general.
In fact, gregarious and amatory as are the Ana, Frogs are
still more so. In short, these two schools raged against each
other, one asserting the An to be the perfected type of the
Frog; the other that the Frog was the highest development
of the An. The moralists were divided in opinion with the
naturalists, but the bulk of them sided with the Frog-prefer-
ence school. They said, with much plausibility, that in
moral conduct (namely, in the adherence to rules best adapted
to the health and welfare of the individual and the community) there could be no doubt of the vast superiority of the
Frog. All history showed the wholesale immorality of the
human race, the complete disregard, even by the most renowned among them, of the laws which they acknowledged
to be essential to their own and the general happiness and
well-being; but the severest critic of the Frog race could not
detect in their manners a single aberration from the moral
law tacitly recognized by themselves. And what, after all,
can be the profit of civilization if superiority in moral con-

duct be not the aim for which it strives, and the test by which its progress should be judged?

"In fine, the adherents to this theory presumed that in some remote period the Frog race had been the improved development of the Human; but that, from causes which defied rational conjecture, they had not maintained their original position in the scale of nature; while the Ana, though of inferior organization, had, by dint less of their virtues than their vices, such as ferocity and cunning, gradually acquired ascendancy, much as among the human race itself tribes utterly barbarous have, by superiority in similar vices, utterly destroyed or reduced into insignificance tribes originally excelling them in mental gifts and culture. Unhappily these disputes became involved with the religious notions of that age; and as society was then administered under the government of the Koom-Posh, who, being the most ignorant, were of course the most inflammable class, the multitude took the whole question out of the hands of the philosophers; political chiefs saw that the Frog dispute, so taken up by the populace, could become a most valuable instrument of their ambition; and for not less than one thousand years war and massacre prevailed, during which period the philosophers on both sides were butchered, and the government of the Koom-Posh itself was happily brought to an end by the ascendancy of a family that clearly established its descent from the aboriginal tadpole, and furnished despotic rulers to the various nations of the Ana. These despots finally disappeared, at least from our communities, as the discovery of vril led to the tranquil institutions under which flourish all the races of the Vril-ya."

"And do no wranglers or philosophers now exist to revive the dispute; or do they all recognize the origin of your race in the tadpole?"

"Nay, such disputes," said Zee, with a lofty smile, "belong to the Pah-bodh of the dark ages, and now only serve for the amusement of infants. When we know the elements out of which our bodies are composed, elements common to the humblest vegetable plants, can it signify whether the All-Wise combined those elements out of one form more than another, in order to create that in which He has placed the capacity to receive the idea of Himself, and all the varied grandeurs of intellect to which that idea gives birth? The An in reality commenced to exist as An with the donation of that capacity, and, with that capacity, the sense to acknowledge that, however through the countless ages his race may improve in wisdom, it can never combine the elements at his command into the form of a tadpole."

"You speak well, Zee," said Aph-Lin; "and it is enough for us short-lived mortals to feel a reasonable assurance that whether the origin of the An was a tadpole or not, he is no more likely to become a tadpole again than the institutions of the Vril-ya are likely to relapse into the heaving quagmire and certain strife-rot of a Koom-Posh."

CHAPTER XVII.

THE Vril-ya, being excluded from all sight of the heavenly bodies, and having no other difference between night and day than that which they deem it convenient to make for themselves, do not, of course, arrive at their divisions of time by the same process that we do; but I found it easy, by the aid of my watch, which I luckily had about me, to compute their time with great nicety. I reserve for a future work on the science and literature of the Vril-ya, should I live to complete it, all details as to the manner in which they arrive at their notation of time; and content myself here with saying, that in point of duration, their year differs very slightly from ours, but that the divisions of their year are by no means the same. Their day (including what we call night) consists of twenty hours of our time, instead of twenty-four, and of course their year comprises the correspondent increase in the number of days by which it is summed up. They subdivide the twenty hours of their day thus: eight hours,[1] called the "Silent Hours," for repose; eight hours, called the "Earnest Time," for the pursuits and occupations of life; and four hours, called the "Easy Time" (with which what I may term their day closes), allotted to festivities, sport, recreation, or family converse, according to their several tastes and inclinations. But, in truth, out of doors there is no night. They maintain, both in the streets and in the surrounding country, to the limits of their territory, the same degree of light at all hours. Only, within doors, they lower it to a soft twilight during the Silent Hours. They have a great horror of perfect darkness, and their lights are never wholly extinguished. On occasions of festivity they continue the duration of full light, but equally keep note of the distinction between night and day, by mechanical contrivances which answer the purpose of our clocks and watches. They are very fond of music; and it is by music that these chronometers strike the principal division of time. At every one of their hours, during their day, the sounds coming from all the timepieces in their public buildings, and caught up, as it were, by those of houses or hamlets scattered amidst the landscapes without the city, have an effect singularly sweet, and yet singularly solemn. But during the Silent Hours these sounds are so subdued as to be only faintly heard by a waking ear. They have no change of seasons, and, at least in the territory of this tribe, the atmosphere seemed to me very equable,—warm as that of an Italian summer, and humid rather than dry; in the forenoon usually very still, but at times invaded by strong blasts from the rocks that made the borders of their domain. But time is the same to them for sowing or reaping as in the Golden Isles of the ancient poets. At the same moment you see the younger plants in blade or bud, the older in ear or fruit. All fruit-bearing plants, however, after fruitage, either shed or change the colour of their leaves. But that which interested me most in reckoning up their divisions of

---

[1] For the sake of convenience, I adopt the words hours, days, years, etc., in any general reference to subdivisions of time among the Vril-ya,—those terms but loosely corresponding, however, with such subdivisions.

time was the ascertainment of the average duration of life amongst them. I found on minute inquiry that this very considerably exceeded the term allotted to us on the upper earth. What seventy years are to us, one hundred years are to them. Nor is this the only advantage they have over us in longevity, for as few among us attain to the age of seventy, so, on the contrary, few among them die before the age of one hundred; and they enjoy a general degree of health and vigour which makes life itself a blessing even to the last. Various causes contribute to this result: the absence of all alcoholic stimulants; temperance in food; more especially, perhaps, a serenity of mind undisturbed by anxious occupations and eager passions. They are not tormented by our avarice or our ambition; they appear perfectly indifferent even to the desire of fame; they are capable of great affection, but their love shows itself in a tender and cheerful complaisance, and, while forming their happiness, seems rarely, if ever, to constitute their woe. As the Gy is sure only to marry where she herself fixes her choice, and as here, not less than above ground, it is the female on whom the happiness of home depends, so the Gy, having chosen the mate she prefers to all others, is lenient to his faults, consults his humours, and does her best to secure his attachment. The death of a beloved one is of course with them, as with us, a cause of sorrow; but not only is death with them so much more rare before that age in which it becomes a release, but when it does occur the survivor takes much more consolation than, I am afraid, the generality of us do, in the certainty of reunion in another and yet happier life.

All these causes, then, concur to their healthful and enjoyable longevity, though, no doubt, much also must be owing to hereditary organization. According to their records, however, in those earlier stages of their society when they lived in communities resembling ours, agitated by fierce competition, their lives were considerably shorter, and their maladies more numerous and grave. They themselves say that the duration of life, too, has increased, and is still on the increase, since their discovery of the invigorating and medicinal properties of vril, applied for remedial purposes. They have few professional and regular practitioners of medicine, and these are chiefly Gy-ei, who, especially if widowed and childless, find great delight in the healing art, and even undertake surgical operations in those cases required by accident, or, more rarely, by disease.

They have their diversions and entertainments, and, during the Easy Time of their day, they are wont to assemble in great numbers for those winged sports in the air which I have already described. They have also public halls for music, and even theatres, at which are performed pieces that appeared to me somewhat to resemble the plays of the Chinese, —dramas that are thrown back into distant times for their events and personages, in which all classic unities are outrageously violated, and the hero, in one scene a child, in the next is an old man, and so forth. These plays are of very ancient composition. They appeared to me extremely dull, on the whole, but were relieved by startling mechanical contrivances, and a kind of farcical broad humour, and detached passages of great vigour and power expressed in language highly poetical, but somewhat overcharged with metaphor and trope. In fine, they seemed to me very much what the plays of Shakspeare seemed to a Parisian in the time of Louis XV., or perhaps to an Englishman in the reign of Charles II.

The audience, of which the Gy-ei constituted the chief portion, appeared to enjoy greatly the representation of these dramas, which, for so sedate and majestic a race of females, surprised me, till I observed that all the performers were under the age of adolescence, and conjectured truly that the mothers and sisters came to please their children and brothers.

I have said that these dramas are of great antiquity. No new plays, indeed no imaginative works sufficiently important to survive their immediate day, appear to have been composed for several generations. In fact, though there is no lack of new publications, and they have even what may be called newspapers, these are chiefly devoted to mechanical science, reports of new inventions, announcements respecting various details of business,— in short, to practical matters. Sometimes a child writes a little tale of adventure, or a young Gy vents her amorous hopes or fears in a poem; but these effusions are of very little merit, and are seldom read except by children and maiden Gy-ei. The most interesting works of a purely literary character are those of explorations and travels into other regions of this nether world, which are generally written by young emigrants, and are read with great avidity by the relations and friends they have left behind.

I could not help expressing to Aph-Lin my surprise that a community in which mechanical science had made so marvellous a progress, and in which intellectual civilization had exhibited itself in realizing those objects for the happiness of the people, which the political philosophers above ground had, after ages of struggle, pretty generally agreed to consider unattainable visions, should nevertheless be so wholly without a contemporaneous literature, despite the excellence to which culture had brought a language at once rich and simple, vigorous and musical.

My host replied: "Do you not perceive that a literature such as you mean would be wholly incompatible with that perfection of social or political felicity at which you do us the honour to think we have arrived? We have at last, after centuries of struggle, settled into a form of government with which we are content, and in which, as we allow no differences of rank, and no honours are paid to administrators distinguishing them from others, there is no stimulus given to individual ambition. No one would read works advocating theories that involved any political or social change, and therefore no one writes them. If now and then an An feels himself dissatisfied with our tranquil mode of life, he does not attack it; he goes away. Thus all that part of literature (and to judge by the ancient books in our public libraries, it was once a very large part) which relates to speculative theories on society is become utterly extinct. Again, formerly there was a vast deal written respecting the attributes and essence of the All-Good, and the arguments for and against a future state; but now we all recognize two facts,— that there *is* a Divine Being, and there *is* a future state, and we all equally agree that if we wrote our fingers to the bone, we could not throw any light upon the nature and conditions of that future state, or quicken our apprehensions of the attributes and essence of that Divine Being. Thus another part of literature has become also extinct, happily for our race; for in the times when so much was written on subjects which no one could determine, people seemed to live in a perpetual state of quarrel and contention. So, too, a vast part of our ancient literature consists of historical records of wars and revolutions during the times when the Ana lived in large and turbulent societies, each seeking aggrandizement at the expense of the other. You see our serene mode of life now; such it has been for ages. We have no events to chronicle. What more of us can be said than that 'they were born, they were happy, they died'? Coming next to that part of literature which is more under the control of the imagination, such as what we call ' Glaubsila,' or colloquially 'Glaubs,' and you call 'poetry,' the reasons for its decline amongst us are abundantly obvious.

"We find, by referring to the great masterpieces in that department of literature which we all still read with pleasure, but of which none would tolerate imitations, that they consist in the portraiture of passions which we no longer experience,— ambition, vengeance, unhallowed love, the thirst for warlike renown, and such like. The old poets lived in an atmosphere impregnated with these passions, and felt vividly what they expressed glowingly. No one can express such passions now, for no one can feel them, or meet with any sympathy in his readers if he did. Again, the old poetry has a main element in its dissection of those complex mysteries of human character which conduce to abnormal vices and crimes, or lead to signal and extraordinary virtues; but our society, having got rid of temptations to any prominent vices and crimes, has necessarily rendered the moral average so equal, that there are no very salient virtues. Without its ancient food of strong passions, vast crimes, heroic excellences, poetry therefore is, if not actually starved to death, reduced to a very meagre diet. There is still the poetry of description,—description of rocks, and trees, and waters, and common household life; and our young Gy-ei weave much of this insipid kind of composition into their love verses."

"Such poetry," said I, "might surely be made very charming; and we have critics amongst us who consider it a higher kind than that which depicts the crimes, or analyzes the passions, of man. At all events, poetry of the insipid kind you mention is a poetry that nowadays commands more readers than any other among the people I have left above ground."

"Possibly; but then I suppose the writers take great pains with the language they employ, and devote themselves to the culture and polish of words and rhythms as an art?"

"Certainly they do: all great poets must do that. Though the gift of poetry may be inborn, the gift requires as much care to make it available as a block of metal does to be made into one of your engines."

"And doubtless your poets have some incentive to bestow all those pains upon such verbal prettinesses?"

"Well, I presume their instinct of song would make them sing as the bird does; but to cultivate the song into verbal or artificial prettiness probably does need an inducement from without, and our poets find it in the love of fame,— perhaps, now and then, in the want of money."

"Precisely so. But in our society we attach fame to nothing which man, in that moment of his duration which is called 'life,' can perform. We should soon lose that equality which constitutes the felicitous essence of our commonwealth if we selected any individual for pre-eminent praise: pre-eminent praise would confer pre-eminent power, and the moment it were given, evil passions, now dormant, would awake; other men would immediately covet praise, then would arise envy, and with envy hate, and with hate calumny and persecution. Our history tells us that most of the poets and most of the writers who, in the old time, were favoured with the greatest praise, were also assailed by the greatest vituperation, and even, on the whole, rendered very unhappy, partly by the attacks of jealous rivals, partly by the diseased mental constitution which an acquired sensitiveness to praise and to blame tends to engender. As for the stimulus of want, in the first place, no man in our community knows the goad of poverty; and, secondly, if he did, almost every occupation would be more lucrative than writing.

"Our public libraries contain all the books of the past which time has preserved; those books, for the reasons above stated, are infinitely better than any can write nowadays, and they are open to all to read without cost. We are not such fools as to pay for reading inferior books, when we can read superior books for nothing."

"With us, novelty has an attraction; and a new book, if bad, is read when an old book, though good, is neglected."

"Novelty to barbarous states of society struggling in despair for something better has no doubt an attraction denied to us, who see nothing to gain in novelties; but, after all, it is observed by one of our great authors four thousand years ago, that 'he who studies old books will always find in them something new, and he who reads new books will always find in them something old.' But to return to the question you have raised: there being then among us no stimulus to painstaking labour, whether in desire of fame or in pressure of want, such as have the poetic temperament, no doubt, vent it in song, as you say the bird sings; but for lack of elaborate culture it fails of an audience, and, failing of an audience, dies out, of itself, amidst the ordinary avocations of life."

"But how is it that these discouragements to the cultivation of literature do not operate against that of science?"

"Your question amazes me. The motive to science is the love of truth apart from all consideration of fame, and science with us too is devoted almost solely to practical uses, essential to our social conservation and the comforts of our daily life. No fame is asked by the inventor, and none is given to him; he enjoys an occupation congenial to his tastes, and needing no wear and tear of the passions. Man must have exercise for his mind as well as body; and continuous exercise, rather than violent, is best for both. Our most ingenious cultivators of science are, as a general rule, the longest lived and the most free from disease. Painting is an amusement to many, but the art is not what it was in former times, when the great painters in our various communities vied with each other for the prize of a golden crown, which gave them a social rank equal to that of the kings under whom they lived. You will thus doubtless have observed in our archæological department how superior in point of art the pictures were several thousand years ago. Perhaps it is because music is, in reality, more allied to science than it is to poetry, that, of all the pleasurable arts, music is that which flourishes the most amongst us. Still, even in music the absence of stimulus in praise or fame has served to prevent any great superiority of one individual over another; and we rather excel in choral music, with the aid of our vast mechanical instruments, in which we make great use of the agency of water,[1] than in single performers. We have had scarcely any original composer for some ages. Our favourite airs are very ancient in substance, but have admitted many complicated variations by inferior, though ingenious, musicians."

"Are there no political societies among the Ana which are animated by those passions, subjected to those crimes, and admitting those disparities in condition, in intellect, and in morality, which the state of your tribe, or indeed of the Vril-ya generally, has left behind in its progress to perfection? If so, among such societies perhaps Poetry and her sister arts still continue to be honoured and to improve?"

"There are such societies in remote regions, but we do not admit them within the pale of civilized communities; we scarcely even give them the name of Ana, and certainly not that of Vril-ya. They are barbarians, living chiefly in that low stage of being, Koom-Posh, tending necessarily to its own hideous dissolution in Glek-Nas. Their wretched exist-

---

[1] This may remind the student of Nero's invention of a musical machine, by which water was made to perform the part of an orchestra, and on which he was employed when the conspiracy against him broke out.

ence is passed in perpetual contest and perpetual change. When they do not fight with their neighbours, they fight among themselves. They are divided into sections, which abuse, plunder, and sometimes murder each other, and on the most frivolous points of difference that would be unintelligible to us if we had not read history, and seen that we too have passed through the same early state of ignorance and barbarism. Any trifle is sufficient to set them together by the ears. They pretend to be all equals; and the more they have struggled to be so, by removing old distinctions and starting afresh, the more glaring and intolerable the disparity becomes, because nothing in hereditary affections and associations is left to soften the one naked distinction between the many who have nothing and the few who have much. Of course the many hate the few, but without the few they could not live. The many are always assailing the few; sometimes they exterminate the few; but as soon as they have done so, a new few starts out of the many, and is harder to deal with than the old few. For where societies are large, and competition to have something is the predominant fever, there must be always many losers and few gainers. In short, the people I speak of are savages groping their way in the dark towards some gleam of light, and would demand our commiseration for their infirmities, if, like all savages, they did not provoke their own destruction by their arrogance and cruelty. Can you imagine that creatures of this kind, armed only with such miserable weapons as you may see in our museum of antiquities, clumsy iron tubes charged with saltpetre, have more than once threatened with destruction a tribe of the Vril-ya, which dwells nearest to them, because they say they have thirty millions of population,— and that tribe may have fifty thousand,— if the latter do not accept their notions of Soc-Sec (money-getting) on some trading principles which they have the imprudence to call a 'law of civilization' ? "

"But thirty millions of population are formidable odds against fifty thousand! "

My host stared at me astonished. "Stranger," said he, "you could not have heard me say that this threatened tribe belongs to the Vril-ya; and it only waits for these savages to declare war, in order to commission some half-a-dozen small children to sweep away their whole population."

At these words I felt a thrill of horror, recognizing much more affinity with "the savages" than I did with the Vril-ya, and remembering all I had said in praise of the glorious American institutions, which Aph-Lin stigmatized as Koom-Posh. Recovering my self-possession, I asked if there were modes of transit by which I could safely visit this temerarious and remote people.

"You can travel with safety, by vril agency, either along the ground or amid the air, throughout all the range of the communities with which we are allied and akin; but I cannot vouch for your safety in barbarous nations governed by different laws from ours,— nations, indeed, so benighted, that there are among them large numbers who actually live by stealing from each other, and one could not with safety in the Silent Hours even leave the doors of one's own house open."

Here our conversation was interrupted by the entrance of Taë, who came to inform us that he, having been deputed to discover and destroy the enormous reptile which I had seen on my first arrival, had been on the watch for it ever since his visit to me, and had begun to suspect that my eyes had deceived me, or that the creature had made its way through the cavities within the rocks to the wild regions in which dwelt its kindred race, when it gave evidences of its whereabouts by a great devastation of the herbage bordering one of the lakes. "And," said Taë, "I feel sure that within that lake it is now hiding. So" (turning to me) "I thought it might amuse you to accompany me to see the way we destroy such unpleasant visitors." As I looked at the face of the young child, and called to mind the enormous size of the creature he proposed to exterminate, I felt myself shudder with fear for him, and perhaps fear for myself, if I accompanied him in such a chase; but my curiosity to witness the destructive effects of the boasted vril, and my unwillingness to lower myself in the eyes of an infant by betraying appre-

hensions of personal safety, prevailed over my first impulse.
Accordingly, I thanked Taë for his courteous consideration
for my amusement, and professed my willingness to set out
with him on so diverting an enterprise.

———◆———

CHAPTER XVIII.

As Taë and myself, on quitting the town, and leaving to
the left the main road which led to it, struck into the fields,
the strange and solemn beauty of the landscape, lighted up,
by numberless lamps, to the verge of the horizon, fascinated
my eyes, and rendered me for some time an inattentive lis-
tener to the talk of my companion.

Along our way various operations of agriculture were being
carried on by machinery, the forms of which were new to me,
and for the most part very graceful; for among these people
art, being so cultivated for the sake of mere utility, exhibits
itself in adorning or refining the shapes of useful objects.
Precious metals and gems are so profuse among them, that
they are lavished on things devoted to purposes the most
commonplace; and their love of utility leads them to beautify
its tools, and quickens their imagination in a way unknown
to themselves.

In all service, whether in or out of doors, they make great
use of automaton figures, which are so ingenious, and so
pliant to the operations of vril, that they actually seem
gifted with reason. It was scarcely possible to distinguish
the figures I beheld, apparently guiding or superintending
the rapid movements of vast engines, from human forms endowed with thought.

By degrees, as we continued to walk on, my attention became roused by the lively and acute remarks of my companion. The intelligence of the children among this race is
marvellously precocious, perhaps from the habit of having

intrusted to them, at so early an age, the toils and responsibilities of middle age. Indeed, in conversing with Taë, I felt as if talking with some superior and observant man of my own years. I asked him if he could form any estimate of the number of communities into which the race of the Vril-ya is subdivided.

"Not exactly," he said, "because they multiply, of course, every year as the surplus of each community is drafted off. But I heard my father say that, according to the last report, there were a million and a half of communities speaking our language, and adopting our institutions and forms of life and government; but, I believe, with some differences, about which you had better ask Zee. She knows more than most of the Ana do. An An cares less for things that do not concern him than a Gy does; the Gy-ei are inquisitive creatures."

"Does each community restrict itself to the same number of families or amount of population that you do?"

"No; some have much smaller populations, some have larger,— varying according to the extent of the country they appropriate, or to the degree of excellence to which they have brought their machinery. Each community sets its own limit according to circumstances, taking care always that there shall never arise any class of poor by the pressure of population upon the productive powers of the domain; and that no State shall be too large for a government resembling that of a single well-ordered family. I imagine that no Vril community exceeds thirty thousand households. But, as a general rule, the smaller the community, provided there be hands enough to do justice to the capacities of the territory it occupies, the richer each individual is, and the larger the sum contributed to the general treasury; above all, the happier and the more tranquil is the whole political body, and the more perfect the products of its industry. The State which all tribes of the Vril-ya acknowledge to be the highest in civilization, and which has brought the vril force to its fullest development, is perhaps the smallest. It limits itself to four thousand families; but every inch of its territory is cultivated to the utmost perfection of garden ground; its ma-

chinery excels that of every other tribe; and there is no product of its industry in any department which is not sought
for, at extraordinary prices, by each community of our race.
All our tribes make this State their model, considering that
we should reach the highest state of civilization allowed to
mortals if we could unite the greatest degree of happiness
with the highest degree of intellectual achievement; and it is
clear that the smaller the society the less difficult that will
be. Ours is too large for it."

This reply set me thinking. I reminded myself of that
little State of Athens, with only twenty thousand free citizens, and which to this day our mightiest nations regard as
the supreme guide and model in all departments of intellect.
But then Athens permitted fierce rivalry and perpetual
change, and was certainly not happy. Rousing myself from
the revery into which these reflections had plunged me, I
brought back our talk to the subjects connected with
emigration.

"But," said I, "when, I suppose yearly, a certain number
among you agree to quit home and found a new community
elsewhere, they must necessarily be very few, and scarcely
sufficient, even with the help of the machines they take with
them, to clear the ground, and build towns, and form a civilized State with the comforts and luxuries in which they had
been reared."

"You mistake. All the tribes of the Vril-ya are in constant communication with each other, and settle amongst
themselves each year what proportion of one community will
unite with the emigrants of another, so as to form a State of
sufficient size; and the place for emigration is agreed upon at
least a year before, and pioneers sent from each State to level
rocks, and embank waters, and construct houses; so that
when the emigrants at last go they find a city already made,
and a country around it at least partially cleared. Our hardy
life as children makes us take cheerfully to travel and adventure. I mean to emigrate myself when of age."

"Do the emigrants always select places hitherto unin-
habited and barren?"

"As yet generally, because it is our rule never to destroy except where necessary to our well being. Of course, we cannot settle in lands already occupied by the Vril-ya; and if we take the cultivated lands of the other races of Ana, we must utterly destroy the previous inhabitants. Sometimes, as it is, we take waste spots, and find that a troublesome, quarrelsome race of Ana, especially if under the administration of Koom-Posh or Glek-Nas, resents our vicinity, and picks a quarrel with us; then, of course, as menacing our welfare, we destroy it: there is no coming to terms of peace with a race so idiotic that it is always changing the form of government which represents it. Koom-Posh," said the child, emphatically, "is bad enough, still it has brains, though at the back of its head, and is not without a heart; but in Glek-Nas the brain and heart of the creatures disappear, and they become all jaws, claws, and belly."

"You express yourself strongly. Allow me to inform you that I myself, and I am proud to say it, am the citizen of a Koom-Posh."

"I no longer," answered Taë, "wonder to see you here so far from your home. What was the condition of your native community before it became a Koom-Posh?"

"A settlement of emigrants,— like those settlements which your tribe sends forth; but so far unlike your settlements, that it was dependent on the State from which it came. It shook off that yoke, and, crowned with eternal glory, became a Koom-Posh."

"Eternal glory! how long has the Koom-Posh lasted?"

"About one hundred years."

"The length of an An's life,— a very young community. In much less than another one hundred years your Koom-Posh will be a Glek-Nas."

"Nay, the oldest States in the world I come from have such faith in its duration, that they are all gradually shaping their institutions so as to melt into ours, and their most thoughtful politicians say that, whether they like it or not, the inevitable tendency of these old States is towards Koom-Posh-erie."

"The old States?"

"Yes, the old States."

"With populations very small in proportion to the area of productive land?"

"On the contrary, with populations very large in proportion to that area."

"I see! old States indeed!—so old as to become drivelling if they don't pack off that surplus population as we do ours. Very old States,— very, very old! Pray, Tish, do you think it wise for very old men to try to turn head-over-heels as very young children do? And if you asked them why they attempted such antics, should you not laugh if they answered that by imitating very young children they could become very young children themselves? Ancient history abounds with instances of this sort a great many thousand years ago, and in every instance a very old State that played at Koom-Posh soon tumbled into Glek-Nas. Then, in horror of its own self, it cried out for a master, as an old man in his dotage cries out for a nurse; and after a succession of masters or nurses, more or less long, that very old State died out of history. A very old State attempting Koom-Posh-erie is like a very old man who pulls down the house to which he has been accustomed, but he has so exhausted his vigour in pulling down, that all he can do in the way of rebuilding is to run up a crazy hut, in which himself and his successors whine out 'How the wind blows! How the walls shake!'"

"My dear Taë, I make all excuse for your unenlightened prejudices, which every schoolboy educated in a Koom-Posh could easily controvert, though he might not be so precociously learned in ancient history as you appear to be."

"I learned! not a bit of it. But would a schoolboy, educated in your Koom-Posh, ask his great-great-grandfather or great-great-grandmother to stand on his or her head with the feet uppermost; and if the poor old folks hesitated, say, 'What do you fear?—see how I do it!'"

"Taë, I disdain to argue with a child of your age. I repeat, I make allowances for your want of that culture which a Koom-Posh alone can bestow."

"I, in my turn," answered Taë, with an air of the suave

but lofty good breeding which characterizes his race, "not only make allowances for you as not educated among the Vril-ya, but I entreat you to vouchsafe me your pardon for insufficient respect to the habits and opinions of so amiable a — Tish!"

I ought before to have observed that I was commonly called Tish by my host and his family, as being a polite and indeed a pet name, metaphorically signifying a small barbarian, literally a Froglet; the children apply it endearingly to the tame species of Frog which they keep in their gardens.

We had now reached the banks of a lake, and Taë here paused to point out to me the ravages made in fields skirting it. "The enemy certainly lies within these waters," said Taë. "Observe what shoals of fish are crowded together at the margin,— even the great fishes with the small ones, who are their habitual prey, and who generally shun them; all forget their instincts in the presence of a common destroyer. This reptile certainly must belong to the class of the Krek-a, a class more devouring than any other, and said to be among the few surviving species of the world's dreadest inhabitants before the Ana were created. The appetite of a Krek is insatiable,— it feeds alike upon vegetable and animal life; but for the swift-footed creatures of the elk species it is too slow in its movements. Its favourite dainty is an An when it can catch him unawares; and hence the Ana destroy it relentlessly whenever it enters their dominion. I have heard that when our forefathers first cleared this country, these monsters, and others like them, abounded, and, vril being then undiscovered, many of our race were devoured. It was impossible to exterminate them wholly till that discovery which constitutes the power and sustains the civilization of our race. But after the uses of vril became familiar to us, all creatures inimical to us were soon annihilated. Still, once a year or so, one of these enormous reptiles wanders from the unreclaimed and savage districts beyond, and within my memory once seized upon a young Gy who was bathing in this very lake. Had she been on land and armed with her staff, it would not have dared even to show itself; for, like all savage creatures, the reptile has a marvellous instinct, which warns it against the bearer of the vril wand. How they teach their young to avoid him, though seen for the first time, is one of those mysteries which you may ask Zee to explain, for I cannot.[1] So long as I stand here, the monster will not stir from its lurking-place; but we must now decoy it forth."

"Will not that be difficult?"

"Not at all. Seat yourself yonder on that crag (about one hundred yards from the bank), while I retire to a distance. In a short time the reptile will catch sight or scent of you, and, perceiving that you are no vril-bearer, will come forth to devour you. As soon as it is fairly out of the water it becomes my prey."

"Do you mean to tell me that I am to be the decoy to that horrible monster which could engulf me within its jaws in a second! I beg to decline."

The child laughed. "Fear nothing," said he; "only sit still."

Instead of obeying this command, I made a bound, and was about to take fairly to my heels, when Taë touched me lightly on the shoulder, and fixing his eyes steadily on mine, I was rooted to the spot. All power of volition left me. Submissive to the infant's gesture, I followed him to the crag he had indicated, and seated myself there in silence. Most readers have seen something of the effects of electro-biology, whether genuine or spurious. No professor of that doubtful craft had ever been able to influence a thought or a movement of mine, but I was a mere machine at the will of this terrible child. Meanwhile he expanded his wings, soared aloft, and alighted amidst a copse at the brow of a hill at some distance.

I was alone; and turning my eyes with an indescribable sensation of horror towards the lake, I kept them fixed on its water, spell-bound. It might be ten or fifteen minutes, to

---

[1] The reptile in this instinct does but resemble our wild birds and animals, which will not come in reach of a man armed with a gun. When the electric wires were first put up, partridges struck against them in their flight, and fell down wounded. No younger generations of partridges meet with a similar accident.

me it seemed ages, before the still surface, gleaming under the lamp-light, began to be agitated towards the centre. At the same time the shoals of fish near the margin evinced their sense of the enemy's approach by splash and leap and bubbling circle. I could detect their hurried flight hither and thither, some even casting themselves ashore. A long, dark, undulous furrow came moving along the waters, nearer and nearer, till the vast head of the reptile emerged,— its jaws bristling with fangs, and its dull eyes fixing themselves hungrily on the spot where I sat motionless. And now its fore feet were on the strand, now its enormous breast, scaled on either side as in armour, in the centre showing corrugated skin of a dull venomous yellow; and now its whole length was on the land, a hundred feet or more from the jaw to the tail. Another stride of those ghastly feet would have brought it to the spot where I sat. There was but a moment between me and this grim form of death, when what seemed a flash of lightning shot through the air, smote, and, for a space in time briefer than that in which a man can draw his breath, enveloped the monster; and then, as the flash vanished, there lay before me a blackened, charred, smouldering mass, a something gigantic, but of which even the outlines of form were burned away, and rapidly crumbling into dust and ashes. I remained still seated, still speechless, ice-cold with a new sensation of dread: what had been horror was now awe.

I felt the child's hand on my head. Fear left me, the spell was broken; I rose up. "You see with what ease the Vril-ya destroy their enemies," said Taë; and then, moving towards the bank, he contemplated the smouldering relics of the monster, and said quietly, "I have destroyed larger creatures, but none with so much pleasure. Yes, it *is* a Krek; what suffering it must have inflicted while it lived!" Then he took up the poor fishes that had flung themselves ashore, and restored them mercifully to their native element.

CHAPTER XIX.

As we walked back to the town, Taë took a new and circuitous way, in order to show me what, to use a familiar term, I will call the "Station," from which emigrants or travellers to other communities commence their journeys. I had, on a former occasion, expressed a wish to see their vehicles. These I found to be of two kinds, one for land-journeys, one for aërial voyages: the former were of all sizes and forms, some not larger than an ordinary carriage, some movable houses of one story and containing several rooms, furnished according to the ideas of comfort or luxury which are entertained by the Vril-ya. The aërial vehicles were of light substances, not the least resembling our balloons, but rather our boats and pleasure-vessels, with helm and rudder, with large wings as paddles, and a central machine worked by vril. All the vehicles both for land or air were indeed worked by that potent and mysterious agency.

I saw a convoy set out on its journey, but it had few passengers, containing chiefly articles of merchandise, and was bound to a neighbouring community; for among all the tribes of the Vril-ya there is considerable commercial interchange. I may here observe, that their money currency does not consist of the precious metals, which are too common among them for that purpose. The smaller coins in ordinary use are manufactured from a peculiar fossil shell, the comparatively scarce remnant of some very early deluge, or other convulsion of nature, by which a species has become extinct. It is minute, and flat as an oyster, and takes a jewel-like polish. This coinage circulates among all the tribes of the Vril-ya. Their larger transactions are carried on much like ours, by bills of exchange, and thin metallic plates which answer the purpose of our bank-notes.

Let me take this occasion of adding that the taxation among the tribe I became acquainted with was very considerable,

compared with the amount of population; but I never heard
that any one grumbled at it, for it was devoted to purposes of
universal utility, and indeed necessary to the civilization of
the tribe. The cost of lighting so large a range of country,
of providing for emigration, of maintaining the public buildings at which the various operations of national intellect were
carried on, from the first education of an infant to the departments to which the College of Sages were perpetually trying
new experiments in mechanical science,— all these involved
the necessity for considerable State funds. To these I must
add an item that struck me as very singular. I have said that
all the human labour required by the State is carried on by
children up to the marriageable age. For this labour the
State pays, and at a rate immeasurably higher than our remu-
neration to labour even in the United States. According to
their theory, every child, male or female, on attaining the
marriageable age, and there terminating the period of labour,
should have acquired enough for an independent competence
during life. As, no matter what the disparity of fortune in
the parents, all the children must equally serve, so all are
equally paid according to their several ages or the nature of
their work. When the parents or friends choose to retain a
child in their own service, they must pay into the public
fund in the same ratio as the State pays to the children it
employs; and this sum is handed over to the child when the
period of service expires. This practice serves, no doubt, to
render the notion of social equality familiar and agreeable;
and if it may be said that all the children form a democracy,
no less truly it may be said that all the adults form an aris-
tocracy. The exquisite politeness and refinement of manners among the Vril-ya, the generosity of their sentiments,
the absolute leisure they enjoy for following out their own
private pursuits, the amenities of their domestic intercourse,
in which they seem as members of one noble order that can
have no distrust of each other's word or deed,— all combine
to make the Vril-ya the most perfect nobility which a political disciple of Plato or Sidney could conceive for the
ideal of an aristocratic republic.

CHAPTER XX.

From the date of the expedition with Taë which I have just narrated, the child paid me frequent visits. He had taken a liking to me, which I cordially returned. Indeed, as he was not yet twelve years old, and had not commenced the course of scientific studies with which childhood closes in that country, my intellect was less inferior to his than to that of the elder members of his race, especially of the Gy-ei, and most especially of the accomplished Zee. The children of the Vril-ya, having upon their minds the weight of so many active duties and grave responsibilities, are not generally mirthful; but Taë, with all his wisdom, had much of the playful good-humour one often finds the characteristic of elderly men of genius. He felt that sort of pleasure in my society which a boy of a similar age in the upper world has in the company of a pet dog or monkey. It amused him to try and teach me the ways of his people, as it amuses a nephew of mine to make his poodle walk on his hind legs, or jump through a hoop. I willingly lent myself to such experiments, but I never achieved the success of the poodle. I was very much interested at first in the attempt to ply the wings which the youngest of the Vril-ya use as nimbly and easily as ours do their legs and arms; but my efforts were attended with contusions serious enough to make me abandon them in despair.

The wings, as I before said, are very large, reaching to the knee, and in repose thrown back so as to form a very graceful mantle. They are composed from the feathers of a gigantic bird that abounds in the rocky heights of the country,— the colour mostly white, but sometimes with reddish streaks. They are fastened round the shoulders with light but strong springs of steel; and, when expanded, the arms slide through loops for that purpose, forming, as it were, a stout central membrane.   As the arms are raised, a tubular lining beneath the vest or tunic becomes, by mechanical contrivance, inflated with air, increased or diminished at will by the movement of the arms, and serving to buoy the whole form as on bladders. The wings and the balloon-like apparatus are highly charged with vril; and when the body is thus wafted upward, it seems to become singularly lightened of its weight.   I found it easy enough to soar from the ground; indeed, when the wings were spread it was scarcely possible not to soar, but then came the difficulty and the danger.   I utterly failed in the power to use and direct the pinions, though I am considered among my own race unusually alert and ready in bodily exercises, and am a very practised swimmer.   I could only make the most confused and blundering efforts at flight.   I was the servant of the wings; the wings were not my servants,— they were beyond my control; and when by a violent strain of muscle, and, I must fairly own, in that abnormal strength which is given by excessive fright, I curbed their gyrations and brought them near to the body, it seemed as if I lost the sustaining power stored in them and the connecting bladders, as when air is let out of a balloon, and found myself precipitated again to earth; saved, indeed, by some spasmodic flutterings, from being dashed to pieces, but not saved from the bruises and the stun of a heavy fall.   I would, however, have persevered in my attempts, but for the advice or the commands of the scientific Zee, who had benevolently accompanied my flutterings, and indeed, on the last occasion, flying just under me, received my form as it fell on her own expanded wings, and preserved me from breaking my head on the roof of the pyramid from which we had ascended.

"I see," she said, "that your trials are in vain, not from the fault of the wings and their appurtenances, nor from any imperfectness and malformation of your own corpuscular system, but from irremediable, because organic, defect in your power of volition.   Learn that the connection between the will and the agencies of that fluid which has been subjected .to the control of the Vril-ya was never established by the first discoverers, never achieved by a single generation; it has gone on increasing, like other properties of race, in proportion as it has been uniformly transmitted from parent to child, so that, at last, it has become an instinct; and an infant An of our race wills to fly as intuitively and unconsciously as he wills to walk. He thus plies his invented or artificial wings with as much safety as a bird plies those with which it is born. I did not think sufficiently of this when I allowed you to try an experiment which allured me, for I longed to have in you a companion. I shall abandon the experiment now. Your life is becoming dear to me." Herewith the Gy's voice and face softened, and I felt more seriously alarmed than I had been in my previous flights.

Now that I am on the subject of wings, I ought not to omit mention of a custom among the Gy-ei which seems to me very pretty and tender in the sentiment it implies. A Gy wears wings habitually while yet a virgin; she joins the Ana in their aërial sports; she adventures alone and afar into the wilder regions of the sunless world: in the boldness and height of her soarings, not less than in the grace of her movements, she excels the opposite sex. But from the day of marriage she wears wings no more; she suspends them with her own willing hand over the nuptial couch, never to be resumed unless the marriage tie be severed by divorce or death.

Now when Zee's voice and eyes thus softened — and at that softening I prophetically recoiled and shuddered — Taë, who had accompanied us in our flights, but who, child-like, had been much more amused with my awkwardness than sympathizing in my fears or aware of my danger, hovered over us, poised amidst the still radiant air, serene and motionless on his outspread wings, and hearing the endearing words of the young Gy, laughed aloud. Said he, "If the Tish cannot learn the use of wings, you may still be his companion, Zee, for you can suspend your own."

CHAPTER XXI.

I HAD for some time observed in my host's highly informed and powerfully proportioned daughter that kindly and protective sentiment which, whether above the earth or below it, an all-wise Providence has bestowed upon the feminine division of the human race. But until very lately I had ascribed it to that affection for "pets" which a human female at every age shares with a human child. I now became painfully aware that the feeling with which Zee deigned to regard me was different from that which I had inspired in Taë; but this conviction gave me none of that complacent gratification which the vanity of man ordinarily conceives from a flattering appreciation of his personal merits on the part of the fair sex; on the contrary, it inspired me with fear. Yet of all the Gy-ei in the community, if Zee were perhaps the wisest and the strongest, she was, by common repute, the gentlest, and she was certainly the most popularly beloved. The desire to aid, to succour, to protect, to comfort, to bless, seemed to pervade her whole being. Though the complicated miseries that originate in penury and guilt are unknown to the social system of the Vril-ya, still, no sage had yet discovered in vril an agency which could banish sorrow from life; and wherever amongst her people sorrow found its way, there Zee followed in the mission of comforter. Did some sister Gy fail to secure the love she sighed for? Zee sought her out, and brought all the resources of her lore, and all the consolations of her sympathy, to bear upon a grief that so needs the solace of a confidant. In the rare cases when grave illness seized upon childhood or youth, and the cases, less rare, when, in the hardy and adventurous probation of infants, some accident attended with pain and injury occurred, Zee forsook her studies and her sports, and became the healer and the nurse. Her favourite flights were towards the extreme boundaries of the domain, where children were stationed on guard against outbreaks of warring forces in nature, or the invasions of devouring animals, so that she might warn them of any peril which her knowledge detected or foresaw, or be at hand if any harm should befall. Nay, even in the exercise of her scientific acquirements there was a concurrent benevolence of purpose and will. Did she learn any novelty in invention that would be useful to the practitioner of some special art or craft? She hastened to communicate and explain it. Was some veteran sage of the College perplexed and wearied with the toil of an abstruse study? She would patiently devote herself to his aid, work out details for him, sustain his spirits with her hopeful smile, quicken his wit with her luminous suggestion, be to him, as it were, his own good genius made visible as the strengthener and inspirer. The same tenderness she exhibited to the inferior creatures. I have often known her bring home some sick and wounded animal, and tend and cherish it as a mother would tend and cherish her stricken child. Many a time when I sat in the balcony, or hanging garden, on which my window opened, I have watched her rising in the air on her radiant wings, and in a few moments groups of infants below, catching sight of her, would soar upward with joyous sounds of greeting; clustering and sporting around her, so that she seemed a very centre of innocent delight. When I have walked with her amidst the rocks and valleys without the city, the elk-deer would scent or see her from afar, come bounding up, eager for the caress of her hand, or follow her footsteps, till dismissed by some musical whisper that the creature had learned to comprehend. It is the fashion among the virgin Gy-ei to wear on their foreheads a circlet, or coronet, with gems resembling opals, arranged in four points or rays like stars. These are lustreless in ordinary use, but if touched by the vril wand they take a clear lambent flame, which illuminates, yet not burns. This serves as an ornament in their festivities, and as a lamp, if, in their wanderings beyond their artificial lights, they have to traverse the dark. There are times, when I have seen Zee's thoughtful majesty of face lighted up by this crowning halo, that I could scarcely believe her to be a creature of mortal birth, and bent my head before her as the vision of a being among the celestial orders.

But never once did my heart feel for this lofty type of the noblest womanhood a sentiment of human love. Is it that, among the race I belong to, man's pride so far influences his passions that woman loses to him her special charm of woman if he feels her to be in all things eminently superior to himself? But by what strange infatuation could this peerless daughter of a race which, in the supremacy of its powers and the felicity of its conditions, ranked all other races in the category of barbarians, have deigned to honour me with her preference? In personal qualifications, though I passed for good-looking among the people I came from, the handsomest of my countrymen might have seemed insignificant and homely beside the grand and serene type of beauty which characterized the aspect of the Vril-ya.

That novelty, the very difference between myself and those to whom Zee was accustomed, might serve to bias her fancy was probable enough, and as the reader will see later, such a cause might suffice to account for the predilection with which I was distinguished by a young Gy scarcely out of her childhood, and very inferior in all respects to Zee. But whoever will consider those tender characteristics which I have just ascribed to the daughter of Aph-Lin, may readily conceive that the main cause of my attraction to her was in her instinctive desire to cherish, to comfort, to protect, and, in protecting, to sustain and to exalt. Thus, when I look back, I account for the only weakness unworthy of her lofty nature, which bowed the daughter of the Vril-ya to a woman's affection for one so inferior to herself as was her father's guest. But be the cause what it may, the consciousness that I had inspired such affection thrilled me with awe,— a moral awe of her very perfections, of her mysterious powers, of the inseparable distinctions between her race and my own; and with that awe, I must confess to my shame, there combined the more material and ignoble dread of the perils to which her preference would expose me.

Could it be supposed for a moment that the parents and

friends of this exalted being could view without indignation and disgust the possibility of an alliance between herself and a Tish? Her they could not punish, her they could not confine nor restrain. Neither in domestic nor in political life do they acknowledge any law of force amongst themselves; but they could effectually put an end to her infatuation by a flash of vril inflicted upon me.

Under these anxious circumstances, fortunately, my conscience and sense of honour were free from reproach. It became clearly my duty, if Zee's preference continued manifest, to intimate it to my host, with, of course, all the delicacy which is ever to be preserved by a well-bred man in confiding to another any degree of favour by which one of the fair sex may condescend to distinguish him. Thus, at all events, I should be freed from responsibility or suspicion of voluntary participation in the sentiments of Zee; and the superior wisdom of my host might probably suggest some sage extrication from my perilous dilemma. In this resolve I obeyed the ordinary instinct of civilized and moral man, who, erring though he be, still generally prefers the right course in those cases where it is obviously against his inclinations, his interests, and his safety to elect the wrong one.

CHAPTER XXII.

As the reader has seen, Aph-Lin had not favoured my general and unrestricted intercourse with his countrymen. Though relying on my promise to abstain from giving any information as to the world I had left, and still more on the promise of those to whom had been put the same request, not to question me, which Zee had exacted from Taë, yet he did not feel sure that, if I were allowed to mix with the strangers whose curiosity the sight of me had aroused, I could sufficiently guard myself against their inquiries. When I went out, therefore, it was never alone; I was always accompanied

either by one of my host's family, or my child-friend Taë.
Bra, Aph-Lin's wife, seldom stirred beyond the gardens which
surrounded the house, and was fond of reading the ancient
literature, which contained something of romance and adventure not to be found in the writings of recent ages, and presented pictures of a life unfamiliar to her experience and
interesting to her imagination,— pictures, indeed, of a life
more resembling that which we lead every day above-ground,
coloured by our sorrows, sins, and passions, and much to her
what the Tales of the Genii or the Arabian Nights are to us.
But her love of reading did not prevent Bra from the dis-
charge of her duties as mistress of the largest household in
the city. She went daily the round of the chambers, and
saw that the automata and other mechanical contrivances
were in order, that the numerous children employed by Aph-
Lin, whether in his private or public capacity, were carefully
tended. Bra also inspected the accounts of the whole estate,
and it was her great delight to assist her husband in the business connected with his office as chief administrator of the
Lighting Department, so that her avocations necessarily kept
her much within doors. The two sons were both completing
their education at the College of Sages; and the elder, who
had a strong passion for mechanics, and especially for works
connected with the machinery of timepieces and automata,
had decided on devoting himself to these pursuits, and was
now occupied in constructing a shop, or warehouse, at which
his inventions could be exhibited and sold. The younger
son preferred farming and rural occupations; and when not
attending the College, at which he chiefly studied the theories
of agriculture, was much absorbed by his practical application
of that science to his father's lands. It will be seen by this
how completely equality of ranks is established among this
people, a shopkeeper being of exactly the same grade in esti-
mation as the large landed proprietor. Aph-Lin was the
wealthiest member of the community, and his eldest son preferred keeping a shop to any other avocation; nor was this
choice thought to show any want of elevated notions on his
part.

This young man had been much interested in examining my watch, the works of which were new to him, and was greatly pleased when I made him a present of it. Shortly after, he returned the gift with interest, by a watch of his own construction, marking both the time as in my watch and the time as kept among the Vril-ya. I have that watch still, and it has been much admired by many among the most eminent watchmakers of London and Paris. It is of gold, with diamond hands and figures, and it plays a favourite tune among the Vril-ya in striking the hours; it only requires to be wound up once in ten months, and has never gone wrong since I had it. These young brothers being thus occupied, my usual companions in that family, when I went abroad, were my host or his daughter. Now, agreeably with the honourable conclusions I had come to, I began to excuse myself from Zee's invitations to go out alone with her, and seized an occasion when that learned Gy was delivering a lecture at the College of Sages to ask Aph-Lin to show me his country-seat. As this was at some little distance, and as Aph-Lin was not fond of walking, while I had discreetly relinquished all attempts at flying, we proceeded to our destination in one of the aërial boats belonging to my host. A child of eight years old, in his employ, was our conductor. My host and myself reclined on cushions, and I found the movement very easy and luxurious.

"Aph-Lin," said I, "you will not, I trust, be displeased with me, if I ask your permission to travel for a short time, and visit other tribes or communities of your illustrious race. I have also a strong desire to see those nations which do not adopt your institutions, and which you consider as savages. It would interest me greatly to notice what are the distinctions between them and the races whom we consider civilized in the world I have left."

"It is utterly impossible that you should go hence alone," said Aph-Lin. "Even among the Vril-ya you would be exposed to great dangers. Certain peculiarities of formation and colour, and the extraordinary phenomenon of hirsute bushes upon your cheeks and chin, denoting in you a species of An distinct alike from our race and any known race of barbarians yet extant, would attract, of course, the special attention of the College of Sages in whatever community of Vril-ya you visited; and it would depend upon the individual temper of some individual sage whether you would be received, as you have been here, hospitably, or whether you would not be at once dissected for scientific purposes. Know that when the Tur first took you to his house, and while you were there put to sleep by Taë in order to recover from your previous pain or fatigue, the sages summoned by the Tur were divided in opinion whether you were a harmless or an obnoxious animal. During your unconscious state your teeth were examined, and they clearly showed that you were not only graminivorous, but carnivorous. Carnivorous animals of your size are always destroyed, as being of dangerous and savage nature. Our teeth, as you have doubtless observed,[1] are not those of the creatures who devour flesh. It is, indeed, maintained by Zee and other philosophers that as, in remote ages, the Ana did prey upon living beings of the brute species, their teeth must have been fitted for that purpose; but, even if so, they have been modified by hereditary transmission, and suited to the food on which we now exist; nor are even the barbarians, who adopt the turbulent and ferocious institutions of Glek-Nas, devourers of flesh like beasts of prey.

"In the course of this dispute it was proposed to dissect you; but Taë begged you off, and the Tur being, by office, averse to all novel experiments at variance with our custom of sparing life, except where it is clearly proved to be for the good of the community to take it, sent to me, whose business it is, as the richest man of the State, to afford hospitality to strangers from a distance. It was at my option to decide whether or not you were a stranger whom I could safely admit. Had I declined to receive you, you would have been handed over to the College of Sages, and what might there have befallen you I do not like to conjecture. Apart from

---

[1] I never had observed it; and, if I had, am not physiologist enough to have distinguished the difference.

this danger, you might chance to encounter some child of four years old, just put in possession of his vril staff; and who, in alarm at your strange appearance, and in the impulse of the moment, might reduce you to a cinder. Taë himself was about to do so when he first saw you, had his father not checked his hand. Therefore I say you cannot travel alone; but with Zee you would be safe, and I have no doubt that she would accompany you on a tour round the neighbouring communities of Vril-ya (to the savage States, No!). I will ask her."

Now, as my main object in proposing to travel was to escape from Zee, I hastily exclaimed, "Nay, pray do not! I relinquish my design. You have said enough as to its dangers to deter me from it; and I can scarcely think it right that a young Gy of the personal attractions of your lovely daughter should travel into other regions without a better protector than a Tish of my insignificant strength and stature."

Aph-Lin emitted the soft sibilant sound which is the nearest approach to laughter that a full-grown An permits to himself ere he replied: "Pardon my discourteous but momentary indulgence of mirth at any observation seriously made by my guest. I could not but be amused at the idea of Zee, who is so fond of protecting others that children call her 'THE GUARDIAN,' needing a protector herself against any dangers arising from the audacious admiration of males. Know that our Gy-ei, while unmarried, are accustomed to travel alone among other tribes, to see if they find there some An who may please them more than the Ana they find at home. Zee has already made three such journeys, but hitherto her heart has been untouched."

Here the opportunity which I sought was afforded to me, and I said, looking down, and with faltering voice, "Will you, my kind host, promise to pardon me, if what I am about to say gives you offence?"

"Say only the truth, and I cannot be offended; or, could I be so, it would be not for me, but for you to pardon."

"Well, then, assist me to quit you, and, much as I should

have liked to witness more of the wonders, and enjoy more of the felicity, which belong to your people, let me return to my own."

"I fear there are reasons why I cannot do that; at all events, not without permission of the Tur, and he probably would not grant it. You are not destitute of intelligence; you may (though I do not think so) have concealed the degree of destructive powers possessed by your people; you might, in short, bring upon us some danger; and if the Tur entertains that idea, it would clearly be his duty either to put an end to you, or enclose you in a cage for the rest of your existence. But why should you wish to leave a state of society which you so politely allow to be more felicitous than your own?"

"Oh, Aph-Lin! my answer is plain. Lest in aught, and unwittingly, I should betray your hospitality; lest, in that caprice of will which in our world is proverbial among the other sex, and from which even a Gy is not free, your adorable daughter should deign to regard me, though a Tish, as if I were a civilized An, and — and — and — "

"Court you as her spouse," put in Aph-Lin, gravely, and without any visible sign of surprise or displeasure.

"You have said it."

"That would be a misfortune," resumed my host, after a pause; "and I feel that you have acted as you ought in warning me. It is, as you imply, not uncommon for an unwedded Gy to conceive tastes as to the object she covets which appear whimsical to others; but there is no power to compel a young Gy to any course opposed to that which she chooses to pursue. All we can do is to reason with her, and experience tells us that the whole College of Sages would find it vain to reason with a Gy in a matter that concerns her choice in love. I grieve for you, because such a marriage would be against the Aglauran, or good of the community, for the children of such a marriage would adulterate the race: they might even come into the world with the teeth of carnivorous animals; this could not be allowed. Zee, as a Gy, cannot be controlled; but you, as a Tish, can be destroyed. I advise you, then, to resist her addresses; to tell her plainly that you can never return her love. This happens constantly. Many an An, however ardently wooed by one Gy, rejects her, and puts an end to her persecution by wedding another. The same course is open to you."

"No; for I cannot wed another Gy without equally injuring the community, and exposing it to the chance of rearing carnivorous children."

"That is true. All I can say, and I say it with the tenderness due to a Tish, and the respect due to a guest, is frankly this,— if you yield, you will become a cinder. I must leave it to you to take the best way you can to defend yourself. Perhaps you had better tell Zee that she is ugly. That assurance on the lips of him she woos generally suffices to chill the most ardent Gy. Here we are at my country-house."

———◆———

CHAPTER XXIII.

I confess that my conversation with Aph-Lin, and the extreme coolness with which he stated his inability to control the dangerous caprice of his daughter, and treated the idea of the reduction into a cinder to which her amorous flame might expose my too seductive person, took away the pleasure I should otherwise have had in the contemplation of my host's country-seat, and the astonishing perfection of the machinery by which his farming operations were conducted. The house differed in appearance from the massive and sombre building which Aph-Lin inhabited in the city, and which seemed akin to the rocks out of which the city itself had been hewn into shape. The walls of the country-seat were composed by trees placed a few feet apart from each other, the interstices being filled in with the transparent metallic substance which serves the purpose of glass among the Ana. These trees were all in flower, and the effect was very pleasing, if not in the best taste. We were received at the porch by lifelike automata, who conducted us into a chamber, the like to which I never saw before, but have often on summer days dreamily imagined. It was a bower,— half room, half garden. The walls were one mass of climbing flowers. The open spaces, which we call windows, and in which, here, the metallic surfaces were slided back, commanded various views,— some, of the wide landscape with its lakes and rocks; some, of small limited expanse answering to our conservatories, filled with tiers of flowers. Along the sides of the room were flower-beds, interspersed with cushions for repose. In the centre of the floor were a cistern and a fountain of that liquid light which I have presumed to be naphtha. It was luminous, and of a roseate hue; it sufficed without lamps to light up the room with a subdued radiance. All around the fountain was carpeted with a soft deep lichen, not green (I have never seen that colour in the vegetation of this country), but a quiet brown, on which the eye reposes with the same sense of relief as that with which in the upper world it reposes on green. In the outlets upon flowers (which I have compared to our conservatories) there were singing-birds innumerable, which, while we remained in the room, sang in those harmonies of tune to which they are, in these parts, so wonderfully trained. The roof was open. The whole scene had charms for every sense,— music from the birds, fragrance from the flowers, and varied beauty to the eye at every aspect. About all was a voluptuous repose. What a place, methought, for a honey-moon, if a Gy bride were a little less formidably armed not only with the rights of woman, but with the powers of man! but when one thinks of a Gy so learned, so tall, so stately, so much above the standard of the creature we call woman, as was Zee,— no! even if I had felt no fear of being reduced to a cinder, it is not of her I should have dreamed in that bower so constructed for dreams of poetic love.

The automata reappeared, serving one of those delicious liquids which form the innocent wines of the Vril-ya.

"Truly," said I, "this is a charming residence, and I can scarcely conceive why you do not settle yourself here instead of amid the gloomier abodes of the city."

"As responsible to the community for the administration

of light, I am compelled to reside chiefly in the city, and can only come hither for short intervals."

"But since I understand from you that no honours are attached to your office, and it involves some trouble, why do you accept it?"

"Each of us obeys without question the command of the Tur. He said, 'Be it requested that Aph-Lin shall be Commissioner of Light,' so I had no choice; but having held the office now for a long time, the cares, which were at first unwelcome, have become, if not pleasing, at least endurable. We are all formed by custom,— even the difference of our race from the savage is but the transmitted continuance of custom, which becomes, through hereditary descent, part and parcel of our nature. You see there are Ana who even reconcile themselves to the responsibilities of chief magistrate; but no one would do so if his duties had not been rendered so light, or if there were any questions as to compliance with his requests."

"Not even if you thought the requests unwise or unjust?"

"We do not allow ourselves to think so; and indeed, everything goes on as if each and all governed themselves according to immemorial custom."

"When the chief magistrate dies or retires, how do you provide for his successor?"

"The An who has discharged the duties of chief magistrate for many years is the best person to choose one by whom those duties may be understood, and he generally names his successor."

"His son, perhaps?"

"Seldom that; for it is not an office any one desires or seeks, and a father naturally hesitates to constrain his son. But if the Tur himself decline to make a choice, for fear it might be supposed that he owed some grudge to the person on whom his choice would settle, then there are three of the College of Sages who draw lots among themselves which shall have the power to elect the chief. We consider that the judgment of one An of ordinary capacity is better than the judgment of three or more, however wise they may be; for among three there would probably be disputes, and where there are disputes, passion clouds judgment. The worst choice made by one who has no motive in choosing wrong, is better than the best choice made by many who have many motives for not choosing right."

"You reverse in your policy the maxims adopted in my country."

"Are you all, in your country, satisfied with your governors?"

"All! certainly not; the governors that most please some are sure to be those most displeasing to others."

"Then our system is better than yours."

"For you it may be; but according to our system a Tish could not be reduced to a cinder if a female compelled him to marry her; and as a Tish I sigh to return to my native world."

"Take courage, my dear little guest; Zee can't compel you to marry her,— she can only entice you to do so. Don't be enticed. Come and look round my domain."

We went forth into a close, bordered with sheds; for though the Ana keep no stock for food, there are some animals which they rear for milking and others for shearing. The former have no resemblance to our cows, nor the latter to our sheep, nor do I believe such species exist amongst them. They use the milk of three varieties of animal: one resembles the antelope, but is much larger, being as tall as a camel; the other two are smaller, and, though differing somewhat from each other, resemble no creature I ever saw on earth. They are very sleek and of rounded proportions; their colour that of the dappled deer, with very mild countenances and beautiful dark eyes. The milk of these three creatures differs in richness and in taste. It is usually diluted with water, and flavoured with the juice of a peculiar and perfumed fruit, and in itself is very nutritious and palatable. The animal whose fleece serves them for clothing and many other purposes is more like the Italian she-goat than any other creature, but is considerably larger, has no horns, and is free from the displeasing odour of our goats. Its fleece is not thick, but very long and fine; it varies in colour, but is never white, more generally of a slate-like or lavender hue. For clothing it is usually worn dyed to suit the taste of the wearer. These animals were exceedingly tame, and were treated with extraordinary care and affection by the children (chiefly female) who tended them.

We then went through vast storehouses filled with grains and fruits. I may here observe that the main staple of food among these people consists, firstly, of a kind of corn much larger in ear than our wheat, and which by culture is perpetually being brought into new varieties of flavour; and, secondly, of a fruit of about the size of a small orange, which, when gathered, is hard and bitter. It is stowed away for many months in their warehouses, and then becomes succulent and tender. Its juice, which is of dark-red colour, enters into most of their sauces. They have many kinds of fruit of the nature of the olive, from which delicious oils are extracted. They have a plant somewhat resembling the sugarcane, but its juices are less sweet and of a delicate perfume. They have no bees nor honey-kneading insects, but they make much use of a sweet gum that oozes from a coniferous plant, not unlike the araucaria. Their soil teems also with esculent roots and vegetables, which it is the aim of their culture to improve and vary to the utmost. And I never remember any meal among this people, however it might be confined to the family household, in which some delicate novelty in such articles of food was not introduced. In fine, as I before observed, their cookery is exquisite, so diversified and nutritious that one does not miss animal food; and their own physical forms suffice to show that with them, at least, meat is not required for superior production of muscular fibre. They have no grapes,— the drinks extracted from their fruits are innocent and refreshing. Their staple beverage, however, is water, in the choice of which they are very fastidious, distinguishing at once the slightest impurity.

"My younger son takes great pleasure in augmenting our produce," said Aph-Lin, as we passed through the storehouses, "and therefore will inherit these lands, which constitute the chief part of my wealth. To my elder son such inheritance would be a great trouble and affliction."

"Are there many sons among you who think the inheritance of vast wealth would be a great trouble and affliction?"

"Certainly; there are indeed very few of the Vril-ya who do not consider that a fortune much above the average is a heavy burden. We are rather a lazy people after the age of childhood, and do not like undergoing more cares than we can help, and great wealth does give its owner many cares. For instance, it marks us out for public offices, which none of us like and none of us can refuse. It necessitates our taking a continued interest in the affairs of any of our poorer country-men, so that we may anticipate their wants and see that none fall into poverty. There is an old proverb amongst us which says, 'The poor man's need is the rich man's shame—'"

"Pardon me, if I interrupt you for a moment. You then allow that some, even of the Vril-ya, know want, and need relief?"

"If by want you mean the destitution that prevails in a Koom-Posh, *that* is impossible with us, unless an An has, by some extraordinary process, got rid of all his means, cannot or will not emigrate, and has either tired out the affectionate aid of his relations or personal friends, or refuses to ac-cept it."

"Well, then, does he not supply the place of an infant or automaton, and become a labourer, a servant?"

"No; then we regard him as an unfortunate person of un-sound reason, and place him, at the expense of the State, in a public building, where every comfort and every luxury that can mitigate his affliction are lavished upon him. But an An does not like to be considered out of his mind, and therefore such cases occur so seldom that the public building I speak of is now a deserted ruin, and the last inmate of it was an An whom I recollect to have seen in my childhood. He did not seem conscious of loss of reason, and wrote glaubs (poetry). When I spoke of wants, I meant such wants as an An with desires larger than his means sometimes entertains,— for ex-pensive singing-birds, or bigger houses, or country-gardens;

and the obvious way to satisfy such wants is to buy of him something that he sells. Hence Ana like myself, who are very rich, are obliged to buy a great many things they do not require, and live on a very large scale where they might prefer to live on a small one. For instance, the great size of my house in the town is a source of much trouble to my wife, and even to myself; but I am compelled to have it thus incommodiously large, because, as the richest An of the community, I am appointed to entertain the strangers from the other communities when they visit us, which they do in great crowds twice a year, when certain periodical entertainments are held, and when relations scattered throughout all the realms of the Vril-ya joyfully reunite for a time. This hospitality, on a scale so extensive, is not to my taste, and therefore I should have been happier had I been less rich. But we must all bear the lot assigned to us in this short passage through time that we call life. After all, what are a hundred years, more or less, to the ages through which we must pass hereafter? Luckily, I have one son who likes great wealth. It is a rare exception to the general rule, and I own I cannot myself understand it."

After this conversation I sought to return to the subject which continued to weigh on my heart,—namely, the chances of escape from Zee; but my host politely declined to renew that topic, and summoned our air-boat. On our way back we were met by Zee, who, having found us gone, on her return from the College of Sages, had unfurled her wings and flown in search of us.

Her grand, but to me unalluring, countenance brightened as she beheld me, and poising herself beside the boat on her large outspread plumes, she said reproachfully to Aph-Lin, "Oh, Father, was it right in you to hazard the life of your guest in a vehicle to which he is so unaccustomed? He might, by an incautious movement, fall over the side; and, alas! he is not like us,—he has no wings. It were death to him to fall. — Dear one!" she added, accosting my shrinking self in a softer voice, "have you no thought of me, that you should thus hazard a life which has become almost a part of mine? Never again be thus rash, unless I am thy companion. What terror thou hast stricken into me!"

I glanced furtively at Aph-Lin, expecting, at least, that he would indignantly reprove his daughter for expressions of anxiety and affection, which, under all the circumstances, would, in the world above ground, be considered immodest in the lips of a young female, addressed to a male not affianced to her, even if of the same rank as herself.

But so confirmed are the rights of females in that region, and so absolutely foremost among those rights do females claim the privilege of courtship, that Aph-Lin would no more have thought of reproving his virgin daughter than he would have thought of disobeying the Tur. In that country, custom, as he implied, is all and all.

He answered mildly, "Zee, the Tish was in no danger, and it is my belief that he can take very good care of himself."

"I would rather that he let me charge myself with his care. O heart of my heart, it was in the thought of thy danger that I first felt how much I loved thee!"

Never did man feel in so false a position as I did. These words were spoken aloud in the hearing of Zee's father, in the hearing of the child who steered. I blushed with shame for them, and for her, and could not help replying angrily: "Zee, either you mock me, which, as your father's guest, misbecomes you, or the words you utter are improper for a maiden Gy to address even to an An of her own race, if he has not wooed her with the consent of her parents. How much more improper to address them to a Tish, who has never presumed to solicit your affections, and who can never regard you with other sentiments than those of reverence and awe!"

Aph-Lin made me a covert sign of approbation, but said nothing.

"Be not so cruel!" exclaimed Zee, still in sonorous accents. "Can love command itself where it is truly felt? Do you suppose that a maiden Gy will conceal a sentiment that it elevates her to feel? What a country you must have come from!"

Here Aph-Lin gently interposed, saying, "Among the Tish-a the rights of your sex do not appear to be established; and at all events my guest may converse with you more freely if unchecked by the presence of others."

To this remark Zee made no reply, but, darting on me a tender reproachul glance, agitated her wings and fled homeward.

"I had counted, at least, on some aid from my host," said I, bitterly, "in the perils to which his own daughter exposes me."

"I gave you the best aid I could. To contradict a Gy in her love affairs is to confirm her purpose. She allows no counsel to come between her and her affections."

———◆———

CHAPTER XXIV.

On alighting from the air-boat, a child accosted Aph-Lin in the hall with a request that he would be present at the funeral obsequies of a relation who had recently departed from that nether world.

Now, I had never seen a burial-place or cemetery amongst this people, and, glad to seize even so melancholy an occasion to defer an encounter with Zee, I asked Aph-Lin if I might be permitted to witness with him the interment of his relation; unless, indeed, it were regarded as one of those sacred ceremonies to which a stranger to their race might not be admitted.

"The departure of an An to a happier world," answered my host, "when, as in the case of my kinsman, he has lived so long in this as to have lost pleasure in it, is rather a cheerful though quiet festival than a sacred ceremony, and you may accompany me if you will."

Preceded by the child-messenger, we walked up the main street to a house at some little distance, and, entering the hall, were conducted to a room on the ground-floor, where we found several persons assembled round a couch on which was laid the deceased. It was an old man, who had, as I was told, lived beyond his one hundred and thirtieth year. To judge by the calm smile on his countenance, he had passed away without suffering. One of the sons, who was now the head of the family, and who seemed in vigorous middle life, though he was considerably more than seventy, stepped forward with a cheerful face and told Aph-Lin that the day before he died his father had seen in a dream his departed Gy, and was eager to be reunited to her, and restored to youth beneath the nearer smile of the All-Good.

While these two were talking, my attention was drawn to a dark metallic substance at the farther end of the room. It was about twenty feet in length, narrow in proportion, and all closed round, save, near the roof, there were small round holes through which might be seen a red light. From the interior emanated a rich and sweet perfume; and while I was conjecturing what purpose this machine was to serve, all the timepieces in the town struck the hour with their solemn musical chime; and as that sound ceased, music of a more joyous character, but still of a joy subdued and tranquil, rang throughout the chamber, and from the walls beyond, in a choral peal. Symphonious with the melody, those present lifted their voice in chant. The words of this hymn were simple. They expressed no regret, no farewell, but rather a greeting to the new world whither the deceased had preceded the living. Indeed, in their language, the funeral hymn is called the "Birth Song." Then the corpse, covered by a long cerement, was tenderly lifted up by six of the nearest kinsfolk, and borne towards the dark thing I have described. I pressed forward to see what happened. A sliding door or panel at one end was lifted up, the body deposited within, on a shelf, the door reclosed, a spring at the side touched, a sudden *whishing*, sighing sound heard from within; and lo! at the other end of the machine the lid fell down, and a small handful of smouldering dust dropped into a *patera* placed to receive it. The son took up the *patera* and said (in what I understood afterwards was the usual form of words), "Behold how great is the Maker!   To this little dust He gave form and life and soul.   It needs not this little dust for Him to renew form and life and soul to the beloved one we shall soon see again."

Each present bowed his head and pressed his hand to his heart. Then a young female child opened a small door within the wall, and I perceived, in the recess, shelves on which were placed many *paterœ* like that which the son held, save that they all had covers. With such a cover a Gy now approached the son, and placed it over the cup, on which it closed with a spring. On the lid were engraven the name of the deceased, and these words: "Lent to us" (here the date of birth). "Recalled from us" (here the date of death).

The closed door shut with a musical sound, and all was over.

———◆———

CHAPTER XXV.

"And this," said I, with my mind full of what I had witnessed,— "this, I presume, is your usual form of burial?"

"Our invariable form," answered Aph-Lin. "What is it amongst your people?"

"We inter the body whole within the earth."

"What! to degrade the form you have loved and honoured, the wife on whose breast you have slept, to the loathsomeness of corruption?"

"But if the soul lives again, can it matter whether the body waste within the earth or is reduced by that awful mechanism, worked, no doubt by the agency of vril, into a pinch of dust?"

"You answer well," said my host, "and there is no arguing on a matter of feeling; but to me your custom is horrible and repulsive, and would serve to invest death with gloomy and hideous associations. It is something, too, to my mind, to be able to preserve the token of what has been our kinsman or friend within the abode in which we live. We thus feel more sensibly that he still lives, though not visibly so to us. But our sentiments in this, as in all things, are created by custom. Custom is not to be changed by a wise An, any more than it is changed by a wise Community, without the gravest deliberation, followed by the most earnest conviction. It is only thus that change ceases to be changeability, and once made is made for good."

When we regained the house, Aph-Lin summoned some of the children in his service and sent them round to several of his friends, requesting their attendance that day, during the Easy Hours, to a festival in honour of his kinsman's recall to the All-Good. This was the largest and gayest assembly I ever witnessed during my stay among the Ana, and was prolonged far into the Silent Hours.

The banquet was spread in a vast chamber reserved especially for grand occasions. This differed from our entertainments, and was not without a certain resemblance to those we read of in the luxurious age of the Roman empire. There was not one great table set out, but numerous small tables, each appropriated to eight guests. It is considered that beyond that number conversation languishes and friendship cools. The Ana never laugh loud, as I have before observed, but the cheerful ring of their voices at the various tables betokened gayety of intercourse. As they have no stimulant drinks, and are temperate in food, though so choice and dainty, the banquet itself did not last long. The tables sank through the floor, and then came musical entertainments for those who liked them. Many, however, wandered away: some of the younger ascended on their wings, for the hall was roofless, forming aërial dances; others strolled through the various apartments, examining the curiosities with which they were stored, or formed themselves into groups for various games, the favourite of which is a complicated kind of chess played by eight persons. I mixed with the crowd, but was prevented joining in their conversation by the constant companionship of one or the other of my host's sons, appointed to keep me from obtrusive questionings. The guests, however, noticed me but slightly; they had grown accustomed to

my appearance, seeing me so often in the streets, and I had
ceased to excite much curiosity.

To my great delight Zee avoided me, and evidently sought
to excite my jealousy by marked attentions to a very handsome young An, who (though, as is the modest custom of the
males when addressed by females, he answered with downcast eyes and blushing cheeks, and was demure and shy as
young ladies new to the world are in most civilized countries,
except England and America) was evidently much charmed
by the tall Gy, and ready to falter a bashful "Yes" if she
had actually proposed. Fervently hoping that she would,
and more and more averse to the idea of reduction to a cinder
after I had seen the rapidity with which a human body can be
hurried into a pinch of dust, I amused myself by watching the
manners of the other young people. I had the satisfaction
of observing that Zee was no singular asserter of a female's
most valued rights. Wherever I turned my eyes, or lent
my ears, it seemed to me that the Gy was the wooing party,
and the An the coy and reluctant one. The pretty innocent
airs which an An gave himself on being thus courted, the
dexterity with which he evaded direct answer to professions
of attachment, or turned into jest the flattering compliments
addressed to him, would have done honour to the most accomplished coquette. Both my male *chaperons* were subjected
greatly to these seductive influences, and both acquitted
themselves with wonderful honour to their tact and self-
control.

I said to the elder son, who preferred mechanical employ-
ments to the management of a great property, and who was of
an eminently philosophical temperament, "I find it difficult
to conceive how at your age, and with all the intoxicating
effects on the senses, of music and lights and perfumes, you
can be so cold to that impassioned Gy who has just left you
with tears in her eyes at your cruelty."

The young An replied with a sigh, "Gentle Tish, the greatest misfortune in life is to marry one Gy if you are in love
with another."

"Oh, you are in love with another?"

“Alas! yes.”

“And she does not return your love?”

“I don’t know. Sometimes a look, a tone, makes me hope so; but she has never plainly told me that she loves me.”

“Have you not whispered in her own ear that you love her?”

“Fie! what are you thinking of? What world do you come from? Could I so betray the dignity of my sex? Could I be so un-Anly, so lost to shame, as to own love to a Gy who has not first owned hers to me?”

“Pardon; I was not quite aware that you pushed the modesty of your sex so far. But does no An ever say to a Gy, ‘I love you,’ till she says it first to him?”

“I can’t say that no An has ever done so, but if he ever does, he is disgraced in the eyes of the Ana, and secretly despised by the Gy-ei. No Gy, well brought up, would listen to him; she would consider that he audaciously infringed on the rights of her sex, while outraging the modesty which dignifies his own. It is very provoking,” continued the An, “for she whom I love has certainly courted no one else, and I cannot but think she likes me. Sometimes I suspect that she does not court me because she fears I would ask some unreasonable settlement as to the surrender of her rights; but if so, she cannot really love me, for where a Gy really loves she foregoes all rights.”

“Is this young Gy present?”

“Oh, yes. She sits yonder talking to my mother.”

I looked in the direction to which my eyes were thus guided, and saw a Gy dressed in robes of bright red, which among this people is a sign that a Gy as yet prefers a single state. She wears gray, a neutral tint, to indicate that she is looking about for a spouse; dark purple if she wishes to intimate that she has made a choice; purple and orange when she is betrothed or married; light blue when she is divorced or a widow and would marry again. Light blue is of course seldom seen.

Among a people where all are of so high a type of beauty, it is difficult to single out one as peculiarly handsome. My young friend's choice seemed to me to possess the average of good looks; but there was an expression in her face that pleased me more than did the faces of the young Gy-ei generally, because it looked less bold, less conscious of female rights. I observed that, while she talked to Bra, she glanced, from time to time, sidelong at my young friend.

"Courage," said I; "that young Gy loves you."

"Ay, but if she will not say so, how am I the better for her love."

"Your mother is aware of your attachment?"

"Perhaps so. I never owned it to her. It would be un-Anly to confide such weakness to a mother. I have told my father; he may have told it again to his wife."

"Will you permit me to quit you for a moment and glide behind your mother and your beloved? I am sure they are talking about you. Do not hesitate. I promise that I will not allow myself to be questioned till I rejoin you."

The young An pressed his hand on his heart, touched me lightly on the head, and allowed me to quit his side. I stole unobserved behind his mother and his beloved. I overheard their talk.

Bra was speaking; said she, "There can be no doubt of this: either my son, who is of marriageable age, will be decoyed into marriage with one of his many suitors, or he will join those who emigrate to a distance and we shall see him no more. If you really care for him, my dear Lo, you should propose."

"I do care for him, Bra; but I doubt if I could really ever win his affections. He is fond of his inventions and time-pieces; and I am not like Zee, but so dull that I fear I could not enter into his favourite pursuits, and then he would get tired of me, and at the end of three years divorce me, and I could never marry another,— never!"

"It is not necessary to know about timepieces to know how to be so necessary to the happiness of an An who cares for timepieces that he would rather give up the timepieces than divorce his Gy. You see, my dear Lo," continued Bra, "that precisely because we are the stronger sex, we rule the other, provided we never show our strength. If you were superior to my son in making timepieces and automata, you should, as his wife, always let him suppose you thought him superior in that art to yourself. The An tacitly allows the pre-eminence of the Gy in all except his own special pursuit. But if she either excels him in that, or affects not to admire him for his proficiency in it, he will not love her very long; perhaps he may even divorce her. But where a Gy really loves, she soon learns to love all that the An does."

The young Gy made no answer to this address. She looked down musingly, then a smile crept over her lips, and she rose, still silent, and went through the crowd till she paused by the young An who loved her. I followed her steps, but discreetly stood at a little distance while I watched them. Somewhat to my surprise, till I recollected the coy tactics among the Ana, the lover seemed to receive her advances with an air of indifference. He even moved away; but she pursued his steps, and, a little time after, both spread their wings and vanished amid the luminous space above.

Just then I was accosted by the chief magistrate, who mingled with the crowd distinguished by no signs of deference or homage. It so happened that I had not seen this great dignitary since the day I had entered his dominions; and recalling Aph-Lin's words as to his terrible doubt whether or not I should be dissected, a shudder crept over me at the sight of his tranquil countenance.

"I hear much of you, stranger, from my son Taë," said the Tur, laying his hand politely on my bended head. "He is very fond of your society, and I trust you are not displeased with the customs of our people."

I muttered some unintelligible answer, which I intended to be an assurance of my gratitude for the kindness I had received from the Tur, and my admiration of his countrymen, but the dissecting-knife gleamed before my mind's eye and choked my utterance. A softer voice said, "My brother's friend must be dear to me;" and looking up I saw a young Gy, who might be sixteen years old, standing beside the magistrate and gazing at me with a very benignant countenance.

She had not come to her full growth, and was scarcely taller than myself (namely, about five feet, ten inches), and, thanks to that comparatively diminutive stature, I thought her the loveliest Gy I had hitherto seen. I suppose something in my eyes revealed that impression, for her countenance grew yet more benignant.

"Taë tells me," she said, "that you have not yet learned to accustom yourself to wings. That grieves me, for I should have liked to fly with you."

"Alas!" I replied, "I can never hope to enjoy that happiness. I am assured by Zee that the safe use of wings is a hereditary gift, and it would take generations before one of my race could poise himself in the air like a bird."

"Let not that thought vex you too much," replied this amiable princess, "for, after all, there must come a day when Zee and myself must resign our wings forever. Perhaps when that day comes we might be glad if the An we chose was also without wings."

The Tur had left us, and was lost amongst the crowd. I began to feel at ease with Taë's charming sister, and rather startled her by the boldness of my compliment in replying "that no An she could choose would ever use his wings to fly away from her." It is so against custom for an An to say such civil things to a Gy till she has declared her passion for him, and been accepted as his betrothed, that the young maiden stood quite dumfounded for a few moments. Nevertheless she did not seem displeased. At last recovering herself, she invited me to accompany her into one of the less crowded rooms and listen to the songs of the birds. I followed her steps as she glided before me, and she led me into a chamber almost deserted. A fountain of naphtha was playing in the centre of the room; round it were ranged soft divans, and the walls of the room were open on one side to an aviary in which the birds were chanting their artful chorus. The Gy seated herself on one of the divans, and I placed myself at her side. "Taë tells me," she said, "that Aph-Lin has made it the law [1]

---

[1] Literally "has said, In this house be it requested." Words synonymous with law, as implying forcible obligation, are avoided by this singular people.

of his house that you are not to be questioned as to the
country you come from or the reason why you visit us.
Is it so?"

"It is."

"May I, at least, without sinning against that law, ask at
least if the Gy-ei in your country are of the same pale colour
as yourself, and no taller?"

"I do not think, O beautiful Gy, that I infringe the law of
Aph-Lin, which is more binding on myself than any one, if I
answer questions so innocent. The Gy-ei in my country are
much fairer of hue than I am, and their average height is at
least a head shorter than mine."

"They cannot then be so strong as the Ana amongst you?
But I suppose their superior vril force makes up for such extraordinary disadvantage of size?"

"They do not profess the vril force as you know it. But
still they are very powerful in my country, and an An has
small chance of a happy life if he be not more or less governed
by his Gy."

"You speak feelingly," said Taë's sister, in a tone of voice
half sad, half petulant. "You are married, of course?"

"No, certainly not."

"Nor betrothed?"

"Nor betrothed."

"Is it possible that no Gy has proposed to you?"

"In my country the Gy does not propose; the An speaks
first."

"What a strange reversal of the laws of nature!" said the
maiden, "and what want of modesty in your sex! But have
you never proposed, never loved one Gy more than another?"

I felt embarrassed by these ingenuous questionings, and
said, "Pardon me, but I think we are beginning to infringe
upon Aph-Lin's injunction. Thus much only will I say in
answer, and then, I implore you, ask no more. I did once

Even had it been decreed by the Tur that his College of Sages should dissect
me, the decree would have ran blandly thus : "Be it requested that, for the
good of the community, the carnivorous Tish be requested to submit himself
to dissection."

feel the preference you speak of; I did propose, and the Gy would willingly have accepted me, but her parents refused their consent."

"Parents! Do you mean seriously to tell me that parents can interfere with the choice of their daughters?"

"Indeed they can, and do very often."

"I should not like to live in that country," said the Gy, simply; "but I hope you will never go back to it."

I bowed my head in silence. The Gy gently raised my face with her right hand, and looked into it tenderly. "Stay with us," she said; "stay with us, and be loved."

What I might have answered, what dangers of becoming a cinder I might have encountered, I still tremble to think, when the light of the naphtha fountain was obscured by the shadow of wings; and Zee, flying through the open roof, alighted beside us. She said not a word, but, taking my arm with her mighty hand, she drew me away, as a mother draws a naughty child, and led me through the apartments to one of the corridors, on which, by the mechanism they generally prefer to stairs, we ascended to my own room. This gained, Zee breathed on my forehead, touched my breast with her staff, and I was instantly plunged into a profound sleep.

When I awoke some hours later, and heard the song of the birds in the adjoining aviary, the remembrance of Taë's sister, her gentle looks and caressing words, vividly returned to me; and so impossible is it for one born and reared in our upper world's state of society to divest himself of ideas dictated by vanity and ambition, that I found myself instinctively building proud castles in the air.

"Tish though I be," thus ran my meditations,— "Tish though I be, it is then clear that Zee is not the only Gy whom my appearance can captivate. Evidently I am loved by A PRINCESS, the first maiden of this land, the daughter of the absolute Monarch whose autocracy they so idly seek to disguise by the republican title of 'chief magistrate.' But for the sudden swoop of that horrible Zee, this Royal Lady would have formally proposed to me; and though it may be very well for Aph-Lin, who is only a subordinate minister, a mere Commissioner of Light, to threaten me with destruction if I accept his daughter's hand, yet a Sovereign, whose word is law, could compel the community to abrogate any custom that forbids intermarriage with one of a strange race, and which in itself is a contradiction to their boasted equality of ranks.

"It is not to be supposed that his daughter, who spoke with such incredulous scorn of the interference of parents, would not have sufficient influence with her Royal Father to save me from the combustion to which Aph-Lin would condemn my form. And if I were exalted by such an alliance, who knows but what the Monarch might elect me as his successor? Why not? Few among this indolent race of philosophers like the burden of such greatness. All might be pleased to see the supreme power lodged in the hands of an accomplished stranger who has experience of other and livelier forms of existence; and, once chosen, what reforms I would institute! What additions to the really pleasant but too monotonous life of this realm my familiarity with the civilized nations above ground would effect! I am fond of the sports of the field. Next to war, is not the chase a king's pastime? In what varieties of strange game does this nether world abound! How interesting to strike down creatures that were known above ground before the Deluge! But how? By that terrible vril, in which, from want of hereditary transmission, I could never be a proficient? No, but by a civilized handy breech-loader, which these ingenious mechanicians could not only make, but no doubt improve; nay, surely I saw one in the Museum. Indeed, as absolute king, I should discountenance vril altogether, except in cases of war. *A propos* of war, it is perfectly absurd to stint a people so intelligent, so rich, so well armed, to a petty limit of territory sufficing for ten thousand or twelve thousand families. Is not this restriction a mere philosophical crotchet, at variance with the aspiring element in human nature, such as has been partially, and with complete failure, tried in the upper world by the late Mr. Robert Owen. Of course one would not go to war with neighbouring nations as well armed as one's own subjects; but then, what of those regions inhabited by races unacquainted with vril, and apparently resembling, in their democratic institutions, my American countrymen? One might invade them without offence to the vril nations, our allies, appropriate their territories, extending, perhaps, to the most distant regions of the nether earth, and thus rule over an empire in which the sun never sets. (I forgot, in my enthusiasm, that over those regions there was no sun to set.) As for the fantastical notion against conceding fame or renown to an eminent individual, because, forsooth, bestowal of honours insures contest in the pursuit of them, stimulates angry passions, and mars the felicity of peace,— it is opposed to the very elements, not only of the human but the brute creation, which are all, if tamable, participators in the sentiment of praise and emulation. What renown would be given to a king who thus extended his empire! I should be deemed a demigod." Thinking of that, the other fanatical notion of regulating this life by reference to one which, no doubt, we Christians firmly believe in, but never take into consideration, I resolved that enlightened philosophy compelled me to abolish a heathen religion so superstitiously at variance with modern thought and practical action. Musing over these various projects, I felt how much I should have liked at that moment to brighten my wits by a good glass of whiskey-and-water. Not that I am habitually a spirit-drinker, but certainly there are times when a little stimulant of alcoholic nature, taken with a cigar, enlivens the imagination. Yes; certainly among these herbs and fruits there would be a liquid from which one could extract a pleasant vinous alcohol; and with a steak cut off one of those elks (ah, what offence to science to reject the animal food which our first medical men agree in recommending to the gastric juices of mankind!) one would certainly pass a more exhilarating hour of repast. Then, too, instead of those antiquated dramas performed by childish amateurs, certainly when I am king, I will introduce our modern opera and a *corps de ballet*, for which one might find, among the nations I shall conquer, young females of less formidable height and thews than the Gy-ei,— not armed with vril, and not insisting upon one's marrying them.

I was so completely wrapped in these and similar reforms, political, social, and moral, calculated to bestow on the people of the nether world the blessings of a civilization known to the races of the upper, that I did not perceive that Zee had entered the chamber till I heard a deep sigh, and raising my eyes, beheld her standing by my couch.

I need not say that, according to the manners of this people, a Gy can, without indecorum, visit an An in his chamber, though an An would be considered forward and immodest to the last degree if he entered the chamber of a Gy without previously obtaining her permission to do so. Fortunately I was in the full habiliments I had worn when Zee had deposited me on the couch. Nevertheless I felt much irritated, as well as shocked, by her visit, and asked in a rude tone what she wanted.

"Speak gently, beloved one, I entreat you," said she, "for I am very unhappy. I have not slept since we parted."

"A due sense of your shameful conduct to me as your father's guest might well suffice to banish sleep from your eyelids. Where was the affection you pretend to have for me, where was even that politeness on which the Vril-ya pride themselves, when, taking advantage alike of that physical strength in which your sex, in this extraordinary region, excels our own, and of those detestable and unhallowed powers which the agencies of vril invest in your eyes and fingerends, you exposed me to humiliation before your assembled visitors, before Her Royal Highness,— I mean, the daughter of your own chief magistrate,— carrying me off to bed like a naughty infant, and plunging me into sleep, without asking my consent?"

"Ungrateful! Do you reproach me for the evidences of my love? Can you think that, even if unstrung by the jealousy which attends upon love till it fades away in blissful trust when we know that the heart we have wooed is won, I could be indifferent to the perils to which the audacious overtures of that silly little child might expose you?"

"Hold! Since you introduce the subject of perils, it perhaps does not misbecome me to say that my most imminent perils come from yourself, or at least would come if I believed in your love and accepted your addresses. Your father has told me plainly that in that case I should be consumed into a cinder with as little compunction as if I were the reptile whom Taë blasted into ashes with the flash of his wand."

"Do not let that fear chill your heart to me," exclaimed Zee, dropping on her knees and absorbing my right hand in the space of her ample palm. "It is true, indeed, that we two cannot wed as those of the same race wed; true that the love between us must be pure as that which, in our belief, exists between lovers who reunite in the new life beyond that boundary at which the old life ends. But is it not happiness enough to be together, wedded in mind and in heart? Listen: I have just left my father. He consents to our union on those terms. I have sufficient influence with the College of Sages to insure their request to the Tur not to interfere with the free choice of a Gy, provided that her wedding with one of another race be but the wedding of souls. Oh, think you that true love needs ignoble union? It is not that I yearn only to be by your side in this life, to be part and parcel of your joys and sorrows here: I ask here for a tie which will bind us forever and forever in the world of immortals. Do you reject me?"

As she spoke, she knelt, and the whole character of her face was changed,— nothing of sternness left to its grandeur; a divine light, as that of an immortal, shining out from its human beauty. But she rather awed me as angel than moved me as woman, and after an embarrassed pause, I faltered forth evasive expressions of gratitude, and sought, as delicately as I could, to point out how humiliating would be my position amongst her race in the light of a husband who might never be permitted the name of father.

"But," said Zee, "this community does not constitute the whole world. No; nor do all the populations comprised in the league of the Vril-ya. For thy sake I will renounce my country and my people. We will fly together to some region where thou shalt be safe. I am strong enough to bear thee on my wings across the deserts that intervene. I am skilled enough to cleave open, amid the rocks, valleys in which to build our home. Solitude and a hut with thee would be to me society and the universe. Or wouldst thou return to thine own world, above the surface of this, exposed to the uncertain seasons, and lit but by the changeful orbs which constitute by thy description the fickle character of those savage regions? If so, speak the word, and I will force the way for thy return, so that I am thy companion there, though, there as here, but partner of thy soul, and fellow-traveller with thee to the world in which there is no parting and no death."

I could not but be deeply affected by the tenderness, at once so pure and so impassioned, with which these words were uttered, and in a voice that would have rendered musical the roughest sounds in the rudest tongue. And for a moment it did occur to me that I might avail myself of Zee's agency to affect a safe and speedy return to the upper world. But a very brief space for reflection sufficed to show me how dishonourable and base a return for such devotion it would be to allure thus away, from her own people and a home in which I had been so hospitably treated, a creature to whom our world would be so abhorrent, and for whose barren, if spiritual love, I could not reconcile myself to renounce the more human affection of mates less exalted above my erring self. With this sentiment of duty towards the Gy combined another of duty towards the whole race I belonged to. Could I venture to introduce into the upper world a being so formidably gifted,—a being that with a movement of her staff could in less than an hour reduce New York and its glorious Koom-Posh into a pinch of snuff? Rob her of one staff, with her science she could easily construct another; and with the deadly lightnings that armed the slender engine her whole frame was charged. If thus dangerous to the cities and populations of the whole upper earth, could she be a safe companion to myself in case her affection should be subjected to change or embittered by jealousy? These thoughts, which it takes so many words to express, passed rapidly through my brain and decided my answer.

"Zee," I said, in the softest tones I could command, and pressing respectful lips on the hand into whose clasp mine had vanished, — "Zee, I can find no words to say how deeply I am touched, and how highly I am honoured, by a love so disinterested and self-immolating. My best return to it is perfect frankness. Each nation has its customs. The customs of yours do not allow you to wed me; the customs of mine are equally opposed to such a union between those of races so widely differing. On the other hand, though not deficient in courage among my own people, or amid dangers with which I am familiar, I cannot, without a shudder of horror, think of constructing a bridal home in the heart of some dismal chaos, with all the elements of nature, fire and water and mephitic gases, at war with each other, and with the probability that at some moment, while you were busied in cleaving rocks or conveying vril into lamps, I should be devoured by a krek which your operations disturbed from its hiding-place. I, a mere Tish, do not deserve the love of a Gy so brilliant, so learned, so potent as yourself. Yes, I do not deserve that love, for I cannot return it."

Zee released my hand, rose to her feet, and turned her face away to hide her emotions; then she glided noiselessly along the room, and paused at the threshold. Suddenly, impelled as by a new thought, she returned to my side and said, in a whispered tone, —

"You told me you would speak with perfect frankness. With perfect frankness, then, answer me this question. If you cannot love me, do you love another?"

"Certainly I do not."

"You do not love Taë's sister?"

"I never saw her before last night."

"That is no answer. Love is swifter than vril. You hesitate to tell me. Do not think it is only jealousy that prompts me to caution you. If the Tur's daughter should declare love to you, if in her ignorance she confides to her father any preference that may justify his belief that she will woo you, he will have no option but to request your immediate destruction, as he is specially charged with the duty of consulting the good of the community, which could not allow a daughter of the Vril-ya to wed a son of the Tish-a, in that sense of marriage which does not confine itself to union of the souls. Alas! there would then be for you no escape. She has no strength of wing to uphold you through the air; she has no science wherewith to make a home in the wilderness. Believe that here my friendship speaks, and that my jealousy is silent."

With those words Zee left me. And recalling those words, I thought no more of succeeding to the throne of the Vril-ya, or of the political, social, and moral reforms I should institute in the capacity of Absolute Sovereign.

----•----

CHAPTER XXVI.

After the conversation with Zee just recorded, I fell into a profound melancholy. The curious interest with which I had hitherto examined the life and habits of this marvellous community was at an end. I could not banish from my mind the consciousness that I was among a people who, however kind and courteous, could destroy me at any moment without scruple or compunction. The virtuous and peaceful life of the people which, while new to me, had seemed so holy a contrast to the contentions, the passions, the vices of the upper world, now began to oppress me with a sense of dulness and monotony. Even the serene tranquillity of the lustrous air preyed on my spirits. I longed for a change, even to winter, or storm, or darkness. I began to feel that, whatever our dreams of perfectibility, our restless aspirations towards a better and higher and calmer sphere of being, we, the mortals of the upper world, are not trained or fitted to enjoy for long the very happiness of which we dream or to which we aspire.

Now, in this social state of the Vril-ya, it was singular to mark how it contrived to unite and to harmonize into one system nearly all the objects which the various philosophers of the upper world have placed before human hopes as the ideals of a Utopian future. It was a state in which war, with all its calamities, was deemed impossible,— a state in which the freedom of all and each was secured to the uttermost degree, without one of those animosities which make freedom in the upper world depend on the perpetual strife of hostile parties. Here the corruption which debases democracies was as unknown as the discontents which undermine the thrones of monarchies. Equality here was not a name; it was a reality. Riches were not persecuted, because they were not envied. Here those problems connected with the labours of a working class, hitherto insoluble above ground, and above ground conducing to such bitterness between classes, were solved by a process the simplest,— a distinct and separate working class was dispensed with altogether. Mechanical inventions, constructed on principles that baffled my research to ascertain, worked by an agency infinitely more powerful and infinitely more easy of management than aught we have yet extracted from electricity or steam, with the aid of children whose strength was never overtasked, but who loved their employment as sport and pastime, sufficed to create a Public-wealth so devoted to the general use that not a grumbler was ever heard of. The vices that rot our cities here had no footing. Amusements abounded, but they were all innocent. No merry-makings conduced to intoxication, to riot, to disease. Love existed, and was ardent in pursuit, but its object, once secured, was faithful. The adulterer, the profligate, the harlot, were phenomena so unknown in this commonwealth, that even to find the words by which they were designated one would have had to search throughout an obsolete literature composed thousands of years before. They who have been students of theoretical philosophies above ground, know that all these strange departures from civilized life do but realize ideas which have been broached, canvassed, ridiculed, contested for; sometimes partially tried, and still put forth in fantastic books, but have never come to practical result. Nor were these all the steps towards theoretical perfectibility which this community had made. It had been the sober belief of Descartes that the life of man could be prolonged, not, indeed, on this earth, to eternal duration, but to what he called the age of the patriarchs, and modestly defined to be from one hundred to one hundred and fifty years average length. Well, even this dream of sages was here fulfilled,— nay, more than fulfilled; for the vigour of middle life was preserved even after the term of a century was passed. With this longevity was combined a greater blessing than itself, that of continuous health. Such diseases as befell the race were removed with ease by scientific applications of that agency — life-giving as life-destroying — which is inherent in vril. Even this idea is not unknown above ground, though it has generally been confined to enthusiasts or charlatans, and emanates from confused notions about mesmerism, odic force, etc. Passing by such trivial contrivances as wings, which every schoolboy knows has been tried and found wanting, from the mythical or prehistorical period, I proceed to that very delicate question, urged of late as essential to the perfect happiness of our human species by the two most disturbing and potential influences on upper-ground society, Womankind and Philosophy,— I mean, the Rights of Women.

Now, it is allowed by jurisprudists that it is idle to talk of rights where there are not corresponding powers to enforce them; and above ground, for some reason or other, man, in his physical force, in the use of weapons offensive and defensive, when it comes to positive personal contest, can, as a rule of general application, master women. But among this people there can be no doubt about the rights of women, because, as I have before said, the Gy, physically speaking, is bigger and stronger than the An; and her will being also more resolute than his, and will being essential to the direction of the vril force, she can bring to bear upon him, more potently than he on herself, the mystical agency which art can extract from the occult properties of nature. Therefore all that our female philosophers above ground contend

for as to rights of women, is conceded as a matter of course
in this happy commonwealth. Besides such physical powers,
the Gy-ei have (at least in youth) a keen desire for accom-
plishments and learning which exceeds that of the male; and
thus they are the scholars, the professors,— the learned portion, in short, of the community.

Of course, in this state of society the female establishes,
as I have shown, her most valued privilege, — that of choosing and courting her wedding partner. Without that privilege she would despise all the others. Now, above ground,
we should not unreasonably apprehend that a female, thus potent and thus privileged, when she had fairly hunted us down
and married us, would be very imperious and tyrannical.
Not so with the Gy-ei: once married, the wings once suspended, and more amiable, complacent, docile mates, more
sympathetic, more sinking their loftier capacities into the
study of their husband's comparatively frivolous tastes and
whims, no poet could conceive in his visions of conjugal
bliss. Lastly, among the more important characteristics of
the Vril-ya, as distinguished from our mankind,— lastly, and
most important on the bearings of their life and the peace of
their commonwealths, is their universal agreement in the existence of a merciful beneficent Deity, and of a future world
to the duration of which a century or two are moments too
brief to waste upon thoughts of fame and power and avarice;
while with that agreement is combined another,— namely,
since they can know nothing as to the nature of that Deity
beyond the fact of His supreme goodness, nor of that future
world beyond the fact of its felicitous existence, so their reason forbids all angry disputes on insoluble questions. Thus
they secure for that State in the bowels of the earth what no
community ever secured under the light of the stars,— all
the blessings and consolations of a religion without any of
the evils and calamities which are engendered by strife between one religion and another.

It would be, then, utterly impossible to deny that the state
of existence among the Vril-ya is thus, as a whole, immeasurably more felicitous than that of super-terrestrial races, and,

realizing the dreams of our most sanguine philanthropists, almost approaches to a poet's conception of some angelical order; and yet, if you would take a thousand of the best and most philosophical of human beings you could find in London, Paris, Berlin, New York, or even Boston, and place them as citizens in this beatified community, my belief is, that in less than a year they would either die of *ennui*, or attempt some revolution by which they would militate against the good of the communty, and be burned into cinders at the request of the Tur.

Certainly I have no desire to insinuate, through the medium of this narrative, any ignorant disparagement of the race to which I belong. I have, on the contrary, endeavoured to make it clear that the principles which regulate the social system of the Vril-ya forbid them to produce those individual examples of human greatness which adorn the annals of the upper world. Where there are no wars there can be no Hannibal, no Washington, no Jackson, no Sheridan; where States are so happy that they fear no danger and desire no change, they cannot give birth to a Demosthenes, a Webster, a Sumner, a Wendell Holmes, or a Butler; and where a society attains to a moral standard, in which there are no crimes and no sorrows from which tragedy can extract its aliment of pity and sorrow, no salient vices or follies on which comedy can lavish its mirthful satire, it has lost the chance of producing a Shakspeare, or a Molière, or a Mrs. Beecher Stowe. But if I·have no desire to disparage my fellow-men above ground in showing how much the motives that impel the energies and ambition of individuals in a society of contest and struggle, become dormant or annulled in a society which aims at securing for the aggregate the calm and innocent felicity which we presume to be the lot of beatified immortals, neither, on the other hand, have I the wish to represent the commonwealths of the Vril-ya as an ideal form of political society, to the attainment of which our own efforts of reform should be directed. On the contrary, it is because we have so combined, throughout the series of ages, the elements which compose human character, that it would be utterly impossible for us to adopt the modes of life, or to reconcile our passions to the modes of thought, among the Vril-ya,—that I arrived at the conviction that this people — though originally not only of our human race, but, as seems to me clear by the roots of their language, descended from the same ancestors as the great Aryan family, from which in varied streams has flowed the dominant civilization of the world; and having, according to their myths and their history, passed through phases of society familiar to ourselves — had yet now developed into a distinct species, with which it was impossible that any community in the upper world could amalgamate; and that if they ever emerged from these nether recesses into the light of day, they would, according to their own traditional persuasions of their ultimate destiny, destroy and replace our existent varieties of man.

It may indeed be said, since more than one Gy could be found to conceive a partiality for so ordinary a type of our super-terrestrial race as myself, that even if the Vril-ya did appear above ground, we might be saved from extermination by intermixture of race. But this is too sanguine a belief. Instances of such *mésalliance* would be as rare as those of intermarriage between the Anglo-Saxon emigrants and the Red Indians. Nor would time be allowed for the operation of familiar intercourse. The Vril-ya, on emerging, induced by the charm of a sunlit heaven to form their settlements above ground, would commence at once the work of destruction, seize upon the territories already cultivated, and clear off, without scruple, all the inhabitants who resisted that invasion. And considering their contempt for the institutions of Koom-Posh, or Popular Government, and the pugnacious valour of my beloved countrymen, I believe that if the Vril-ya first appeared in free America — as, being the choicest portion of the habitable earth, they would doubtless be induced to do — and said, "This quarter of the globe we take; Citizens of a Koom-Posh, make way for the development of species in the Vril-ya," my brave compatriots would show fight, and not a soul of them would be left in this life to rally round the Stars and Stripes at the end of a week.

I now saw but little of Zee, save at meals, when the family assembled, and she was then reserved and silent. My apprehensions of danger from an affection I had so little encouraged or deserved, therefore, now faded away, but my dejection continued to increase. I pined for escape to the upper world, but I racked my brains in vain for any means to effect it. I was never permitted to wander forth alone, so that I could not even visit the spot on which I had alighted, and see if it were possible to reascend to the mine. Nor even in the Silent Hours, when the household was locked in sleep, could I have let myself down from the lofty floor in which my apartment was placed. I knew not how to command the automata who stood mockingly at my beck beside the wall, nor could I ascertain the springs by which were set in movement the platforms that supplied the place of stairs. The knowledge how to avail myself of these contrivances had been purposely withheld from me. Oh, that I could but have learned the use of wings, so freely here at the service of every infant! then I might have escaped from the casement, regained the rocks, and buoyed myself aloft through the chasm of which the perpendicular sides forbade place for human footing!

CHAPTER XXVII.

One day, as I sat alone and brooding in my chamber, Taë flew in at the open window and alighted on the couch beside me. I was always pleased with the visits of a child in whose society, if humbled, I was less eclipsed than in that of Ana who had completed their education and matured their understanding; and as I was permitted to wander forth with him for my companion, and as I longed to revisit the spot in which I had descended into the nether world, I hastened to ask him if he were at leisure for a stroll beyond the streets of the city. His countenance seemed to me graver than usual as he replied, "I came hither on purpose to invite you forth."

We soon found ourselves in the street, and I had not got far from the house when we encountered five or six young Gy-ei, who were returning from the fields with baskets full of flowers, and chanting a song in chorus as they walked. A young Gy sings more often than she talks. They stopped on seeing us, accosting Taë with familiar kindness, and me with the courteous gallantry which distinguishes the Gy-ei in their manner towards our weaker sex.

And here I may observe that, though a virgin Gy is so frank in her courtship to the individual she favours, there is nothing that approaches to that general breadth and loudness of manner which those young ladies of the Anglo-Saxon race, to whom the distinguished epithet of "fast" is accorded, exhibit towards young gentlemen whom they do not profess to love. No: the bearing of the Gy-ei towards males in ordinary is very much that of high-bred men in the gallant societies of the upper world towards ladies whom they respect but do not woo; deferential, complimentary, exquisitely polished,— what we should call "chivalrous."

Certainly I was a little put out by the number of civil things addressed to my *amour propre*, which were said to me by these courteous young Gy-ei. In the world I came from, a man would have thought himself aggrieved, treated with irony, "chaffed" (if so vulgar a slang word may be allowed on the authority of the popular novelists who use it so freely), when one fair Gy complimented me on the freshness of my complexion, another on the choice of colours in my dress, a third, with a sly smile, on the conquests I had made at Aph-Lin's entertainment. But I knew already that all such language was what the French call *banal*, and did but express in the female mouth, below earth, that sort of desire to pass for amiable with the opposite sex which, above earth, arbitrary custom and hereditary transmission demonstrate by the mouth of the male. And just as a high-bred young lady, above earth, habituated to such compliments, feels that she cannot, without impropriety, return them, nor evince any great satisfaction at receiving them, so I, who had learned polite manners at the house of so wealthy and dignified a Minister of that nation, could but smile and try to look pretty in bashfully disclaiming the compliments showered upon me. While we were thus talking, Taë's sister, it seems, had seen us from the upper rooms of the Royal Palace at the entrance of the town, and, precipitating herself on her wings, alighted in the midst of the group.

Singling me out, she said, though still with the inimitable deference of manner which I have called "chivalrous," yet not without a certain abruptness of tone which, as addressed to the weaker sex, Sir Philip Sidney might have termed "rustic," "Why do you never come to see us?"

While I was deliberating on the right answer to give to this unlooked-for question, Taë said quickly and sternly, "Sister, you forget,—the stranger is of my sex. It is not for persons of my sex, having due regard for reputation and modesty, to lower themselves by running after the society of yours."

This speech was received with evident approval by the young Gy-ei in general; but Taë's sister looked greatly abashed. Poor thing!—and a Princess too!

Just at this moment a shadow fell on the space between me and the group; and, turning round, I beheld the chief magistrate coming close upon us, with the silent and stately pace peculiar to the Vril-ya. At the sight of his countenance, the same terror which had seized me when I first beheld it returned. On that brow, in those eyes, there was that same indefinable something which marked the being of a race fatal to our own,—that strange expression of serene exemption from our common cares and passions, of conscious superior power, compassionate and inflexible as that of a judge who pronounces doom. I shivered, and, inclining low, pressed the arm of my child-friend, and drew him onward silently. The Tur placed himself before our path, regarded me for a moment without speaking, then turned his eye quietly on his daughter's face, and, with a grave salutation to her and the other Gy-ei, went through the midst of the group,—still without a word.

CHAPTER XXVIII.

WHEN Taë and I found ourselves alone on the broad road that lay between the city and the chasm through which I had descended into this region beneath the light of the stars and sun, I said under my breath, "Child and friend, there is a look in your father's face which appalls me. I feel as if, in its awful tranquillity, I gazed upon death."

Taë did not immediately reply. He seemed agitated, and as if debating with himself by what words to soften some unwelcome intelligence. At last he said, "None of the Vril-ya fear death: do you?"

"The dread of death is implanted in the breasts of the race to which I belong. We can conquer it at the call of duty, of honour, of love. We can die for a truth, for a native land, for those who are dearer to us than ourselves. But if death do really threaten me now and here, where are such counter-actions to the natural instinct which invests with awe and terror the contemplation of severance between soul and body?"

Taë looked surprised, but there was great tenderness in his voice as he replied, "I will tell my father what you say. I will entreat him to spare your life."

"He has, then, already decreed to destroy it?"

"'T is my sister's fault or folly," said Taë, with some petulance. "But she spoke this morning to my father; and, after she had spoken, he summoned me, as a chief among the children who are commissioned to destroy such lives as threaten the community, and he said to me, 'Take thy vril staff, and seek the stranger who has made himself dear to thee. Be his end painless and prompt.'"

"And," I faltered, recoiling from the child, "and it is, then, for my murder that thus treacherously thou hast invited me forth? No, I cannot believe it. I cannot think thee guilty of such a crime."

"It is no crime to slay those who threaten the good of the community; it would be a crime to slay the smallest insect that cannot harm us."

"If you mean that I threaten the good of the community because your sister honours me with the sort of preference which a child may feel for a strange plaything, it is not necessary to kill me. Let me return to the people I have left, and by the chasm through which I descended. With a slight help from you, I might do so now. You, by the aid of your wings, could fasten to the rocky ledge within the chasm the cord that you found, and have no doubt preserved. Do but that; assist me but to the spot from which I alighted, and I vanish from your world forever, and as surely as if I were among the dead."

"The chasm through which you descended! Look round; we stand now on the very place where it yawned. What see you? Only solid rock. The chasm was closed, by the orders of Aph-Lin, as soon as communication between him and yourself was established in your trance, and he learned from your own lips the nature of the world from which you came. Do you not remember when Zee bade me not question you as to yourself or your race? On quitting you that day, Aph-Lin accosted me, and said, 'No path between the stranger's home and ours should be left unclosed, or the sorrow and evil of his home may descend to ours. Take with thee the children of thy band, smite the sides of the cavern with your vril staves till the fall of their fragments fills up every chink through which a gleam of our lamps could force its way.'"

As the child spoke, I stared aghast at the blind rocks before me. Huge and irregular, the granite masses, showing by charred discolouration where they had been shattered, rose from footing to roof-top; not a cranny!

"All hope, then, is gone," I murmured, sinking down on the craggy wayside, "and I shall nevermore see the sun." I covered my face with my hands, and prayed to Him whose presence I had so often forgotten when the heavens had declared His handiwork. I felt His presence in the depths of the nether earth, and amid the world of the grave. I looked up, taking comfort and courage from my prayers, and gazing with a quiet smile into the face of the child, said, "Now, if thou must slay me, strike."

Taë shook his head gently. "Nay," he said, "my father's request is not so formally made as to leave me no choice. I will speak with him, and I may prevail to save thee. Strange that thou shouldst have that fear of death which we thought was only the instinct of the inferior creatures, to whom the conviction of another life has not been vouchsafed. With us, not an infant knows such a fear. Tell me, my dear Tish," he continued, after a little pause, "would it reconcile thee more to departure from this form of life to that form which lies on the other side of the moment called 'death,' did I share thy journey? If so, I will ask my father whether it be allowable for me to go with thee. I am one of our generation destined to emigrate, when of age for it, to some regions unknown within this world. I would just as soon emigrate now to regions unknown in another world. The All-Good is no less there than here. Where is He not?"

"Child," said I, seeing by Taë's countenance that he spoke in serious earnest, "it is crime in thee to slay me; it were a crime not less in me to say, 'Slay thyself.' The All-Good chooses His own time to give us life, and His own time to take it away. Let us go back. If, on speaking with thy father, he decides on my death, give me the longest warning in thy power, so that I may pass the interval in self-preparation."

We walked back to the city, conversing but by fits and starts. We could not understand each other's reasonings, and I felt for the fair child, with his soft voice and beautiful face, much as a convict feels for the executioner who walks beside him to the place of doom.

CHAPTER XXIX.

In the midst of those hours set apart for sleep, and constituting the night of the Vril-ya, I was awakened from the disturbed slumber into which I had not long fallen, by a hand on my shoulder. I started, and beheld Zee standing beside me.

"Hush," she said, in a whisper; "let no one hear us. Dost thou think that I have ceased to watch over thy safety because I could not win thy love? I have seen Taë. He has not prevailed with his father, who had meanwhile conferred with the three sages whom, in doubtful matters, he takes into council, and by their advice he has ordained thee to perish when the world re-awakens to life. I will save thee. Rise and dress."

Zee pointed to a table by the couch, on which I saw the clothes I had worn on quitting the upper world, and which I had exchanged subsequently for the more picturesque garments of the Vril-ya. The young Gy then moved towards the casement, and stepped into the balcony while hastily and wonderingly I donned my own habiliments. When I joined her on the balcony, her face was pale and rigid. Taking me by the hand, she said softly, "See how brightly the art of the Vril-ya has lighted up the world in which they dwell. To-morrow that world will be dark to me." She drew me back into the room without waiting for my answer, thence into the corridor, from which we descended into the hall. We passed into the deserted streets and along the broad upward road which wound beneath the rocks. Here, where there is neither day nor night, the Silent Hours are unutterably solemn,— the vast space illumined by mortal skill is so wholly without the sight and stir of mortal life. Soft as were our footsteps, their sounds vexed the ear, as out of harmony with the universal repose. I was aware in my own mind, though Zee said it not, that she had decided to assist my return to the upper world, and that we were bound towards the place from which I had descended. Her silence infected me, and commanded mine. And now we approached the chasm. It had been reopened; not presenting, indeed, the same aspect as when I had emerged from it, but through that closed wall of rock before which I had last stood with Taë, a new cleft had been riven, and along its blackened sides still glimmered sparks and smouldered embers. My upward gaze could not, however, penetrate more than a few feet into the darkness of the hollow void, and I stood dismayed, and wondering how that grim ascent was to be made.

Zee divined my doubt. "Fear not," said she, with a faint smile; "your return is assured. I began this work when the Silent Hours commenced, and all else were asleep; believe that I did not pause till the path back into thy world was clear. I shall be with thee a little while yet. We do not part until thou sayest, 'Go, for I need thee no more.'"

My heart smote me with remorse at these words. "Ah," I exclaimed, "would that thou wert of my race or I of thine, then I should never say, 'I need thee no more.'"

"I bless thee for those words, and I shall remember them when thou art gone," answered the Gy, tenderly.

During this brief interchange of words, Zee had turned away from me, her form bent and her head bowed over her breast. Now, she rose to the full height of her grand stature, and stood fronting me. While she had been thus averted from my gaze, she had lighted up the circlet that she wore round her brow, so that it blazed as if it were a crown of stars. Not only her face and her form, but the atmosphere around, were illumined by the effulgence of the diadem.

"Now," said she, "put thine arms around me for the first and last time. Nay, thus; courage, and cling firm."

As she spoke her form dilated, the vast wings expanded. Clinging to her, I was borne aloft through the terrible chasm. The starry light from her forehead shot around and before us through the darkness. Brightly and steadfastly and swiftly as an angel may soar heavenward with the soul it rescues from the grave, went the flight of the Gy, till I heard in the distance the hum of human voices, the sounds of human toil. We halted on the flooring of one of the galleries of the mine, and beyond, in the vista, burned the dim, rare, feeble lamps of the miners. Then I released my hold. The Gy kissed me on my forehead passionately, but as with a mother's passion, and said, as the tears gushed from her eyes, "Farewell forever! Thou wilt not let me go into thy world,— thou canst never return to mine. Ere our household shake off slumber, the rocks will have again closed over the chasm, not to be reopened by me, nor perhaps by others, for ages yet unguessed. Think of me sometimes, and with kindness. When I reach the life that lies beyond this speck in time, I shall look round for thee. Even there, the world consigned to thyself and thy people may have rocks and gulfs which divide it from that in which I rejoin those of my race that have gone before, and I may be powerless to cleave way to regain thee as I have cloven way to lose."

Her voice ceased. I heard the swan-like sough of her wings, and saw the rays of her starry diadem receding far and farther through the gloom.

I sat myself down for some time, musing sorrowfully; then I rose and took my way with slow footsteps towards the place in which I heard the sounds of men. The miners I encountered were strange to me, of another nation than my own. They turned to look at me with some surprise, but finding that I could not answer their brief questions in their own language, they returned to their work and suffered me to pass on unmolested. In fine, I regained the mouth of the mine, little troubled by other interrogatories,— save those of a friendly official to whom I was known, and luckily he was too busy to talk much with me. I took care not to return to my former lodging, but hastened that very day to quit a neighbourhood where I could not long have escaped inquiries to which I could have given no satisfactory answers. I regained in safety my own country, in which I have been long peacefully settled, and engaged in practical business, till I retired, on a competent fortune, three years ago. I have been little invited and little tempted to talk of the rovings and adventures of my youth. Somewhat disappointed, as most men are, in matters connected with household love and domestic life, I often think of the young Gy as I sit alone at night, and wonder how I could have rejected such a love, no matter what dangers attended it, or by what conditions it was restricted. Only, the more I think of a people calmly developing, in regions excluded from our sight and deemed uninhabitable by our sages, powers surpassing our most disciplined modes of force, and virtues to which our life, social and political, becomes antagonistic in proportion as our civilization advances, the more devoutly I pray that ages may yet elapse before there emerge into sunlight our inevitable destroyers. Being, however, frankly told by my physician that I am afflicted by a complaint which, though it gives little pain and no perceptible notice of its encroachments, may at any moment be fatal, I have thought it my duty to my fellow-men to place on record these forewarnings of The Coming Race.

THE END.